Most Greatly
Lived

Most Greatly Lived

A Biographical Novel of Edward de
Vere, Seventeenth Earl of Oxford,
whose pen name was William
Shakespeare

Paul Hemenway Altrocchi

Contents

To Julia Cooley Altrocchi, poet and author,
1893 - 1972
whose research, writings, and stimulating
conversations kindled my
perplexity and lifelong interest in the mysterious
and fascinating
story of Edward de Vere.

Small time, but in that small most greatly lived
This star of England. Fortune made his sword,
By which the world's best garden he achieved.

-Henry V

Heraldic Crest of Edward de Vere
for 43 years as Viscount Bolebec.

Edward de Vere's Coat-of-Arms:
Nothing Truer Than Truth
Nothing Truer Than Vere

Acknowledgments

The author is grateful to the following individuals for very helpful editorial advice rendered during this seven-year project: Ruth Loyd Miller, William Greenleaf, Catherine Altrocchi Waidyatilleka, Penelope Huneke, Dr. John Altrocchi, Robin Pennell, Dorothy Norton, Laurel Altrocchi, Geoffrey Altrocchi and Gene Thompson.

Many thanks also to Dorothy Norton for the fine art work.

But stay, I see thee in the hemisphere
Advanced, and made a constellation there:
Shine forth, thou star of poets.

Ben Jonson

I overtook
In Germany a great and famous Earl
Of England; the most goodly fashion'd man
I ever saw: from head to foot in form
Rare and most absolute; he had a face
Like one of the most ancient honour'd Romans
From whence his noblest family was deriv'd;
He was beside of spirit passing great,
Valiant and learn'd, and liberal as the sun,
Spoke and writ sweetly, or of learned subjects,
Or of the discipline of public weals :
And 'twas the Earl of Oxford.

George Chapman

Chapter 1

Come what come may,
Time and the hour runs through the roughest day.
— Macbeth

In the deep end of July, 1561, the villagers of Castle Hedingham were reaching a fevered pitch of excitement. In two days their young Queen would pay them a personal visit while on Royal Progress. This might be the only time in their lives they could see, talk to and perhaps even touch a divinely-inspired monarch.

John de Vere, the jovial and distinguished Sixteenth Earl of Oxford, walked through the village encouraging them in the painting of their houses with bright new colors. He cheered them on as they trimmed hedges and spruced up their gardens in honor of the peace-loving and friendly Elizabeth, Queen for the past three years.

While chatting in his lively laughing manner, Earl

John suddenly clutched his chest for the second time that morning. He turned away quickly so others would not see, but the eclipse of mortality was not lost in the moment. Fear followed the slice of pain as it cut its path through the ribbon of his heart.

The first painful spasm had been easy to explain away: too much ale from the night before, overly spicy sauce on the lamb eaten too gluttonously. But the second intense pain, starting under his breastbone, radiating into his jaw and down his left arm, instantly gasped his breath and iced his smiling countenance in a cold sweat.

Edward, he thought with an unaccustomed feeling of impending doom. *I must speak to my son. . . .*

Half a mile away, eleven-year-old Edward de Vere sat on a grassy bank of the River Colne watching the shimmering images of scattered clouds in the clear water. His face was sensitive and comely, with straight Roman nose and full lips. His dark hair glinted a tinge of Viking red. His countenance was serious but his luminous brown eyes hinted a quick wit.

Years before, Edward decided to make Wednesdays and Saturdays his alone-days which he called "Bolebec Days," named after his title of Viscount Bolebec, hereditarily assumed by the oldest de Vere son since the late 1100's. He loved word-origins and he often savored the mental image evoked by Bolebec, derived from the Old Norwegian words *bolr*, meaning trunk of a tree, and *bec*, meaning small brook with a rocky bed.

On Bolebec Days, weather permitting, he walked or rode to a favorite scenic knoll or spot on the Colne where he would contemplate, write and read. It was a privileged time to dream of possibilities, expand creative boundaries and think about the endless potential of the human mind.

On other mornings, often arranged by his father, he gained exposure to crafts such as carpentry, brickwork, or butchering, or learned about birds and insects. If the weather was too cold or rainy, he isolated himself in the castle-keep and let his imaginings and writings freely roam. Late mornings and afternoons were for tutorial and study. Half of each year he spent in residence at Queen's College, Cambridge, where he looked forward to beginning his fourth year in September.

His gaze wandered along the river's edge where clusters of water grasses danced slowly and sinuously, brushed softly by silent currents. He glanced at the pond which he and Old John, the white-haired, pink-cheeked family falconer, had laboriously shoveled and channeled to the Colne to provide a resting and feeding area for the local mallards and other ducks flying by. The river itself was only twenty-five feet wide as it followed its ancient meandering course toward the sea.

Edward basked happily in the day's warmth, both pacified and activated by the inexhaustible splendor of nature's surround. His mind drifted with the gentle breezes into a contented reverie, ruminating on his own purpose in a world so full of beauty.

He wondered why words were so easy for him to learn and remember in any language, why pleasing word-combinations harmonized so easily in his mind. Appealing phrases and poetic rhyme seemed to penetrate his brain like illuminated arrows. At times his pen was unable to keep pace with the relentless volleys of ideas which demanded written permanency.

He was elated that his parents constantly encouraged his linguistic skills and writing talents.

He was roused out of his thoughts by the familiar hoofbeats of Raven, his father's black stallion. Raven always tapped his hooves in a brief syncopated rhythm when he approached Edward, followed by a reverential bow of his head. Edward had taught Raven this little trick when the colt had been left with him several years before, while his father attended to his duties as a royal courtier.

Surprised that his Bolebec time was being interrupted, Edward gazed admiringly at his father's handsome face, his long curled chestnut mustache, his blue eyes. Edward had always felt a special bond with his father. John had spent abundant time with him since Edward's earliest childhood, teaching him the noble sports of horsemanship, tilting at the quintain, fencing, archery, tennis and bowls.

Whenever father and son were both in residence at Castle Hedingham, the de Vere family seat for 450 years, Edward relished accompanying his father three mornings each week on visits to his tenants and to conduct business in nearby towns.

Edward did not share such a close relationship with his mother. Margery Golding, second wife of John, was a dignified, shy, reserved intellectual who bought books for Edward in any language and often spoke Latin with him. But he felt strained and awkward with her. His seven-year-old sister Mary, on the other hand, had a strong bond with their mother, often sitting contentedly with her for hours going over lessons.

When Earl John dismounted, Edward got to his feet. He noted that his forty-five-year-old father seemed subdued and uncharacteristically pensive, his usual charisma lacking.

John placed his arm affectionately around his son as he guided him silently along the river past Edward's favorite gnarled yew tree to the top of a slight rise. A field of wheat stretched out before them. They paused and watched the slowly moving folds of silvered green roll across the shallow valley, the quiet breaths of wind lovingly touching and curving the stalks like gentle waves on a tranquil estuary during an incoming tide. Beyond, the smoothly rolling countryside was interspersed with patches of oaks and elms, hedgerowed pastures, and small clusters of houses surrounding steepled churches.

But the world as Edward knew it—safe, constant and consistent—was about to tilt precariously.

"Many Englishmen find Essex tiresome," John said with a sigh. He patted Edward's back tenderly, always feeling a special comradeship with his only son. "But I have always loved its gentle landscape. It is a beautiful and fertile area of England." He gently tipped Edward's chin upward so that his son's vision would duplicate his own. "I pray that this lovely countryside has entranced your soul . . . as it has mine."

"It already has, Father," Edward assured him, "just as the ocean captures the mind and spirit of the mariner."

A wandering twinge of John's heart suddenly reminded him of his mission: the serious job of letting go. He placed his hand on his chest in hopes of steadying the tenuous rhythm of life. He stole a glance at his beloved son, wondering if this boy was yet ready to hear such vital inner thoughts.

"I must share something with you, Edward. This morning I experienced two episodes of chest pain."

Edward turned to look up at him and said quickly, "But it's gone now?"

"Yes . . . for now. It is not the pain which concerns me, but its implications. For many generations in our family, few of our men have lived longer than four years after such pain or after an episode of weakness of an arm or leg."

A cold sweat broke out on Edward's forehead, followed by a sudden chill. "But that's impossible! You are so young!"

"I plan to be an exception to the four-year rule, Edward."

"I'm sure you will be, Father."

John's voice thickened at the blend of fear and hopefulness in his young son's voice. "I must mention an item of great importance. Henry Hastings and I have produced what we feel is an excellent marriage arrangement for you with either of his two youngest sisters, Elizabeth or Mary. As you know, they are of royal blood and both girls are bright and charming. Either one will make you a lovely wife."

Edward cocked his head. "I like them both, especially Mary. But do we have to talk about marriage? I am only eleven!"

John smiled wistfully. "Of course you are only eleven. But it is essential that we speak of such things. If I die while you are under the age of twenty-one, you will be taken away from your mother and sister to become a royal ward."

"Father, that will not be—"

"If that happens, your wardship will be purchased and you must live in your guardian's home. All decisions about finance, education and marriage can be forced upon you by him under the laws of England."

Edward filled with disgust. He turned and threw

a rock forcefully into the river below and watched it sink in the shallow water. "How disgraceful! Whenever a nobleman dies, his children become little more than slaves, without even a choice of whom to marry!"

"We can do something about that, Edward. Listen carefully. A pre-existing marriage contract will free you to choose, after the age of eighteen, either Mary or Elizabeth. Henry and I detest the concept of forced marriage, so we have added the unusual option that both individuals must agree and freely consent or the contract becomes non-binding."

"Thank you for that!"

"There are three copies of the marriage contract," John continued. "You will have one, Henry Hastings has one, and I have given the third to a trusted family friend. It is essential that you keep your copy of the contract securely locked in your chest. You must not lose it."

"But if there are two others—"

"Yes, yes," his father said with uncharacteristic impatience. "But this matter is ultimately your responsibility. Unfortunately, loyalties can be bought and documents can be intentionally lost or destroyed. This contract is a powerful legal instrument. It cannot be overruled by any greedy individual or even the Court of Wards. You must protect it at all costs or your entire life could be adversely affected."

"Yes, Father," Edward said solemnly, shaking his head from side to side and looking at the ground.

Only then did John seem to relax a little. They stood together as the sun touched the western horizon. Shadows pooled and thickened as the sky reddened, forming a flaming russet backdrop for darting swallows.

John reflected that the goodnight kiss of the sun

was one less for him to enjoy. But he knew that this afternoon was an important moment of transition, as father and son became man to man.

After an affectionate hug, Earl John rode off toward Great Yeldham to confirm food supplies for the large entourage on Royal Progress about to visit the de Vere household.

Edward walked sluggishly toward home, angling away from the river along a narrow path up the hill, hands clasped behind him. He passed through the ancient brick entrance gate to Castle Hedingham and watched a pair of stockdoves glide to the edge of the smallest fishpond, gracefully land and sip. The sun's rays scintillated off the small patch of iridescent green below their beaks.

A beautiful vignette, thought Edward, *but my own throat is not scintillating; it is tight and my mouth dry.* He had started the beautiful summer day filled with growing excitement over the Queen's impending visit to their castle. Now he felt a foreboding sense of disquiet about his own future and a much bleaker sense of apprehension about the fate of his youthful, convivial companion-father.

He walked up the gravel road, across the arched brick bridge over the dry moat and past the stately castle-keep to the elegant towered manor house. He slowly ascended the stairs to his book-shelved room and sat at his desk, fighting back tears as he gazed at the peaceful darkening countryside.

After a few moments, he pushed up his sleeves and began to write:

> *What plague is greater than the grief of mind?*
> *The grief of mind that eats in every vein;*
> *In every vein that leaves such clots behind;*

Such clots behind as breed such bitter pain;
So bitter pain that none shall ever find,
What plague is greater than the grief of mind?

As he softly put down his pen, a tranquil confidence pervaded him and his throat no longer felt constricted.

Chapter 2

The purest treasure mortal times afford
Is spotless reputation: that away,
Men are but gilded loam or painted clay.
- Othello

Thirteen-year-old Edward sat down on a red brick wall in front of Whitehall Palace on a gray squally day in March, 1563, early for his royal appointment. A brief shaft of sunlight gleamed into the choppy waters of the Thames and sparkled off the back of a darting trout. Edward smiled as he thought that it must be a native English fish, so startled did it seem by a ray of sunshine.

As a light rain began to fall, he let his mind drift. How quickly his life had changed when his father had died suddenly seven months before, one year after telling him of his first chest pains. Edward had immediately been acquired as a ward of the Queen. He was purchased by William Cecil, Principal Secretary of

England and new Master of the Court of Wards, the most powerful man in the country, for not even a farthing.

A few days after his father's burial, obeying Cecil's request, Edward had ridden to London during two days of rain with 140 black-garbed retainers, all riding horses richly caparisoned in black. Sitting erect, wet and dignified, the new premier earl of the realm traversed the entire length of London past gaping gossiping commoners to Cecil House, his new home in Westminster.

Cold spray blew on his face, interrupting his unhappy remembrance. He licked his lips and tasted the river's mild saltiness. The rain had stopped. A gust of wind rippled the feathers of the many white swans bobbing on the dark river and reminded him of his appointment with the Queen.

He straightened his purple jacket, jumped down from the wall and strolled confidently through Whitehall's northern Holbein Gate. He saluted the red-and-yellow-clad guards who smiled and returned the salute. He climbed a long staircase, walked along the familiar portrait-lined gallery and was admitted to the Queen's crowded presence chamber.

Queen Elizabeth was magnificently attired in a bejeweled pink skirt ribbed by whale bone farthingales jutting out at the hips and falling perpendicularly to the floor. Kneeling in front of her were two French diplomats, restlessly taking the pressure off each knee in turn as Elizabeth, pacing back and forth, gave long answers in French to their brief statements. She seemed overly serious, lacking her usual flair.

Elizabeth was indeed in a domineering negative mood, this one triggered by one of her recurrent headaches. She was brusque in her Latin conversation with the German emissaries and in her Italian comments to the papal envoy.

Edward looked around the room and admired the ten tall battle-axe carrying gentlemen pensioners on either side of the chair of state, the brilliantly-colored tapestries with scenes of Africa, and the white-clad maids of honor whispering with the Queen's courtiers.

Elizabeth had acceded to the throne in 1558 at the age of twenty-five. With his mother a lady in waiting and his father a courtier, Edward had interacted with the Queen on many occasions and was very familiar with palace activities. Her five-day visit to Castle Hedingham in the summer of 1561 had been eminently successful. She had enthusiastically complimented him on the interlude he had written for the occasion and the humorous performance he had given with his father's acting troupe, playing the role of jester. He happily recalled how often he had acted on the stage since earliest childhood, his father encouraging his natural acting ability and comic bent. As the last foreign emissary arose and backed away, Edward's name was called. He came forward and knelt.

"Stand up, Viscount Bolebec," said Elizabeth fondly. She was the same height as Edward but her high-soled chopines made her taller. Because of his keen mind, quick wit, and maturity of conversation, she had talked to him for many years as an adult. "What earth-shaking message have you brought your Queen today which will rock our staid court's complacency?"

Edward admired her strong face, pleasingly handsome and elegant. Her forehead was high, her eyelashes thin, her Tudor nose somewhat prominent, her mouth narrow. Her eyes were lovely emerald-green counterpoints to her high-tiered, flaming orange-golden hair inherited from her grandmother, Elizabeth of York. He felt comfortable and relaxed with her.

"I would seek Your Majesty's permission to leave Cambridge for a term to begin work translating Ovid's *Metamorphoses,* an assignment my Latin tutor, Uncle Arthur Golding, has challenged me to do."

Well-knowing Edward's precocity, having heard reports of his clever original student dramas at Cambridge and having recently read his pseudonymously-published 3000 line narrative poem on Romeus and Juliet, the Queen decided to tease him. "And what will be your essential role in the endeavor, punctuation?" She threw her head back and laughed shrilly with a metallic vibrancy that flickered the torch flames and accentuated her headache.

Edward enjoyed wit-games but decided that seriousness was more appropriate to the learned Queen's tenuous mood. "Your Majesty, most translations are too literal, completely losing the flavor and essence of the original. Uncle Golding has an unparalleled knowledge of Latin but he realizes that his type of formal verbatim translation would not do Ovid justice. He wants me to translate all fifteen books as part of my training in the classics. We both think I can add meter, melody, rhyme and a dash of novelty to the *Metamorphoses,* creating a work of art true to Ovid's beautiful poetry."

Elizabeth, with hands pressing on her temples to attenuate her pulsing headache, felt acerbic. Was this interview worthy of Queenly time? "An ambitious idea but why not just ask William Cecil?"

"Approval by you is much more meaningful to me, Your Majesty."

Edward hesitated, then decided to speak forthrightly. "William Cecil has little tolerance for creativity and despises all poetry, poets and writers." He thought of Cecil's many derogatory remarks about his poetry. He reached into his jacket pocket, pulled out a clove and placed it between his teeth to add flavor to his drying mouth and to remind him to be careful with his major weapon, his words.

The Queen's eyes glazed. She was well aware of the strengths and weaknesses of her Principal Secretary but her trusted and most relied-upon councilor must not be criticized in any manner in public, especially by a mere boy.

"You have my permission, Edward," she said with penetrating coldness. "And does our little bastard want anything more from us today?"

A strained silence permeated the room. No movement could be seen, as if everyone in the presence chamber had become marbleized. Edward's shoulders stiffened upward, his lips firmly set. His eyes narrowed, infused with the confident look of generations of pride, like those of a peregrine about to strike its prey.

Edward thought for a moment: he wished he could be as patient as a gentle meandering stream but he *could not*, and *would not*, accept the biting edge of slander.

"Your Majesty, you are my Queen and I am your loyal subject. But I am also Edward de Vere, Seventeenth Earl of Oxford and Lord Great Chamberlain of England. I respectfully request that you *never* call me bastard again. You trample my good name with no just cause and deride with contempt my honorable family."

Taken aback, Elizabeth stared at Edward. She knew her remark was inappropriate. How sharply she personally had felt the venomous sting of illegitimacy-accusations! *What courage he shows,* she thought, *to stand his ground at age thirteen against the Queen of England! What a unique combination of talents and traits he has. . . . I wonder what role I can find for him in my court?*

A sudden throbbing pain lanced behind her eyes. *God's wounds! Why are divinely-inspired monarchs impaled by headaches?* She squinted her eyes against the sudden brightness of the torches and clenched her teeth to distract her pain. *By God's precious soul, Queens do not apologize!* She gestured him away, turned around with a rustling swirl of her immense skirt, and disappeared into her private chambers.

*   *   *

Edward walked firmly from the presence chamber, then ran from the palace into a downpour. A servant let him into elaborately-turreted, massive Cecil House on the Strand in Westminster. He changed his wet clothes and put on his crimson velvet night-robe. He was appalled at the Queen's totally undeserved public assault on his honor. He tried to elevate his thoughts by looking at the small white busts of Ovid and Plautus on the green marble mantle.

He lit a fire. As he was warming his hands, his guardian barged into the room without knocking. *If private sanctuaries can be invaded with impunity,* thought Edward, *civility in the Cecil household certainly has a thin veneer.*

Cecil was wearing his familiar long black robe, lined and collared with brown rabbit fur. He was stout with graying hair, pointed silver beard and disquieting eye-movements. Edward respected him and, at times, thought he might even be fond of him.

"I understand you have offended, yes, grievously offended, the Queen."

"Hardly accurate, Sir," Edward responded, impressed at the speed with which Cecil's highly organized spy-system kept him informed.

"Then what is your version, yes, your fanciful tale?"

"For no reason whatsoever she offended me and my family by calling me bastard. I courteously but forcefully requested that she cease slandering me. She had no cause to denigrate me."

"She had all the cause she requires, Edward. She is Queen. She can do and say anything she wants without the expert guidance of a thirteen-year-old. Although I am her principal, yes, her chief councilor, I am often battered by her tongue and deem it prudent not to respond."

Edward aggressively rubbed the de Vere ring on his left thumb with its incised family rebus of a boar. "Verbal dishonoring of my name, despite my youth, cannot and will not be accepted from any source. The Queen clearly is aware that my older half-sister's ill-advised bastardy suit has been dismissed."

Edward shook his head in disgust over Katherine's greed in claiming the de Vere inheritance after their father's death, and the disgracing bastardy claims with which he and Mary had to live for an entire year. "Surely she knows that Uncle Arthur Golding has proved in court the validity of my father's second marriage, to Arthur's sister Margery."

Edward motioned to his guardian to sit down and Cecil continued. "I am not in favor of your ill-considered request to drop out of Cambridge to spend time on a silly poem, a silly ancient poem."

"Poems are not silly, sir. Throughout recorded history poetry often represents the finest writing a culture produces." He was amazed at Cecil's crenelated mind, with such strong merlons of political wisdom alternating with devastating gaps of intellectual emptiness.

"It is time to become serious, Edward. Yes, pasttime. You have a brilliant future in the Queen's court but you must give up this wasteful writing habit, squandering your time and talent."

"Hardly squandering. It is a mind-elevating and stimulating pursuit."

Cecil tightened his grip on his long white staff. "As you know well, Edward, nobles are not allowed to use their hands in a craft. That is for the lewd lesser classes. And if you do write anything worthwhile, you know it is a disgrace to the nobility to attach one's name to a product of hand-work. Yes, quite disgraceful!"

Edward stuck a clove between his teeth. Who was Cecil, grandson of a tavern-owner, to tell England's prime earl how to behave? "These strange ideas are passing fads, sir. Poets in ancient Greece and Rome were heaped with honors! England is a young country with little literature, no drama and a word-starved language."

Cecil looked at him with disdain. "Who benefits from pretty phrases and asinine jingles? Edward, we enjoy having you live with us but please don't embarrass us further with posies." Cecil limped slowly from the room, stomping his white staff on the floor.

Edward gritted his teeth and paced the floor. *First a bastard, now a useless waster of words.* A poem began forming in his mind. He closed his eyes and savored its development for a few minutes.

He sat at his desk, dipped his quill pen in his inkwell, titled his poem *Loss of Good Name* , and began to write:

> *Fram'd in the front of forlorn hope past all recovery,*
> *I stayless stand, to abide the shock of shame and infamy.*
> *My sprites, my heart, my wit and force, in deep distress are drown'd;*
> *The only loss of my good name is of these griefs the ground.*
> *And since my mind, my wit, my head, my voice and tongue are weak,*
> *To utter, move, devise, conceive, sound forth, declare and speak,*
> *Such piercing plaints as answer might, or would my woeful case,*
> *Help crave I must, and crave I will, with tears upon my face,*
> *Of all that may in heaven or hell, in earth or air be found,*
> *To wail with me this loss of mine, as of these griefs the ground.*

Edward put down his pen, his muscles no longer tense.

Chapter 3

Thou wretched, rash, intruding fool, farewell !
- Hamlet

Seventeen-year-old Edward felt both relieved and sad to be leaving the stimulating intellectual companionship of Publius Ovidius Naso, born 1500 years ago, but he knew that Ovid had become an intimate part of his writing core. As he completed the final lines of his own original *Preface* to Ovid's *Metamorphoses,* his absorbing four year literary task was finally finished:

> *Considering what a sea of goods and jewels thou shalt find,*
> *Not more delightful to the ear than fruitful to the mind.*
> *For this do learned persons deem of Ovid's present work.*

*That in no one of all his books, the which he
wrote, do lurk*

*More dark and secret mysteries, more counsels
wise and sage,*

*More good examples, more reproves of vice in youth
and age.*

*More fine inventions to delight, more matters
clerkly knit,*

*No, nor more strange variety to show a learned
wit.*

*The young, the old, the good, the bad, the war-
rior strong and stout;*

*The wise, the fool, the country clown, the learned
and the lout,*

*With constellations of the stars and planets in
their climes.*

*Moreover thou mayst find herein descriptions of
the times.*

Exhausted, Edward slowly stretched his legs, smiled
with satisfaction, and placed his pen on his desk. He
wondered whether any human pleasure could surpass
the overwhelming joy of creativity fulfilled. He put the
morning writings into his special walnut chest and
locked its double bolts with different keys.

Draping a green velvet cape over his shoulders
he strode jauntily out of the room. He closed the
door, jumped down the balustraded stairs two at a
time, and walked briskly out the back door to his
favorite flowered nook in the garden of Cecil House.

He sat on a black marble bench damp with rain
and admired the droplet-adorned red and white
roses sparkling in the sunshine. How right the Greeks
were to design gardens as places for mental recre-
ation. No wonder they called them *paradeisoi* !

He rubbed his shoes on the purple-flowered thyme and water mint that were carefully planted between the path's gravel squares. He got down on his hands and knees to inhale the mind-invigorating sweet spiciness.

"What entrancing senses combine to fragrance the elixir of life," he whispered softly. He sat back on the bench, listened attentively to the faint buzz of a few industrious bees, and tried to absorb fully nature's endless banquet for the human spirit.

Edward let his mind drift into his creative world of words and remained there until raindrops began to sprinkle his reflective mood. With a poem forming in his mind, Edward walked happily from the garden and bounded up the stairs.

As he arrived in front of his room, he was surprised to see that the door was ajar. A boy about his own age was kneeling over Edward's now wide-open storage chest, searching through his private papers. The young intruder was scattering his best literary creativity and most important family documents across the floor.

For a moment, Edward's rage was so great that he could not speak. Blood pulsed loudly in his ears. He reached for his sword but quickly remembered that he was not wearing it.

"My God, are you stealing from my private chest?" he said sharply. "I keep no jewels or money there!"

The youth, garbed in a greasy apron, leapt up wide-eyed.

"Speak! Identify yourself, you scurvy knave!" Edward shouted as he clenched his fists. He watched the boy's jaws working wordlessly, like a loathsome rat gnawing on stolen cheese.

Edward shouted, "Repulsive rodent, do you work in the kitchens? Speak!"

Beads of sweat popped out on the lad's pale face. "My name is Tom Bricknell, sir," he rasped. "I am an apprentice cook and have worked for Mr. Cecil for only a month."

"God's wounds, why are you robbing me?" Edward squeezed the iron keys in his pocket. His heart was pounding. "How did you unlock my chest?"

Receiving no answer, he moved firmly toward a pair of crossed swords on the wall. Tom Bricknell staggered backward toward a tapestry of Troy hanging a foot from the wall.

"Answer me!" Edward demanded. "Do you know England's penalty for stealing, you foul felon? Hanging! You throw down your gauntlet at the Seventeenth Earl of Oxford's feet? I accept your challenge!"

Tom reached for the tapestry, his eyes wide, his mouth agape.

Edward grabbed the two swords and tossed one at the feet of the boy. Edward's fury had cooled into a hard knot in his stomach.

He visualized himself as a knight defending virtue against evil. "He who steals my writings steals my soul! The time is *now*, Tom. Tell me the truth!" Bending his knees, he took the *en garde* position.

Tom looked wildly around the room, like a fox surrounded by baying hounds. His body quivering, he glanced helplessly at the sword he knew not how to use, then jumped behind the tapestry.

Edward moved forward, feeling the full insult to himself and his noble heritage. *By Jesus, a despicable brigand stealing my most precious documents!* "One last chance, Tom! Defend yourself with *truth,* and life is yours! Do so now or prepare to die!"

No sound came forth.

"Thou wretched, rash, intruding fool, farewell!"

bellowed Edward as he lunged forward, thrusting his sword through the tapestry. He felt it plunge into yielding flesh, then heard a soft gasp as Tom fell to the floor and rolled into view. A rapidly expanding crimson stain spread over the left side of his chest. His astounded eyes flickered twice, and a soft sigh, too quiet to be a groan, escaped him. He twitched and lay still.

Edward instantly dropped the bloodied sword as a cold comber of astonishment washed over him. "My God, what have I done?" He stood as silent as death itself as the room around him seemed to transform itself into a tomb. Had he just taken a human life? *What a split-second brevity there is between life's vitality and death's sudden stillness* !

He tried to form a prayer but only the grief of silence drifted spiritless inside him. The young man's blood formed a transfixing stain on the rug. He thought of the garden and his tranquil savoring of nature's endless beauty. Now in a flicker of time the miracle of life itself had been extinguished.

He bent down low near the body and spoke the only word that would come forth: "Why?"

But there was no answer from this innocent-appearing youth. Edward noticed the boy's small hands, almost childlike and sinless, yet caught in a sinful act. He suddenly felt bitter bile force itself into his throat as he began to retch. He ran to the corner and vomited into the washbasin.

Lingering over the bowl for several moments, he splashed cold water onto his face from a pitcher and walked slowly to his walnut chest, staring at the inlaid ivory boars, the de Vere rebus.

Then he quickly looked through his family documents, his translation of Ovid's *Metamorphoses,* his one-act plays, and his poetry. Nothing seemed to be missing, but nothing seemed to be important at this moment, either. A cursory search disclosed no stolen papers on Tom's body.

God's blood! What was he trying to find? He stared at the unreal scene, his heart racing, his body trembling.

He knew he would have to tell his guardian, William Cecil.

*   *   *

Edward walked slowly to the other end of the house, hesitating outside Cecil's study door. A wave of despair engulfed him and he had to lean against the wall, afraid his knees would buckle. Finally he replenished his inundated strength and rapped on the door.

He heard a groan and then: "Enter."

Plumped up at his desk as though it were his own personal throne was England's portly, white-bearded, 47 year-old Principal Secretary, England's most powerful politician for the past nine years.

Cecil was grimacing and grasping his inflamed gouty right foot above a pewter basin filled with warm water, vinegar and floating daisies.

"Must you knock the door off its hinges, Edward?" Cecil said crankily. "Are you so eager to read me your latest childish verses that you jerk my toe into torment?" Cecil proudly looked around his room. No tapestries or artwork interrupted its Spartan décor. The purpose of books was to impart useful knowledge—architecture, horticulture, and government, such as Machiavelli's *The Prince* .

Cecil put his foot back in the basin and groaned again. "You seem troubled, Edward. Sit down. Yes, do sit down. Why so distraught?"

"I have . . ." Edward felt suddenly speechless and vacant as the act rewound itself through his mind. Words had always been his life and now they abandoned him. He cleared his throat, walked across the room and stood with his back against a colorful arras showing Dutch fishing vessels leaving harbor. "I have sad news," he said in a voice unlike his own. "I caught the new undercook, Tom Bricknell, trying to rob my room. I allowed emotions to overwhelm me and . . . and I killed him."

Cecil's eyebrows lifted momentarily but no other emotion crossed his face. He straightened his black robe and slowly stroked his beard. "Are you sure he is quite dead?"

"Yes."

Cecil toweled his foot tenderly. "Let us go to your room. Did he say anything before he died?"

"No. He was too frightened."

Edward walked slowly behind a hobbling Cecil who leaned heavily on his long white stave. When they reached Edward's room, Cecil gazed down at the bloody body.

"Tom seemed like such a nice shy lad," he said. "Yes, quiet and shy. I hired him myself. Hard to believe he was a thief, a common felon."

"Would that I could move time backwards!" Edward blurted. He felt warm tears swim across his vision, threatening to spill across his face. He turned to stare out the window and blinked once, twice.

"I wonder what he was searching for," Cecil said with a shrug as his eyes flitted about. "This might not have happened if you didn't misuse your time writing poetry and translating meaningless ancient poems, keeping them in your chest—which I'm sure Tom thought was full of precious stones."

Edward turned to stare at him, finding it hard to believe that Cecil was once again deriding his writing, this time in the midst of such a sorrowful scene. He briefly recalled how Cecil, before enrolling at Cambridge, had legally rejected his family name of Sitsilt, connoting being mired in dark murky water, and changed it to Cecil with an iron determination to forge the Cecils from commoners into a leading noble family. Edward had never thought it prudent to point out to his legal guardian that the word 'cecil' was derived from the Latin *caecilius,* meaning dimsighted.

Edward pulled a clove out of his pocket and stuck it forcefully between his teeth, deciding it was best not to respond.

Cecil's eyes returned to Tom's bloody body. "This killing must be managed immediately and calmly. I will do my best to ensure a verdict of *se defendendo* at the inquest."

"But that is not the truth!" exclaimed Edward. "It was not a case of self-defense! I must testify and declare the facts!"

Cecil gave him a look of arrogant disdain, reminding Edward of a venomous toad lurking in the shadows beneath a bridge. "And I must emphatically insist that you leave it to me alone. Truth often only complicates matters. Muddies the waters, so to speak." Without another word, he limped slowly from the room, stomping his staff on the floor.

*   *   *

With Edward being a minor in wardship, Cecil forbade his presence at the hearing. The jury reached a verdict of *felo-de-se,* a felony against one's self through one's own fault. Tom Bricknell had died from falling upon the point of a sword during the commission of an unlawful act. The details leading up to the killing had not been provided to the jury by the Principal Secretary and did not become part of the legal record.

That night, Edward sat in his elaborately carved maple chair and watched the dark rain cascade over the two stained glass panes which he had copied from St. Nicholas Church in his home village of Castle Hedingham. He looked at the round Earl of Oxford pane, a brown ox fording a blue stream. His eyes moved to the square pane containing the simple red and gold de Vere heraldic shield with a five-pointed silver star in the upper dexter red quarter, the fierce blue boar above, and the family motto below: *Vero Nihil Veritas*–Nothing Truer Than Truth. He wondered why truth was such a rarity, why the world was so given to lying.

As the rain slashed at the window, he felt a cold perfusion of loneliness. He was perplexed by God's strange and often sad ways. He pondered the words he had written *To The Reader* of his first long narrative poem, *Tragicall Historye of Romeus and Juliet*, published under a coerced pseudonym five years before:

> *So the good doings of the good and the evil acts*
> *of the wicked, the happy success of the blessed*
> *and the woeful proceedings of the miserable, do*
> *in diverse sort sound one praise of God.*

He lowered his eyes to the bare oak floor as he sadly reflected upon his recent consolatory visit with Tom Bricknell's parents, simple barley farmers in Fiddlers Hamlet outside of London. They were as baffled as Edward.

"Tom was God-fearin' and completely honest all

his short life," said his mother as she wiped away her tears. "Stealin' would never've occurred to 'im."

Edward solemnly vowed on his chivalric honor to unravel the mystery of Tom's inexplicable behavior.

Chapter 4

Come now, what masques, what dances shall we have
To wear away this long age of three hours
Between our after-supper and bed-time?
Where is our usual manager of mirth?
What revels are in hand? Is there no play
To ease the anguish of a torturing hour?
- A Midsummer Night's Dream

Lightning split the sky and thunder exploded against the mullioned panes of Whitehall Palace as if Zeus were making one final tumultuous objection to the end of a particularly rainy English spring.

In the great hall, the head table was tense with its own kind of storm. Even the light of tapers along the walls and the flare of black iron chandeliers hanging from the high-beamed ceiling could not diminish the murk of quarrel in the room.

Edward watched as the Queen tried to distract her somber mood. One of the major goals of her reign, to keep England at peace both at home and abroad, was in jeopardy.

It was June of 1569, and William Cecil's spies had confirmed that the powerful Catholic earls of Northumberland, Cumberland, and Westmoreland were massing their troops along the Scottish border for an invasion south to London. Their goal was to take over the Crown and re-establish Catholicism under Mary Queen of Scots, now detained under house arrest in England.

Elizabeth, the daughter of Henry VIII and Anne Boleyn, was aware that they regarded her as a bastard. Her father's divorce from Catherine of Aragon and marriage to Anne had never been ratified by the Pope.

Edward listened to the storm rage outside as he shifted his glance to Robert Dudley, master of the horse, enriched in one year by Elizabeth with grants of sixteen landed estates, 12,000 pounds in currency, a manor house on the Thames, the Earldom of Leicester, and a Knighthood. Elizabeth and Robert had been childhood friends, born in the same hour on the same day. Edward was aware that there were few members of inner Court circles who didn't believe they were long-time lovers.

Edward also knew that Lord Robert had often been given rooms adjacent to hers in palaces and on progresses. And hadn't she been observed quietly tickling the back of his neck? Hadn't Leicester been seen early in the morning in the royal bedchamber handing the Queen her shift as she arose out of bed naked? Hadn't she admitted to the Spanish ambassador, "I wish to confess to you my secret, which is that I am no angel and do not deny that I have some affection for Lord Robert."

Edward had heard that the Queen told Kat Ashley, her former governess, that if she had decided to lead an unchaste life, she did not know of anyone who could forbid her. Most courtiers and maids of honor believed that the Queen had been delivered of a son fathered by her "Sweet Robin" in 1561, secretly giving up the child immediately for adoption by a non-noble family.

Leicester took a final bite out of a roasted swan breast and threw it on the floor, causing a wild snarling scramble by half a dozen dogs. Downing a full goblet of wine, he waved his knife at Christopher Hatton, the rising new favorite of the Queen seated on her left.

"You want to lead our troops to battle against the Northern Rebels?" Leicester said in a mocking tone. "That's the first joke I've ever heard from your lips! You couldn't lead a troop of pigs across a farmyard!"

The room grew silent, the diners waiting tensely for the Queen's reaction. Both men, tall and handsome, were tactfully dressed in black velvet to allow Elizabeth's gold-embroidered, red satin dress to appear more magnificent. Each now sought opportunities to prove his masculine supremacy, like two antlered stags in the rut.

"And you, Lord Leicester, who have never won a jousting tournament except perhaps in a linen closet, desire to be anointed an instant general?" answered Hatton haughtily. "Will you lead your men with your earring or your codpiece?"

Leicester's cheeks reddened. He cast a sidelong glance at the Queen, refilled his goblet and plunged ahead. "And will you frighten away the northern rebels with one of your effeminate dancing capers?"

Hatton was incensed that Leicester was making

fun of his invitation from the Queen to become a courtier after she had become attracted to his dancing in a masque at Gray's Inn. He drew up his chest and replied, "And you, sir, will you try to make as many openings in enemy battle lines as you have in women's apparel?" Hatton laughed and his nostrils flared. "And does your dark skin hint a Moorish derivation?"

A sudden clap of thunder shattered the silence as both men reached for their daggers. Hatton and Leicester were perilously close to a forbidden weapon-drawing confrontation before the sovereign.

Edward was confident that the Queen would cleverly ease the tension. But it was William Cecil who quickly stood, raised his hand and said, "Please, please. Meals are times for relaxation and entertainment." He beckoned for the minstrels to begin their strolling singing. "All of us want to serve our Queen on the battlefield. Why, if it weren't for my gout . . ."

The Queen rinsed her sticky hands in a silver basin of water with floating rose petals. Alluding to Cecil's only exercise—riding his mule—she said, "It's not *your* gout, Spirit, but your *mule's* gout which would prevent your leading my troops into battle!"

The royal entourage burst into relieved laughter.

The Queen's diverting sally set Edward's mind wandering. At age nineteen, he was partially content with his present life as a courtier, one of the few professions open to noblemen which allowed time for study and writing.

He was frustrated, however, that he was not free to learn more about the world's fascinating diversities. He was constantly reminded that Elizabeth was very possessive of her courtiers and demanded that their total energies be devoted to

her and her Court. But why had she allowed several courtiers to leave for their tour of Europe at
age seventeen, and not him?

He realized suddenly that the Queen's attention
had turned to him. With her green eyes sparkling,
she said, "And you, Edward de Vere, with all of your
university degrees at such a young age, I suppose
you also want to be commander-in-chief and take on
the rebels all by yourself, pen in hand!"

When he didn't answer immediately, she added,
"Please join us, Commander Edward! Are you dream-
ing of fairies in enchanted forests?"

"Begging your pardon, Majesty. My only wish is
to serve England faithfully, as all de Veres have done
for five hundred years. But I doubt that I could conquer your foes with pen only. I would need parchment as well!"

The crowd laughed. Edward was pleased that
Elizabeth was indirectly honoring his recent comple-
tion of three years of law studies at Gray's Inn following his MA from Oxford at sixteen and his BA from
Cambridge at fourteen.

The Queen tipped her head in acknowledgment
of his witticism. Her golden hair was intertwined with
strings of glistening pearls. "And will the heavenly
power of your wit and poetry numb the rebels' minds
into stupefied paralysis?"

Edward was well acquainted with the Queen's
verbally frisky moods. Although he loved being on
stage and swaying a crowd's emotions, he was aware
that she had consumed more than her usual single
glass of wine and he decided to defer oral jousting.
"I would do anything to be allowed to participate in
that campaign, my Queen. But in order to relax my

brain for that endeavor, may I now join the maids of honor for sweets?"

The Queen nodded. Soon, repeated giggles emanated from Edward's group at the next table as they munched marchpane, a molded confection of pounded almond paste and sugar.

Finally a loud burst of laughter prompted Elizabeth to tap the ivory handle of her ostrich-feathered fan on the table. With an imperious but subtle smile, she said, "Lord Edward, we would know your gibe that set the maids in stitches. Stand and proclaim it loudly so that all of us may share in your thigh-slapping witticism!"

Edward and the maids had been making jokes about Hatton's and Leicester's glowering faces, dour and sour senses of humor, and how their black attire made them look like undertakers during a pestilence.

Edward pushed back his stool from the table but continued to sit, rubbing his de Vere boar seal-ring. He hesitated, knowing how the Queen enjoyed overpowering and embarrassing members of her entourage.

"Rise, my Lord of Oxford, and regale us," the Queen prompted. "In a voice as ringing as that of Aubrey de Vere enjoining his First Crusade troops to victory at Antioch, the fateful five-pointed star shining on his shield, tell us your mirth-provoking tidbit. I so command!"

Edward walked over to Patch, the royal jester, grabbed his cap and placed it on his head. "A quip, my gracious liege, melts like a flake of hapless snow when gazed upon by the Sun of Royalty!"

The flattered Queen smiled and waved her fan for him to continue.

"A transient joke, my Queen, is a bird of passage, sprite of wing, a mere flicker of ephemeral beauty. Shot down, it is mute feathers." He pretended to sit down. His mind was racing.

"S'death! You have audacity, young Bolebec-Patch, to parry my royal command! We would be tickled with those very feathers! Quickly, my Lord of Oxford, let us convulse with your jest."

All could see the glint of pleasure, mixed with challenge, in the eyes of the two wit-combatants.

"Most verbally incomparable and beauteous Queen," said Edward, doffing his jester's cap and bowing low. "I merely was telling a tale which came into my head today when I was walking through your royal orchard and an apple fell on my head."

"Continue. My laughter is not yet exhausted." She slowly opened and closed her fan.

"A husband is found kneeling and weeping in his orchard next to the body of his wife, who has just hanged herself from his apple tree. His neighbor walks over to comfort him, pats him consolingly on the back, and says, 'Friend, may I take a portion of your apple tree to graft on some stock in mine own orchard?'"

The banquet hall erupted in laughter. Even the smile-less Lady Mildred Cecil could not prevent a slight upturn at the corners of her mouth.

"Oh, come now, my young Lord Plagiarist," said the Queen, fanning herself rhythmically. "Think you that I sit all day sewing and spinning? That same story is in Baldassare Castiglione's *The Courtier*, except that with de Verean magic, you have changed figs into apples!"

She paused and regarded him thoughtfully for a moment. "Although I do congratulate you on your familiarity with that outstanding book, penalties accrue to plagiarists, and you are hereby sentenced to entertain us this very evening."

During the previous week, with the Queen's urging, Edward had quickly written a thirty-minute, one-act interlude for after-supper entertainment. Co-actors for the performance were his good friends Ned Somerset and Edward Manners, Earl of Rutland, the latter another of Cecil's noble wards.

The drama was a spoof of Philip, former husband of Queen Mary of England and now the fanatically Catholic and aggressive King of Spain. The interlude was a mixture of dialogue and pantomime, with Edward playing black-garbed Philip. One scene showed Philip teaching a new torturer how to operate the rack to extort information, with himself tied to the rack as an example. The novice, however, started the controls, stretching Philip to screaming agony. The final scene showed Philip kneeling next to his bed reading from the Bible, not realizing that he was actually reading from the Koran. The audience, well disinhibited by liberal portions of French wine, laughed appreciatively.

After the performance, Elizabeth stood and congratulated the actors, then waved her gloved hand signaling the end of the evening's formal festivities. She swung her silver scented pomander from side to side in front of her farthingaled bright red dress and allowed the retinue to disperse.

Edward basked in the satisfaction of inner contentment. He had been center stage before the Queen and had performed well. Wasn't it a normal human trait to allow the mellow sweetness of success to linger awhile to savor it fully?

Elizabeth beckoned him to her side. Sudden

understanding tightened his shoulders. He had seen the same glint in her eye at his estate of Havering-Atte-Bower a few months before when he had tactfully but narrowly escaped her amorous advances.

"Edward, you have delighted me tonight with your wit, your acting and your creativity. It would please me even more if you would join me in my antechamber in ninety minutes and read me some poetry."

"Your Majesty, I—"

"I will have a fire well-lit and will change into something more comfortable," she continued briskly, leaving no room for negotiation. "My overly-solicitous attendants will be dismissed so that our minds may blend without intrusion."

Chapter 5

"Fondling," she saith, "since I have hemmed thee here
Within the circuit of this ivory pale,
I'll be a park, and thou shalt be my deer.
Feed where thou wilt, on mountain or in dale;
Graze on my lips, and if those hills be dry,
Stray lower, where the pleasant fountains lie ."
— Venus and Adonis

Edward walked slowly to his room in the palace, tense with a blend of excitement and anxiety. He was totally inexperienced in the art of love and knew not how to please a woman. Clearly the Queen was interested in more than poetry tonight. Was the Goddess of Love—the Greek Aphrodite, the Phoenician Cytherea, the Roman Venus—melting her way to the surface?

Perhaps Elizabeth was merely tired of the tedious talk of Leicester, against whose rigid Calvinistic

gravities her jests and wit-cracks abutted unappreci-
ated. Was she looking for variety and a new challenge?

In his room, Edward undressed and began washing at his basin. He wondered nervously whether he
was Adonis in the Greek myth, who was beloved by
Venus but died of a boar's tusk-wound during a hunt.

He paused and tried to grasp a little courage.
Wasn't his family rebus a blue-tusked boar, derived
from the similarity between Vere and the Latin word
for boar, *verres* ? Why should he fear the wiles of the
Goddess of Love?

He admired the Queen for her learned agile
mind, her linguistic gifts, the truly regal manner in
which she conducted the Court, her political astute-
ness and her intense desire to bring peace and pros-
perity to her realm.

Despite their age difference of seventeen years,
he found her face comely, her presence powerful,
her personal charm captivating. As a loyal courtier
he could overlook her authoritarian ways, her intense
need for flattery and adulation, her frequent and
unrepentant manipulation of truth, and her tramp-
ling underfoot of anyone who stood in her way.

After drying himself, he put on his green jerkin
and breeches, yellow hose and cap. He drew a calm-
ing breath and walked to the Queen's antechamber.
Her door was partially open. He knocked and was
bid to enter.

Elizabeth was seated on a chair wearing a crimson night robe worn loosely in front, with no clothing underneath. The fragrance of several perfumes
filled the air. "Ah, cousin Edward, how handsome
you look!"

Edward noted that no candles were lighted. The
daggers of the fire stabbed the air with blazing gold,

glinting off the gold-embroidered wall tapestries and dancing along the waves of Elizabeth's orange-gold hair. He could see that she still glowed from the evening's wine.

She poured two glasses of dry Spanish sherry. They touched glasses and drank.

In an obvious attempt to put him at ease, Elizabeth began conversation on an intellectual note. "I have only recently finished re-reading *The Courtier.* Thus I could so easily trip you up on your little joke tonight. Do you agree with Duchess Elizabetta of Urbino and her learned friends about the ideal attributes of the perfect courtier?"

Edward sat near the fireplace, feeling the temporary safety of distance. "Yes, Your Majesty, and I am trying my best to emulate them."

"Be a good courtier and summarize them for me." Elizabeth looked admiringly at her long tapering fingers in the flickering firelight and convinced herself that they were pale and smooth, like those of a much younger woman.

Edward took a deep breath and let it out slowly. "The ideal courtier should be nobly-born and skilled in the knightly arts of war and sport. He should show good judgment and grace, and be chivalrous and complimentary to women. He should be learned, multi-lingual, have talents in writing and music and be capable of brilliant conversation. He must adorn and splendify the royal Court, all exhibited with an effortless nonchalance or *sprezzatura.*"

She smiled and beckoned. "Come sit by me and splendify my royal attributes."

Carrying his glass of sherry, Edward left the chair near the fireplace and crossed the room to sit beside her. In the hollow of his back, a single droplet of sweat traced the course of his spine. He wondered if she could hear the thumping of his heart.

"Are you still a virgin, Edward?" Elizabeth asked.

He looked at her for a moment, then dropped his eyes and gulped his sherry. He could feel a flush creeping up his neck into his cheeks. Speaking softly, he asked, "What is the answer you wish, Your Majesty, yea or nay?"

"Nothing truer than truth in my presence! *Vero Nihil Veritas*, or, as you so cleverly changed your family motto so it could also mean Nothing Truer Than Vere, *Vero Nihil Verius.*" She fidgeted with the sash around her robe.

"I don't know whether to be embarrassed or proud of it, Your Majesty, but the answer is 'yes.' I have always given higher priority to intellectual pursuits. I have taken a ribbing about it from my Gray's Inn friends and even from some of the fair damsels at Court."

She smiled faintly. "I sometimes wonder why I dress my maids of honor in white!"

"And might I ask the same question of you?" He surprised himself with his boldness, and took three quick sips of sherry.

The Queen's cheeks instantly reddened. "No, you might not! There are certain behaviors of queens which must remain secret. Our people need a monarch who can command adoration and loyalty." She paused, her gaze steady on his. "Don't you agree?"

"Absolutely."

"I am devoting my whole life to my country. I am already bound unto a husband which is the Kingdom of England! No man shall own me! Look what happened to my mother! The concept of a Virgin Queen is for the English people, who wish it so. It increases their reverence for the monarch, thus enhancing royal governance."

"I fully understand, my Queen."

"Must queens be angels or nuns, forbidden to taste life's sweet pleasures? My unmarried state is my virginity! Surely we who rule by Divine Right may make slight changes in word definitions!" She threw her robe more open at the top.

"Most assuredly, Your Majesty!" he said quickly.

"Well then," Elizabeth demanded, "fill our glasses and read me some stimulating poetry."

Edward quickly poured more sherry for them both. He recited from memory two witty poems in Latin he had written at Oxford, and then a long passage in Greek from *The Iliad*.

Elizabeth found herself carried away by the beauty of expression in these ancient tongues. She began to caress his leg sensitively. Although she felt the strong waves of her own desire, she knew that one must be gentle in coaxing a fawn from the forest.

Moving her hand slowly upward, she said softly, "Edward, I care for you greatly. I want you close to me. You did state, did you not, that you would *do anything* to participate in the northern war? I hereby promise you that it will be arranged."

Edward felt encircled. He looked down from above on the developing drama. What a scene, in the inner sanctum of an absolute monarch! Why not participate fully? Should not poets and dramatists understand and experience life as completely as possible? Why resist? Had he not recently written from his own imaginings:

> *I heartily beseech thee,*
> *To take advantage of presented joy.*

O, learn to love! The lesson is but plain
And once made perfect, never lost again .

Elizabeth got up and went slowly to a cherrywood chest, took out several satin pillows and arranged them in two parallel rows on the floor. "You do believe strongly in the precepts of a perfect courtier developed so clearly and so engagingly by the court of Urbino?"

He tried to speak, cleared his voice and tried again. "Of . . . . . . course, Your Majesty."

"Then you do agree that your major goal as a courtier is to love and obey your ruler, dedicating all of your strength and energy to adoring her above all else and devoting your every talent and ability to serving her?"

"Yes, Your Majesty," said Edward, feeling a growing warmth and a growing confidence.

"Then stand, Edward. Approach me and proudly disrobe in front of your admiring monarch. I would get to know thee better." She stood with legs apart, hands on hips.

Edward again filled both glasses, swirled his sherry, drank it in one swallow, and did as he was told. He felt only a pervading sense of harmony, a sense of unity with the warmth of the fire and the rising heat of his own excitement.

"You are most nobly proportioned, Edward . . . admirably sculpted to serve your Queen. It is time to let love follow its entrancing course."

She embraced him, kissing him tenderly, moving her hands slowly over his shoulders and neck. She stepped back, slipped from her robe and stood sideways in the firelight. She smiled as Edward gazed rapidly up and down and moved to her.

He began kissing and touching her with the haste of youthful inexperience. She tried to slow him down, guiding his hands delicately. But his mind was concentrating totally on his own new sensations. He breathed rapidly and began to tremble, consumed with an ardor quite unfamiliar to him. He could not control the powerful force that was overwhelming him.

Elizabeth smiled and tousled his hair with her right hand, then picked up her robe and placed it over the satin pillows. Putting her arms around him, she held him tightly and kissed him with greater intensity. She relished the moment, savoring it and him. His muscles rippled eagerly beneath her touch.

Elizabeth could feel her own desires mounting as she felt his innocent ardor rising powerfully. She moved backward, lightly massaging his chest and abdomen. She kneeled and caressed him tantalizingly for long moments, moving her body in rhythm with her hands.

Edward felt a fiery craving as she pulled him down gently but firmly to her soft, divinely inspired eyrie and coalesced his fervent passion with her own.

Chapter 6

But what a point, my lord, your falcon made,
And what a pitch she flew above the rest!
To see how God in all his creatures works!
Yea, man and birds are fain of climbing high.
— Henry VI, Part 2

Edward knew he possessed the soul of a writer but in what mode? He felt that he had a natural instinct for poetry but who would read it? Whatever his eventual medium, he was confident that his artistry and creative force would come with maturity. In the meantime, he must read, study, broaden his vocabulary and, like all writers, live life.

As he gazed out of his room at Windsor Castle in December of 1569 and watched the low gray clouds pour forth in heavy rain, Edward once again felt trapped. In early October, he had been afflicted with sweating sickness and was still coughing.

Elizabeth had insisted that he recuperate in her royal apartments at Windsor.

Even after his recovery, she told him to immerse himself in the library, forget about war, and be available for her royal visitations. She emphasized that these were his duties as a courtier, and for her they were necessary respites from the constant strain of statecraft.

He stared at the muddy Thames and impressively antlered royal red deer feeding on tall grasses in the meadow below the castle. He elevated his eyes northward, where he so longed to be. Yes, he loved solitude and the magic of an absolutely solitary day, but he would rather be earning honor in the war against the rebellious Catholic earls.

Edward began to reminisce. In his city-life as Cecil's ward, he had spent half of each year at Cambridge and half at Cecil House with brilliant tutors. He was proud of his unique modernizing of the 12,000 lines of Ovid's *Metamorphoses* and his own addition of 2,500 new lines plus many new coined words. He was grateful to Uncle Arthur Golding for publishing the work under his name, since Edward had been forbidden by Cecil from doing so.

He shook his head in wonderment that his society's guidelines forbade authorship by nobles—such an alien concept to him and to most cultures throughout history. He muttered aloud to himself, "If God endows a man with special writing talent, what purpose lies in denying authorship? Who benefits?"

Edward agreed with his tutors' dismay over the almost complete lack of agreed-upon spelling, punctuation and grammar in English despite William

Caxton's bringing of the printing press to England in 1476.

Languages came easily to him and he was now fluent in Latin, French and Italian, and he could read and write Greek. He knew he had achieved a solid reputation among his classmates as poet, actor and writer of interludes.

Edward agreed thoroughly with Thomas Smith, expert linguist, his tutor from the ages of three to eight, who believed that wardship was contrary to nature, and that a gentleman should not be bought and sold like an ox. But by archaic law revived by Henry VIII for reasons of greed, he was Cecil's ward and must do his bidding. All of his property and its income were in Cecil's control, as were all the major decisions of his life except marriage, since Edward was protected by his legal marriage contract. Although he would have preferred a different life-situation for himself, he admired Cecil's excellent choice of teachers and the intellectual atmosphere of his home.

Edward was aroused from his recollections by a sharp crackling from the fireplace which sent two glowing embers onto the bare floor. As he kicked the embers back into the fireplace, he was thankful that he kept his floors clean of the hated and unsanitary strewn rushes that characterized Elizabeth's palaces.

He settled himself deeper into his soft leather chair and thought about the Queen.

He enjoyed Elizabeth's visits despite the oozing ulcer on her left shin. The various interactions between himself and the Queen were increasingly concordant. The thought came to him that lovemaking was like a child that craved everything it could come by. He was awed by the contrast between the Queen's majestic bearing and her uninhibited love-habits, which he recently described in a poem as *the raging lust wherein thy limbs did rave* .

But Edward also felt more and more ensnared and confined at Windsor. It was as if he were nothing more than a bauble in a velvet box, a plaything for shallow, transient royal amusement. Oftentimes he wished he had a close friend with whom he could share his deepest thoughts. For the present, however, he had learned how to extract exquisite pleasure from carefully crafted words written across a page.

He continued to remind the Queen, tactfully yet forcefully, that royal promises, like all promises, should be kept. He began to feel for the first time the painful rankle of her deception and mendacity. The border war had already been active for two months and he longed to play a military role in the campaign which she had pledged. He wrote firmly in his tablet:

> *He that depends*
> *Upon your favours swims with fins of lead*
> *And hews down oaks with rushes . . . Trust ye?*

If he could not influence her with reminders of the sacredness of promises, Edward decided to appeal to her romantic instincts as a woman. He wrote her a personal poem and sent it by courier:

> *Who taught thee first to sigh alas, my heart?*
> *Who taught thy tongue the woeful words of plaint?*
> *Who filled your eyes with tears of bitter smart?*

Who gave thee grief and made thy joys to faint?
Who first did paint with colours pale thy face?
Who first did break thy sleeps of quiet rest?
Above the rest in court who gave thee grace?
Who made thee strive in honour to be best?

She continued to point out to Edward that his talents as courtier and companion were far more valuable to her than one additional armed horseman. She told him to remain at Windsor for her frequent visits and to refrain from further requests for front-line action in the border war.

* * *

Edward decided to spend considerable time in Windsor's library reading original historic documents. The trend of linguistic decline, as a reflection of English history, was clear to him. The original Celtic language of the Ancient Britons had disappeared after the Roman subjugation in 50 AD except for surviving pockets in Cornwall, Wales and Scotland. The subtlety and elegance of the Latin language during 450 years of Roman occupation was wiped out by the brutal decimation by Angle, Saxon, Frisian and Jute intruders whose intermixed language came to be called Old English.

Viking invasions led to an intermixture of Norse with Anglo-Saxon but it was a peasant-farmer society with no need for linguistic complexity. Grammar, spelling and pronunciation fell into a confused anarchy called Middle English.

Edward knew that William the Conqueror in 1066 brought an infusion of Latin-influenced French, but it was manifestly evident that English was still a crude tongue with an embarrassingly meager vocabulary. How different from the fullness and elegant intricacies of Roman literature, with their Latin so admirably influenced by Cicero's prose, Virgil's poetry, and countless other language-enhancing writers.

Being encompassed by books caused an expression to flash across his mind: *My library is dukedom large enough.* Edward felt that studying was akin to saturation in heaven's glorious sun and he wrote in his tablet:

> *What is the end of study, let me know?*
> *Why, that to know, which else we should not know.*
> *Things hid and barred, you mean, from common sense?*
> *Ay, that is study's godlike recompense.*

Having brought his favorite falcon with him to Windsor Castle and becoming tired of castle confines, one day he suggested to the Queen that they go hunting on the river.

"Wonderful idea, Edward. My leg is bothering me a bit, so I will watch you in action. I will be ready in an hour."

As they rode along the Thames, Elizabeth fanned herself with an emerald-encrusted fan.

"Tell me about your bird," she said. "She seems very comfortable with you."

Edward was carrying his hooded falcon on his gloved left hand. "Old John, our Scottish family falconer, taught me that there is only one choice, namely the noble female peregrine. Her name is Athena, Your Majesty, after the Greek goddess who, as you know, represents human wit and cleverness and is also goddess of the arts."

"How did you capture her?"

"Old John, who knows all the peregrine migration routes, caught her as a haggard when she was about three years old. He taught me that haggards are truly wild birds who fear humans and are difficult to train but are more astute hunters and worth the effort. During training, I never gave her a reprimand or scolding. Now she trusts me completely."

"Old King Harry taught me the same," she said approvingly. One of Elizabeth's heraldic badges was a falcon with crown and scepter. She was well-versed in falconry but enjoyed listening to Edward's descriptions. "How did you teach her to fly so high?"

"She already knew from her wild freedom that the highest flights are best. She quickly learned to wait-on by circling slowly overhead until we could flush a juicy mallard. It took only three days more to teach her that the steepest and fastest stoops are the best and most rewarding."

Edward reined in, signaling that he had spotted a mallard. They dismounted and tied their horses, then made their way in a crouching walk along a path lined with bushes. He unhooded Athena who strained with taut eagerness against her leather jesses. Edward let go, moving his hand upward. Athena took off away from the river and began to climb.

"Fly high and majestically, Athena," whispered Edward with pride, "and match or surpass your noble heritage."

The Queen looked at Edward, nodded her head subtly and smiled.

They watched Athena spiral higher and higher until she was a small dark speck against the brightness of a billowing white cloud. A wind was now blowing in the same direction as the flowing river.

Edward and the Queen stealthily moved forward and saw the single drake swimming restlessly. On the far side of the river were large willow trees and tall elms; on the side nearest the falconers, there were only bushes and shrubs.

Elizabeth exclaimed in a loud whisper, "I have never seen a falcon wait-on so high. She must be a thousand feet in the sky!"

The alert mallard flushed straight out of the water with a great flapping of wings and final noisy push with his splashing feet and headed at a steep angle toward the high trees.

Athena saw the duck's slow upward flight as a perfect opportunity. She immediately turned downward with her sleek, pointed wings partially folded and began to hurtle earthward. The drake, keeping his life-and-death adversary in view, quickly turned downriver and gathered speed. Instead of following the curving river, he cleared the low bushes on the bank and followed the wind precisely, his bright blue wing-patches and brilliant green head glistening in the sunshine.

Athena plummeted at extraordinary speed toward the mallard.

"Look at that stoop, Your Majesty!" shouted Edward.

"What perfect form!" said the Queen with equal enthusiasm.

But the mallard, aided by the wind, had also attained maximal speed. He flew on a low trajectory over the meadow so the falcon would have to attenuate the steepness of its dive toward the end. Just as the falcon extended her clenched feet to deliver a deadly blow, the mallard suddenly swerved to the left.

Athena came out of her steep dive just above ground

and curved upward two feet behind the mallard. The falcon screeched repeatedly in annoyance, knowing that mallards at full speed on a horizontal course are faster flyers. The mallard began to pull away.

Edward whistled three times and Athena reluctantly headed toward Edward's glove, turning to give one final harsh shriek at the departing mallard.

"Hillo, ho, ho Athena. Well-flown!" said Edward, stroking her neck. Turning toward the Queen, he added, "I have never seen a faster stoop!"

"That was a magnificent and thrilling example of flying at the brook, Edward, although the mallard's crafty strategy earned him his freedom. Are you disappointed in the outcome?"

"Only a little, Your Majesty, for Athena's sake."

"What about your sake?"

"For a true falconer, the major excitement derives from the privilege of watching the unmatchable spectacle of the entire contest: the beautiful ascent of the falcon into the clouded heavens; the majestic, spiraling waiting-on; and then the culminating, deadly stoop, reaching speeds which defy imagination." Edward gave a look of noble pride directly into Athena's eyes.

A gust of wind rippled the Queen's hair. "What now?" she asked.

"It is not good to end a falcon's hunting day with defeat, so let us wander a bit upstream. I am sure we can get her a teal or two."

"Ah, a noble idea, my favorite courtier. Let's find a secluded spot, shall we?"

*   *   *

As the weeks went by, Edward began to think about his relationship with Mary Hastings. When he had reached the age of eighteen in 1568, he had held long discussions with both of the Hastings sisters, Elizabeth and Mary, sixteen and fifteen. Elizabeth was a maid of honor to the Queen, and Mary a gentlewoman of the royal bedchamber.

Elizabeth was beginning to form bonds of affection with Edward's friend, Ned Somerset, and had opted out of the marriage contract. But that mattered not to Edward, for his interest was in her sister Mary. He was captivated by Mary's maturation into a slim statuesque young lady with ribbon blue eyes and the regal bearing of her Yorkist heritage. Her hair was long and lightly kissed with the color of rich soil, surrounding a lovely face and gentle smile.

Edward knew that there lived inside that soul a nobility of character and a bright mind. Mary's strong devotion to Edward was discreet and known only to the two of them, along with her sister and Ned.

As Edward felt a growing attraction to Mary, he began to wish that he could break free of the Queen's tight grip. But he thought it imprudent, in such an authoritarian monarchy, to request it openly. Whenever he had hinted at it, the Queen had reminded him that his stature was short enough already without additional shortening by loss of a head. Mary told Edward that time would solve the problem and urged him to handle the Queen with chivalric discretion. But as time passed, he found it increasingly difficult to live as though he were nothing more than a pawn from whom favors were so frequently commanded.

But Edward was increasingly pleased with the

wisdom and farsightedness of the marriage contract between his father and Henry Hastings, Mary's oldest brother and Third Earl of Huntingdon. As stipulated in the document, Edward and Mary pledged their troth within a month of his eighteenth birthday. They agreed to keep it a secret and wait several years to marry, so that he might travel and broaden his horizons for a writing career.

One problem troubled him, though. His copy of the marriage contract was still missing. He chose not to share that with Mary. *I'll find it* , he thought. Besides, before he died, his father had told him that there were two other copies of the contract. Mary's brother Henry had one; another had been left with a family friend whose identity Edward did not know.

Whenever he thought about his contract, he found himself nibbling at his lower lip, trying to will away a tight little knot of dis-ease within.

The contract will turn up, he told himself. *It has to. But how in Hades did I misplace it?*

Chapter 7

In God's name and the King's, say who thou art,
And why thou com'st thus knightly clad in arms,
Against what man thou com'st, and what thy quarrel.
Speak truly on thy knighthood and thy oath,
As so defend thee heaven and thy valour!
              - Richard II

The expectant crowd of 12,000 clamorous English from all walks of life had paid from a penny to a shilling to sit for hours on temporary wooden scaffolding to watch this most thrilling and dramatic of all public sports: a Royal Tournament. The crowd buzzed with restless excitement as the knights entered the tilt-yard of Whitehall Palace on a sunny early afternoon in May, 1571.

Edward de Vere, at twenty-one, was more than ten years younger than any other participant. He had decided to adopt the red gules color of his heraldic shield and the blue boar of the Veres as symbol for his first tournament. He attached long, flaming crimson ostrich plumes to his helm to symbolize his knightly panache. He admired the elegant carriage of his sturdy white courser whom he had named Bucephalus after Alexander the Great's famous white horse, whose square-shaped head and black forehead-patch had reminded Alexander of an ox.

Led by trumpeters and drummers, the knights, clad in crafted steel from head to toe, sparkled in the sun as they walked stiffly toward the royal box. They were followed by lancebearers, armorers, grooms and pages leading their richly caparisoned horses.

To glorify the romantic ideals of chivalry, to celebrate once again the victory over the Northern rebels in 1570, and to enhance public enthusiasm and loyalty to the cult of the Virgin Queen, Sir Henry Lee, the Queen's Champion, had arranged a special tournament.

Edward, the neophyte, reviewed in his mind that the purposes of tournaments had changed over the centuries from killing and violence to those of entertainment. Chivalrous knights displayed their manly valor and skill, fighting in defense of their chaste and beautiful ladies in a highly ceremonial atmosphere. For reasons of safety, spear-tips were changed into three-pronged coronels. Swords were blunted along the edges and squared at the ends. The long central tilt barrier was introduced to separate the combatants.

Trumpets blared as Elizabeth entered her box. The crowd, seated in grandstands at the north end, cheered as she signaled with her fan that the festivities should begin. Sir Henry Lee presented to her his symbolic shield with emblematic picture and Latin motto meaning *Do away with Discontent.*

Christopher Hatton, whose impresa translated as *Eternally Yours,* was given a perfumed handkerchief from the Queen which he devoured with kisses. Elizabeth smiled but thought, *I wish you had one-tenth of Edward's subtlety and intellectual adroitness.*

After the other presentations it was Edward's turn. To many in the crowd, he was known for his comic acting in interludes that were practiced in the taverns before being presented at Court, as well as for his disguised appearances, jokes and wine-exaggerated story-telling.

The crowd began to laugh as Edward rode forward. Elizabeth could not suppress a smile, for she was well aware of Edward's escapes from castle confines to mix with the common people, gather writing material, and enjoy the variety of life. Edward raised his visor and declaimed:

"What stronger breastplate than a heart untainted! Thrice is he armed that hath his quarrel just, and he but naked, though locked up in steel, whose conscience with injustice is corrupted."

Edward turned his horse and motioned to the entrance gate. After a moment, there burst forth two dwarfs riding large pigs jerkily into the tiltyard. One dwarf had the word TRUTH in large blue letters on his back and held a six-foot-long spear made of white ostrich plumes. His pig was draped in crimson ornamented with blue boars. The other dwarf wore an ugly slinking hyena as crest and the word UNTRUTH on his back, with brown hyenas decorating the pig. He carried a silver paper lance.

Each dwarf guided the unruly pigs before the Queen as the crowd howled with laughter. The pigs began to run the course at the south end, with the dwarfs stabbing the air over the six foot tilt in mock battle, neither able to see the other. They confronted each other as they came around the north end. The dwarfs tried to control the confused pigs, finally locking in mortal combat. TRUTH struck the fatal wound with his feather-weapon and UNTRUTH fell onto the ground to breathe his last. The entire crowd, including the Queen and her retinue, cheered loudly.

Edward waited a few moments for emotions to subside. Then, with dramatic timing, he gently turned Bucy around and handed the Queen his impresa with its Latin motto translating as *Virtue is its Own Reward*.

Elizabeth watched with astounded eyes as he turned away from her, rode Bucy to the right and stopped in front of Mary Hastings. Mary smiled radiantly. Edward did not move but Bucephalus, with shaffroned head held erect, tapped his front hooves in a quick rhythm and then bowed reverently.

Mary and Edward had decided to marry at Christmas. In the flowing embellished rhetoric of chivalry, Edward requested a token from his fiancée. She gracefully removed from her finger a specially designed gold ring. The broad gold centerpiece bore a sterling silver reproduction of the Bolebec Heraldic Crest: the fierce and courageous lion sejant brandishing the broken spear of his vanquished enemy in victorious defiance.

Edward smiled appreciatively and placed the ring on his left small finger. Mary lowered her dark lashes and blushed, innocent to the Queen's withering glare.

William Cecil scowled at this spectacle. He gripped his staff tightly and his brow furrowed.

Edward listened as the chief herald reviewed with the participants the official jousting rules. The highest score was given for unhorsing an opponent, the second highest for an attaint to the head with the blunted coronel, the third highest for an attaint to the chest. Such directed blows were risky, leaving one's own upper body unprotected. Most knights chose to garner their points by breaking the adversary's spear. A higher number of points were awarded for breaking the other's spear at the coronel itself.

Earl Marshal Tom Howard, the popular Duke of Norfolk, lifted his staff to silence the crowd and, in a ringing voice, shouted: "Sound, trumpets! Trumpets, sound!"

The trumpets pierced the air with their long vibrating tones, and the crowd sat forward with expectancy. Each challenger was to run six courses with each of five opponents. Sir Henry Lee began the day of jousting. Edward, the youngest and least experienced jouster, was the last to take his oaths.

After observing all of the individual clashes closely, he was helped onto Bucy. He felt calmly confident, enhanced by the gentle beauty of Mary and the lovely ring she had bestowed upon him. He patted Bucy's neck and spoke familiar words to him that they must now merge as one body and one unconquerable spirit.

Both Edward and Robert Colsell raised themselves in their saddles, leveled their long shafts, and pounded down the field. At the last second, fixing his eyes totally on his target, Edward turned his spear downward to the left and splintered Colsell's spear shaft at the coronel.

The tilters rode their horses a short distance beyond the curved end of the barrier to be handed fresh spears. Edward again spoke quietly to Bucy and he sensed the horse responding to the self-assured sound of his voice.

The two combatants began their run on signal, Colsell spurring his horse vigorously, Edward and Bucy gliding gracefully without spurring. Again the pounding hooves, the murmured excitement of the crowd, the splintering sound of wood meeting wood at high speed, the snorting of horses and the staccato crowd exclamations.

In six courses run with Colsell, Edward broke six staves of his adversary, two at the coronel. Then he convincingly beat Thomas Coningsby. Next he defeated Sir Edward Stafford. The crowd began to sense an unexpected skill. Was this the same ale-swilling jokester from the taverns, the comic actor and writer of skits?

Edward prepared himself mentally for his fourth encounter, which was with the ambitious and wily 31-year-old Thomas Knyvet. A lisping flattering courtier, Knyvet ushered visitors to the Queen with an airy walk, mincing steps and a penchant for French phrases and mannerisms, his thin lips crescenting an unremitting smile. But he was tall, strong, and athletic. He and Edward shared a mutual dislike and disrespect.

Knyvet's steel-covered face needs de Verean re-sculpting, thought Edward as he clenched his teeth.

The trumpets sounded and the horses thundered toward each other. Edward extended his legs and stood in the stirrups, his body maintaining a constant level. He glanced over at Mary Hastings, and for a moment his mind turned to the missing marriage contract. He was certain he had never removed it from his walnut chest—suddenly there was the crash of wood and Edward's lance shattered at the base, just above his hand. *How stupid for letting my thoughts stray!* He could almost feel Knyvet's smile of contempt oozing through his visor.

The signal was again given. Edward clenched his spear, tightened his arms and legs, and flew at his adversary. This time he suffered an attaint on his chest and had difficulty remaining in his saddle. The crowd groaned their disappointment.

He shook his head in disgust over his ruinous tenseness, breaking his own basic rules. He took a deep breath and reminded himself that although strategy and strength were important, the real keys to winning tournaments were tranquillity of mind and body, and being totally unified with one's horse.

Edward closed his eyes briefly and reposed himself. He spoke soft, confident words to Bucy and let the heavy spear rest securely but gently on his palm and forearm. Bucy sensed the relaxation of his rider's legs. When the trumpets sounded, the two became one.

Now is the time to witch the world with noble horsemanship, thought Edward. All at once he felt as if, like an ancient Greek god, he had dropped from the clouds onto his saddle and he was now floating through the air on Pegasus. He applied gentle pressure with his legs to Bucy's chest, eliciting subtle changes in speed and direction.

Edward held his spear steadily, pointing slightly upwards as he focused on Knyvet's visor. He suddenly elevated the tip, scoring a powerful, crunching attaint on Knyvet's helmet, violently snapping his head back and forth. A mighty cheer erupted from the bloodthirsty crowd.

Edward's crimson plumes flew proudly upwards and Knyvet's seemed to droop, as Edward then broke two spears at the coronel and unhorsed his opponent in course six. He chivalrously dismounted and helped a groggy Tom Knyvet to his feet as the crowd rose and shouted approval.

Edward then combated his friend Tom Cecil, William Cecil's son by his sudden brief marriage with the impoverished Mary Cheke while he was a student at Cambridge. Edward won easily in a gentlemanly combat, each only aiming at the other's coronel.

In the late afternoon sun, Marshal Tom Howard took the scoring tablets from the herald clerks and read out the final scores. Twenty-one-year-old Edward de Vere, in his first joust, was the clear winner.

Edward removed his helmet and bowed to the crowd, searching amongst the sea of faces for Mary's reaction to his win. Queen Elizabeth fanned herself rapidly, unaccustomed to second place in the esteem of her courtiers.

* * *

Tudor tournaments lasted for three days. The tourney on the second day consisted of a series of mounted encounters between two opponents fighting with swords. Edward and Tom Knyvet were co-winners.

The third day of barriers consisted of battling on foot across short lower wooden barriers, fighting a predetermined number of pushes with pike and strokes with sword. Edward's point total was second best but he was the overall winner of the tournament by a significant margin.

His victory was quite unexpected by the Court because of their premise that intellectual introspective poets who spent their time finding rhymed meaning in stars, flights of butterflies, and the transient aroma of nodding violets were not supposed to be athletic courageous tournament champions in a dangerous sport. Members of the Court, as well as London tavern patrons, were equally astounded that the tournament-neophyte and poet-jokester had performed so far above expectations.

That evening a sumptuous royal banquet was given by the Queen in Whitehall's great hall, with its magnificent tapestries and armorial displays. Mary Hastings, gentlewoman of the bedchamber, tactfully stayed away, although it was not her desire.

All participants were given memorabilia of the tournament. Hatton, a non-winner, was given a silver bell on a silver neck chain. After Sir Henry Lee, the second place winner, was presented with a jewel-studded goblet, Edward was called to the Queen's chair.

With a flourish, he swung his brilliant crimson velvet cape over his shoulders, walked in front of the head table and knelt before his Queen.

"Notably done, my noble and youthful poet!" she proclaimed. "Your most personable and loyal father would indeed be proud, as we all are, of such an unanticipated victor! Do you tilt at dusty books in clandestine libraries? Rise up and receive this tablet to record your poems and random thoughts."

The audience rose and cheered. Glasses filled with the finest French white wine were raised on high and downed as Elizabeth handed him a tablet with a small portrait of herself, circled with emeralds and diamonds set into the white soft leather cover.

Then she leaned forward and gave him an enthusiastic victor's kiss. He felt her desire in the moist heat of her lingering lips. For a brief moment he closed his eyes and visualized Mary's lips as he accepted this royal seal of approval.

"Thank you, Most Kind Majesty, for this thought-provoking table-book graced by your treasured likeness. Yet need I no crafted reminder of my Queen, whose beauty is ever etched into the tablet of my heart!" As he spoke these words, he was thinking of Mary.

Elizabeth beamed. "May my gift stimulate only the most beautiful and creative ideas. Keep it forever in memory of this day and of me."

Edward paused, looked around the great hall and savored the rich fare of Tudor pageantry. He promised the Queen that he would treasure the table-book always as his most prized possession—momentarily forgetting that even the purest courtiers and most gallant knights may sometimes be lured to stray from the noble paths of virtue.

Chapter 8

O, pity, God, this miserable age!
What stratagems, how fell, how butcherly,
Erroneous, mutinous, and unnatural.
- Henry VI, Part 3

William Cecil left the jousting tournament immediately after witnessing Mary Hastings giving Edward the symbolic ring. He returned to high-towered Cecil House on the Strand and went directly to his study.

His usual equanimity was ruffled. For the next hour he limped back and forth, leaning heavily on his cane, muttering to himself. His breath wheezed laboriously from his chest as his mind conjured the next phase of his cunning.

He sat at his desk and looked restlessly at the pile of state papers on his left and the equally tall stack of letters and petitions on his right requesting favors. To each letter and petition was clipped paper money.

Every evening after supper, he processed between fifty and a hundred petitions, returning those with insufficient financial incentive.

Tonight he pushed the stacks aside and jiggled a bell. A servant brought him a plate piled high with cheese. He specifically asked not to be disturbed.

Known for his position papers for the Queen, he was an expert at concisely summarizing the pros and cons of important state matters. He now began to fill sheet after sheet with possible tactics to break any engagement between Edward de Vere and Mary Hastings—and compel Edward to marry his innocent-as-a-lamb daughter, fourteen-year-old Anne.

Under *Purpose,* he wrote, *In one masterful leap, the common Cecils, through kinship with the Premier Earl of England, would have a solid foothold in ancient nobility.*

On another sheet, he tracked the history of ward-ship, a scheme devised to enrich the Royal Treasury and the Crown's favorites. The King or Queen ultimately owned all the land in a kingdom. Land-usage was a temporary privilege granted by the monarchy in return for military availability. When a nobleman died, his children and widow became royal property and could be sold to the highest bidder. Profits from their land went to the guardian until the ward reached the age of twenty-one, at which time he sued for livery and recovery of his landed wealth.

The major purposes of buying wards were financial gain and the opportunity to marry them to your own daughters or others of your choice for social advantage. As Master of the Court of Wards, Cecil rewarded himself without charge the first sons of the richest noblemen.

By law, a guardian could not force a ward into marriage if he was fourteen, the age of consent, or if he had a valid marriage contract. A guardian was forbidden from disparaging a noble ward by marrying him to a commoner.

Cecil wrote down: *Bad mistake! Edward already twenty-one. Thinks he still has legal marriage contract.* After this, he wrote *Options* and filled the sheet.

He was oblivious to the pain in his feet and the deepening beauty of the night sky outside his window.

Twice he re-read passages from Machiavelli describing how leaders of a state must be ready to act contrary to faith, friendship and humanity according to the winds of fortune. He recalled how well this had worked in his twenties when he helped gather evidence against his own Protestant government associates and friends, several of whom were executed, ingratiating himself with the new Queen, fanatically-Catholic Mary Tudor, thus saving his own neck.

Cecil stayed at his desk all night working on the marriage problem. He munched on his cheese and drank weak ale, finally falling asleep at his desk at dawn.

*   *   *

Late the next morning Cecil walked across the recently cobbled Strand and down a path to the Thames. He embarked on his private boat, rowed by eight liveried bargemen, for the short ride upriver to Whitehall. He was the only person in England who could see the Queen promptly without appointment.

They moved into the private red room.

"Your Majesty, I need to talk to you about the Court of Wards and my sweet daughter Anne." Because of his weight and his infirmities, he was allowed to sit.

Elizabeth nodded her pearl-embroidered coiffure. "Yes, that wonderful relic of feudalism which will make my coffers bulge. I understand that you are daily discovering new wards and widows."

Cecil stroked his white beard slowly and sinuously. "I think Edward and my sweet Anne would make an excellent match. Yes, a truly excellent match, Edward and Anne."

Elizabeth tolerated his slow repetitive speech that had led the Court to nickname him Pondus. "But Edward has told me several times that he has a legal marriage contract with the Hastings sisters and that he and Mary intend to honor that pledge." She paused and shot him a measuring stare. "Does such a contract exist?"

"I doubt it. Yes, I doubt it." Cecil twisted his cane with his hands. "Edward often lives in a fantasy world and I suspect he dreamed it up. Can poets distinguish fancy from reality? I have asked him to produce it for me several times and he says he cannot locate it."

He paused and cleared his throat. "There is a minor problem, yes a minor concern that I have . . . ."

Her brow lifted inquisitively as Cecil continued. "Mary's brother Henry Hastings . . . I have reason to believe that he might go along with Edward's contention about the existence of more than one marriage contract. Yes, and he might be persuaded even to produce a forged contract."

"Surely he would not do such a thing!"

"It would be an ugly and distracting inconvenience, Your Majesty . . . . ugly and distracting, indeed. So far, I have been able to keep Edward and Henry Hastings out of touch. But I won't be able to do that much longer, no, not much longer . . . ."

The Queen's brow lowered in thought as she tried to puzzle through the nature of Cecil's intrigue. "What is your suggestion, Spirit?"

"Henry Hastings is most capable, most capable," Cecil said. "I believe that a new post up north might be to his liking, yes in the far north of England. I feel sure that he would serve the Court most competently."

The Queen nodded as a smile tweaked the left edge of her mouth. "Perhaps something could be arranged. And then?"

"My daughter Anne is fourteen and of marriageable age. I think this whole business of the contract should be dropped, yes dropped once and for all." He fingered his cane, tapping it lightly on the floor. "But I am in a quandary, a puzzling quandary. There is a small impediment."

Elizabeth's burst of laughter was sudden and shrill. "So *that's* the point, my sometimes devious adviser! Edward cannot be forced to marry a non-noble!"

Cecil gazed at the floor and spoke in a quiet voice. "Merely seeking advice, my Queen, but there may be benefits. I don't believe Mary and Edward will remain long at Court if they marry."

That was enough to douse her humor. "What are you saying, Leviathan?" She stroked her pearl necklace and contemplated the absence of Edward in her life.

"Forgive me, Your Majesty, but I am not unmindful of the pleasure you find in his personal company and in his adornment of your Court."

She flicked her hand with impatience. "Explain your strategy clearly, Councilor."

"I promise to keep Anne away from Court and away from royal progresses so that Edward will be copious in your service. Anne will do as I say."

"Ah . . .straight to the heart of the matter. Have you been reading *The Prince* again? At times we seem to have similar minds. Only the ultimate goal is important, not the means used to achieve it or the bodies strewn along the pathway!"

Cecil shifted his aching feet. "Marriage should come first, Your Majesty, love later. A match between Edward and Anne would have many advantages. Yes, many advantages."

The Queen fondly studied her long fingers. "And there is only one stumbling block—your lack of a noble superior birth. Your vexing problem requires instant gentility! 'Tis indeed food for thought, since I am not yet finished with the plentiful talents of our champion jouster."

"As you know, my Gracious Majesty, I only want what is best for you and your Royal Court."

Elizabeth pointed at the portrait of Julius Caesar in his military attire. "There, my hard-working Principal Secretary, is a man regarded by history as achieving greatness despite being responsible for a million deaths of those he chose to conquer. As you well know, being a ruler is not easy, constantly made more complex by tedious variables. Life is indeed a chess game but the goal of games is winning."

"Exactly, Your Majesty."

"Then we are of the same mind."

After Cecil left, Elizabeth found herself alone amongst her grandeur. She glanced out the window and admired her large garden of intermixed roses, Yorkist white and Lancaster red, growing together in such harmony. She disregarded a slight ambivalence-induced disquiet in her stomach.

She firmly stood and reminded herself that she was a Tudor. She had been born for greatness. It was

TR

her destiny, her birthright. Fragility of emotion must not interfere with Royal decisions.

Elizabeth gazed at the portrait of Caesar, then abruptly turned and walked firmly out of the room, leaving her weak thoughts behind.

One week later, for the first time in her thirteen years of rule, she elevated a commoner, William Cecil, to the lowest rung of nobility by royal decree, creating him the first Baron Burghley.

Chapter 9

*And I in going, madam, weep o'er my
father's death anew; but I must attend
his majesty's command to whom I am
now in ward, evermore in subjection.*
                    - All's Well That Ends Well

Two weeks after Cecil became Baron Burghley,
Edward de Vere challenged the Queen to a game of
lawn bowls at Whitehall, hoping to ensure her good
mood. It was a game which both particularly enjoyed.
For Edward, though, there was a matter of much
more importance than a game of bowls.

"How many heads shall we play?" he asked.

"A dozen should suffice."

"Cast first, my Queen. Throw out the mistress, so
deceptively white."

In spite of her broadly farthingaled silk dress, tight
corset, large starched linen ruff, and dangling necklaces, Elizabeth took the white target ball and threw

it down the smooth grass lane. She took a bowl, drew up her skirt with her left hand, and rolled the weighted ball with a deft motion. It lightly kissed the mistress and stopped a few inches away.

Edward knew the Queen did not like to lose. He rolled his bowl unevenly on purpose, its one-sided weight giving it an irregular course, even striking a pebble, an interfering rub.

Elizabeth slapped her thigh with a jeweled hand and laughed shrilly. "Ah, Lord Edward, sometimes I see *you* in bowls like that, with such erratic tendencies in your own nature."

The Queen's next throw drew to within a foot of the mistress. After another bowl by each, Edward decided to use more of his skills. With well-aimed cast, he knocked the Queen's ball into the ditch.

"God's bones, beshrew you!" cried the Queen and snatched her next bowl out of Edward's hands. She bowled quickly and her ball went over the rink-line, giving Edward an unplanned victory in the first set.

So they went on, rolling and quibbling and jesting through the remaining sets, the Queen easily winning the majority.

"Are you cozening me, Edward?" she asked suspiciously. "I seem to be conquering you more effortlessly than usual."

Edward laughed. "Must I answer, Your Majesty?"

"Yes, I command so, by the truth of your motto!"

"Were I playing with full intent, I think I might win." He held the bowl carefully, allowing his hands to feel its weight, his eyes calculating distance, texture of lawn and obstructing balls. He then flexed his knees, took his step forward and, with a careful swing curved the bowl to within four inches of the small white mistress.

"And I," said the Queen, with lips set, "would respond like this!" She gently curved her ball adjacent to the mistress to end the match.

They walked along the path to one of the spectators' stone benches. The Queen sat, spreading her dress in careful, circular folds around her. "What is the rub, Edward?"

Edward knelt before her. For days, since learning of the Queen's decision from the triumphant new Baron Burghley, Edward had been depressed and embittered. He knew his only hope was to influence Elizabeth to change her mind and he knew that his chances were slim.

He decided to be direct. "Your Majesty, I *implore* you not to force me to marry Anne Cecil."

"The decision has been made and you must obey it. Burghley is your royal guardian. He may choose brides for his wards."

"But Anne and I are incompatible, without a single common bond. You know that as well as I."

"Now Edward, she is a virtuous girl and will make you a fine wife. I agree with Burghley that marriage comes first, love later."

Edward vigorously massaged the ring Mary had given him, which he now wore in the middle of his left index finger. Elizabeth had shared with him more than once her own strong feelings about the endless hell of an unhappy marriage. "But de Veres marry nobility, not commoners."

"The Cecils are no longer commoners, Edward."

He got up from his knees, digging his fingernails into his palms. In a voice suddenly thickened with anger, he said, "By a mere pen-stroke, you can create instant gentleness? Can the same be done with street dogs and stray cats?"

Elizabeth restlessly rearranged her hooped dress. "Were the de Veres nobles when they swept down as raiding conquering Vikings in the 800's and settled in what is now Normandy, land of Norsemen? No, Edward, nobility always derives from, and at the discretion of, royalty."

Edward swallowed another angry reply and instead stuck a clove in his mouth. Somehow, he had to convince the Queen to change her mind. He had been forced to join the Cecil household when he became Cecil's ward at the age of twelve. Anne was only six at the time and there had never been any kind of special friendship or relationship between them. At best, Edward felt like a distant older brother to her. Her mother was a cold Puritan and a fierce, rigid, unattractive woman. Edward felt desperately sure that Anne would be the same.

"Good God!" he burst out, "Anne sprinkles her slow speech with Puritan platitudes and rarely harbors an original thought. And only her father calls her 'sweet.' Mary Hastings is not only captivatingly lovely but her mind is as beautiful as an illuminated manuscript. I beg you, Your Majesty, to allow me to refuse the marriage to Anne. I will pay the penalty."

Elizabeth rested her chin in her right hand and stroked her cheek with her index finger. "Ever since Henry VII's huge fine of the Thirteenth Earl of Oxford, more than half of your properties have been encumbered. Your landed wealth is rather tenuous, Edward." She turned her face away.

Edward bit so hard on the clove that he jarred his teeth. *Is this why de Veres have fought with such valor for five hundred years in all of the great crises and battles of English history? To be ordered about like serfs?*

"I care not a whit for land when my whole life

and my posterity are in jeopardy! What about my contract with Mary Hastings? That is a legal binding agreement, Your Majesty, not to be superseded by a guardian's greed. Mary and I have pledged ourselves to each other for years and recently exchanged vows to marry at the end of this year. I believe we would wondrously enhance your Court."

Elizabeth's lips tightened. She was tiring of Edward's pleas. "Our new baron assures me there never was such a marriage contract. Can you produce it?"

"I have kept it in my chest of valuables ever since my father gave it to me at the age of eleven. I brought it to Cecil House. It has subsequently disappeared, I know not how. Believe me, Your Majesty! I do not lie. *Vero Nihil Verius!*" He closed his eyes and prayed that the Queen would change her mind . . .but he knew that she rarely did.

"Was there but one copy of such an important document?"

He felt the knot tighten inside him. "My father said there were two more. Henry Hastings has one, of course. Father said he had also given one to a family friend, but he did not identify the friend—"

"How unfortunate," Elizabeth said. "And what of the one held by Mary's brother Henry?"

"I cannot reach Henry." Did he dare share his suspicion that Burghley had arranged for Henry Hastings to be far away from London?

"I feel one of my headaches commencing." She pressed with the heel of her hand into her left eye.

Edward set his jaw. "This decision will affect my entire life! The law states that after the age of fourteen a male is free to choose his own mate. Even a monarch does *not* have the right to abrogate that legal process. I am twenty-one!"

A cold look came over her features, with muscles drawing taut at the corners of her mouth and eyes. "God's death, Bolebec! 'Not' is *not* a word to use with princes! Despite your age, you are the *Queen's ward*. *No* contract and *no* law supersedes my royal will! My decision is final. Obey your Queen, courtier!" She turned her head and spit on the ground.

Edward forced himself to breathe more slowly. What authoritarian times! Whether pauper or leading earl of the realm, all must grovel before an autocratic monarch and her Divine Right! He felt as if a regal elephant were squashing his chest and his soul. *What is her worst trait, her mendacity or her scheming chicanery? Why is the world so full of rubs? Why do the weighted biased coils of fortune smother me so adversely?*

Then he recalled his father's important advice, rendered to him many times. Total loyalty to King or Queen, even unto death, formed the very essence of their family philosophy since Alberic de Vere came to England with William the Conqueror.

Dropping to his knees, he said quietly, "Your Majesty, de Veres have steadfastly obeyed their monarchs for five hundred years. Forgive my youthful intransigence. I accept your decision and ever will be true."

* * *

Edward brooded, pacing his room, his mood matching the dark clouds and frequent rainstorms. A rising sense of indignation and injustice pervaded him. He had a valid legal marriage contract under the laws of England! He was a legal adult! Why have laws, if they can be so whimsically and illegally circumvented by those in power?

Wardship was intolerably wrong and disgracefully archaic. *Why don't they rip off my clothes, check my teeth, wave a hand in front of my eyes to make sure I don't have epilepsy, and auction me off as in ancient slave markets?* He felt like totally destroying London, as Boudica and her British Iceni tribes had done to Roman Londinium in 60 AD.

To regain his composure, he retreated for several weeks to Castle Hedingham. There he found the manor house depleted of lead, iron and some antique furniture. He learned that Cecil, as Edward's guardian, had sold to Leicester the rights to Castle Hedingham, as well as to several of Edward's Essex estates. He was dismayed to see the disintegrated roof of Earl's Colne, laying bare to the weather the priory containing the stone coffins, remains and carved effigies of twenty generations of de Veres.

Edward recalled the words of Cicero, that we must keep our spirits free from anger so that peace, serenity, steadfastness and dignity may reign in our souls. *Easy to say, harder to do!* He clenched his fists and muttered oaths. Finally he sought emotional outlet in poetry:

> *Fain would I sing, but fury makes me fret,*
> *And rage hath sworn to seek revenge of wrong;*
> *My mazèd mind in malice so is set,*
> *As Death shall daunt my deadly dolours long;*
> *Patience perforce is such a pinching pain,*
> *As die I will, or suffer wrong again.*

*   *   *

One week later, he rode northwest to visit Mary and Elizabeth Hastings. They sat around a gray marble table on the terrace above their spacious garden.

Elizabeth Hastings, who was now completely in love with Edward's close friend Ned Somerset, shook her head and said, "The whole concept of wardship is an insulting disgrace, designed solely to enrich the royal coffers. And now it is being siphoned to satisfy the endless avarice of our new Baron Burghley."

"In the grip of absolute power, what are my options?" asked Edward.

"Flee to Italy," responded Elizabeth, with simple logic. "Mary will join you, and you can marry in beautiful Florence. The Queen will forgive you."

Even as the bitterness burned like an inflamed canker inside him, Edward knew that course of action was impossible for a de Vere. "If only we could," he murmured.

The dark mood settled over them entirely, and nobody spoke for a long time. Only the wind voiced opinions as it rustled through the trees. Mary, who had fled heartbroken from the Court to her home upon hearing the news of Edward's betrothal to Anne Cecil, held Edward's hand tenderly.

Finally she turned to look at him, her eyes glistening with tears. She spoke in a soft but even tone. "Edward, we both know how long there has been a special affinity between us. Even as a child, whether you were sad or joyous, serious or joking, I always felt a warm and comfortable happiness in your presence. For the past ten years, I have never thought about anyone else."

"Such a singular harmony between two individuals

must be rare indeed," Edward answered. He stood and began to pace, clenching his fists. "Imposed marriage is absolute anathema! Our self-centered Queen has become an intolerable despot!"

"You must marry Anne," answered Mary, her voice breaking.

"No!" He smashed his fist on the table. "We must find Henry and settle this dispute about the marriage contract." He spun to face her. "Have you heard any word from him? Doesn't he realize the desperate situation we are in?"

Mary's looked down at her hands clasped in her lap. "I fear that the wily Baron Burghley has somehow subjugated Henry to his will. I know not how."

"Just as he convinced the Queen to command the marriage!" Edward fumed. "What a vile viper! There is no other interpretation! Total dictatorial injustice! Endless avaricious greed!" He strode to the edge of the garden and furiously plucked a rose, bringing blood to his hand. He threw the rose into a bird bath.

"Although my entire being aches, I must release you from our contract," Mary said quietly. "But . . ." She lowered her face into her ivory hands and softly sobbed. "I will always love you, Edward. Until the day I die . . . I shall always love only you."

Edward bent down and took her hands into his own. He felt the ache of loss as never before, tight in his throat and face, hot in his chest. He felt tears of loss and grief form as he shook his head in sorrow that someone as gentle as Mary, someone so rare and ethereal, could not be his lifelong partner.

As she finally lifted her brimming azure eyes to his, he thought, *She is too noble for this place.*

* * *

He rode west for two days to his isolated country retreat at Bilton in Warwickshire, bordering the River Avon. For the next two months, he walked contemplatively along its banks and strolled slowly over the hills and through the forests, reveling in the quiet beauties of nature and wondering why the presence of man so denigrated earthly magnificence.

He was not in a creative mood but whenever he felt particularly upset and helpless, he eased his emotional turmoil by writing poetry. Often, however, the words would not come and he learned a new truth—sometimes no words can describe the profoundness of one's own heartache.

* * *

On September 22, 1571, the Queen and her retinue arrived on Progress at Theobalds, Burghley's unfinished mansion twelve miles from London, for several days of wedding festivities.

Theobalds was already England's largest private home. It was built of pink brick and white stone standing at the end of a one-mile curving gravel road lined by cedars, with impressive turrets of blue slate on the corners, endless bayed windows, and multiple chimneys. The walls of its long stately gallery featured illustrated lineages of all of England's monarchs on one wall and Burghley's fictitious ancient noble lineage, purchased from the College of Heraldry, on the opposite wall.

An artificial waterway for boats wended its way for two miles through flowers, hedges, arbors and orchards. The summer house entry was lined by white marble statues of the twelve Roman emperors. Fish ponds and swimming pools dotted the landscape.

Fountains jetted water in elaborate displays. Different-toned bells chimed the onset of each new hour.

Festivities before the wedding included hunting, tennis, bowls and boating. Lavish feasts, music, masques, jesters and dancing entertained England's festive nobility until midnight.

There was only one item missing: Edward de Vere, the groom.

Search parties failed to locate him. A confused fourteen year-old Anne wept and prayed. The new baron, a meticulous planner, was purple-cheeked. The Queen, alone in her room, laughed at Edward's dramatic retaliatory scenario.

The wedding was canceled and the Royal Progress moved on.

Edward had concluded in Bilton that he *must* follow the 500-year-old de Vere ethic of being loyal to the monarch in *all* circumstances. But he could not suppress a final act of defiance.

One week after the wedding postponement he rode slowly to join the Royal Progress. He begged the Queen's pardon and Burghley's.

Just before Christmas, a few days after Ned Somerset happily married Elizabeth Hastings in a true love-match, Edward married Anne Cecil on her fifteenth birthday, in Westminster Abbey. Queen Elizabeth sat in a chair of state, the lords and ladies of the Court lining both sides of the taper-lighted chapel.

Through all the conjoining words and sacred pageantry, Edward felt completely entrapped by forces beyond his control, bound by the onerous weight of invisible chains.

The ritual was followed by a magnificent feast at Cecil House. The guests were hailed into the banquet hall by trumpets and drums. The tables were decorated with holly, evergreen and wheat sheaves. Sprays of mixed herbs were placed in brackets along the walls, alternating with torches.

A proud Baron Burghley escorted Queen Elizabeth to her seat at his left. On his right were Lady Burghley and Leicester. On the Queen's left were a somber Edward and a frightened fidgeting Anne.

When those at the head table were seated, Burghley rose, signaled for another trumpet flourish, then gave his simple welcome. "Good friends, be placed. Be welcome. The Cecils and de Veres all give you a hearty hospitable welcome on this historic uniting day!"

At the end of each table was a large molded sugar model of one of the five major royal palaces on the Thames: Windsor, Hampton Court, Richmond, Whitehall, and Greenwich.

The first course consisted of boar-pies brought in at shoulder height on silver trays, symbolic to Edward that the boar, namely himself, had indeed been slain.

Trumpets heralded each subsequent course as waiters served endless meats from stags, goats, cattle, herons, swans, cranes, curlews, pheasant and partridge. Sturgeon, salmon, trout, lampreys, lobsters, oysters and prawns were served from gigantic silver trays lined with ginger, an esteemed aphrodisiac, much jested over by courtiers and maids of honor.

Elaborate salads contained as many as thirty vegetables. Beverages included beer, ale, the best red and white wines of France, and hippocras, a red wine made spicey and aromatic.

Edward, as a loyal courtier, felt he must act the scene. He tried his best to smile and pay attention to his bride and make animated conversation. At the request of the Queen, he played one of his original compositions on the virginal.

When the time for dancing began, Burghley withdrew to his study and penned a letter to his former ward Edward Manners, Earl of Rutland: *I think it doth seem strange to your Lordship to hear of a determination in my Lord of Oxford to marry with my daughter. I could not well imagine what to think, considering I never meant to seek it nor hoped for it.*

He completed the letter, rang the brass bell on his desk, and told the servant to fetch his in-house biographer. Burghley handed him the letter and told him to follow the usual special procedure.

The biographer read the letter, then asked, "You mean write a copy of it, file the copy in our archives and then destroy the original without sending it?"

"Yes, of course, of course," Burghley snapped. "Isn't that our special procedure?"

"Begging your pardon, sir, and with all due respect, I recall Cicero's first law for the historian, that he shall never record a known untruth. I find this somewhat distasteful."

Puffing up his chest, the Queen's Principal Secretary said, "You seem to be forgetting one of the great lessons of history, my good man. To the victor goes not only the spoils but also the opportunity of writing the history of his era . . . yes, the definitive history, in the manner of his choice."

Chapter 10

He was a scholar, and a ripe and good one;
Exceeding wise, fair-spoken, and persuading :
Lofty and sour to them that loved him not;
But, to those men that sought him, sweet as summer.
                                    - Henry VIII

Edward felt that his forced marriage to Anne was an obnoxious tyrannical intrusion into his life but he was determined to try to make it work.

They spent their initial married days at his favorite country estate at Wivenhoe in Essex. Edward loved the quiet quaint village with its mixture of daub-and-wattle and brightly painted houses, its pleasure craft and fishing fleet, and the River Colne broadening quietly to greet the incoming tides.

The wall-encircled, stately red brick de Vere manor house stood on top of the hill. Edward converted its tall watchtower, a landmark used for generations by North Sea ship captains, into his writing room. He hoped his creativity would be inspired by the view of the sea four miles away, the curving river, and the gentle hills of eastern Essex dotted with hamlets.

One day, as was often the case, Anne insisted on joining Edward in the watchtower, promising not to interrupt him. Although she was quiet, the encroachment into his exhilarating mental universe disconcerted him. Instead of writing, he found himself watching her sew.

He liked Anne's dark brown hair but her nose was too large and her mouth too small in a long narrow face very similar to her mother's. Her conversation, albeit restrained by immaturity and insecurity, was laced with ancient classical lore, especially Greek. This was inspired by her mother, Mildred Cooke Cecil, who was fluent in classical tongues.

Anne devoted most of her time to Mildred's Puritan religious books which were full of diatribes against evil and the thousands of ways to offend God by sin. Even marital relations for other than the purpose of creating life were frowned upon by Puritan dogma.

On their first night together he had tried to make love with her. He winced thinking about it. He had watched as she brushed her hair and the curls tumbled below her waist. He had come up behind her as she sat at her dressing table and slowly bent down near the nape of her neck. She radiated purity but with an aura of repelling coolness. Edward knew that he must be gentle and coax her, just as the Queen had once coaxed him over the dividing line of innocence.

As he put his hands on her shoulders and bent

down to kiss the soft indentation below her ear, she let out a startled giggle and pushed him away.

"But, Anne, surely your idealistic religion does not want to hinder newlyweds learning to love each other, does it?" Her answer was a startled, frightened and naive glance in the mirror at his looming reflection. It had chilled his ardor instantly. He realized that Anne was too young, especially with such strong-willed parents, to have formed her own value system and had not received any instruction about marital interaction. Any form of pleasure was, by definition, sinful. She was afraid of long-lasting penalties, in this life and the next, for any transgression.

Edward knew that religious discussion with the overly-pious was doomed to failure, but he couldn't stop himself from asking, "How does one reach salvation, Anne? Am I eligible?"

Her face confident but dour, she answered sweetly, "Edward, dearest, there is no salvation except for those of the righteous whom God deems saints."

Edward realized the futility of further discourse or further interplay on their wedding night. He saw formidable barriers working against their developing any form of love relationship. Anne only knew what her father had told her, that love would inevitably follow the marriage ritual.

Although Anne eventually submitted to him, it was in a cool dutiful way that brought no satisfaction to either one and only increased the obstacles to marital harmony.

Edward reacted by plunging himself into his work. He now underwrote the publication by his former tutor at Cambridge, Bartholomew Clerke, of

Baldassare Castiglione's *The Courtier* from Italian into the more widely understood Latin.

Edward was proud that this was the first time in England's history that a nobleman had sponsored publication of such a book. In his Introduction in Latin, Edward commended Castiglione for defining the most perfect type of man, the courtier, and praised Clerke's eloquent use of Latin:

> *When he writes with precise and well-chosen words, with skillfully constructed and crystal-clear sentences, and with every art of dignified rhetoric, it cannot be but that some noble quality should be felt to proceed from his work. To me, indeed, it seems when I read this courtly Latin that I am listening to Crassus, Antonius, and Hortensius discoursing on this very theme.*

When Edward and Anne returned to London, he funneled his energies into becoming an ideal courtier. Wasn't striving for perfection a realistic goal? Did not Xenophon devise criteria for a perfect king, and Cicero strive all his life to become a perfect orator?

Edward helped entertain visiting dignitaries. His poems were passed around the Court and he elevated the level of conversation. He wrote and acted in interludes. He danced exhibitions, alone or with the Queen, who astonished all with her high agile leaps and spins in the air. And in the evening hours, he relieved his frustration in the arms of an uninhibited and demanding Elizabeth.

Edward went on each annual Progress, usually without Anne, and he followed every shift in the Court from palace to palace, upriver from Whitehall to Richmond, Hampton Court or Windsor, downriver to Greenwich, or sometimes to multi-spired Nonsuch in the Surrey countryside.

By the age of twenty-two, Edward's eagerness to prove his de Verean courage in battle had not abated. His brief assignment to the northern insurrection occurred after the war was over. His major memory was witnessing the repugnant hanging of innocent men in every village, ordered by Cecil as a warning against future insurrection, leaving their bodies on the ropes until they rotted and fell off.

Edward repeatedly requested military duty but was turned down by Cecil and the Queen. While walking with the Queen around Whitehall's court-yard one day, Edward showed her his latest poems. The Queen read them eagerly and asked, "How will we ever find scope for your writing talents?"

"Your Majesty, my goals in life and at your Court are still frosted with disclarity. One of my puzzlements is that if all is fair in politics, war and love, shouldn't *all* be allowed in writing?"

"Meaning?" Elizabeth asked as the wind sent fallen leaves scurrying across their path.

Edward pushed up his sleeves. "In the fifth century BC, at times of celebration, after several days of tragedies by Aeschylus, Sophocles and Euripides, comic poets and playwrights were brought in on the last day of drama-festivals to lighten the atmosphere with humor."

"Good idea!" Elizabeth bent over to inhale the scent of a red rose. Edward noticed the traces of gray about the crown of her head and the slight stooping of her shoulders.

"They were free to mock both men and gods,

even naming them in the process. Beneficial social change occurred as a result."

"Social change?" she repeated doubtfully. "I would need time to think that over. Perhaps it would depend upon the quality of the writing."

"I want to describe what I see around me, as Ovid did, but I would need freedom to encourage my creativity. My inventive resolution longs to soar at a high pitch, but the medium escapes me!"

"Your unusual creativity *will* take flight, my favorite Seventeenth Earl of Oxford!" Reaching up, Elizabeth stroked his cheek with her cool pale hand. "Most esteemed courtier, I shall *guarantee* your opportunity to soar. But first you must please your Queen."

The Court was well aware of the affair between the Queen and Edward. Everyone in court knew that the Queen delighted more in Edward's personage, his quick mind, his dancing and all of his many courtier-attributes than any other. It was obvious and accepted. Each inspired the other, elevating the atmosphere of the entire Court. Anne heard rumors but was too naive to believe them. The truth of carnality was lost upon her, now protected by layers of devout piety.

Burghley kept his bargain with the Queen, keeping Anne away from Court, and he was made Lord Treasurer. Also retaining his position as Master of the Court of Wards, he now held the two most lucrative posts in the realm. Having already achieved one lifetime goal of noble status for endless generations of Cecils, henceforth he could concentrate on acquiring unrivaled riches.

Mildred Cecil made open remarks about the Queen's behavior with a married Edward and was banned from Court. Robert Dudley sought solace successfully with many ladies. Christopher Hatton used every opportunity to remind the Queen of his devotion. He ended a recent letter to Elizabeth, "Bear with me, my most dear sweet Lady. Passion overcometh me. I can write no more. Love me, for I love you."

For several weeks, to Edward's annoyance, Hatton became her number one favorite, having ready access to the Queen day and night. One day Edward was walking in the privy garden at Hampton Court, admiring its dazzling display of sculpted heraldic beasts, including lions, tigers, boars, wolves, stags, eagles and falcons, all impaled on long poles and painted bright colors. He rounded a hedge and encountered Elizabeth and Hatton holding hands on a bench.

The Queen spoke coldly, with embarrassed haste. "Why waste such talent by walking alone, courtier? Why not bowl with the maids of honor?"

Edward spun on his heels and retreated to his palace room. He slammed the door and pondered the Queen's fickleness and evanescent loyalty.

He paced about the room, weary of the confusion in his life. He missed Mary Hastings and wished that she were his steadfast loving wife. But he knew that could never be and that he would never derive comfort or happiness from Anne.

Perplexity and doubt swirled inside his head. He sat down at his desk, tapping his foot restlessly, and wrote about *Woman's Changeableness:*

> *If women could be fair and yet not fond,*
> *Or that their love were firm not fickle, still,*
> *I would not marvel that they make men bond,*

By service long to purchase their good will;
But when I see how frail those creatures are,
I muse that men forget themselves so far.
To mark the choice they make, and how they
change,
How oft from Phoebus do they flee to Pan,
Unsettled still like haggards wild they range,
These gentle birds that fly from man to man . . .
And then we say when we their fancy try,
To play with fools, O what a fool was I.

When Edward locked the poem in his double-padlocked chest, a brief vignette of Tom Bricknell kneeling on the floor, scattering his treasured papers, flashed into his mind. *What the devil was he trying to steal and how did he open that chest?*

Although the questions came back to him often, even after so many years, he had not yet found the answers.

A few days later the Queen was stricken with smallpox and lapsed into stupor. The Court was immobilized and stunned into silence by Elizabeth's grave illness. She was a popular sovereign and England was at peace. All were also well aware that tenure at Court, power, influence, wealth and status depended upon a personal relationship with the monarch.

With the Queen so ill, Edward felt guilty about the poem he had written. But the strong Queen rallied and was left with only a few facial pock-marks which she covered with a mixture of egg white, alum, borax, poppy seeds and powdered eggshell.

* * *

At the age of twenty-three, Edward decided to break English precedent by supporting aspiring writers, both intellectually and financially. He took out long-term leases on several rooms at the old Savoy Hospital on the Thames. Here he placed, as his first impoverished protégés, Thomas Twyne and Thomas Watson.

Edward was trying hard to develop an affection for Anne and he suggested that they return to the quiet environs of Wivenhoe. She was pure of heart but without panache in any arena of life. There had been many frustrating nights that lacked the fulfillment of passion or even the comfort of warmth.

And yet he knew that he was partially to blame, for he still craved Mary Hastings. In dreams that even he was too ashamed to pen, it was Mary who came to him. With her dark hair cascading entrancingly about her shoulders, she reached for him, desiring him in the way that love commands. But the dream always ended with a sudden awakening, legs trembling, his frustration etched in sweat across his brow.

His complicated relationship with Elizabeth was also a major impediment to improving his marriage. He continued to hint at ending the affair but the vain Queen immediately countered by suggesting that the Tower had need for younger guests. He well knew that she used the Tower both as a governance and personal weapon and that she had inherited a generous dose of calculating coldness and callous disdain from her father, Henry VIII.

At this time, Edward agreed to sponsor Thomas Bedingfield's translation from Latin into English of *Cardanus Comfort* by the great Italian philosopher Gerolamo Cardanus. Edward thought of himself as carrying on the tradition of patrons like Lorenzo de Medici, who spent much of his life bringing forgotten writings out of oblivion to enflame the minds of readers eager for exposure to past literary beauty.

Edward retreated to Wivenhoe, climbed the stairs to his tower-study and contemplated his *Introduction*. Looking out over the peaceful landscape, he watched a kestrel rapidly fanning its wings in hover-flight above a field. He sat down at his desk and began to write:

> *To my loving friend Thomas Bedingfield: You amongst men, I do not doubt, will aspire to follow the virtuous path, to illuster yourself with the ornaments of virtue. In mine opinion, as it beautifieth a fair woman to be decked with pearls and precious stones, so much more it ornifieth a gentleman to be furnished with glittering virtues. For when all things shall else forsake us, virtue will ever abide with us, and when our bodies fall into the bowels of the earth, yet that shall mount with our minds into the highest heavens.*

Edward leaned back in his chair. He knew that his writing skills were improving, but too slowly. His unsettled feet longed to travel and his mental wings to fly high into the heavens.

To write well, he was completely convinced that it was essential for him to cross the Rubicon to see, feel, hear, smell and taste the world.

Chapter 11

The thieves have bound the true men; now
could thou and I rob the thieves, and go merrily
to London. It would be argument for a week,
laughter for a month, and a good jest for ever.
- Henry IV, Part 1

Edward had hoped that over time he might be permitted to acknowledge his writing more openly. But much to his rankling annoyance, Baron Burghley created a tight censorship over all publishing and insisted on enforcing the rules forbidding acknowledged authorship by nobles.

Edward detested the strange concept of pseudonymity, which was fostered by the even more bizarre idea that creative writing was manual labor not to be done, or admitted to, by the exalted noble class. He was unable to comprehend the concept that it was degrading for members of the gentle class to publish the product of their pens, as if they were money-grubbing merchants trying to market their brains.

Who benefited from namelessness? Did Virgil, Ovid, and Horace write their great poetry anonymously? Was Homer despised through the centuries for having his name attached to The Iliad and The Odyssey? He shook his head in complete mystification.

Now, in 1573, for the third time in his life, Edward was compelled to publish a book under a pseudonym—this time *Meritum Petere Grave* (To Seek Serious Reward). The book, *A Hundreth Sundrie Flowers,* contained several poems by George Gascoigne under his own name and a few by Hatton, Thomas Watson, and Gervase Holles. The majority were Edward's under such pseudonyms as Ever or Never, Ignoto, and *Meritum Petere Grave.*

Edward wondered how many years such irrational artistic suppression would last before new ideas could burst forth out of their arbitrary restraints. How he loathed the narrowness of repressive cultural dogma and the rigidity of societal rules!

The learned Queen Elizabeth, an avid reader of great literature, had told him often that she would eventually exempt him from literary pseudonymity because of her enthusiasm for his talents in poetry and interludes.

He hoped that basic honesty would inspire her to comply with these words but in his late nights of solitary thinking with pen in hand, he often wondered whether she ever really intended to keep her word.

After long hours of writing isolation, Edward frequently felt the need for his social self to emerge. At such times, he gathered his friends, or went alone, for long hours of talks, drinks and jests at a tavern.

TR

Sometimes they would ride out Drury Lane past Covent Garden to Bermoothes, that district west of Westminster which was privileged against arrest. It was an area of felons and other criminals, escapists and prostitutes. Edward's group made no attempt to disguise itself.

Sitting with the outcasts and drinking their crude but strong whiskey called dew, made in their own stills, the nobles greatly enjoyed the underworld cast of characters in the Bermoothes.

They wouldn't dare visit the area without Edward, who knew most of the inhabitants by name. He did not regard them as base dunghill villains but as unique, often eloquent, portrayers of their way of life. Edward always enjoyed the Bermoothians' love of fun and laughter, their mixture of dialects and quaint use of words. He wrote in his tablet:

> *The prince but studies his companions*
> *Like a strange tongue wherein, to gain the*
> *language*
> *'Tis needful that the most immodest word*
> *Be lookd upon and learn'd.*

At the end of an hour or two of banter and discussing topics as diverse as the excitement of piracy and the relative merits of different weapons for committing a murder, Edward would often buy a few bottles of dew and head back to his London home, Oxford Court, with his companions.

One evening in May 1573, Edward had a rendezvous with four friends at The Boar's Head Tavern in Eastcheap, near Oxford Court. The Boar's Head was one of his favorite haunts, having good food, excellent wines, pleasant host William Brooks, amiable vintner Thomas Wright, and that indefinable but essential ingredient—atmosphere. The habitués, from many walks of life, were fun-loving and boisterous. Impromptu wit contests were common, as were stories, anecdotes, brief impersonations, skits or monologues, with Edward often a participant or stimulator.

On that particular evening, Edward was waiting for the bright and jovial kin to the Queen, Thomas Sackville, Lord Buckhurst, whose relish for life was attested by his easy laughter and notable potbelly. An able poet, sonnetist and sometime dramatist, he had been knighted in 1567 and was a competent diplomat for the Queen on special assignments to France. His sense of humor and good fun were irrepressible. He loved taverns and had been heard to say, "I'll drink as long as there is passage in my throat."

Ned Somerset and Edward Seymour were also expected. Ned was now Earl of Worcester and always brought with him a relaxed conversational style and the infectious joy of his happy marriage with Elizabeth Hastings. Thirty-four-year-old Seymour had secretly married, in 1560, Catherine Grey, Henry VII's granddaughter and an heir to the throne. The potential threat to Elizabeth's sovereignty caused the Queen to consign them to the Tower where she died and he spent the next eleven years. Despite this flagrant injustice, he was always brimming with *joie-de-vivre*.

Before the others had arrived, while sipping a glass of canary, the sweet Spanish white wine from the Canary Islands, Edward recognized voices at a corner table as those of his own servants, Daniel Wilkins, John Hannam and Morris Denys. They were discussing two of Edward's former servants, William

Faunt and John Wotton, who had gone over to Burghley's household under pressure from the Principal Secretary.

Hannam was talking. "Faunt and Wotton are on assignment for Burghley carrying the Queen's gold to the treasury. It would be easy and good fun to waylay them and steal their bags of gold."

"It's government gold, John. Do you want to entertain the crowds at Tyburn, hanging from a hemp tippet?" warned Denys.

"Both of them annoy me and even seem to be adopting a high-toned accent since their move to Cecil House," declared Dan Wilkins.

"Let's steal the gold, hold it long enough to ice their innards, then charitably donate it back to them," suggested Hannam.

"Let's ask the Seventeenth Earl for the day off," said Wilkins. "Faunt and Wotton should be coming over Gad's Hill at about twilight, a good place to waylay them."

Thomas Sackville soon arrived and gave Edward a resounding smack on the back.

"Gad, Thomas!" Edward exclaimed. "Have you nothing better to do than jolt me to jelly?"

"Being jolted out of stale complacencies is good for the appetite! I feel mischief in my guts. Have you any diabolical schemes to digest?"

"Yes, indeed I do," Edward said, his eyes moving to the corner table where Wilkins, Hannam, and Denys were still plotting. "But bide some time until Seymour and Ned appear."

"Then let's crush a cup of Madeira." Thomas was a blackbearded, captivatingly merry fellow whose long mustache seemed to twirl upward as he laughed, and whose rotundity kept him two feet from the table.

At just this moment, Ned and Seymour entered The Boar's Head and came over to the table. Seymour was tall, seemingly reserved but with brown eyes that held both intelligence and sparkle. Ned was a handsome fellow with light brown hair. Like de Vere, his closest friend, Ned alternated between adventure and books.

"What, ho! Good cheer! I smell sulfur so I know who's here," laughed Ned.

"What deviltry's afoot, you pranksters from Hades?" asked Seymour.

The evening wore on until Edward thought his table-mates were sufficiently mellow. Sackville had eaten a platter of capon smothered with sugar-sweetened bitter oranges, plus anchovies and cheeses, and was now emitting table-shaking belches.

Edward related the plot he had overheard, then broached his plan for surprising his own thieving servant-plotters at Gad's Hill and pretending to rob the robbers.

"Well," he concluded, "what say you all? What says Sir Thomas Fillbelly, Sir Thomas Sackbelch?"

Sackville laughed. "I say, my merry madcap Lord, that it consorts not well with one to whom his cousin-Queen recently said that she would never know me until I knew myself and could separate myself from my misdemeanors."

"But this is something we've never tried before, you adventurous eructation! Truly a highway robbery! In pretense, of course, but the double-twisted drama takes me quite. Surely our inspired cleverness can manage to keep our identities eternally secret!"

Sackville and the others, flush with wine and the joy of life, agreed. None of them could resist a good romp enlivened by the excitement of mischievous misdemeanor.

The next afternoon, the four conspirators, dressed in black kirtles, jackets, and riding pants, met on the Surrey side of London Bridge. They rode off at a good gait, turning into Borough High Street to ride south past the Tabard Inn and then toward Rochester on the old Roman road. They galloped into open moor country interspersed with scraggly bushes and midland hawthorn in white bloom. Four miles out, they skirted the Park of Greenwich Palace, rode past the wilds of Blackheath and finally galloped into Gravesend.

They put on full black facial masks as they came over Gad's Hill in the late dusk. They were just in time to witness the initial robbery that was taking place. The figures of Faunt and Wotton and their horses and those of the attackers with flourishing swords were visible against the deep violet haze of the sky.

Shortly, the three scheming robbers turned and rode back toward Gravesend. The four highwaymen drew into the bushes in pairs on either side of the road. Along came the trio. Suddenly out came the four menacing horsemen, swords whistling in the evening air. Horses reared amidst exclamations of surprise and fear. Bags of gold thudded to the ground.

"Prithee, *messieurs*," cried Denys, "it is Government gold we be carrying. You rob the Queen, messieurs!"

"*You* robbed the Queen, *monsieur!* And a dastardly Frenchman it is, no doubt planning to use the money to make war against us," cried Edward, deepening his voice and thoroughly enjoying the comedy. Raising his sword, he shouted, "Cut the villains' throats! Ah, you heavy-headed moldwarps, you grizzled hedgepigs! Fleece them!"

Denys tried with all his might to fight his way clear but Edward immediately struck down Denys' sword and held him in a strong grip.

Nearby, Dan Wilkins was pleading for his life from Seymour, who held his dagger against the fellow's throat. Sackville and Somerset together had unhorsed and disarmed John Hannam.

Sackville bellowed: "How now, you onion-eyed rogues, you bacon-fed knaves, you rake-pockets and hell-scum of the devil! Steal the Queen's money, would you? That deserves rack or thumbscrews!"

"Have mercy!" pleaded Hannam. "Keep the gold and let us go! We be not thieves. We took the money as a joke. They are friends of ours!"

Ned gave their grazing horses good whacks with his riding stick and they galloped away. Then, like cats at play with mice, the four adventurers toyed with the fears and guilts of their three captives. Only Denys, with tenacious French pride, stood up bravely in the ordeal.

After a few minutes, Edward said, "Let us be magnanimous and add meaning to the great quality of sweet mercy. We will spare your lives."

"Only," menaced Seymour, "if they seem truly repentant."

Edward continued. "There is your gold. Take it and be cursed, for gold is the hex of man. Those who seek it for its own sake will pay a heavy price. To etch this episode in your memories forever, each of you will walk the twenty-five miles back to London carrying two bags of gold. Tomorrow you will return the gold in its entirety to Lord Burghley. There you shall admit your sin and beg his forgiveness. And do remember:

> *All that glitters is not gold;*
> *Often have you heard that told.*
> *Many a man his life hath sold,*
> *Gilded tombs do worms infold."*

The three thieves, heavily weighted down, began the long walk back to London. The four black-clothed protectors of the Queen's Treasury rode silently past them, shaking their heads.

Down the road, the four cavaliers broke out into loud guffaws.

"Who called us reckless adventurers?" said Edward. "Were we not all day and evening ensconced amongst the dusty basement bookshelves of Lambeth Palace, tracing the mysterious disappearance of the Holy Grail? Are not all four of us ideal candidates to pursue such a quest, being perfectly pure in thought, word, and deed?"

"Well done, lads," said Sackville. "Bermoothes will be proud of us when they hear our tale!"

"Indeed, gentlemen," Edward agreed, "this episode will engender hearty laughs in us and others for many weeks or months. Certainly, from my standpoint, it is a good jest for E. Vere!"

Chapter 12

And from the forlorn world his visage hide,
Stealing unseen to west with this disgrace,
Even so my sun one early morn did shine
With all triumphant splendour on my brow;
But out, alack, he was but one hour mine;
The region cloud hath masked him from me now.
                              - Sonnet 33

But my sword burns in my belt from my ardor to help protect your realm," said Edward to the Queen, pleading for a military assignment with the English contingent helping Protestant Netherlands defend itself against the Spanish invasion. "It is my heritage and, like my Bolebec lion triumphantly brandishing his foe's broken spear, I long to show my courage in battle." He slapped his leg forcefully, rippling his purple velvet breeches.

The Queen and Edward were walking in St. James

Park behind Whitehall Palace in December, their feet scrunching through a foot of snow.

"I admire your devotion to me and to England, Edward," Elizabeth responded. "But you are much more valuable to me right here as my favorite and most gifted courtier. War is not glorious."

Edward began to pace nervously. "But fanatic Spanish Catholicism is the chief threat to your reign! Rowland Yorke and Roger Williams are already winning battles! So can I!"

"Your greatness will come here at home, Edward. Be patient. Your unusual talents will not find appropriate expression on the fields of war."

He implored Elizabeth, as an alternative, to allow him to travel. "For God's sake and for mine, Your Majesty, grant me freedom to see the glories of Europe, Greece and Istanbul! My horizons and writing scope need broadening, away from this lovely but small and isolated island!"

The Queen considered his request. "Next year, perhaps. The heavens are full of days!" She slowly opened and closed her fan.

The knot of frustration tightened inside Edward, punishing him with sensations of rough, grating futility. "Your Majesty, you can't imagine how much I crave to savor the world and its wisdom!"

"How young and rash you are, especially when you know how much you please me here at Court and how much I need you with me at this time."

"Pray tell, how do you need me at this time?" Edward queried, turning to face Elizabeth. "Have I not fulfilled your needs? Have I not provided for your desires?"

Elizabeth inhaled softly and felt the cool air glide

down her throat. With her eyes cast firmly on Edward, she said, "I need you not only for my own self but for yet another, as well."

Edward knew her words before she spoke them, felt the words before they had fallen from her lips. "Elizabeth . . . are you with . . ."

"With child?" she said and tossed her head back, laughing shrilly. "Three months with your child! So now you see, Edward, why your request to wander is inappropriate. I am forty-one years old and do not intend to go through this alone."

Edward could think of no reply to this astonishing news.

Later, in the privacy of his room, he felt the gentle nudge of pride for an heir being produced from his loins. He became more and more intrigued by the idea of a de Vere becoming royalty after serving the English monarchy so loyally for five hundred years. Edward also saw this as a way out of his woeful marriage.

After six weeks of intense matrimonial discussion, Elizabeth finally agreed to wed him if his marriage to Anne Cecil could be annulled by the Church of England without significant rancor.

But she had a caution to add. "If we marry, Edward, there can be only one Monarch of England. My word on state matters must be final without dissent from you."

"I solemnly swear, Your Majesty, that I will never interfere in any manner with affairs of government. I am totally committed to life as a literary artist and have less than zero interest in politics."

In March, they talked at length with Matthew Parker, Archbishop of Canterbury, and visited him for three days in early April at his home in Croydon, south of London.

The Archbishop accepted the Queen's generous offer of financial help to enlarge his manor house, and readily agreed to annul Edward's marriage by reason of Anne's natural frigidity enhanced by unyielding Puritan beliefs. The Queen promised Edward that she would find a noble husband for Anne of sufficient stature and wealth that Burghley would concur.

The Queen had her farthingaled dresses redesigned with hoops higher on the abdomen. Only her two senior maids of honor knew of her condition. Elizabeth cut back on her work schedule and granted only the most essential diplomatic interviews.

In mid-May, the Queen went to visit Edward at his estate near London, Havering-Atte-Bower, where she spent the next two months to her Court's puzzlement. All diplomatic visits were canceled. She sent Christopher Hatton to the continent and commanded the Privy Council, Burghley, and her new Principal Secretary Francis Walsingham to remain in London and communicate with her by courier. Her retinue was told that she was pensive and melancholy and needed to be alone. Burghley said that he was surprised by this unusual request but would do as he was commanded.

Elizabeth told them by dispatch that her Royal Progress to Bristol and western England would be postponed for two months and would begin in late July.

Elizabeth took daily walks and rides with Edward over the low hills, inhaling the fragrance and relishing the beauty of spring's burst of life: fresh green grass shimmering wetly in the intermittent sun, tousled by wandering breezes; spring flowers of all colors; and endless white-blossomed hawthorn trees. She admired the magnificent views over five counties and the broad serpentine Thames, busy with sailing vessels from many countries.

These were quiet moments that they both shared and Edward felt closer to her than ever. Elizabeth's pregnancy seemed to produce a youthfulness in her demeanor, a playful and carefree femininity that Edward found appealing. For the first time in many years, he felt connected to something greater than he had ever known. He daydreamed of this child of royal birth whom he would soon call his own.

In late June, the Queen gave birth to a plump orange-haired son. Later that day, an exhausted and pale Elizabeth told Edward to view the baby and then come to her bedroom to talk.

With the iron will of personal resolve in her eyes, Elizabeth said, "Edward, I can not go through with our plans. I am an able monarch, not a doting mother."

Edward was momentarily struck speechless. "But Your Majesty, the baby is beautiful and will enhance our lives. All of England loves you and will be thrilled with a Tudor heir."

"An heir is not essential to my life! I am quite content being the last of the Tudors."

"But I thought everything was agreed upon between us! Is this why you insisted on waiting until the baby's birth before having my marriage to Anne annulled?"

Elizabeth sighed deeply and fidgeted with her handkerchief. "Yes, and to make sure the baby and I survived the birthing."

Edward sensed a deep sadness and decided to

push further. "But our marriage will enrich the Court! What a partnership we would have!"

"When I think of marriage, I visualize my mother's bloody murder. Should she have been beheaded because she did not produce an immediate royal son? She was a completely loyal wife and was cleft in two by a husband-tyrant! I will *not* trust my body or my soul to any man in the world, Edward, even you."

Edward knew it was fruitless to attempt to influence the Queen in her present state, but he put a clove in his mouth and decided to continue. "Think of our son's magnificent ancestry! How could he not be an extraordinary king?"

"Edward, enough. I feel tired. I have spoken. There will be no marriage. I am resolved to marry only when the necessity of my governing and the welfare of my subjects absolutely require it."

"Then I plead with you, Your Majesty, not to make him disappear into the morass of mediocrity. Allow him to be raised in a noble family and nearby the Court so we may watch him grow."

She nodded wearily. "I am way ahead of you, Edward. I already have a patrician family in mind with a newborn son who represents a festering legitimacy problem. Our son will be a changeling. You may interact with him but must never publicly acknowledge him. The subject is now closed. I need to rest."

Despite the emotions tumulting inside him, Edward knew he must desist and yield. Utmost loyalty was hammered into de Veres from earliest childhood. "So be it, Your Majesty. I am deeply honored to be the father of your son. May he exceed our expectations and bring great credit to England."

* * *

Edward rode slowly back to London, eyes moist and downcast. He lay on his bed at Oxford Court, hands behind his head, staring at the molded plaster boars and lions on the ceiling. At sunset, he sat dejectedly at his desk and wrote part of a sonnet for future revision:

Even so my son one early morn did shine
With all triumphant splendour on my brow;
But out, alack, he was but one hour mine;
Regina's cloud hath masked him from me now.

He took a long evening walk through the foul, horse-manured, garbage-strewn streets of Eastcheap, returned to his study and, gripping his pen firmly, wrote in his tablet:

Truth will come to light; murder cannot be hid
long—
a man's son may, but in the end truth will out .

He underlined it forcefully, scattering tiny ink droplets on the page. Then he hurled himself into bed and threw the covers over his head.

Chapter 13

Farewell the plumed troop and the big wars
That make ambition virtue! O, farewell,
Farewell the neighing steed and the shrill trump,
The spirit-stirring drum, the ear-piercing fife,
The royal banner and all quality,
Pride, pomp and circumstance of glorious war!
- Othello

After a fitful sleep, the next morning Edward mulled his options. He decided he needed a dramatic diversion far away from the autocratic decisions and mendacity which permeated royal courts.

He contemplated who would be the best available companion for an exciting adventure. He decided upon Edward Seymour, who had not remarried and had been given no official job since his long Tower sojourn. Edward sent Seymour a message to meet him as soon as possible at Wivenhoe on an urgent matter.

Edward abruptly left London and rode circui-
tously with two doublings-back to avoid Burghley's
intricate spy network, arriving at Colchester late the
next evening. He spent the night in the old Celtic
capital of Boudica and Cunobelinus. In the morning, wearing a disguise, he made some purchases
and rode to Wivenhoe.

When Seymour arrived a day later, Edward led
him up to his tower-study. Pacing back and forth,
Edward shared his recent tribulations. "It is time for
an escapade! I'm tired to death of beating my
pounces on the floor of the mews, my wings against
the stifling, ensnaring cage of authority! I must fly
into the limitless skies of freedom, a falcon liberated!
Come with me! We are going to Flanders for a taste
of the real world!"

An astounded look came over Seymour's face.
"Flanders? To be killed or brought back in disgrace
by some sniveling informant of Burghley?"

"Death is not on the agenda, my friend," Edward
assured him. "We both have a further role in the
script of life. From time to time, however, we must
burst the chains of courtly captivity, with which you
are so profoundly familiar, to maintain our sanity and
dignity as humans!"

"Would Castiglione approve?"

"That chapter was stolen by a deranged monk
from the original manuscript on its way from Urbino
to the printer!"

Seymour laughed. "And how are we traveling, by
coach or litter?"

Edward's mood suddenly elevated as he saw that
Seymour was hooked. "Have I ever led you astray to
your later regret? The boat is already arranged with
an old acquaintance of my father, one of the few in

England who can keep a secret. Let us ready our costumes to add theater to our adventure and a few days to our liberty!"

"Perhaps we should both go as fools since I smell dangerous folly in the air. Being with you is being perpetually on stage, playing new parts almost every time we meet!"

Edward bowed low, pretending to sweep a hat before an audience. "Life is a series of roles, and danger adds to the dramatic tension and luster! Do you want to be a friar or a pilgrim?"

"I'll be the friar. Then that large pillow can protect my belly from your rapier-wit!" Seymour donned the rough black gown, put the pillow underneath, and tied the girdle-sash tightly. He then put on the wide-brimmed friar's hat and grabbed the amber-headed walking stick.

"Say a few Hail Marys and I'll follow you to the Holy Land!" exclaimed Edward. "And remember, fat friars always laugh loudly and uncontainedly at my witticisms!" Edward threw a brown smock and simple cloak over his riding clothes. Then, with a dramatic flourish, he added a hat with cockle-shells.

As darkness descended, the two devout travelers were rowed out from Wivenhoe's pier to an unlanterned gray sloop in the Colne. The boat quietly left Wivenhoe, floating with the outgoing tide.

In fog the next day the boat sailed into a small cove in Ostend and the friar and pilgrim waded ashore. They walked at a good clip the twelve miles to Bruges. Seymour soon pulled the hot sweaty pillow from his abdomen and threw his fat jolly belly into a ditch.

Edward thought how many men throughout history, with ideas different from the norm, had fled the coils of circumstance filled with fear—like the hunted stag, the hounded fox, the hawk-stooped heron.

With each friendly salutation to travelers they encountered, Edward entertained his companion by changing the pitch of his voice from highest falsetto to lowest vibrating basso, in several different languages.

They discarded their disguises when they reached the outskirts of Antwerp. It was time to seek officer-friends who might be resting between battles. They also needed to buy horses. They knew that the superior Spanish army had been brought to a stalemate, with English troops making the difference. It was a key element of Burghley's and Elizabeth's foreign policy to keep the Spanish army bogged down as long as possible to delay Catholic Philip's inevitable invasion of heretic England.

They entered the towered city in the late afternoon and sought out the best tavern in town.

Seated at the Golden Stag, they had just quaffed their second beer when a voice boomed: "Lord Edward of Oxenford! And my Lord Edward of Hertford! God bless you both! Are you here to buy wooden shoes or just out for a stroll in tulip-time?"

They turned in surprise at the familiar voice.

"Roger! Roger Williams!" Edward exclaimed.

The three of them embraced as old comrades.

"*Colonel* Roger Williams, I will have you know, my good friends!"

"Colonel!" Seymour exclaimed.

"An officer, no less!" cried Edward jubilantly. Encountering Roger boosted his spirits considerably. He had become acquainted with him when Roger was a picturesque member of the household of Sir William

Herbert, Earl of Pembroke. He was a large well-muscled Welshman with chunky cheeks, broad smile, twinkling eyes and accented English. "You must have wounded a stalwart Spanish mule or two! But you're just the man we're looking for!"

"Indeed!" Seymour added. "We are eager for posts of command to defend our Queen against the Spanish knaves!"

Roger thrust out his right hand, palm out. "Now wait a minute, my noble lords. One just doesn't walk to the front lines, wave a wand and have the enemy run in fear from the great jousting knights who have a lady's velvet bodkin flying from their crest! This is a messy war with acres of dead bodies and ditches running with blood."

"We came to fight!" declaimed Edward, slamming his fist on the table and feeling the courage of beer in his blood.

"Ah, Edward, you're a gallant lad and you can't resist trying to be a noble warrior, just like your ancestors! You both look so fierce, you already frighten me to death!" Roger guffawed like the hairy, raucous, engaging Celtic giant that he was, and sat down at their table.

"Just like the old Boar's Head," said Seymour, smiling at Roger.

"Such a stupid war!" said Roger. "Religious acrimony between faraway rulers with peasants doing the dying."

"As in all wars," agreed Edward, filling their mugs.

"But now to a more pertinent topic: by St. David's gizzards, this be the utter-damnedest place for digestings I've ever set stomach in. I call for a great joint of mutton, and what do these lousy servitors bring me but a poor creature done out of all resemblance's to a goodly sheep, lying on a platter and crying its heart out in a sodden bed of hot apple sauce, cinnamon, sugar and raisins! I call for a hare most honestly fumed in butter, and they bring me a tricksy thing all flaunting in white grapes and currants and jelly! I ask for an honest leek soup, and I get a potage with all the herbs of Christendom afloat on its ridiculous bosom! Enough, enough, say I!" He mockingly put his hand on his sword.

Edward and Seymour laughed heartily and gulped their beer.

"Here, boy," Williams continued, as he waved a waiter to the table. "I will have a slab of beef, plain and naked as you were on the day you were born. And if you bring me a beef with so much as one little niggling, outlandish, alien barbarian speck of any kind on it, any herb, spice, fruit, or bastard flibbertigibbet, I'll run you through from backbone to belly button!"

* * *

Sitting alone at a corner table was a servant and spy of Henry Neville, Fifth Earl of Westmoreland, who had been attainted for his part in the 1569 rising in the north but had escaped to Brussels. An ardent Catholic, Neville had familial ties with the de Veres. He had gathered around him a sizable group of English Catholics.

When Westmoreland's retainer brought him the news early the next morning of the arrival of two important noble Edwards, he sent a message to arrange a meeting.

Edward read the letter from Westmoreland at dinner the next day at the Golden Stag, passed it to Seymour and announced to the courier in a confident voice: "Tell the Earl of Westmoreland that Edward, Earl of Oxford, and Edward, Earl of Hertford, regret that any kinsmen of theirs should follow any masters or allegiances other than her magnificent Majesty, Queen Elizabeth of England, whom alone we will ever serve."

That evening, in the July moonlight, the two Edwards and Roger Williams rode northeast toward the enemy lines a hundred miles away, arriving in thirty-six hours by frequent changes of horses.

"Now, my two young generals," said Roger, "I will outfit you on one solemn promise: For the first week, you will stay with me and *observe*. We will *then* discuss a more useful role for each of you. Is it agreed?"

It was so agreed.

*   *   *

The battle raged back and forth for several days across the flat fields and a river. Charges by foot soldiers on both sides, led by horsed officers, yielded endless deaths, most of the damage being done by cannonades. The cries and moans of the wounded defiled the beautiful moonlight.

So many frontal assaults, so few ruses and diversions, thought Edward. *Can't one truly strategize even in flat country?* He devised a plan he was sure would succeed, visualizing the surrender to him personally.

The week of observance ended quickly. Edward and Seymour dismounted in front of Roger Williams' tent, eagerly awaiting assignments as captains. Roger emerged, shook their hands and smilingly congratulated them on their cooperation and restraint.

At just that moment, a horseman appeared carrying a black and white banner, Elizabeth's royal colors. "Queen's messenger," he shouted. Thomas Bedingfield rode straight to Edward and handed him a parchment roll bearing the Queen's ribbons and seal. "I regret to inform you, my Lord of Oxford," said Edward's colleague in literature, "that you are hereby placed under my sovereign-commanded authority and ordered to ride with me post-haste to the port of Ostend and thence to England. My Lord of Hertford is free to do as he wishes."

Edward's face reflected absolute dismay. He glanced at the parchment and looked at Seymour in helpless futility. "But Thomas, I have a most imperative action to conclude here that will reflect glory upon the Queen!"

"If I am forced to report that you defied your Queen and delayed one instant in obeying her urgent command, I cannot guarantee the future continuity of your noble head with your youthful body!"

"It would be prudent for you to obey, Edward," advised Seymour. "I think I will opt out of the war idea and taste some adventuring in Italy, far away from the Tower."

"God's Wounds!" exclaimed Edward, dropping the parchment and grinding it into the mud with his boot. "No military success, no honor, no chance to show my patriotism! Is this my destiny, to be hindered, balked, foiled, obstructed, thwarted and suppressed forever?"

Chapter 14

Home-keeping youth have ever homely wits . . .
I rather would entreat thy company
To see the wonders of the world abroad
Than, living dully sluggardized at home,
Wear out thy youth with shapeless idleness.
　　　　- The Two Gentlemen of Verona

As they sailed across the cold choppy channel, Edward felt deeply wronged. Why was he fated never to achieve military honor, so conspicuous in his illustrious family history? Would he never equal that day at Antioch in 1098 when the star suddenly shone on the shield of Alberic's son, the first Aubrey de Vere, who then led the First Crusade to victory? Or achieve fame like John, the outstanding Thirteenth Earl of Oxford, who played such a key role in the battle of Bosworth, ending the War of Roses and handing the monarchy back to the Lancasters, making the Earl of Richmond King Henry VII?

Edward felt that his star always failed him at the decisive moment, reducing him to a Vere boar groveling in the dirt with worthless white tusks.

The ship came around the North Foreland and sailed into the Thames between Gravesend and Tilbury only two weeks after his departure from Wivenhoe. Despite his dark mood, Edward loved the drama of ships of all sizes with orange, red or white sails. He savored the familiar landmarks: the marshes near Gad's Hill; Greenwich Palace, Elizabeth's birthplace and favorite summer residence; and London Bridge, built in the twelfth century with all its shops and dwellings, the symbol of London itself.

It was testimony to the efficiency of Burghley's spies that he and Anne arrived at Belin's dock simultaneously with the ship. Edward could not help noticing their identical expressions of sanctimonious reproach.

The combined odors of fish, tar and wet stone greeted Edward as he stepped onto the landing stairs. He kissed Anne on the forehead and she lowered her eyes as if caught in a sinful act. He held out his hand to Burghley.

But Burghley shook Bedingfield's hand instead and said, "Welcome to you, good Sir Thomas." His eyes flicked to Edward's. "And to you, our prodigal son. Our Queen will begin her Progress soon. We are hoping for a pardon for you but this is serious business, leaving our country without the Queen's license! Such escapades are for schoolboys, not for nobles of England!"

"The glory of war and defending our Queen against her enemies is for earls," Edward shot back. "*Chastisement* is for schoolboys." He snatched the bridle from the startled groom and leaped onto his horse. "By your leave, Bedingfield." He rode briskly home, past the grimy fish markets of Billingsgate, the rank butcher shops of Pudding Lane, the street mongers of Eastcheap shouting "hot mutton pie" and "apples fine," and past the old Roman road-marker, London Stone, to Oxford Court.

*   *   *

Several days later, Burghley brought news of the Queen's acceptance of Edward's apology offered by his father-in-law. Although the Queen seemed to have no intention of punishing Edward, the Lord Treasurer preferred to think that it was the reports of his spies which had influenced her. They had picked up several accounts in Antwerp of Edward's vociferous repudiations of Westmoreland's overtures, and from Colonel Roger Williams of Edward's eagerness to fight.

Edward joined the Queen at Bristol. During the remainder of the Royal Progress, he enjoyed the ardor of Elizabeth's renewed favor, often warm and tender. Although she tired easily, she was her usual spritely self.

It was in her arms that Edward escaped the frustrations of his life, even though Elizabeth was the embodiment of his captivity. At times she held him tightly, clinging to him with a different fervency, making Edward wonder whether she had regrets over her postpartum anti-marriage decision, made so quickly and unilaterally.

She told Edward that their son, Henry, was now indeed a changeling and the only son of the Second Earl of Southampton, whose newborn illegitimate son, conceived while he was in prison, had been given away for adoption.

Edward felt a deep yearning to be absolutely free to experience the world and improve his languages. He longed to flavor the country of Ovid, Virgil and Dante and the fabled land of the ancient Greek dramatists. He wanted to experience the exotic culture of Turkey. Whenever he mentioned to Elizabeth either travel or diplomatic missions, however, conversation abruptly ended.

At the end of the Progress, Edward joined Anne at Theobalds. Since Burghley and his wife Mildred were leaving shortly for London, Edward consented to stay on, at Anne's urging. Both were trying to build an emotional closeness, but Edward became more and more aware of how little they had in common. He still harbored deep resentment over the forced marriage and the commanded obliteration of his engagement vows with Mary Hastings.

Anne had little understanding of how much her Puritan restrictions interfered with true bonding. Edward knew that his heart would never belong to Anne but he did at times make an effort, as did Anne. Emotional closeness did not follow.

*   *   *

Edward was very fond of Theobalds with its elegant manor house skillfully crafted by Burghley's artisans, gathered from all over England and Europe. He admired the elegant charm of Burghley's beautiful gardens, designed by John Gerard, England's finest landscapist and Edward's tutor in the lovely complexities of botany when Edward lived at Cecil house. He walked the house interior and gazed at the walls painted with city plans and landscapes of all the leading towns in Christendom.

But Edward continued to brood over his thwarted

military ambitions. So many tapestries, statues and paintings at Theobalds glorified men of action and great scenes of history. Here depicted were the statues of the Caesars in the pavilion, the tapestries of Roman victories in the dining hall, the painted emblems of the great kings of England in the gallery. Whenever Edward walked through this long hall he paused at the shield of Henry V and the depiction of the remarkable Battle of Agincourt. How much he had in common with Henry V—lover of life, bookreader, dreamer and man of action.

One morning a thought struck him. Could he write a drama about Henry V so vividly that the Queen would, for the first time, feel his heartfelt enthusiasm for tasting the world outside of England? Might she then relax her tight constraints and allow him to experience the diversity he felt he needed to become a truly effective creative artist?

Edward began work on the manuscript immediately, closing the door to his room so he could be alone with his mental energy. For this was to be his first real play, a form best calculated to engage the Queen's involvement and excitement. English theater was extremely simple and basic, without cleverness in plot, dialogue or character portrayal. Edward began to feel a growing sense of the potential power of a longer dramatic presentation, including the contrapositives of circumstance and character, the ironic emotion-arousing dissymmetries of life.

He tried to make the play, which he entitled *The Famous Victories of Henry V*, well balanced. He included witty, earthy scenes from The Boar's Head Tavern and a description of the Gad's Hill escapade. He used some of the bibulous, genial, verbally fluent qualities of Tom Sackville for one of his characters. He included the war against France and credited Richard de Vere, Eleventh Earl of Oxford, with an important role which had been overlooked by *Hall's Chronicles*. Accurately reflecting his own family archives, he portrayed the earl as Henry V's chief military adviser who devised the strategic defensive palisade of stakes at Agincourt. This so decisively jammed together the vast French army that they were annihilated by endless cascades of long-bow arrows from the small English force.

Edward was moving along briskly and happily with the play when he received a letter from his friend Tom Radcliffe, now Lord Chamberlain of the Royal Household. The letter notified him that the Queen desired his attendance at Hampton Court.

Edward ruminated for days. In his writing enthusiasm, he had laid aside all thoughts of the fawning, self-seeking frivolities of the Court. Now so desirous of winning over the Queen with his play, however, he realized that he had no choice but to obey.

Edward did love Hampton Court with the original opulence of Cardinal Wolsey and superimposed luxuriance of Henry VIII who had spared nothing to make it one of his own showpieces. He knew that this was Elizabeth's least favorite palace since her illness with smallpox there.

The time Edward could spend in creative solitude, however, was severely limited. Courtiers were expected to pay continual attention to the Queen's self-centered whimsies in a perpetual minuet of observances. He could not bear the sycophants like Thomas Knyvet, who were forever bidding hail or farewell with their civet-reeking handkerchiefs and their outflung, daintily postured hands. He hated the peacock-strutters and imitators of Don John of

Austria, who were forever pushing real or imaginary locks back from their foreheads. He amused his friends with imitations of Knyvet's exaggerated obeisances, Hatton's gooey flatteries, and Burghley's ponderous repetitions.

Edward even gave a few imitations for the Queen, usually in private. Try as she would, she could not rebuke him. He knew that Elizabeth loved laughter, which always seemed to ride in like a rollicking wave over the reefs of reproach. No matter what her faults or how much she craved and demanded adulation, she always appreciated true talent and creativity, and she encouraged their appearance and development.

"Oh, Edward," she told him, "you do make me laugh! You are my favorite fool!"

To serve its purpose of influencing the Queen's mind soon, Edward felt that his drama must be presented as part of the annual Christmas entertainment. Edward was determined to play the role of his hero, Henry V. Although writing was his favorite pastime, acting followed close behind.

The night before Christmas at Whitehall Palace the Queen and her Court saw the first production of *The Famous Victories of Henry V.* Patch the Jester took the part of Derick, Sackville was Henry IV, and Edward played Henry V. A willowy young boy played the King's daughter, Kate, since women were forbidden on the English stage. Edward supervised the production.

The Queen was totally engrossed and intrigued. She laughed loudly at the brief comic scenes and leaned forward eagerly for the scenes of dramatic dialogue and war. She became captivated by Edward's energetic and realistic impersonation of Henry V.

But in a scene in which Henry was making a

declaration of his now double kingship—of both England and France—and of his intention to win the French Princess Katherine to be his Queen, Elizabeth could not resist an attempt to disconcert him.

"Ah, Harry!" declared Edward, striking his heart with the flat of his hand, his voice ringing to the farthest carved oak beam of the banqueting hall. "Hast thou conquered the French King, and begun a fresh attack upon his daughter?" Edward, lost in the part, had come so close to the Queen's Chair of State that she received a thrill almost of personal declaration.

At the peak of Edward's stage-intensity, she threw one of her long pearled gloves directly in front of him. Edward bent forward and picked up the glove, his mind rhythmically responding to the unfailing stimulation of the Queen's mind.

He returned the glove with a bow and the flowing words:

"And though now bent on this high embassy, yet stoop we to take up our cousin's glove; but here she comes, that other fair. How now, faire Ladie, Katherine of France?"

Delighted, the Queen thought how often that bright-minded Edward of Oxford picked up the gauntlet, the challenge of mind and wit! *I can use such minds to adorn and enrich my Court with his special flare, his exceptional creative talent. A wild youth, yes! But so was Harry the Fifth! Perchance we have, after all, held him on too tight a rein. Lest we lose him permanently, perhaps he does need wider pastures for his gallops, more freedom and scope to bring his full capacities to fruition.*

The very next day, Elizabeth signed a grant of permission for Edward to travel on an extended tour of the continent.

*   *   *

Edward was pleased and excited that he had finally won his point and achieved his travel ambition with a play. He wrote in his tablet:

> *There is a tide in the affairs of men*
> *Which, taken at the flood, leads on to fortune.*
> *On such a full sea are we now afloat,*
> *And we must take the current where it serves.*

Before his departure, he had several private sessions with Elizabeth during which she suggested an overseas political assignment to be planned in cooperation with Burghley.

Edward agreed readily and proposed an additional diplomatic task to be known only to himself and the Queen.

Chapter 15

*A traveler! By my faith, you have great reason
to be sad. I fear you have sold your own lands to
see other men's. Then to have seen much and to
have nothing is to have rich eyes and poor hands.*
                                    - As You Like It

"Be wary of the seductions," Burghley expounded, "of strange cultures and voluptuous women tempting you in a hot climate, Edward. Yes, tempting women. And be warned against alien religions which are little more than papal political and financial ambitions hidden behind sanctimonious ceremonies."

Burghley was now entirely white-haired and white-bearded at the age of fifty-four. He had the same unsettled and unsettling eyes and was seated at his desk in Cecil House. As usual, he had two tall piles of papers in front of him with a plate of cheese between.

"My goals are otherwise," Edward responded indignantly.

"We have high hopes for you, Edward, yes, high hopes. Anne needs you and you need your own de Vere sons, so we hope you will keep your trip short. A few months in France and Germany should suffice, especially since you have had to sell several estates to finance your trip. Italy used to have a great deal to offer but that was long ago. I would suggest quickly fulfilling your diplomatic mission with Venice, having a bowl of spaghetti or two, and promptly returning home."

Edward requested and received Burghley's meticulously prepared notes on the history of failed previous attempts to establish ambassadorial relations with Venice. He respected Burghley's expertise in practical politics and international relations but he shook his head in wonderment over some of these lean-witted travel comments coming from someone who had never traveled.

"While you are in Venice," Burghley continued importantly, "I want you to learn as much as you can about their highly sophisticated, closely guarded shipbuilding methods which have been the best in the world for centuries."

"You mean become a spy?" Edward frowned. "I like not that role."

"Don't regard it as spying, Edward." Burghley brushed away the comment with a wave of his corpulent hand. "Just keep your eyes open. England is going to be attacked by the Spanish navy and invaded one of these years. We *must* begin to build up our own navy soon, for our own survival. We can learn much about that from the Venetians."

"I detest the concept of spying."

"You have wanted to serve England in war in the great tradition of your ancestors. This could represent your greatest military contribution to England. It would be much more important than fighting on any battlefield. Do it, Edward, for England. I will duly reward you."

Edward remained silent, reflecting upon his continuing mixed feelings about his coerced father-in-law and guardian.

*   *   *

Each year on January 1, Elizabeth reaped her annual harvest of presents and gave silver plate in return. Edward gave her a gold brooch in the shape of a woman holding a ship of diamonds, rubies and pearls. It was symbolic of her bestowal on him of the long-awaited voyage of freedom.

His previous pre-trip sessions with the Queen had been encouraging and stimulating, bordering on maternal at times. She had given him sage strategic advice on his political assignments. She now waved everyone out of the presence chamber and beckoned Edward to come forward.

"Edward, you mean a great deal to me and my Court. You do have rough edges, though. You must learn to control your quick mind and in-born gifts. I now realize that I have kept you on too tight a leash. Enrich your mind, hone your skillful sword of words, and drink deeply the draughts of wisdom and tempered sobriety of ancient lands. I shall miss your talents and yourself."

"I shall try to return as a more mature and mellow Castiglione courtier, Your Majesty."

* * *

Six days later, the Queen gave Edward personal
letters to Valentine Dale, her Ambassador in Paris,
to Luigi Mocenigo, Doge of Venice, and others. Edward then departed for Paris with his good friend
Will Russell plus Morris Denys, who had behaved so
well as a victim at Gad's Hill. Edward's retinue consisted of two grooms for the horses, a harbinger to
arrange lodging, a housekeeper, and a trencherman
to arrange food.

He had been unable to find a suitable payend to
handle expenses until Burghley arranged for William Lewyn to join the group in Paris. Lewyn, a former
tutor of Anne Cecil, could also speak several languages, including German which Edward did not
speak.

Edward intended to stay in Paris only a brief time
but the city and the Court of Henri III and his bride,
Louise of Lorraine, bewitched him. The dowager
Queen, Catherine de Medici, despite her sinister
ways and diabolical schemes, oversaw a highly cultured Court with frequent plays, musical events and
dances.

It was a rich feast, and Edward was asked to con-
tribute to the intellectual banquet by translating into
French, directing, and acting in *The Famous Victories
of Henry V.* It was well received despite its theme of
English victory over the French.

Edward obtained diplomatic papers and intro-
ductions from the King and Ambassador Dale to
Venice, Greece and Istanbul.

Just before leaving Paris, he received by courier
a letter on March 17 from his father-in-law, telling

him that Anne was pregnant and urging his immediate return.

The news struck no particular chord of joy in
Edward and that troubled him. But he felt it was
understandable, given the circumstances. He and
Anne had never formed an intimate bond. Their
marriage was a legal arrangement, nothing more,
and he found it difficult to bring forth feelings of
real warmth toward potential offspring from an enforced marriage without love. How different he would
feel if Mary Hastings were his wife and she had become pregnant!

It was a disquieting insight. *I will have to try to rec-
tify that when I return home,* he told himself. The child
Anne was carrying was innocent of Burghley's scheming, and deserved to have the same attentive father
that Edward had enjoyed.

He had no intention of cutting short his travels,
however. He answered by return letter to Burghley
that the unexpected news had made him a happy
man, *"for now that it hath pleased God to give me a son of
my own, methinks I have the better occasion to travel, sith
whatsoever becometh of me I leave behind one to supply my
duty and service to my country."*

Edward lingered in Strasbourg for a month attending lectures and taking every opportunity for
conversation with the great Protestant leader and
intellectual, John Sturmius, using Latin as their common language.

At the end of April, 1575, Edward and his companions rode south past the snow and the pine and
birch forests. They saw first-hand the balconied
houses, red-and-green-cupolaed churches, and
winter of the Brenner Pass, and followed the Adige

River into the vineyards, flowers, blossoming fruit trees and spring of Italy.

In Venice, they rented rooms at the Hotel Danieli, a renovated small palace near Piazza San Marco.

Edward knew that Venice was a beautiful city but he was quite unprepared for its endless splendor. He quickly realized that every public building was an architectural gem like ancient Athens, with ornate white columns and many-colored marble and bronze statues. A constantly shifting rainbow of yellow, orange and blue houses, all with red-tiled roofs, emerged directly from the water of myriad canals large and small.

What an assault on the senses! He loved the baskets of bright flowers which hung in every alcove. Fragrant orange, lemon and pomegranate trees blossomed in the courtyards and enclosed gardens. Varnished black gondolas were propelled rhythmically by their gondoliers. And Venice had none of the stenches of London, which Edward felt was the rankest compound of villainous smells that ever offended nostril!

Edward was fascinated by the people, who represented the cosmopolitan mixture of east and west: the turbaned Levantine Jews, the Moors and Ethiopians with glistening pearls in their brown ears, the white-robed Arabs and the brightly clothed Venetian citizens. How openly respected were the courtesans, the ladies of the night and day, who were listed by name and address in annual published directories and who wore their touch of obligatory yellow.

Edward was staggered by the interiors of Venetian buildings. They exuded grandeur with their marble stairs, the crusted gold of elaborate walls and ceilings, the blazing red of tapestries and curtains, and endless magnificent paintings. Here was dramatized in vivid color the triumphant emergence of man from the dismal repressions and disarray of centuries of anarchy into the glorious re-awakening of the individual with his free creative talent and limitless potential.

At sunset as the buildings became aflame with reds and pinks reflected in the quiet waters, Edward saw that the entire city was not only a vast panorama of beauty but a work of art itself. He was determined to learn how such aesthetic elegance was fostered.

* * *

On the third afternoon, Edward decided to send a letter to Burghley since he had been badly remiss in following Burghley's instructions for regular reports on the group's activities. After writing the letter, he asked the manager to mail it.

"Certainly," the manager said. "Your letter will go out with the other to Baron Burghley."

Edward nodded his thanks and turned to go. Then a sudden chill of suspicion coursed its way down his spine and he turned back. "Someone else in my group asked you to mail a letter to Baron Burghley?"

"Yes, my Lord, right here." The manager reached under the counter and handed Edward a letter from William Lewyn to Burghley. Edward took it, walked upstairs and knocked on Lewyn's door. He was bid to enter.

Waving the letter in front of Lewyn, Edward said, "May I assume that you are assuring our esteemed Principal Secretary that you have not yet seen me in conference with any known enemies of England?"

Lewyn's eyes lowered instantly to the floor. "I am afraid so, sir."

"The long tentacles of our noble Baron Burghley have slithered all the way to this entrancing city! I knew that a spy within our small entourage was almost inevitable but how dispiriting. But also how fortunate to have discovered such a collusion so early in our travels!"

"I'm sorry, Your Lordship, I—"

"I accept your apology, William." The anger dissipated as quickly as it had come. "Say no more. I am well aware—more than you can imagine—of the overwhelming coercion, connivance and festering malintent of the politically powerful. Pack your bags and be gone. Perhaps you should limit your future efforts to tutoring."

That evening, at the end of an alfresco supper with the rest of the group, including the servants, Edward stood up, wineglass in hand, and said: "My companions, look around you and let the beauty sink into your hearts and souls. I am sure that the magnificence of Venice has affected each of us profoundly in a different manner.

"I have thought much today about our further travels and now deem it wise that we each go our own way. I will provide enough money for many weeks of travel for all of you. Farewell and fare thee well!"

The next day, he presented his letters of introduction at the Doge's palace and also gave a letter from Henri III to Francesco Foscari, who had hosted Henri the previous year. The handsome, elegantly bearded and mustached Francesco promptly invited Edward to be his guest for as long as he wished at Palazzo Foscari on the Grand Canal. This immediately admitted Edward into the active social and intellectual life of Venice.

Edward asked Foscari why such immense weight of their large public buildings didn't sink into the fragile, sandy reed-beds of the 117 islets upon which the city was built.

Foscari laughed. "It was clever planning and the luck of nature! The first builders hammered thousands of wooden piles into the shallow sand and deep into the layer of clay below, which we call *caranto.* Instead of rotting in a generation or two, the minerals infiltrated the poles and fossilized them into stone, lasting hundreds of years!"

Edward tried to grasp the aesthetic explosion which was based upon the classical art of ancient Greece and Rome but infused with emphasis on the individual and his creative energy. Edward was stimulated and deeply moved by his visits with Bassano, Jacopo Tintoretto, Paolo Veronese and especially by Titian Vecellio, still alert in mind and still producing masterpieces at the age of eighty-eight.

Ten days after his arrival, Edward was invited to meet the Doge to discuss the purpose of his diplomatic mission to Venice. Edward was personal emissary from the Queen to seek the permanent establishment of an official ambassadorial relationship.

The dreadful fire of 1574 had destroyed the Golden Staircase and Hall of the Ante-College, where diplomats were usually received. The Doge greeted him instead in the Hall of the Great Council. The entire gold-painted room was covered by gild-framed paintings and frescoes, as if the artistic geniuses of the world had imbedded their masterpieces in an all-encompassing vein of gold.

"Welcome, my Lord of Oxford!" Luigi Mocenigo

announced with a smile. "I'm glad that your Queen sent you instead of one of her regular emissaries. Those officials are so worried about putting a word out of place that they never seem to enjoy the lovely surroundings of these chambers! Tell me your mission."

Edward thanked the Doge for allowing him to experience such beauty. He then told him that Elizabeth intended to pull England out of its insular and strife-filled ways. England wanted and needed to learn from the impressive international experience of Venice. Edward described the potentially huge market for Venetian products now that England's success in exporting its wool and cloth was more evenly distributing its wealth. Edward also pointed out the strategic advantage of an alliance with England against the increasing strength and insatiable land-grabbing hunger of King Philip of Spain.

Edward tried to make his points with quiet grace, fluent Italian and an actor's well-timed use of hand gestures which were dear to the heart of Italians.

The Doge promised to give the matter serious consideration, send it through the many required committees and discuss it with his entire council. The Doge later told Francesco Foscari that his own positive presentation to the Council was in no small part influenced by Edward's personal dignity, charm and persuasive eloquence in a foreign tongue.

"He is a man who seems more Venetian than English!" the Doge declared.

The interview went so smoothly and so well that Edward asked the Doge if he might see their famous ship-building Arsenal, consisting of sixty acres of sheds and buildings where 15,000 men worked. One hundred ships at a time could be built or repaired.

Edward already knew that they could start with six keels in the morning and float six completed galleys out to sea that evening fully sailed, armed and provisioned.

Edward had decided to disregard Burghley's suggested spying maneuvers and instead to be open and direct in his questions. The Doge agreed with Edward's request on one condition: that Edward would put on a special performance of *The Famous Victories of Henry V.*

Edward was allowed to spend two profoundly impressive days at the Arsenal. He memorized even the finest details of their remarkably efficient production methods.

Fulfilling the Doge's request, Edward translated into Italian, staged and two weeks later acted in *Famous Victories* . The play was particularly appreciated by the Venetian patricians for its unusual combination of comedy, war and romance.

When Edward stepped out with his fellow actors for the final applause and saw the enthusiastic facial expressions of the Doge and his Council, he knew that the exchange of ambassadors would be approved.

A powerful question occurred to him as he felt the thrill of success and absorbed the artistic splendor of the room. *Could plays and other forms of literature trigger a rise toward greatness by England, just as art in the form of inspired painting, sculpture and architecture had stimulated the rebirth of Venice and all of Italy?*

He vowed to pursue the answer.

Chapter 16

How sweet the moonlight sleeps upon this bank!
Here we will sit and let the sounds of music
Creep in our ears: soft stillness and the night
Become the touches of sweet harmony.
- The Merchant of Venice

Beautiful women played by attractive and seductive ac-
tresses—not by wigged boys, as in England! What a wider
scope that gives to the playwright and how much more plea-
sure to the audience, Edward thought. *And what stimu-*
lation and laughter emerge without censorship!

Night after night, Edward attended plays presented by the Commedia dell'Arte, or comedy of the
art of acting. Every performance was improvised from
a stock of possible conversations and dramatic scenarios by a set of masked basic characters such as
Pantaloon the Jokester, Harlequin the Braggart Soldier, and the tedious Pedant.

Every production was different, for those on stage

knew not what witty and satirical interaction was coming next. Each actor had the opportunity to change direction and all others had to respond immediately to the comedy's new situation. Edward was impressed with the skill, memory and ingenuity required. What a marvelous demonstration of the intelligence and talent of the acting profession, not demeaned and scorned as in London but held in great respect as a form of high artistry.

One of the amusing stock characters was Graziano the talkative Bolognese doctor who told long tales, hardly stopping to take a breath. One evening while Edward was attending the Commedia with Foscari and a packed audience, Graziano began one of his typical descriptions of a tournament.

"I found myself ambassador of my illustrious country of Bologna at the court of Emperor Polidor of Trebizond and attending the great tournament celebrating his marriage to Irene, Empress of Constantinople. Present were many great worthies: Basil, King of Zelconda; Doralba, Princess of Dacia; Isuf, Pasha of Aleppo; Fatima, Sultan of Persia; Elmond, Milord of Oxford."

Edward blushed as he realized Graziano was referring directly to him! An impossibility on the English stage, it reminded him of the free atmosphere in which Aristophanes wrote in the fifth century BC in Athens.

He began to smile as the impudent doctor described the horse of Milord of Oxford as faun-colored and going by the name of Oltramarin, Beyond-the-Sea. The English lord carried a large sword and wore a maroon costume. His worthy opponent in the joust was the ferocious Lady Alvilda, Countess of Edemburg. She was mounted on a dapple gray, dressed in bright yellow armor shining like the sun, and armed with a Frankish lance. After a long struggle, the noble lord and lady speared each other simultaneously off their horses, both landing face down in the dust!

Laughing, Edward stood and applauded vigorously, then turned and bowed in each direction, hand on heart, as the audience laughed and also applauded. After the Commedia performance ended, Edward immediately went backstage and enthusiastically congratulated all of the entertainers, especially the Bolognese doctor.

On their way home, Foscari said, "Edward, I agree with the Doge. You are truly Italian in spirit! Next on the menu is a masked ball I am giving at my Villa Malcontenta on the Brenta, built for my father by Palladio."

* * *

One week later, costumed and masked as Pan the god of flocks, and appropriately carrying a shepherd's flute, Edward was gondoliered slowly up the willow-lined River Brenta. They passed pale marble villas and vineyards, reaching Malcontenta as the glow of sunset was subsiding. Costumed guests were walking up and down the matched pair of white marble stairs on either side of the immense Ionic-columned loggia and facade. A glow of bonfire and torchlight arose from the esplanade beyond the house itself, from which the sounds of music drifted. Mixed fragrances hung on the warm evening air from the resin of torches, the smoke of burning incense, and from roses and honeysuckles in a row of large jardinieres standing along the river embankment wall.

Edward greeted his host warmly and, after enjoying Foscari's sumptuous buffet, strolled through the elegant garden. When he heard shouts and applause, he proceeded to the plaza, where he arrived in time to witness a *Bergamasca,* a very athletic dance, including twisting gyrations and somersaults, performed by several pairs of acrobatic young peasants from Bergamo.

This was followed by the *Cappello,* or Dance of the Hat, performed by a dozen pairs of men and women. It was one of those joyously obscene and uninhibited country dances to ensure the fecundity of their crops. Music was provided by drummers and a dozen flutists and pipers dressed in goatskins. The men kissed their hats and placed them on the heads of the girls, thus transferring male behaviors to the girls. The girls kissed the bare heads of the men, transferring female characteristics to them. The men became shy and coy, pretending to run away. As the music beat faster and faster, the women pursued, becoming more and more wild in their actions, catching the men to kiss their necks and stroking their backs as the men pretended to try to escape. Finally, as the music rose toward a crescendo, the women twisted their men to the ground, lying upon them with increasingly amorous contortions until they finally rolled off in pretended, and sometimes actual, contented exhaustion.

As the dance was finishing, Edward felt an arm slip through his. He turned and saw an elegant figure, somewhat taller than him, with ruby and emerald jeweled grapes wreathing long black curled hair, an obvious wig. But the woman's face remained a mystery, covered by a purple mask. Her silver gown was heavily embroidered with clusters of artificial dark red grapes and green leaves.

In a melodic but clearly disguised throaty voice, she said, "They don't look very malcontenta! Nor do I, now that I have captured my partner for the evening according to Foscari's rules!"

"And do I struggle, run, or shall I yield to the charming Princess of the Vineyard?"

"That depends upon what your inner sense tells you." She had a confident grace of body-carriage and used her hands softly and sensitively while speaking. "If I am not mistaken, I have been fortunate enough to encounter Pan, lover of music and of all things pastoral. Surely such a creature as Pan would not flee from the Princess of the Vineyard."

He smiled agreement. "Surely not."

"Then my suggestion would be to yield to your good fortune before a courtesan captures you." She nodded subtly to her right at a group of invited courtesans who had come as Amazons, with bleached hair piled high in curled pyramids with a yellow ribbon on top. Tiger-skins covered one shoulder, leaving the other shoulder and breast tantalizingly bare, the nipple pinked with rouge.

When trumpets sounded, all the guests in their masks and masquerade costumes gathered in the torch-lit courtyard. Foscari gave a brief welcoming speech and suggested that for anyone still without a partner, only ten minutes remained to pair up. He reminded his guests that coupling-up was a mandatory rule, detailed on the invitations, as a continuing attempt by his generation of Foscaris to deserve a name-change of the villa from Malcontenta to Contenta.

Trumpets announced the beginning of dancing. The musicians took their places on the terrace behind the villa, on the plaza in front and on wooden decks laid over chained flat-boats in the river, reached by a carpeted bridge.

Edward and his partner danced the stately pavane and the livelier coranto and lavolta. They seemed to float across every dance floor with a harmony of mutual rhythm. At breaks in the music they walked along the river or among the trees or sat on the grassy bank.

She spoke easily and with confidence on many subjects. Whenever he asked questions about herself—her name, her background, her place of abode or her special interests—she answered silently by placing a finger on his lips.

He looked over her shoulder at the moonlight shimmering on the river, at the villa and the dancers, the torches and bonfires. He imagined watching the enchanting scene from above, engraving the beauty of the enchanting dream-world of wealthy Venetians indelibly in his memory.

"I know what you are thinking, my puzzled minstrel," she said softly. "It *is* almost an illusion, so beautiful the scene, so lovely the warm night."

"What else am I thinking?" asked Edward, feeling a comfortable compatibility and pull of attraction despite the conversational blocks.

"You are wondering when I will unmask and identify myself! Foscari's rules forbid unmasking before midnight. After that, individual discretion prevails."

"And if I choose to unmask, are you required to follow suit?" Edward asked playfully, enjoying the game.

"At that point, all pros and cons must be carefully weighed, the Gods consulted and the choice freely made. If I am married with ten children, or if I decide that the best strategy is to continue to tantalize my mystified partner, the mask may remain in place. Forcible removal of my mask, incidentally, represents a personal insult to Bacchus and condemns the sinner to a lifetime of crushing grapes with his feet!"

Edward smiled. "I'll toast to that! Let's find a passing wine servant, acquire two glasses of Foscari's noblest *blanco,* and stroll through yonder forest. Perhaps the God of Branches will conspire with my fondest wish and accidentally de-mask you."

Time passed quickly as they walked on a path through the trees, strolling slowly in the lights and shadows of the moonlight. The villa was long out of sight but the music, now slower again, softly embroidered a gentle breeze.

They stepped into a clearing. Above them the sky was blazing with thousands of stars, most twinkling, a few bright and steady. Looking up and gently holding her hand, Edward felt a special glow.

He hesitated a few moments, then fixed his eyes directly on the eyes behind the mask and, speaking in a soft voice, said:

> *"Look how the floor of heaven*
> *Is thick inlaid with patens of bright gold.*
> *There's not the smallest orb which thou behold*
> *But in his motion like an angel sings."*

*   *   *

At midnight, they heard the trumpets sound. Edward immediately removed his mask and put his arms around her. She moved toward him and held him. His lips brushed her hair and he immediately recognized the wild and erotic aroma of jasmine.

She finally pulled away. In a voice laced with

smoky desire, she said, "Handsome minstrel-knight, I wish to thank you for the happy rapport we have enjoyed together on this magical night. Will you now promise me, on your chivalric honor, to keep your eyes closed for the next minute?"

"A tigered courtesan would not insist upon that!" he protested. "Must I?"

"Yes, for the sake of international relations and the fecundity of our grape crop, you must!"

Edward laughed and did as he was told. He then felt the warm lips of his lady press gently to his. It moved him in a way that was foreign to him and caused him to inhale the scent of her being. Her arms delicately encircled him as they kissed more intensely. Her right hand moved upward to stroke the back of his neck. She tried her best to express with her lips and hand the tender feelings he had elicited.

She then slowly removed her lips from his, waited a few seconds, and watched his expression reflected in the glow of the moon's alluring sheen. She kissed him briefly once more, replaced her mask and drew back.

"You may open your eyes now and fulfill my final chivalric request," she said, her voice low and husky. "I want you to hold my hand as we walk quietly to the villa. You may then escort me to my waiting gondola but no further conversation shall intrude on our special mood."

Edward bowed in silence.

As they walked slowly towards Malcontenta, hand in hand, Edward did as he was told, except that twice he tried to speak. Each time a gentle finger touched his lips. She retrieved her scarf and jacket and he walked her to the gondolier.

As she headed upriver, just before rounding a curve, he saw her remove her mask and then her wig. He strained to identify the color of her hair, but could not. A verse quickly traversed his brain like a ray of moonlight:

> *O, speak again, bright angel; for thou art*
> *As glorious to this night, being o'er my head,*
> *As is a wingèd messenger of heaven*
> *Unto the white upturnéd wond'ring eyes*
> *Of mortals.*

He watched her disappear and drew three conclusions: he was full of powerful conflicting emotions; the mystery woman was headed toward Padua, not Venice; and he knew that he must, and would, see her again.

Chapter 17

. . . since for the great desire I had
To see fair Padua, nursery of arts,
I am arrived here fore fruitful Lombardy,
The pleasant garden of great Italy . . .
Here let us breathe, and haply institute
A course of learning and ingenious studies.
                    - The Taming of the Shrew

As Edward rode his new horse Oltramarin through the Lombardian countryside toward Mantua, he pondered the eruption of art throughout Italy over the past 150 years. How had so many extraordinarily gifted artists sprung forth almost simultaneously in the cultural rebirth of the Italian city-states?

After deep thought, Edward finally found a satisfactory answer. In every human population, there must be a small percentage of people with exceptional creative gifts in diverse fields. Geniuses are most likely to emerge when two necessary factors are present: an encouraging enlightened government and patronage of the arts. Individuals must be free to reach their artistic potential not encumbered by economic concerns.

How stimulating to be in the midst of such artistic splendor! He felt his own surge of creativity stirring inside, longing to emerge in full blossom.

He visited the Palazzo de Te in Mantua and was overwhelmed by the extraordinary three-dimensional paintings of Giulio Romano, especially his horses which appeared to leap forth from the walls so fully alive that one could hear their snorting and their hoof beats. He allowed himself the thought, *I wonder whether I can do the same with my writing.*

While in Genoa, he played a minor role in stopping an impending civil war between Genoa's old patrician families and the *nouveaux riches* . They accepted his suggestion to halt the strife and write a new state constitution under the mediation of a Vatican envoy, Cardinal Morone.

*   *   *

Edward rode back toward Padua wondering what Epicurean delights he might be served on the dining table of life. He hoped that the purple-masked mystery maiden from Malcontenta might be included in the menu.

After renting a small room in the Hotel Vulcanus near the university, he began attending lectures on law and Italian poetry. There he met thirty-year-old Ottonello Falconetto after his lecture on civil law.

Edward congratulated him. "Well done, Professor! A complex subject simplified and edified! My name is Edward de Vere. I am trying to escape from soaking up rain in favor of soaking up learning at your world-famous institution."

"Ah . . . Milord of Oxford, your reputation precedes you!"

"And which particular reputation is that—the devil or the archangel?"

Nello laughed. He was tall and dark-haired with brown eyes, tan skin and handsome Italian features. "My charming sister Serena was visiting friends recently in Venice and happened to attend your *Famous Victories,* which she enjoyed immensely. She still rattles on about it, just like Graziano, your Bolognese doctor-friend!"

"Good Lord, was she at that Commedia performance also?"

"Yes, and she still laughs over your unhorsing by the muscular Alvilda! You must come and have dinner with us tomorrow night."

"Only if your sister promises not to unhorse me, and only if she is as charming as you say!"

Nello laughed heartily, slapping Edward on the shoulder. "I shall let you be the judge, but I don't think she will disappoint you."

* * *

Edward loved Italy, greatly enjoyed the exuberant Italian people and was in a happy mood the next night as he rode Oltramarin two miles to the Falconetto family villa of Bellaria on the Brenta.

He was quite taken aback when Nello introduced him to Serena. She was tall and notably beautiful, with sparkling green eyes, long blonde hair, a Roman nose and appealingly full lips.

How truly lovely, thought Edward as he noted her poise, her olive skin and her slender classical figure.

Her black dress dramatically complemented her blonde hair as it cascaded to her shoulders. A necklace of glittering silver-white pearls added elegance to her graceful neck. A green emerald brooch nearly matched her eyes.

Bowing low, he kissed Serena's hand.

"Oh, Edward, it is such a wonderful treat to meet you and have you as a guest in our home," she said in a melodic alluring voice. "I have been so excited since Nello told me yesterday that you would be joining us for dinner."

"You certainly don't remind me of Lady Alvilda!"

She smiled broadly. "I suggested corned beef, cabbage, stale bread and weevils, but Nello insisted on fresh bread and weevils!"

Dinner passed quickly for the compatible laughing threesome. Edward learned that 24-year-old Serena was widowed and studying to be a lawyer.

Before the evening was over, Edward had made two promises: he would give two guest lectures on law and he would spend every weekend as a guest in their villa. He extracted only one promise from Serena: that she would have dinner with him the next evening.

* * *

Edward lectured on *Land Tenure in England,* the main emphasis at Gray's Inn, and *The Petition Process in Britain,* summarizing knowledge gained from his chairmanship of the Parliamentary Committee on Petitions.

When Serena congratulated him, he answered, "I feel far more natural in any acting role, even playing a court jester holding a monkey!"

Each afternoon Serena tried to study in the

university's renowned library; Edward insisted that she spend every free evening with him. They felt more and more comfortable with each other. She now slipped her arm through his when they walked.

One evening they sipped wine and talked deep into the night on his hotel balcony. The warm air was filled with odors of spaghetti and frying oil from the noisy restaurant below.

Serena hesitated, then said, "If you promise not to be upset with me, I will share a plan which began forming in my mind the very first time you came to our house. Will you forgive my boldness?"

"On my noble Etruscan honor!" Edward vowed with his hand across his heart.

"Then here is my plan." She drew a breath as if to steady her nerves. "I invite you to leave with me next week after the university lectures finish and let me show you Verona, which is more your kind of city than Padua. After a few days in Verona I have rented for a month from family friends the lovely Castle of the Scaglieri in Malcesine on Lake Garda. It is intended just for the two of us. You must agree to spend half of each day alone with your thoughts and your writing. The rest of each day and night is open for negotiation. Perhaps we should ask Cardinal Morone to mediate!"

Edward was stunned into silence. He rubbed his boar ring. Loud laughter erupting from diners below brought him back into the moment.

"Serena, you astound me with your forthrightness and insight. These past weeks in Italy have filled my mind with new ideas, new aspirations and new thoughts for poems and plays. It is time for me to set them down in writing but I didn't wish to leave you."

"Then my plan is not too brash?"

"Your solution sounds perfect. Your knight, I think, was too busy trembling in fear inside his armor to devise a creative solution! Let us seal the agreement with our first kiss!" Edward got up from his chair. His kiss was gentle, lingering; hers equaled in perfect rhyme.

Serena stood up, looked fondly into his eyes and said, "Would you do me a favor, my dear Edward, and close your eyes?"

Edward did as he was asked. Serena's arms encircled him as she pulled her body into every contour of his. Her right hand gently massaged the back of his neck as she kissed him with tender fervency.

Edward suddenly pulled away, raised his arms in triumph, and shouted, "Ah-hah, the mystery maiden appears at last and without her ten children!" They laughed as he pulled her to him eagerly. "How unforgettable is the music two blended hearts create!"

They breathed softly and clung together in reunion.

*   *   *

With Serena as his guide, Edward immediately felt comfortable in Verona, the beautiful old city tucked into a bend of the Adige River, blending gently with the surrounding hills. He admired the venerable city's charm with its red-tiled roofs, marble balconies overlain with flowers, streets of red and white marble, brightly painted stucco houses, beautiful cathedrals and even traces of doubly-rutted Roman roads.

Serena pointed out three city gates crafted by her grandfather, Giovanni Falconetto.

While having lunch in the fragrant Piazza delle Erbe, Edward finished his salad and wondered why Italian olive oil was so superior. "Serena, this whole city, like Venice, is a work of art. I doubt that any country in the world has such civic pride, such far-sighted leaders and such intense beauty."

Edward took in the scene around them in the piazza: the old lady sitting under a tented stall, hands stained black, cutting the leaves swiftly off artichokes and dropping the hearts into a pail of water; a dog with a little basket tied around its neck quietly walking from table to table begging for coins; the vegetable sellers calling out their wares; the short-skirted self-sellers walking tantalizingly past the diners.

"This used to be the old Roman Forum," said Serena. "Now they sell herbs, vegetables and fruits from all over Italy. Those large oranges come from Sicily and are called 'tarocco.' They have a sweet purple juice."

"The oranges we get in England come from Spain and are quite bitter, like Spanish foreign policy. They are best used for marmalade, a word we borrowed from 'marmelo,' the Portuguese word for quince."

She turned to him, fondling her hair with her left hand. "You love words and their derivations, don't you, Edward?"

"Nothing intrigues me more! English is such an insubstantial language. I find it much easier to express myself in Latin or your beautiful Italian."

"Why don't you do something about it?"

He nodded thoughtfully. "I hope to do just that but the mechanism escapes me. I am looking forward to the peace of Malcesine to inspire me."

At night they watched plays superbly staged in front of thousands at the first century Roman Arena. They saw comedies of Plautus at the small unrestored semicircular Teatro Romano overlooking the river.

One evening after a play at the Arena, they

walked slowly back through the old city full of con-versing gesticulating people. Serena asked Edward into her room in the Albergo Due Torre for a glass of Soave Blanco.

As they sat on her small balcony, she said, "Ed-ward, you have been very circumspect about my past. It is time to fill in the missing years."

"It is not necessary, my love," Edward said as he kissed her gently on the forehead. A whisper of her hair fell across her left eye. He blew the tendril softly with his breath; it fell into place, nestling at her temple.

"For me and for us, I feel that it is," she said. "My family lived a life of wealth but my widowed father foolishly over-speculated, bringing us to near-bank-ruptcy and him to despondency. I was fourteen. A very wealthy acquaintance of my father from Mirandola, Pietro, a childless widower in his midsixties, asked to marry me. As part of the mar-riage contract, he promised to leave his entire wealth to me. I pleaded with my father but he saw it as the only way to recoup the family fortune—to keep Villa Bellaria and continue our elegant lifestyle. I had no choice."

He took her hand. "Was it as unpleasant as you feared?"

"Worse. He had no interests, drank heavily and kept pawing me." Serena shuddered as if a cold wind had passed through the memory so painfully im-planted in her mind.

"There was nothing you could do?"

"Nothing. I was helpless. There was no tenderness, no words. Just unshaven beard, bad breath, clumsy grabbing and impotence." She drew a breath and let it out in a long sigh.

"Did it mar your feelings about men for life?"

This brought a fragile smile. "No. My father died a few months after the marriage and Pietro died soon after. I split his fortune equally with Nello but made him promise never to interfere with my complete freedom in choice of men and mate."

"It is none of my business, but may I ask . . ." Edward hesitated. "Have you spent much time with other men?"

She responded instantly. "Many men have sought my company. Some for the usual reasons, others with higher aspirations. But I have not shared my love with any man."

Still holding her hand, Edward led her into the bedroom. He began kissing her, his hand roaming softly over her back. She hesitated, then kissed him with increasing passion until her ardor matched his. He teased her earlobe with his tongue, his warm breath in her ear. He trailed kisses down her neck and felt her body shiver.

Breathing more rapidly and beginning to tingle all over, she said, "Edward, you are such a tender and loving man." She pressed her body against his as his warmth melted away her memories of the past.

Edward unbuttoned the back of her dress and nudged it forward gently over her shoulders. Her eyes locked on his as she let it fall to the floor.

She held him tightly for a long moment, then gently whispered, "I have never felt closer to anyone, Edward. I want you as much as you want me, if not more. I believe we have a beautiful compatibility which deserves only the finest milieu. But, my darling . . . this isn't it."

Chapter 18

Thy love is better than high birth to me,
Richer than wealth, prouder than garments cost,
Of more delight than hawks or horses be.
                                        - Sonnet 91

Holding candles in their hands, Edward and
Serena climbed the narrow, twisting wooden staircase toward the top of the castle's tall tower. They
had arrived at Castle Scaglieri in Malcesine after dark
and it was Serena's idea to see their new surroundings at dawn.

Edward pushed back the oak cover and they
climbed onto the marble terrace. Dawn was tinctur-
ing the eastern sky with delicate rose tones. In front
of them was narrow Lake Garda, turning from black
to dark blue; behind were the steep slopes of Mt.
Baldo. On both sides of the castle lay the scattered
houses of the fishing village.

Holding hands, they stood entranced as the

massive jagged, pinnacled limestone cliffs rising above the opposite shore turned purple, red, pink, orange and finally yellow. It was a kaleidoscope of God's wondrous palette.

Serena turned to Edward and, with her cheek against his, whispered, "This is indeed our castle in the sky. This tower top will be *our place* . . . but you may not join me here without my permission!"

"And when might that be?"

"When the time is right, my dear Edward. Women know such things!"

They watched fishermen, with piled corked nets stashed in the sterns of their boats, push off from the pebbled shore and raise their red and orange sails. Olive groves and small vineyards were interspersed with the red-tiled houses. Roosters crowed in the distance.

Suddenly the vibrant ringing of bells from two churches jarred them. "There must be a bell-war here between two priests!" Edward said with a laugh. "He who rings first and loudest saves the most souls!"

Edward noted the castle crenelations with the attractive Scaglieri swallow-tail design sculpted at all the corners. The castle itself was constructed on four levels of the sloping rock shoreline.

"There are my two writing areas," he said, peering down. "At each end of the major courtyard, see how those curved white marble staircases end in small flat hideaways with red marble benches overlooking the lake? Perfect for a thinker, philosopher, writer or lover!"

"And which might you fancy yourself?" asked Serena, smiling.

"All four, of course!" They both laughed.

"What are your writing plans?"

"I will spend at least the first two days thinking and planning. I have some important questions to resolve."

"Whenever you want to rest your weary brain, you may accompany your serene tower owner on a stroll through this picturesque village. In the meantime, you will live on the second floor of the castle and I will sleep in the silk-quilted four-poster on the third floor."

Edward lifted an eyebrow. "Are you a Spanish general trained by the Duke of Alva?"

Serena laughed. "No, my ardent admirer, but we both need time to relax our city tensions and blend our souls into the calm beauty of these lovely surroundings."

Edward hesitated a few moments, then responded, "*I am giddy. Expectation whirls me round. The imaginary relish is so sweet that it enchants my sense.*"

* * *

Edward spent most of each day in his hideaway basking in the sunshine, thinking of Virgil, Horace, Ovid and Plautus. He leaned on the iron grillwork and gazed down at the many turquoise blues and emerald greens of the clear lake and the dark, slowly moving shapes of pike and trout.

He knew that he must continue to be a poet and writer, and develop and sharpen his inborn gifts. But in what form? *Poet, I am, but where does poetry lead? Yes, I must remain a courtier, to remain loyal to my Queen. The Court does provide incomparably delicious material for any form of writing! But not indefinitely; one can only digest so many flittery-flatteries!*

Yes, I still want a chance for heroism in defense of my monarch. That is the knightly de Vere tradition. But am I pursuing transient mists like those shadowing Lake Garda, quickly scattered into disappearance by sun or breeze?

By writing plays infused with the beauties of poetic expression and by stimulating the writings of others, won't I be fulfilling some of Castiglione's criteria for the ideal courtier? My plays would entertain and uplift the Court and delight Londoners.

If a high level of literary caliber is achieved, could plays become a highly valued form of art? Wasn't England, under the leadership of an intellectual and cultured Queen, ready for an artistic rebirth itself? Could the art of literature lead the way?

Edward breathed with new enthusiasm as he walked back and forth across the white marble of his hideaway, unaware that Serena was peering down at him from behind third-floor curtains. She could feel the power of his energy and across her body swept a wave of admiration and desire.

Yes, thought Edward, the times were right. His maturity had ripened and Italy was providing the necessary spark.

Then another thought rose to the surface of his mind like an unstoppable bubble. The implications intrigued him but were not without peril.

His plays would be *chronicles of the times,* like the ancient Greek dramatists and great Roman writers and poets. No bias and falsification, but the truth. *Vero Nihil Verius!* He would include real people. He would dramatize their strengths, weaknesses and foibles.

His mind began to soar. *For entertainment, especially during the long dreary winter months in the cold palaces, I will first write comedies. When my creativity and style sufficiently mature, I will write tragedies, a combination the great Greek playwrights never attempted.*

That evening at their candle-lit shoreline table behind the tavern-inn, Edward shared his new ideas with Serena. She kissed him enthusiastically and moved her chair next to his. Holding hands in silence, they admired the castle's majestic outline against the moonlit sky, so stately on its rocky promontory overlooking the sparkling silver waters of the lake. Tiny waves lapped gently against the shore. A warm breeze rustled the olive leaves. Miniature torchlights from scattered houses on the opposite shore shined between the quietly rocking fishing boats. Moonlight reflected off glistening limestone cliffs created a dark ragged outline of the mountains.

"This is an enchanting moment," Serena murmured, "one long to be remembered. I have waited many years for you to come into my life and my heart. Tomorrow, your most serene Queen of the Castle earnestly invites her favorite King from a nearby principality to join her for breakfast on the tower top, bringing with him only his most honeyed mood."

*   *   *

The next morning Edward eagerly climbed the tower staircase. Serena wore a white satin nightrobe, a red ruby brooch and a garland of pink honeysuckle flowers.

Edward gasped as he beheld her radiant loveliness. He took her two small hands and held them between his own. Her fingers were reminiscent of the petals of a rose, kissed of dew and velvet. The desire echoed with each syllable as he said, "Your luminous beauty quite stuns my senses!"

"Not all of them, I hope, my handsome courtier!"

Edward pressed his lips softly to her forehead. The breakfast table overlooking the lake held a pitcher of tarocco juice, bread and cheeses. Adjacent to the opposite wall, with steep Mount Baldo as a backdrop, lay a thick mattress covered with a white silk sheet embroidered with a red heart.

During breakfast, each savored the loveliness of their surroundings. Afterward, Serena stood, kissed Edward gently, and led him to the soft mattress. She removed her brooch and put it by a rose-filled terracotta pot. She untied her satin robe and stepped slowly out of it, standing before him naked, her olive skin lightly pinked. She walked to a swallowtail corner and picked up a jar which had been warming in the sun.

"Is that a Falconetto passion potion?" asked Edward, smiling.

"We need not such, my rhythmical poet! It is a mixture of red rose petals, white rose buds, sweet mint and ros-marinus, our herb of the sea which you call rosemary. All are lightly crushed in a small amount of water and mixed into a jar of our finest olive oil. The jar is left in the sun each morning for several weeks. Yesterday I strained out all of the solid particles and removed the residual water. Smell it."

Edward inhaled deeply the sweet herbal aroma, then began to remove his clothes hastily. "It works quickly!"

"Lie down on your stomach, my helpless knight, and let me fulfill my longtime fantasy." Serena took a small bit of oil and began to massage his feet slowly and tenderly. The sun was warm but not yet hot. A quiet wind breezed around the tower. No sound interrupted Serena's dedicated task. She used both hands to massage his legs, then straddled him to rub her aromatic oil into his neck. Edward sighed quietly.

Smoothly she rubbed his shoulders and moved her hands down his back.

"Now turn over, my dearest."

An excited Edward did so and faced Serena and the sky. Serena still straddled his legs. She emitted a soft gasp.

After a long moment of silence, she said, "Oh, Edward, forgive me, but my husband was puny and powerless. Most of my knowledge of male anatomy has come from statues!"

Edward started to say something but she quickly put her left index finger over his lips. Placing more scented oil on her fingers, she caressed his feet, moving slowly upward, frequently unable to resist exploring and loving her new area of fascination. Edward had to concentrate on the wall, on darting blue swallows, on her flower garland.

After she had finally worked her way up to his chest, he took her hands gently in his and said, "Now it is time for my own voyage of discovery, Serena. And it is your turn to lie on your stomach."

Edward began an unhurried sensual massage, starting at her feet, slowly moving up her long tan legs to the gentle rise of her finely formed buttocks, her back, her neck. She breathed faster as she moved each body part toward him.

By the time he turned her over onto her back, her breathing had become rapid, her body restless. He began to worship her firm full breasts with his lips and tongue. She sighed more eagerly and her hips began to roll. He kissed her softly, starting at the left corner of her mouth and working slowly across.

He added oil to his hands, lay down, and kissed her more deeply, more intensely. He prolonged each moment, whispering softly into her ear tender words of endearment. With their lips softly touching again, he inhaled as she exhaled, blending their breath.

Serena turned toward him, encouraging him, relishing this entirely new world. Edward caressed her totally and teasingly while kissing her eyes, her eyelids, her earlobes. Her sighs became louder and more rhythmical. Her knees flexed, and her hips moved with a sense of urgency.

"Please, Edward, now" she whispered eagerly.

Edward and Serena merged with all the flaming enthusiasm of newborn love, soaring far beyond their dreams and fantasied expectations. Edward was amazed at the spontaneous unrestrained responsiveness of such an exquisite inexperienced woman.

Serena shuddered and gasped, "Oh, Edward. It is so wonderful. Please, please don't stop."

Edward visualized in his mind the scene from the top of Mt. Baldo—the dark blue lake gleaming in the sunshine, the peaceful orange and red villages coloring the curving shoreline, the brightly-dyed sails, the picturesque Scaglieri Castle with its high stone tower. There, two loving humans crescendoed their uniting in a burst of unimagined pleasure, remaining intertwined in joyful exhaustion, clinging tightly to the happy afterglow.

*   *   *

For the next three days, Edward and Serena rarely left the castle. Every morning they walked down the twisting stone path to their private cove, swam naked, then walked up to the tower top for breakfast and love. At night they paid blissful homage to their down-mattressed four-poster, reveling in isolated togetherness. One night, too excitedly tired to sleep, he wrote in his tablet:

> *So we grew together,*
> *Like to a double cherry, seeming parted,*
> *But yet an union in partition;*
> *Two lovely berries molded on one stem.*

On the fourth day, Serena reminded him of their covenant about writing. Edward retreated to his red and white marble hideaway.

The Commedia dell'Arte had opened up a witty, inventive, exhilarating world of comic drama. All the drolleries of human nature were performed with light-hearted whimsy and satire.

The hidden laughter of *situation* fired Edward. The Commedia's standard characters derived from stereotypes used in ancient Greece. But they reminded him of colorful attributes of the myriads of people who walked the streets of London, the corridors of Queen Elizabeth's palaces, the canal banks of Venice, the piazzas of Padua, Verona, and Malcesine, the thoroughfares of all humanity. Edward's mind became a crowded stage with whirling plots and swirling figures.

He decided to title his first comedy *The Historie of Error*. He borrowed plots from two plays by Plautus, the celebrated comic poet and playwright of third century BC Rome, his *Menaechmi* and *Amphitruo*. He liked the comic twists of long-lost identical twins interacting with wife, mistress and father.

Edward wondered how Plautus had developed such skill in coining new words. *Could I stimulate an enrichment of English with the language of my artistry? Why not write my dramas in poetic verse, thus combining my major inborn talents? What a challenging and exciting thought!*

Edward decided to work diligently for three half-days in a row, then take an entire day off to experience the countryside with Serena.

One day was spent riding up a twisting path to the top of Mt. Baldo for a glorious panoramic view of Lake Garda and the snowcapped Alps of northern Italy rising in the distance. Other days were spent talking with peasants to learn the techniques of cultivating and processing grapes and olives.

When he had half-finished with *The Historie of Error*, he began to plot an unusual love story involving a dominant suitor and an unwilling, objecting, shrewish woman. Edward wanted to honor three of his favorite Italian cities, so he set the play in Padua, Mantua and Verona. He tentatively titled it *A Morrall of the Marryage of Mynde and Measure*. He liked some of his lines:

> *Our purses shall be proud, our garments poor,*
> *For 'tis the mind that makes the body rich,*
> *And as the sun breaks through the darkest clouds,*
> *So honour peereth in the meanest habit.*

As the end of August approached, Edward and Serena became more tender and clinging. They took walks along the shore and through olive groves, or sailed quietly wherever the breezes beckoned.

But Edward knew that he would have to continue his journey soon. His destiny was immutably bedrocked in England. Torturing as their disjoined world would be, Serena could only be a passing interlude.

Serena knew also and she hid her sadness when

he sighed heavily over breakfast one morning and said, "*Tempus fugit* , my Darling. Time does fly, and now we must write the epilogue to this beautiful and unforgettable drama in our lives."

* * *

They hired groomsmen to guide the pack-horses. After turning to catch a final glimpse of Malcesine, they headed south along the lake past Assenza and Magugnano to Brenzone, then rode over the mountains. They followed the Adige River, rode past the sycamore groves on the western outskirts of Verona, and reached Villa Bellaria in three days.

The next morning before Edward boarded the traghetto for Venice, he kissed Serena gently on both cheeks and softly and lovingly on her lips. When she gazed into his eyes and tried to speak, Edward placed his finger gently on her lips, lingered a moment, then turned and walked up the gangplank.

As the boat sailed slowly down the Brenta, and Serena disappeared from view, Edward felt a deep chasm of profound emptiness. He paid little attention to the beautiful Venetian summer villas on the river, the passing gondolas or the cargo boats being pulled slowly upstream by horses. As much as he desired happiness, it always seemed to elude him like a mirage dancing in the distance. He wondered whether such pinching pain was a necessary torment in the evolution of a writer.

He leaned his elbows on the rail and lost himself in reverie as the traghetto quietly passed Malcontenta. Suddenly he raised his right arm, imitating the Bolebec lion defiantly shaking the broken spear, and cried out to the heavens, "If mental anguish is a prerequisite to artistic creativity, so be it!"

He watched the water churned into evanescent white foam, a final salute to a fleeting Epicurean interlude, now only a memory but indelibly etched into his mind and his writing soul. And his heart beat the drum of an artist, a synchronicity of rhythm and rhyme, portending the creation of new lettered images to inspire his countrymen.

He was captivated by his next thought: *How presumptuous but what a mind-expanding intellectual adventure, to attempt to portray the infinite complexity of human emotions and interactions on a tiny stage!*

Chapter 19

Our remedies oft in ourselves do lie
Which we ascribe to heaven. The fated sky
Gives us free scope, only doth backward pull
Our slow designs when we ourselves are dull.
 - All's Well That Ends Well

Upon his return to Venice, Edward decided to keep a low profile. He rented a room at the Aeolian Inn on the island of Murano in the Venetian lagoon. Having already tasted and enjoyed the social, cultural and artistic life of Venice, he wanted a nearby but peaceful environment in which to plan the rest of his journey.

It was now September 15, 1575. He had been gone from England for eight months but it seemed like only a fortnight.

Sitting in the inn's grape-trellised courtyard, he savored the memories of his four months in Italy. His literary soul was fired by the explosion of arts all around him and the essence of his being fit perfectly with Italy's artistic reawakening. But Greece and Turkey were essential to his plans, not only to carry out his private diplomatic mission but also to enrich further his aesthetic self.

One morning Edward awoke with drenching sweats and powerful shaking chills. An Arabic physician diagnosed swamp fever and treated him with herbs and bitter liquid extracts from plants. He didn't recover his full energy for many days but, although fatiguing quickly, he began hiring a gondola daily to visit the shipping docks. No captain was interested in a special voyage to Turkey during the season of bad weather.

Edward finally enticed gray-bearded ship owner and captain Domenico Panaiotis by personally guaranteeing both trading profit and reimbursement for any damages to his ship, the *Signora Fortuna.*

"The only reason I'm doing this, my Lord, is because I admire your spirit," Domenico said. "I ran away to sea at age twenty to follow my inclinations and have never regretted it."

"Then, Captain Domenico," said Edward, "you will surely accept an extra one hundred pounds to sail your noble craft via Ephesus and return by way of Athens! And part of our bargain is that I may interact with the ordinary seamen, even work alongside them at times and share their meals to learn their skills, lore and elegant vocabulary!"

When Domenico objected to this, Edward said, "As a writer, I must acquire the true feel of ship and sea, sights, sounds, smells, bilge, rats and jargon. But I would welcome learning navigation and salty swear words from you!"

When Edward returned that evening to Murano,

the innkeeper handed him a packet of letters from England. One letter from Burghley dated September 2 announced the birth to Anne on July 2 of a daughter named after the Queen. He suggested that Edward return home promptly. Edward folded the letter and held it in his hand.

He sat in the silence of his room for long moments, wondering again why this news did not evoke stronger feelings. The stern, sour Puritan visage of his mother-in-law came to him and his mind shrank away from it as from contamination. He had seen the same rigid reproachful look on Anne's face so often! He vowed to prevent his daughter from wearing such a constant judgmental expression of disapproval. She would feel the influence of a warm caring father. He would not let her become yet another Mildred Cecil.

But he was definitely not yet done with his trip. The next day he arranged loans from London banker Baptista Spinola's representatives in Venice, based upon further sales of his landed estates. He also purchased gifts to be shipped to Palermo. For Anne there were richly colored satins, silks and velvets, Murano glassware, and those intriguing novelties, Venetian forks. For the Queen, he selected earrings with roses of gold, and Venetian gloves embroidered with four rose tufts of colored silk, perfumed with Persian jasmine.

He also bought for himself a chest filled with velvet and silk material, capes, cloaks and hats of the latest Italian style, and two boxes of Latin and Italian books.

*　*　*

After only three days at sea a violent storm struck. Edward marveled at Captain Domenico's remarkable seamanship of the *Signora Fortuna,* which withstood forceful gales and rain for thirty-six hours. They finally safely entered the protected harbor of Delos.

A completely drenched Edward said, "My God, Domenico, the force of that storm was incredible! All of us should now be giving personal greetings to Neptune! You did a masterful job!"

"I've been in worse storms but not many," said the captain. "When the sailors shouted 'St. Elmo's fire!' I knew we'd be safe!"

Edward recalled the faint dancing flame, balls of misty blue and red fire rolling along the yardarms, jumping from mast to mast, signifying protection by the patron saint of sailors.

"Many times during the storm, Edward, I swore I was a damned fool to allow you to stay on deck just to experience it!"

"Now, Capitano, would you really have tied me to my bunk and ordered me to pray? I would not have missed nature's grand display for anything. Never before have I witnessed sky and sea merging with such ferocity and power!"

"Well, you'll have several days to dry out while we repair the ship and re-stow the cargo."

"In that case, I shall visit the ancient Greek ruins on Delos and try to discover how this small island became the mythical birthplace of Apollo as well as the wealthy religious and commercial center of the Cyclades."

Edward wandered through the ruins crumbled by time and earthquakes, past the shattered Temple of Apollo and along the carved stone road flanked by once-pedestaled white marble Naxian lions.

He sat next to a lion, rested his left arm on its still-proud mane, and meditated. He thought of the past and where it had led him in his journey thus far. Then he ruminated on the future and wished he knew in advance the panorama of his own life.

A brown sparrow landed near his feet, hopping and chirping, with no concern over past or future. He was brought back into the present with a new enthusiasm for the exciting breath of the here and now.

*   *   *

The *Signora Fortuna* sailed on to the impressive marble ruins of Ephesus, once a city second to none. Nothing was left of the fabled Temple of Artemis, one of the seven wonders of the ancient world, four times the size of the Parthenon.

As Edward sat in the huge amphitheater where plays had been staged for audiences numbering 24,000, he mused how remarkable it was that words, beautifully assembled or meaningfully combined, could last forever while stone buildings and marble temples, such seemingly permanent structures created by man, crumbled into dust.

How intriguing that the writings of Homer, Plato and the Bible are still extant for man's enlightenment, while of the seven magnificent wonders of the ancient world, only the pyramids had endured. How fascinating words are, with limitless power and majesty, able to elicit the entire gamut of human emotions, the whole range of man's biological responses, create love and life, cause or avert war and death, inspire religious conviction and survive indefinitely through printing.

* * *

As they headed toward Istanbul, Edward planned strategy for his diplomatic assignment. The Queen had eagerly embraced his own idea to try to establish a formal trade relationship with Turkey. Burghley and the Privy Council were not made aware of his goal. On several occasions, they had told the Queen that any interaction with Turkey was premature and doomed to failure.

Edward wondered whether he could act his way through yet another theater of life, this time in the exotic land of viziers, harems, sultans, scimitars and shrewd merchants.

Edward gazed at the multitude of ships anchored in the Golden Horn, its harbor shaped like the horn of an ox, made golden by the world's goods. He looked up at the minarets and domes of this famous promontoried city, so rich in history for both East and West.

"What a marvelous location for a city!" he exclaimed to the captain. "Will you be able to find cargo for our return, Domenico?"

"In Istanbul? This is the greatest trading center in the world! I could fill my ship many times over with silk from China, spices from India, sugar from Persia, grain and furs from Russia, drugs, cotton and carpets from Turkey, and gold, ivory and exotic animals from Africa."

As Edward walked toward the Sultan's palace the next day he became instantly enchanted by Istanbul: endless blends of skin colors and costumes, black-veiled women and turbaned men, shops with aromatic mounds of red, yellow and green spices, intricate rugs displayed in shaded arched corridors, and flute-play-ing cobra charmers from Morocco.

He reached the Sultan's palace and was led into a richly carpeted antechamber. He presented his papers to a red-turbaned official and joined a frustrated crowd of men sitting on cushions.

Edward struck up conversation with a clean-shaven Italian diplomat from Milan who had been waiting ten days. His name was Ricardo.

"Their bureaucracy seems a bit sluggish," commented Edward. "Any suggestions? I leave in six days."

"Come back another year and plan to stay six months!" Ricardo suggested with a flick of his hand at the turbaned official.

Edward learned that Murad III, successor to Selim the Sot, spent much of his time diligently working his way through the harem, sometimes planting his esteemed royal seeds three times a night.

"As an Imperial policy," whispered Ricardo, "the Sultan only spends his time with heads of state, del-egating all other responsibilities to the Grand Vizier, Sokollu Mehmed Pasha, who is worldly-wise and ex-tremely capable."

After several hours, Edward ripped a piece of paper from his tablet, wrote a few sentences and asked Ricardo, "Do any of these turbans speak En-glish, Italian, French, Greek, Latin or Tired-Buttock?"

Ricardo laughed and pointed to a huge eunuch. "Greek." Edward labeled his message in Greek: *For the Honorable Sokollu Mehmed, from a humble petitioner representing a remote tribe of cannibals in England.* He handed it to the statue-like, scimitared eunuch.

Edward spent the next two days in the palace library in company with an elderly Jew with a long white beard. Most of the books were in Arabic although some were in Latin or Greek. Many were written on ancient parchment.

On the second afternoon, Sokollu Mehmed entered the library with his guards. In Italian he welcomed Edward to Turkey. He was of medium height with white mustache and beard and wearing a long green flowered robe.

"Having been in this job for twenty-two years, Lord Oxford, I enjoy original approaches! Your note stating that you felt it a more noble compliment to the Sultan to enrich your mind in our renowned library than to adorn one of his silk pillows with your anatomy, was most amusing."

Edward stood. "Not being a professional diplomat, I am perhaps a bit unorthodox."

"I know a great deal about you, my Lord. Our informants have reported your Queen's and your own great learning and love of knowledge, as well as your sense of humor. Part of our bureaucracy is rather good at spying."

"I hope not *all* of my travel adventures are well known!"

Sokollu laughed. "We use discretion so that other countries will return the favor! But let's talk business. Why should the Turkish empire open trade negotiations with such an isolated self-quarreling island?"

"Our outward-looking Queen is expanding the mental horizons and wealth of our people and is encouraging worldwide trade. Your cottons, carpets and the vast array of products that pass through this great city will have a large market in England. In return, we believe that our raw wool, clothes, armaments, tin and steel will be welcomed in your empire."

"Please continue." Sokollu sat down, inviting Edward to do so also.

Recalling Turkey's devastating naval defeat at Lepanto four years before by a combined European fleet, Edward said, "We can and will represent an important diversion and bulwark against Spanish aggression. We request the same trading privileges you grant the Venetians and French. Sadly, I doubt that our Queen would approve the importing of harems!"

"You do amuse me, my Lord of Oxford! His Eminence looks to your comfort and invites you to be his guest at Castle Rumeli Hisari overlooking the Bosporus. What could be more appropriate, since 'Bosporus' means ox-ford! Is there any activity you seek before leaving?"

"Yes. I would greatly enjoy doing some falconing."

"I will mention this to the Sultan. Good day, my Lord. I wish I encountered more men of learning, especially with a sense of humor, in my line of work! We are honored that you knew of our library, which has kept alive so much ancient wisdom."

*   *   *

Two days after Edward moved to the castle-fortress, a messenger appeared telling him to be ready within the hour. Four royal falconers arrived, each wearing a bright red and blue riding coat. They sat astride richly ornamented horses and brought one for Edward.

Sokollu followed behind, riding next to a smiling Sultan. Murad III was so stout that his head seemed directly joined to his body. His long flowing beard was almost golden in color. He was richly attired in a bright orange riding coat with his brown turban topped by long green plumes adorned with diamonds. He greeted Edward jovially.

"Welcome, Edward de Vere, Count of Oxford and Lord Great Chamberlain of England. I hear you have a love of falconry. It is a pleasure to share this fascinating sport with you. We shall have a pleasant morning's ride and perhaps kill a houbara or two!"

Houbaras, Edward knew, were the largest land birds in Europe, reaching weights of more than thirty pounds.

They crossed the Bosporus in a sailing ferry and rode up the hill onto the sparsely vegetated plain which smelled of hot dry grass. Edward rode alongside the Sultan and asked him many questions. How effective was sealing, or sewing falcons' eyes shut after capture, as opposed to hooding? Did they still capture falcons on the wing with baited nooses dangling from slower-flying hawks? Was it true that the Sultan had four hundred full-time falconers and 3,500 falcons? What were the relative merits of the desert falcons, the sakers, lanners, laggars and luggers?

Horsemen rode ahead to frighten the well-camouflaged birds.

By noon two houbaras weighing twenty pounds each, imported from Bulgaria, had been taken with the short stoops typical of desert falcon hunting.

Although all Edward had done was to keep the Sultan talking, two days later Sokollu told him, "Our esteemed Sultan thinks you are a brilliant conversationalist and among the very few well-informed falconry experts he has ever met. He is particularly pleased that you did not spoil the purity of the hunt by discussing diplomatic business."

Sokollu then delivered to Edward the Sultan's

dispatch to Queen Elizabeth. Sokollu told Edward that the Sultan concurred with the concept of trade agreements and urged the Queen to send a negotiating team to work out the details.

Edward tried to hold his exhilaration in check. Not a premature concept, after all! The first step in establishing trade between an emerging England and the vast markets of the Turkish Empire had now been accomplished.

*   *   *

As the *Signora Fortuna* sailed back toward Venice via Athens, Edward contemplated the panoramic fascinations of his travels, which were exceeding even his own expectations. *What an extraordinary adventure life is, if one has eyes to see, zest to seek, and an inquisitive mind to capture!*

Chapter 20

Kings, princes, lords,
If there be one among the fairest of Greece
That holds his honour higher than his ease,
That seeks his praise more than he fears his peril,
That knows his valour and knows not his fear,
That loves his mistress more than in confession
With truant vows to her own lips he loves,
And dare avow her beauty and her worth
In other arms than hers—to him this challenge .
- Troilus and Cressida

Edward enjoyed Siena and its black and white marble cathedral, marveled at the artistic wonders of Florence, and admired the stately ancient grandeur of the Roman Forum.

He was now in Sicily at the end of January, 1576. He planned to arrive back in London in April.

Edward still craved excitement and he wanted to publicize the new international outreach of

Elizabeth's England. With those goals in mind, he decided to seek knightly combat in tribute to his Queen, and issued his challenge while in Palermo:

Edward de Vere, Seventeenth Earl of Oxford, Viscount Bolebec, Lord Great Chamberlain of England, Courtier and Defender of the Honor of Elizabeth, Queen of England, hereby issues a challenge to any and all persons, from nearby States or afar, with any form of weapon. They may be with or without horse or armour, to fight a combat in any place, at any time, in the defense of his Prince and Country.

On his return to the Hotel Archimedes in Palermo after visiting the beautiful Greek temples at Syracusa and Agrigento, he found a reply to his tournament challenge:

To the Courageous English Knight, Lord Edward de Vere:

> Since, as Ovid said, *Carmina proveniunt animo deducta sereno* (Inspired poetry bursts forth from a serene mind) . . .
>
> Why not, as Persius said, *Indulge genio, carpamus dulcia* (Give your genius an opportunity; let us gather the sweetnesses of life).
>
> Therefore, you are challenged: *Venire, videre, vincere Vulcania in Vulcano statim!* (To come, to see, to conquer Vulcania in Vulcano immediately!)
>
>   -Vulcania

Edward laughed with delight when he read the name Vulcania, Goddess of Fire. Only one grape-draped mystery guest could have composed that!

He knew that Vulcano was the nearest Aeolian

Island off the coast of Sicily. He walked to Palermo's library and studied the history of the Aeolian Islands. They were named after Aeolus, Greek God of Winds, who lived on Stromboli, the most actively volcanic of these seven windy lava isles.

This might be a wild houbara chase, Edward thought, *but since Odysseus spent a month being entertained on the Aeolian Islands, why not me as part of my Homeric adventuring?*

He hired a sailboat and landed at Porto di Levante on Vulcano the next morning. He was greeted by the powerful rotten-egg stench of sulfur gases which he could see rising from the large volcano on his left and from irregular orange and yellow mounds of steaming mud and sulfur on his right. Beyond the layered and pinnacled mounds were the narrow isthmus and then a peninsula with two smaller black and whitish-yellow volcanic cones, from one of which steam was rising. A black rippled stream of hardened lava angled toward the port.

A stark but appealing landscape, Edward said to himself, *if I can just get used to the smell!*

At the port were a few small shops. He inquired at the market and was told that he had been expected. The owner's son rode across the isthmus to take word that Edward had arrived.

Edward looked around him. Three fishermen were sitting on the black sand beach mending their nets. Two others were in boats in the small inlet pulling in their nets with a few small fish wriggling and glinting in the morning sun. Another knelt on the pier sorting crabs into wooden boxes.

An hour passed before he saw two mules crossing the isthmus. The mule behind was saddled but empty. On the front mule rode a strange apparition: a person

R

in flaming red riding-clothes and shining steel helmet with long red plumes on top, a long spear held vertically in the right gloved hand, and a white shield in the left stating: VOLCANIC SERENITY.

The apparition stopped in front of Edward. Trying his best to stifle a laugh, he said, "In the name of Aeolus, God of Winds, and Edward, God of Sulfurous Fumes, say who thou art and why thou comst so frighteningly appareled! What is thy quarrelsome mysterious intent?"

In a gruff voice, the helmet answered: "As said Caecilius, 'A man who does not believe that Love is the greatest of the Gods is either foolish or inexperienced.' Therefore, my Dearest Sulfurous Fume," said Serena, removing her helmet, "join Lady Alvilda in her lair of Venus and provide memories which she will wear forever like a rainbow-colored scarf."

They studied each other's face for a moment and burst out laughing. They embraced and kissed. Then Serena de-armored herself, left the armor at the market, and they rode their mules across the isthmus along a narrow dirt road to the end of the peninsula. On a cliff overlooking the ocean was a red-tiled cottage surrounded by a small vineyard and gardens.

"This belongs to my father's sister who lives in Rome," Serena explained. "She bought it very cheaply after Barbarossa led his North African pirates here in 1544 and carried off hundreds of islanders as slaves. She calls it *Serenitas*. It is ours as long as we want it. In winter it is an isolated retreat of bleak beauty, in spring and summer a fragrant flowered gem of loveliness."

After a loving interlude, Serena and Edward sat sweatered on the grapevine-arbored verandah lined with large terra-cotta pots filled with dirt. They held hands and looked out on the frothy whitecapped waves of the sea. The channel was less than a mile wide between the peninsula of Vulcano and the island of Lipari.

"Oh, Edward, I have thought so much about you. You seemed so happy, so creatively filled with ideas in Malcesine that I thought I could do the same for you here. I also have concerns about certain ideas of yours and wanted to probe a little deeper." Serena smiled and wrapped her arms securely around his neck.

He smiled. "What else has the torridly steaming mind of Vulcania conjured?"

"When the weather allows it, we will take a three-day trip to Stromboli. There we will hire a boat to take us out at night to see the bright orange streams of lava emerge from the cone and slowly wend their way into the ocean. I want you to hear and see the roaring explosions of flaming pitch and fire-balls cast out from earth's very center!"

* * *

Serenitas provided an excellent environment for writing and Edward wanted to get started immediately. Joyously replenished both physically and mentally, he reviewed his tablets filled with thoughts, verses, outlines and character sketches. To use a basic story outline from a prior famous author was to pay him tribute. Was any idea really new?

He decided that he would set most of his plays in areas that he had visited. A pity he couldn't use Istanbul but he wanted nothing to interfere with pending trade negotiations and he wasn't sure the Turks would understand this form of tribute.

He started his writing at Serenitas by taking a story from Giovanni Boccaccio's *Decameron* and changing the setting to France. He would capture the audience with humor and sustain them with winning characters in both farcical and believable situations. He would make the play memorable by commentary on love, honor, courage and chivalry. He decided to name it *The historie of the Rape of the Second Helene.* He included a recent thought about Serena:

> *Those girls of Italy, take heed of them.*
> *They say our French lack language to deny*
> *if they demand.*

With many plots partially developed in his mind, he also began work simultaneously on another play, this time with no literary precedent. He set the play in Navarre and included techniques of the Commedia dell'Arte. He tentatively named it *A Pleasant Conceited Comedie Called Loves Labours Lost.* Despite its farcical orientation, he tried to fill the comedy with a high level of verbal sophistication. Having felt true love's intensity for the first time with Serena, he attempted to describe it:

> *A lover's eyes will gaze an eagle blind.*
> *A lover's ear will hear the lowest sound.*
> *Love's feeling is more soft and sensible*
> *Than are the tender horns of cockled snails.*
> *And when love speaks, the voice of all the gods*
> *Make heaven drowsy with the harmony.*

Three days later, the sun broke free of the gray cloudy skies and Serena suggested that they climb the big steaming volcano. Leaving their horses at the base, they followed a narrow trail that half-circled the mountain. As they walked forward and slid backwards on the gray ash and pumice, they passed low shrubs and brushwood, green and red succulents, sparse heather and an occasional red-barked, dwarf gnarly cedar. Serena carried a blanket and Edward a picnic basket.

They reached thick layers of compacted red and gray ash, where the path narrowed and became steeper. Every few minutes they paused to rest and talk.

Serena shared her worries over his insistence upon including in his plays actual people who were only thinly disguised.

"Most great poets and writers throughout history have recorded the people and thoughts, words and feelings of their times," Edward answered. "That is an essential part of their greatness and their contribution to history and humanity."

"But Edward, your words, verses and insights are beautiful by themselves. There is no need to become a political satirist."

"I hate beheaders of truth."

"I see hints of the revenge motive in you. It isn't necessary, and I foresee danger and harm coming your way."

They reached the rim and were stunned by the view of the pumiced ashy crater colored by brilliant yellow and orange, solid and liquid sulfur. Wisps and clouds of powerfully odoriferous, dense sulfurous steam emerged everywhere from mounds, pinnacles and contorted excrescences making bubbling and sputtering noises.

"Once adapted to, the smell of sulfur has a

strange allure," Edward said as he walked toward the largest billowing cloud of fumes.

"Don't go too close, Edward!" Serena shouted. "Please be careful! The gusts are shifty!"

The winds swirled and Edward vanished in the yellow vapors. Serena heard a paroxysm of coughing. She ran toward the cloud but just then he emerged, bent over, holding his nose, red-faced and gagging. He coughed twice and drew a deep ragged breath.

"I wish I could say 'How exhilarating,' " he said hoarsely. "But that was a bit scary. It was literally impossible to breathe!"

She hugged him. "Come with me, my fumigated knight-errant. Let us move to the outer side of the rim for our wine, salami, cheese and bread. While you de-sulfurize, I will point out the beauty of the islands which are so magnificently displayed today. The six volcanic Aeolian cones look like lonely sentinels in a sea of sapphired blue, guarding the distant misty coast of Sicily."

*   *   *

After a week of good weather, during which they experienced a memorable trip to Stromboli, a storm suddenly erupted an hour after dawn. Rain pelted the leaded windows, whipped by howling winds which loudly banged the bedroom shutters.

Edward and Serena vaulted out of bed and secured all shutters. The skies were so repeatedly shattered by lightning and the house so shaken by rolling explosions of thunder, that Edward and Serena ran to the other side of the house to make sure that Vulcan wasn't expressing himself with his fiery molten weaponry.

The volcanoes, whose dark shapes could barely be distinguished beneath the rapidly moving black clouds, were silent recipients of the wrath of Zeus. They returned to their bedroom and opened the large center window facing Lipari to watch nature's drama.

"Oh, Edward, look!" she cried out. "That ship is headed through the straits trying to reach the Bay of Lipari."

"Those crazy Neapolitans and their winter galley runs!" Edward shook his head wonderingly. "They pray to their saints and off they go!"

"I fear they'll not make it! How do you know they're Neapolitan?"

"By their brightly colored patchwork sails, just as they are a patchwork of races like the Sicilians. Winter trading between Naples and Tunis is profitable if you don't sink! Look, the topsails are coming down and the captain is trying to zigzag through with his main course only."

"I'll put my money on Zeus and Aeolus," exclaimed Serena. "They're being blown directly toward the Faraglione, those two rock pinnacles off Lipari's shore. Isn't there anything we can do?"

"Just what the sailors are doing. Pray! Galleys are top-heavy, and the wind and seas are much too strong. Look! The captain realizes it now and is trying to turn her around and head for the open sea! I think he's too late!"

They stared in horror at the sailors jumping off as the ship was blown sideways into the first pinnacle, where the smashing waves tore it apart.

"How fast tragedy strikes!" said Edward. "The ship is already gone—just a few pieces of wood, a single floating mast, and those little bobbing heads being swept by the waves and current toward that sandy inlet at the base of Lipari's cliffs."

They watched as monks ran down to the inlet from their hilltop monastery and helped the sailors from the surf.

"There must be twenty survivors climbing up the path toward the monastery," observed Serena.

"Pity it's not a convent! They must have prayed to the wrong gods!"

"Oh Edward, you see humor in everything, even during the dark side of nature's tempests. I am emotionally spent. Let's go back to bed."

As they lay in bed holding hands, a contemplative Edward softly said, "Someday I will write a drama in your honor, Serena, and include this moving spectacle. Your name will be silent but you and the tempestuous island of Vulcano will be versed forever."

She soon fell asleep, but Edward's brain began to fill with tributary thoughts about Serena:

> *For several virtues*
> *Have I liked several women; never any*
> *With so full soul but some defect in her*
> *Did quarrel with the noblest grace she owed*
> *And put it to the foil. But you, O you,*
> *So perfect and so peerless, are created*
> *Of every creature's best.*

Chapter 21

There may be in the cup
A spider steeped, and one may drink, depart,
And yet partake no venom, for his knowledge
Is not infected; but if one present
Th'abhorred ingredient to his eye, make known
How he hath drunk, he cracks his gorge, his sides,
With violent hefts. I have drunk and seen the spider.
- The Winter's Tale

Edward leaned against the ornate iron gate of the Duke of Montmorenci's manor house where he was staying and pondered the many charms of Paris, so different in atmosphere from Italy.

He had rested for two days after a long beautiful journey through France surrounded by a warm blossoming spring. The boat trip from Sicily to Naples and thence to Marseilles had been peaceful but poignantly reflective. He was doubtful that he would ever see Italy or Serena again.

The day was sunny and Edward decided to tour an area of Paris he had not seen before. As he left, a man leaning against an elm tree across the avenue mounted his horse and rode in the opposite direction.

After fifteen minutes of quiet riding through parks, meadows and forest, Edward halted at the reeded edge of Lac Superieur. A delicate greenish hue of just-emerging leaves tinted the trees, the water mirroring their promise and their color. As a blackbird flew from a small maple branch, Edward savored the quiet motion of the bird-sprung bough.

A rhythmed thudding of hooves interrupted his peaceful thoughts as a horseman dressed in black raced past, wheeled around and came back.

"Cousin Edward! It is you, indeed! What an unexpected coincidence!"

"Henry! Greetings!" Edward was surprised and happy to see his cousin Henry Howard. " 'Tis good to see a member of my own clan after so many months."

"Let's sit on the grass. I've much to tell you." Henry had dark penetrating eyes, a highly arched right eyebrow, a downpointing mustache and a small beard. "It was a wise move for you to return earlier than expected."

"Why a wise move?" Edward questioned as he dismounted. "For many reasons, cousin. Firstly, Burghley extends his thirsty sticky tongue more and more into the cream of your estates, milking and mulcting, so to speak. He swallows them, ruminates, then makes them disappear in the dark acid of his endless greed." Edward appreciated Henry's verbal imagery, derived from an impressive library and wide reading.

Edward scowled. He wondered who first said,

Falsus in uno, falsus in omnibus, false in one aspect of life, false in everything. "Let's not talk about Burghley. I'm starved for other news! How fares my daughter? And the Queen? And my sister Mary, and Francis and Horatio Vere?"

"All flourishing, Edward. Francis seems to be a soldier-born, like many of your de Vere ancestors. He will be sent to the Netherlands soon. Horatio, though of gentler mettle, is longing to follow."

Henry fingered his mustache and continued. "Your devoted friend Hatton is prospering like all good sycophants. He has grabbed Ely House and its great gardens from Bishop Cox. He now lives there with forty servants. For special services rendered to royalty, he will undoubtedly be knighted soon."

"Enough of greed and flatterers!" Edward said, waving a hand as if to clear away a stench. "Tell me of Anne and my daughter."

"I haven't seen Anne. She retreated rapidly to Theobalds when she became pregnant and has stayed there." He hesitated. "May I be so bold as to share the rumors that are so rampant?"

"Rumors?" An uneasy feeling left a hollow cave in Edward's stomach.

"The rumors about the date and origin of her conception."

Edward stood up abruptly. "What do you mean? I was with her maritally for the last time in October and the baby was born in July."

Henry's eyebrow arched. "Did Burghley really tell you July? Some say the baby was merely overdue by a few weeks. But you know what it's like at Court: chatter, chatter, chatter, like popinjays."

Edward clenched his fists as he felt the biting edge of slander's abrasive sword. He regarded Anne, with all of her shortcomings, as trustworthy. Anne unfaithful to a de Vere? Hard to believe.

"But who, Henry, would wish to besmirch Anne so foully and, through Anne, me? Such rumors fester and become goads, thorns, nettles, tails of wasps." He pounded his fist on the ground. "I will *not* have my name dragged into the mud of Court intrigue!"

Henry put his hand on Edward's shoulder. "I suspect it's all merely gossip." He hesitated. "But certainly everyone is discussing it."

Edward put a clove in his mouth. "I like not what I hear. Let us change the subject."

"Well . . .there is something else," Henry said. "But I fear this may incense your writing soul. While you were gone, with Burghley's urging and money, your protégé George Gascoigne published a new edition of your *A Hundreth Sundrie Flowres* under his own name as sole author."

"Impossible!" Edward burst out. "I wrote most of those poems myself! That is outright thievery, knavery, skullduggery! That rump-fed canker blossom! I'll knock his head from his treacherous shoulders!" He looked out at the tranquil lake and felt mocked by its serene repose.

The ultra-Catholic Henry Howard licked his lips and smiled subtly. "Surely your devout father-in-law has your best interests at heart . . ."

"I would say 'The Devil take Burghley!'" exclaimed Edward, "but he already *is* the Devil incarnate!" Listen to these lines for a future play which just entered my head:

> *This outward-sainted deputy is yet a devil*
> *Whose settled visage and deliberate word*
> *Nips youth i' th' head as falcon doth the fowl .*"

"Right on, Edward! Y'gads, how do lines form so quickly?

Edward continued. "God's precious soul! Burghley is duplicity personified. A veritable quicksand of dissimulation! The world is so easily deceived by external ornaments!" He held his head in both hands and shook it from side to side. "Why do so few see through that self-serving man?"

Henry decided to let Edward's thoughts simmer. They fell into silence as a chilly breeze rippled the lake, blackening the water.

Edward was appalled that Burghley, a master of Machiavellian chicanery, had already achieved his pre-eminent life-goals: to attain a position of political power close to the monarch, thereby becoming immensely wealthy; to lead his family out of the middle class by acquiring an upper class title, thus launching a noble posterity; and to create a dignified, albeit fictitious, ancestry which future generations wouldn't question.

I wonder, Edward reflected gloomily, *whether Burghley will be my endless malignant adversary, my evil shadow, the stifling darkness of my entire life?*

Chapter 22

But ships are but boards, sailors but men. There
be land rats and water rats, water thieves and
land thieves, I mean pirates, and then there
is the peril of waters, winds, and rocks .
    - The Merchant of Venice

Edward usually enjoyed the atmosphere of a busy port—the many kinds of ships bobbing at anchor, the sailors and longshoremen working and cursing, and the intermingled smells of sea, algae, clams, human sweat, paint and cargoes of pungent spices.

But now he sat silently on the dock in Calais, eyes downcast. After arriving in Paris a few days before in a happy travel-exhilarated mood, he had quickly become fractured by mistrust.

He came aboard the French two-master *Galopin,* the Rascal, with his chests and boxes to make sure they weren't placed in a bilgy rat-infested compartment. He made friends with the crew who were surprised by the discrepancy between his nobleman's attire and his mariner's speech.

When *Galopin* escaped the confines of the harbor, picked up the channel wind and had all sails unfurled and trimmed, Edward stood at the bow. To distract his mind he played his childhood game of finding figures, faces and animals in clouds.

Some minutes later, his thoughts were interrupted by black-bearded Captain Pierre Laroux, who pointed out a smaller ship about a mile away headed directly toward them. "What do you make of it, Lord Edward?"

"Perhaps it's only my cynical mood, but I read sinister intent," Edward replied, shading his eyes as he watched the other ship.

"I don't see any pennants flying," the captain said. "I've been makng this run for two years and haven't met a pirate yet. They're probably just delivering a forgotten piece of important cargo."

As the ship drew near, a sailor shouted, "Pirates!"

The other ship was lined with sailors holding either rapiers or muskets. The captain of the vessel signaled the hauling down of sails. Planks were laid between the two vessels, and the pirates swarmed aboard. No resistance was offered.

Captain Laroux walked firmly up to the pirate captain, who was tall, blond-haired and clean-shaven. "Captain, why are you doing this? We are not a Spanish galleon loaded with gold and jewels!"

With almost accentless English, the pirate captain said, "Let me introduce myself. I am Hag Jacobson from a once-wealthy Amsterdam family. My father's business was ruined by the rapacious Spanish invaders. I was about to attend Cambridge when my older

brother was killed. In wartime, only limited opportunities are available to recoup a fortune."

"You call this making your fortune?" Edward demanded, pointing to two pirates who had looted a
lady's trunk, put on expensive dresses and thrown
powder over their faces. They were now dancing a
jig on the deck in front of the tied-up passengers
and a group of clapping pirates.

"Ah, Edward de Vere, Earl of Oxford," Jacobson
said with a grin. "Even pirates are entitled to have
their fun. My men are English and Dutch, all treated
like cockroaches in the navy—low pay, villainous flog-
ging captains, inedible food and sickening water. On
my ship they're treated like men, fed well and have
a chance at earning enough to start a new life."

"What's so appealing about our ship?" asked Captain Laroux.

"We know almost every passenger on board and
most of the cargo." My men hang out in the taverns
of Calais and as far away as Paris. People talk and we
listen. You forget that, like you, we have to eat and
drink. Your ship is full of pork and casks of fine
French wines."

"God's death, look at that!" Edward exclaimed.
"Are they enrobing the murky waters with my silks?"

He pointed at two pirates holding large beer
mugs full of wine. They were plucking with their
swords his own clothes, hats and silk material out of a
smashed box, swirling them over their heads and
hurling them into the sea. Another pirate wrapped
himself in one of Edward's olive green rolls of velvet
and strutted slowly and suggestively past Edward, like
a peacock doing a graceful pavane. The Flushing co-
median then walked to the side of the ship and
flauntingly threw the velvet into the ocean.

"Enough!" shouted Edward, drawing his rapier.

Hag Jacobson gave a quick sign and Edward was immediately surrounded by menacing swords.

"This is now a point of honor," Edward said. "You and your men have offended me and, through me, the Queen of England. I demand satisfaction!"

"Just like your challenge at Palermo!" said Jacobson, laughing. "News spreads rapidly among sailors! Too bad you had no takers!"

Edward's mind was racing but in true crises he remained calm and unruffled. He thought about his four partly-completed plays, his random verses, tablet-lines, observations and ideas, all in his luggage. He visualized his goods and those of the other passengers being thrown into the sea.

"I challenge your best swordsman to a duel, weapon of his choice."

Jacobson lifted an amused inquisitive eyebrow. "And if you win?"

"You may take any items from the ship or its passengers which have value to you but nothing else. The meaningless destruction must cease."

"And if you lose, which you surely shall?"

Edward answered without hesitation. "I die but I retain my honor forever."

Captain Jacobson stared at him for a long moment, as if trying to decide whether or not this crazy English lord was serious. Then he nodded and turned to his men. "Who wants him?"

"I'll take him between drinks," said wine-swilling Petter Scudamore.

"Not this time, Pinot Scudamore," said the Captain. The pirates laughed. "How about you, Benji? You're English, small and frail like our English Lord, and you have a great fencing name!" The captain pointed at Benjamin Parry, six feet ten inches in height with a mustache to match.

The pirate Goliath stripped to his waist, bulged his huge chest and flexed his biceps. "Rapiers, it is," he said in a gravelly voice. "Mine should work well on corned noble beef."

Edward put down his rapier, peeled off his jacket and rolled up his sleeves. He was wearing loose brown breeches and thanked his de Vere crest's silver mullet that he was wearing soft, flat, pliable leather shoes.

Picking up the rapier, he took the *en garde* position and planned his strategy. First, test Benji's style and competence. Is he a thruster or slasher? How fast does he recover his balance? Where does he place his weight, on the forward foot or back-foot? Does he twist sideways to avoid a thrust and throw himself off-center?

"Knock off the Frenchy stuff," Benji growled after Edward had made a few preliminary feints. "Let's fight!" He lunged straight at Edward's heart.

Edward quickly parried and retreated, noting that Benji was momentarily off-balance forwards. Edward feinted a thrust and Benji jerked backward, keeping his knees straight.

Edward circled slowly. Benji raised his sword, opening up his entire right side, and slashed downward toward Edward's ribs. Edward retreated quickly, and easily parried as the weapons clanged loudly together.

Now let's do some dueling, decided Edward.

Moving his feet rapidly, constantly maintaining his center of gravity, he feinted twice toward the abdomen. Benji twisted to the side, leaving his chest wide open for an easy kill. But Edward decided against it. He initiated a leaping *flèche* and thrust his rapier into Benji's right biceps.

Benji howled in pain and dropped his sword. Edward placed his rapier point at Benji's throat, just nicking the skin as he picked up his opponent's sword with his left hand.

"A lucky stroke," said Edward, bowing formally and handing the sword back to Benji, who looked puzzled. "You forgot to parry!"

Hag Jacobson couldn't stifle a quick smile.

"En garde!" said Edward, as he again assumed the classic position of readiness and balance.

He allowed Benji to regain his over-confidence as they moved back and forth across the deck at an increasing pace. Edward invited a slash as he backed toward the main mast, then jumped sideways at the last moment as Benji's sword gashed the mast. Despite the excitement of danger, Edward breathed quietly, his muscles relaxed.

They fought their way to the forecastle wall, with Edward backed against it. Benji lunged forward with his sword headed for Edward's navel. Edward leaped to his right, centered himself quickly and directed a *stoccata* into the thickest portion of Benji's bare right forearm, transecting muscles and tendons. Benji's sword struck the wall as he fell to his knees and grabbed his forearm.

"This duel is now declared terminated," said Edward. He turned his back on Benji, bowed to both captains and started walking back into the semicircle of the crowd.

"Look out!" Captain Laroux shouted.

Edward turned just in time to see Benji launch a savage two-handed horizontal slash toward Edward's legs. Edward had no time to defend himself. He jumped straight up with both legs flexed as the sword cut the air underneath.

Now Benji was slashing wildly with both hands. Edward could easily have killed him with a thrust to heart or throat, but he feared piratical revenge on all passengers and crew of the *Galopin*. Instead, he parried and retreated strategically. He was just about to perform a *stramazzone,* then flick his wrist and send Benji's rapier flying when one of the pirates poured a large mug of French Chablis on the deck around his feet. Edward slipped and landed on his back.

The giant straddled him, stepped on his right wrist, and said: "Well, maties, Little Lord Eddie with all of his *en garde* this and *en garde* that, learned in the bedrooms of London and Paris, forgot about what us pirates are made of: courage, guts and plenty of extra blood. Now shall I cut out his gizzard or his liver before tossing him to the fishies?"

Captain Hag Jacobson put his left hand on Benji's shoulder. "Well done, Benjamin Parry, but now I'm asking all of my officers and crew to join me in the aftercastle for discussion." He helped Edward to his feet. "Nobly fought, Lord Oxford. Pirates make decisions by vote and now we shall vote on what we are to do."

The crew and passengers congratulated Edward but looked worried. They knew the pirate vote would affect them all. Some of the crew pleaded with Edward to untie their hands and let them fight it out but Laroux cautioned against such a bloody futile effort.

They watched the conference at the rear of the ship which continued for many minutes. Shouts and oaths were heard. Captain Hag Jacobson exerted his authority and made the pirates express their opinions in sequence.

Finally Edward and the others saw a vote being taken, then a speech by Jacobson, then a final vote.

The passengers quietly stared as the pirate captain walked forward. Then he smiled broadly and said, "It is the decision of Captain Jacobson, his officers and crew that this well-fought duel resulted in a draw. Because of the closeness of the fight, all of Edward de Vere's conditions of victory will be honored."

Captain Jacobson reached out and shook Edward's hand. "I must say, Lord Edward, that was an impressive performance! What my crew didn't realize, and I had to explain, is that you had many opportunities to kill the non-parrying Parry, but you refused to take advantage of them. Many of my crew now want to take fencing lessons."

"Better for them to take cooking lessons!" Edward suggested. "Once the Spanish war is over, the English navy will likely turn its weeviled, scurvied attention to pirates. Your occupation may become rather hazardous."

Chapter 23

There have been,
Or I am much deceived, cuckolds ere now
And many a man there is, even at this present,
Now, while I speak this, holds his wife by th'arm,
That little thinks she has been sluiced in's absence,
And his pond fished by his next neighbor, by
Sir Smile.
       - The Winter's Tale

Edward paced the floor of his room at Whitehall Palace muttering oaths. His name was being dragged through the mud. To a chivalric knight and noble courtier, personal integrity meant everything. Just thinking about his perpetually scheming father-in-law spasmed his jaws. The calmness he had achieved during his travels was fast disappearing and his brain was beginning to seethe.

He had been looking forward to seeing his new daughter for the first time, holding her and cooing to her and doing all those things that proud fathers do. But now he had reason to doubt that the baby girl was even his. *Why does life have to be so convoluted and troublesome?*

He went over in his mind Anne's possible unfaithfulness to him. If she became pregnant in early October, the last time they were intimate, why hadn't she informed him before he left for Paris three months later? Why the notable delay of two months by Burghley in notifying Edward of the actual birthday and gender of the baby, if she was born July 2?

Edward talked with Dr. Masters, the Court physician, who said, "I confirmed the pregnancy in March, Edward. Anne told me she was in doubt whether you would accept the baby as your own."

"Good God, why?"

"She wouldn't tell me. My examination suggested only a three months pregnancy, not the five months she claimed. I was so puzzled by the time-sequence she gave that I discussed it with the Queen."

"Did you deliver the baby?"

"No. Anne disappeared. I was told she went to Theobalds. Burghley brought me a birth certificate in early September, told me that Anne had delivered with the help of a midwife, and asked me to sign the document which had a birth-date of July 2."

"Did you?"

"No. He offered me a hundred pounds but I told him I could not. He was displeased but, since I am the Queen's physician, he did not push me further."

"You are one of the few in England with sufficient integrity to resist such a combination of implicit threat, power and money."

Edward brooded about the misfortunes that had befallen him. Mary Hastings and Serena were both far superior women and would have been magnificent wives, creating a true marital alliance, each partner enhancing the other's abilities, potential and happiness. Burghley and the Queen had jointly chained his entire life to a permanent anchor of incompatibility. Didn't they know that love was a compelling but *not* compellable emotion?

With his legal training, Edward knew that all of the evidence against Anne was circumstantial. But it was more than impressive. Whether Anne was guilty or innocent, the Cecils had besmirched the de Vere shield of honor.

He wrote Burghley that what they could have solved in private conference was now a fable of the world. He continued:

> *"I must let your lordship understand this much: until I can better satisfy myself of some mislikes, I am determined, as touching my wife, not to accompany her. What they are—because some are not to be spoken of or written upon as imperfections—I will not blaze or publish until it pleases me. And last of all, I mean not to weary my life any more with such troubles and molestations as I have endured."*

Edward strongly suspected a far more damning scenario about the source of Anne's pregnancy but thought it prudent to show restraint. It was clearly time, however, to separate himself from the Cecils and seek his destiny alone. Henceforth, he and Anne would live apart.

*   *   *

As Edward waited for his audience with the forty-three-year-old Queen in Whitehall's presence chamber, he thought how much he cared for and respected her despite her shortcomings and volatility. She had been Queen for eighteen years, since 1558, and had brought peace and stability to her troubled kingdom. She ruled by intellectual prowess, perceptive insight, charisma, craftiness in creating ambiguities, and careful sifting of advice.

Edward knew that she was not as vacillating and delaying as she seemed. She often allied herself with time, deferring major decisions until the problem solved itself. He recalled her motto which had served her well, *Video et taceo* . I see and am silent.

Edward was less approving of her and Burghley's Machiavellian approach to governance—that the ultimate result was the only meaningful goal. Lies, deception and crushing of enemies were an inevitable part of ruling. But she was successful and all of England benefited from her wisdom and foresight. He looked at the tapestry of English royal genealogy and knew she would hold an honored place in that distinguished list.

Elizabeth was in a jovial mood when Edward's turn finally came. As he kneeled, he noted that her Tudor nose had become more hooked and the shadows under her eyes betrayed the strain of being monarch.

"Stand up, Edward, my handsome roving ambassador! Your admirable diplomatic performances in Venice and Turkey have set a high standard."

"You are most kind, Your Majesty," Edward said.

"I found diplomacy interesting and challenging but I think my talents lie elsewhere."

Elizabeth smiled broadly. "I am well acquainted with your talents on many levels, Edward, and I have missed them. Your long absence has impressed upon me how much the Court needs your gifts. Fawned and flattered queens surrounded by dronish overbuzzing attendants also spend many hours in isolated aloneness. I have chosen to use many of those hours for thinking and creative planning."

"Your more mature courtier awaits your conclusions with eagerness, Your Majesty."

Elizabeth paused as she lifted her bejeweled arms and inhaled the fragrance of her civet-scented hands. "My Court is glamorous but lacks cultural and intellectual innovation. Pleasant and joyous atmosphere it has, like a perpetual castle party, but I want, and will have, something more mind-elevating, artistically innovative and enduring."

"Do continue, Your Majesty." Edward's curiosity was genuine. She seemed never to tire of surprising him.

"First comes state business." She straightened her broadly hooped yellow dress with her favorite red acorn pattern. "My dispatches from Venice mentioned how different you were from the usual ambassador. The Doge especially appreciated how truly Venetian you are. He will send his first ambassador to London soon. Even our Lord Treasurer is pleased!"

Edward murmured something about the Lord Treasurer not meant for her ears. If she heard, she ignored it.

"He and the Privy Council are most impressed with your detailed description of ship production at the Arsenal. We shall be adopting some of their techniques."

Burghley must also be annoyed, thought Edward, for my escaping so adroitly his spying surveillance, like a stag leaping free from encircling bush-beaters!

"The Grand Vizier wrote that it was your learning, your love of books, your sense of humor and your uniqueness which allowed you to breach so many tight bureaucratic barriers so swiftly."

"My diplomatic unorthodoxy seemed to be an asset, not an encumbrance, strange as it may seem, Your Majesty."

Elizabeth began swinging the sweet-scented pomander hanging by a silver chain from her dress. "The Sultan is still talking about your remarkable knowledge of desert falconry! I informed the Privy Council of our secret negotiations. They were stunned into unaccustomed and most refreshing silence by your accomplishment! They immediately accepted the Sultan's invitation to send a negotiating team to Istanbul."

Edward rubbed the boar ring on his left thumb. "The falconry gambit was good fortune at its highest pitch, quite a providential bit of luck by your haggard ambassador."

Elizabeth opened and closed her fan slowly. "England is beginning to take its place on the world scene. That has been one of my fondest goals and now we are being regarded with new international respect. I think that from this time forward, my chief nickname for you will be my 'Turk.'"

Edward opened a package he had brought and gave her three Murano red glass swans for dining table decorations, the perfumed gloves and gold rose earrings. "Please accept these small gifts not thrown overboard by the pirates, at least half of whom were English!"

"They are lovely, Edward." She admired the gifts, then set them aside. "I would like you to devote more time to your writing. You may live outside of the palace. May we hope you will have a play for our Christmas festivities?"

"It was a thought I dared to entertain, Your Majesty."

"Please accompany me to dinner. I will not be eating alone today."

*   *   *

As they entered the dining area, a screened-off sector of the Great Hall, Edward saw Thomas Knyvet talking to his nephew, Tom Vavasour. He noted how Knyvet's left hand rose to his forehead, with the index finger and little finger protruding, the whole hand then sliding into his hair. *The devil damn him for making the sign of the horns, the cuckold sign!*

Christopher Hatton was making the same sign— or was he? Edward smiled, though his mouth felt like a clam shell washed with sea brine. He briefly thought that to die with mocks would be as bad as to die from tickling.

Edward was given a seat beside Hatton, who was on the Queen's right, with Henry Howard seated on his other side. Edward noted that Hatton was wearing the bell on a silver chain which had been presented to him after the 1571 tournament. As Hatton helped seat the Queen and sat himself down with a flourish, the bell jangled.

Turning toward Edward, Hatton said, "Did you hear that?"

"What, the chain?" asked Edward.

"No, the *bell*," Hatton said with a tone that suggested Edward was as dumb as Burghley's mule.

Edward smiled and mused that the Queen's nickname for Hatton, "my Sheep," must have been chosen because he was so mutton-headed. *My God, his brain is as dry as the remainder-biscuit after a voyage!*

"You look fairer tonight, dear my Queen, than all the roses in my garden on Holborn Hill," said Hatton, bowing so low that his forehead nearly knocked over his wine.

"The rose garden that Bishop Cox spent years in developing and from which he is now allowed to pick only a single annual rose?" Edward said, thinking that Hatton's major gifts were fawning behavior and base spaniel flattery. *Lord help you, shallow man, who hath more earwax than wit!*

"Our Blue Boar is barbed tonight, is he not, my dearest Majesty? The horned boar apparently thinks that his tusks and brain are sharper than the rest of us do!" Hatton laughed, scratching his forehead with index and little finger extended, his black beard twitching its approval.

"Where the blue boar razes, let the bleating sheep be wary," said Edward firmly, his eyes piercing, his right hand moving toward his dagger. *Enough of these cuckold references!*

Henry Howard gripped Edward's wrist below the table.

"Peace, gentlemen!" hissed the Queen. "Where the lion roars, let both the boar and sheep beware! Come, let us drink down all incivilities."

After dinner, several maids of honor sang. During

a brief recess, George Gascoigne came up to Edward. Looking embarrassed but not remorseful over *A Hundreth Sundrie Flowres,* Gascoigne said, "It was Burghley's idea, not mine." Gascoigne was following one of the current fashions of immensely bulging clothes, his pants filled with bran and chaff. *What a shrunken head on a bloated carcass,* Edward thought.

"I understand the situation well, George." Edward hugged him in friendly fashion, patted him on the back and, noticed only by Henry Howard, quickly slit Gascoigne's pants across the buttocks with his dagger.

After the break, Sussex conducted the Queen to the harpsichord. Gascoigne took his position on her left as turner of pages. As the Queen played and sang, Edward suddenly realized that she was singing his own poems from *A Hundreth Sundrie Flowres.* Like a frosty blast of wintry wind, he recognized that she was paying tribute to Gascoigne!

At the end of three songs, the Queen finished to applause and said, "Is not George a pretty poet?"

"Writing is hard work more than inspiration, Your Majesty." Facing the Queen, Gascoigne bowed low twice, each time pouring an avalanche of bran and chaff onto the floor. The assembled throng broke into an uproar of laughter. Gascoigne was mystified.

Henry grabbed Edward's arm and said, "Let's get out to the stables fast! Your jokestering tickles my kidneys but is fraught with imperial peril!"

As they left the great hall, walking rapidly, Henry added, "But let's change the subject. How did you like the Queen's singing?"

"It reminded me of a raven with laryngitis," Edward replied. "It's a wonder the wine glasses didn't shatter!"

"God's body, Edward, take heady care! All women have vanity and a queen's pride is that of a thousand peacocks!"

"Where are we going?" Edward demanded. "I am suffocating with falsity."

"You need a change of atmosphere. A group of us is gathering at the Stillyard tonight. Why not join us?"

Edward agreed but told Henry that he needed an hour to regain his composure. He rode off swiftly to Oxford Court and the exquisite serenity of silence.

Chapter 24

I am known to be a humorous patrician, and one that loves a cup of hot wine with not a drop of allaying Tiber in't . . . one that converses more with the buttock of the night than with the forehead of the morning.
— Coriolanus

Edward rode through the great arched gateway of the Stillyard, the steep-gabled German building between Thames Street and the waterfront which, for three centuries, had belonged to the Teutonic Guild of the Hanseatic Merchants. He dismounted and made straight for the vaulted cellars. An open space for tables was squared among the rows of casks. The room was full of rich smells of foaming beer, cheeses, sausages, pickled fish and roasting meats.

The grilled window openings on the upper walls were covered with oiled paper. Candles stuck into flasks provided flickering light as did large open fires at each end where cooks were turning ducks, geese, swans, pigs and lambs on spits. Laughter and loud voices permeated the large room. Edward always enjoyed the Stillyard's robust uninhibited ambiance.

Henry Howard stood and waved Edward to his table, where also sat Charles Arundel and Philip Howard, Henry's nephew, now twenty-two. Soon three others were waved over by Henry.

"Francis Southwell!" Edward exclaimed. "What a pleasant surprise. Heaven save you and your good digestion! And Tom Vavasour! By Adam's fig, do join us!"

Francis introduced the third man, a handsome red-bearded young man with keen eyes. "And this is my newcomer-guest, Walter Raleigh of Fardell, Devon. He has come to London to seek his fortune."

"Pick up your fardel and head back to Devon is my advice," said Edward. "There is no fortune to be found in London but ill fortune."

"Fortune is where you make it, not find it, my Lord," said Walter. "If I fail, I'll head for the open seas and see the world!"

Two rotund German servers appeared with bowls of anchovies and caviar to whet the thirst. The table was soon crowded with wooden platters of steaming meats and carafes of Rhine wine.

Conversation flowed freely and happily, far away from palace restraints. At a pause in the talking, Henry asked Edward to launch a series of toasts in the usual serious vein.

Edward stood with wine glass in hand and said, "Would that I, like Homer, had a posset of Pramnian wine to make a proper classical toast and to sip while eating grated goat's cheese and white barley meal!

But, to start, here's to the pig which used to be connected to the pickled pig's foot Henry is eating."

Henry led a toast to the Queen, but didn't identify whether it was Elizabeth or Mary, Queen of Scots. Edward toasted the Gaelic proverb, *Tri ghalar gan naire: Gra, tochas, agus tart*—To the three maladies without shame: love, itch and thirst. They downed their wine and refilled.

Edward stood again. "And now I give a toast to words and word origins. Let us toast the Celts for allowing us to create the word 'whiskey' from their *uisge-beatha,* water of life."

Edward downed more wine and briefly worried about ever-present spies. But he decided to go ahead and toast the Queen's beautiful singing voice and her pendulous ears, longer than her dangling pearl necklaces, able to hear all gossip in England.

Before he could do so, however, a wary Henry intervened and asked, "Edward, tell us what really happened in Genoa's civil conflict and what role you played in its solution."

"Ah, yes, Genoa," Edward said. "A mixture of war and peace. The old nobles were trying to maintain the *status quo* against the *nouveaux riches,* desirous of instant change. No sooner had I arrived than Prince Andrea Doria sought me out, having heard of my impressive achievements in the border war and in Flanders. He offered me command of his thirty thousand troops. I normally refuse such small assignments but finally yielded."

"A wise decision, General Edward. What next?" asked a smiling Charles Arundel.

Edward wondered whether he should continue his cupshott-embellished story but smiled to himself and went on. "While marching towards the conflict,

I reviewed in my mind the great battles of history. I decided to choose Hannibal's tactics at Cannae, where he so cleverly surrounded and slaughtered seventy thousand Roman troops.

"When we arrived at the plain east of Genoa's mountains we were astounded at the size of the enemy's hordes, including a hundred thousand mercenaries. In a stirring oration equal to Cicero's best, I told my small army what a magnificent opportunity this was for endless fame. I then formed my lines in a long convexity with the weakest troops in the center and my finest on the wings, including my best cavalry.

"We allowed the enemy to attack our center. We gave way before them, becoming a deep concave crescent, following Hannibal's strategy perfectly. At my signal, our cavalry and infantry wings completed the encirclement."

"What did you do then?" asked Philip, grinning.

"I felt myself pulled upward into the sky. I looked down upon the valley as if it were a gigantic tapestry by that rare Italian master Giulio Romano. I knew I held the fate of this tragic human drama in my hand."

Edward refilled his glass of wine. "After a few moments of philosophic reflection, I had our trumpeters and standard-bearers signal an immediate cessation of conflict. With Caesar's concise, carefully chiseled use of words, I pointed out that a dreadful slaughter was imminent which would create generations of enmity between the two Genoese factions. I requested an instantaneous disbanding of armies and a prompt beginning of mediated negotiations."

"Hear, hear!" shouted Henry, grabbing a piece of cheese and placing an anchovy on it. "And you, no doubt, were the mediator!"

TR

"Not alone," answered Edward, as he sat down in triumph. "I didn't want to appear too conspicuous so I asked the Pope to join me!"

"Well told," said Charles Arundel, laughing. "What then?"

"The troops of both sides marched back to Genoa together and paraded through the streets as the crowds cheered. Have you ever seen an Italian marching?" Edward got up from the table, pulled his plumed cap down slantwise and, pacing alongside the table, caricatured a leisurely, devil-may-care Italian soldier with a glass of wine in his hand, throwing kisses to the crowd. The surrounding habitués, who had been listening to the tale, laughed and clapped. Edward bowed and sat down. The show was over.

Raleigh shook hands around the table and excused himself. "Men from Dover can handle only so much caviar but I did enjoy the Genoese ham!"

Edward stopped drinking and let the others dominate the lighthearted interchange.

After an hour, Henry said, "Let's go to my place. I've invited a few friends over."

The six of them rode along the river through London to Westminster and along the Strand to the old Hospital of St. Mary de Rouncival near Charing Cross. Henry had shrewdly wangled the hospital, a place of hospitality for the needy, from the Queen and was changing it into a magnificent mansion.

Henry led them up three flights and along dark hallways to the rear of the building. Through a closed door came the sound of a man's deep reverberant voice chanting. Edward and the others walked into the improvised chapel. Candles were set on a white damask-covered table along with a gold crucifix, gold patens, a holy chalice and a bowl of lilies. Fastened to the dark paneling above was a marble crucified Christ.

A Jesuit priest sat at a spinet striking the faint chords accompanying his fine voice. In the shadowy room sat a group of Edward's acquaintances: Henry Percy, Earl of Northumberland, Anthony Browne, and John Lumley.

Edward, in a mellow mood, was swept with the beauty of the music and the shining symbols. He dropped to one knee and silently prayed. Charles Arundel gave Henry Howard a congratulatory look.

The young singing priest was lost in his music. He moved from song to song, explaining as he went along, seeming to direct his words toward the figure of the pendant Christ rather than his audience.

After the music the priest moved to the altar for mass. He intoned the Kyrie eleison and the Gloria as if he were offering every word as an oblation.

When he reached the ceremony of the Elevation of the Host, Edward found himself deeply emotional. His spiritual self seemed to be reaching out for the time-honored comfort of the old established Mother Church.

John Lumley held the breviary with him. At first Edward murmured the words quietly but gradually he began repeating the fine old Latin phrases with full resonance and commitment.

The service ended, and Father Leo came to him with hands extended. "Welcome, my son."

Edward rode home after midnight, wondering what it mattered that this was a Catholic group. After all, God the Father, Son and Holy Ghost belonged to all men. The Church of England had broken away not because of different beliefs of faith but for

TR

mundane reasons of divorce, financial greed and termination of Vatican control.

How could it be construed a heresy to turn away from sterner, less-forgiving Protestantism and return to all of the warmth, color and compassion of the old religion? Wasn't Catholicism the religion of all of his noble and heroic ancestors except his father, who had loyally changed to the Church of England immediately after Henry VIII founded it?

What harm could possibly derive from the spiritual beauty of private worship in association with those who were sincerely religious?

Chapter 25

How many ages hence
Shall this our lofty scene be acted over,
In states unborn and accents yet unknown!
       - Julius Caesar

Edward found considerable solace and a warm candle-lighting of the darkness of his personal worries by attending private Catholic services with his friends, including Thomas Sackville and Ned Somerset. He read books of Catholic doctrine loaned to him by Father Leo. He studied his Geneva Bible, covered with maroon velvet and decorated with a silver boar engraving, underlining and annotating it for future use in his plays. He considered confirmation but hesitated to go against the Church of England with the Queen as its head.

Financial worries continued to plague him. The huge unjust fine imposed by Henry VII upon the Thirteenth Earl of Oxford for having too many men in liveried service was a small amount compared to Burghley's continuing thefts of his lands and income. By law, wardships were supposed to end at age twenty-one. Edward had filed the required petitions with the Court to free himself and his lands. Burghley, however, for reasons of personal greed and against the laws of England, used his power as head of the Court of Wards to block it.

Edward began to ruminate about his father-in-law. He found it difficult to forgive Burghley for refusing to pay him the promised dowry of 10,000 pounds. Burghley had said that the gift of his daughter was quite sufficient. Edward knew that Burghley accepted large bribes—up to 6,000 pounds in one instance—from foreign suitors of the Queen and worked late every night processing up to a hundred lucrative petitions for favors, land or jobs.

Edward had heard Burghley say several times that nobility is nought but ancient riches and he was gobbling up the riches of others faster than any man in English history. Edward knew that Burghley grumbled and mumbled in Parliament about evaders of taxes on goods and services but, despite an official salary of 4000 pounds and illegal income in excess of 50,000 pounds, he stated his income year after year, for the historical record, as 133 pounds, six shillings and eight pence.

Edward was quite aware that Burghley's Machiavellian approach allowed him to act contrary to morality, personal feelings or religious faith according to the intended goal. After the unexpected and unexplained death of his first wife, hadn't Burghley soon married the stern Mildred Cooke to place himself strategically in the inner circle of the boy-King, Edward VI? Hadn't this resulted in his becoming, at age twenty-eight, the youngest Principal Secretary in England's history?

Edward felt grudging admiration for the tenacity with which Burghley reaped his riches by maintaining his good grace with the Queen. Through hard work and good judgment, he had gained Elizabeth's complete trust. Although Burghley was not an original thinker, he was an excellent councilor, the best option-analyzer in England. The ultimate political realist, he was feared by associates and enemies alike. No distinction need be drawn between truth and lies. Only the end result mattered; details would be provided by himself and his personal librarian.

Even though anyone who stood in his way was ruthlessly suppressed or eliminated, Edward realized that Burghley's meticulously selected and altered files would guarantee his place in history. It occurred to Edward that while the malice in Burghley's heart and his unending guilty deeds might be unknown to most of his contemporaries, they could not be hidden from the sight of God. He wondered how long they would remain invisible to the eyes of history. He wrote in his tablet:

> *Now in his mouth he carries pleasing words,*
> *Which pleasing words do harbor sweet conceits,*
> *Which sweet conceits are limed with sly deceits.*

Elizabeth had loaded down Robert Dudley and Christopher Hatton with estates, palaces and trading monopolies and had allowed Burghley to accumulate immense landed wealth, although Edward was certain that the Queen did not know how much.

Wasn't Edward one of her favorites? Why hadn't a single penny come his way?

To save money, Edward closed up Oxford Court and moved to a small house in Charing Cross. He tried to concentrate on writing but found his mind too frequently distracted by courtiership, repetitive pleas from Burghley to get back together with Anne and create an heir, and Henry Howard's interruptive social invitations.

Edward was in a creative mood and decided that he must find privacy. He rode the forty miles to the invigorating isolation of Wivenhoe and spent his days writing in his study-tower overlooking the peaceful meandering River Colne.

First he completed *The Historie of Error,* which he had begun at Malcesine and now sub-titled *The Comedy of Errors* . It was set in Ephesus and all the action took place in a few hours. The humor derived from the tortuous twists of mistaken identities and illusion.

Against Serena's strong advice, he included himself and other real people in the play. Edward believed that any playwright who deliberately chose to describe his times must scrutinize himself at least as critically as others. If the character flaws outweighed the strengths, so be it.

Edward realized all too well that he sometimes drank too much wine and exaggerated stories. At times he was filled with overwhelming anger and need for vengeance, self-justified by feudal codes of honor. He was often too proud, critical, cynical and overly quick with biting verbal commentary. He'd spent enough time alone to understand the inner workings of his own self and had comfortably reached the conclusion that he, like most men, was half sinner and half saint.

Edward decided to change his money worries into a positive force by writing *The Life of Timon of Athens,* briefly mentioned in Plutarch's *Life of Mark Antony* . He recalled commentary by Plautus: "On anyone's financial status hangs his status with his friends. If he is in a solid financial condition, his friendships are sound; once that state begins to waver, his friends waver likewise."

Sailing alone one day down the Colne past sheep quietly browsing along its banks, he gradually visualized an entire play based upon this theme. He decided to praise the one servant who remained true to Timon and the three common thieves honest enough to practice openly their chosen trade. He compared the unjust hanging every year in England of over 800 lower-class citizens for petty thievery to the hidden never-punished stealing and legalized murder by politicians.

Edward was satisfied with his writing. He believed his words were flowing more smoothly, more meaningfully and with increasing relevance. He felt happy and decided that contentment depended upon inner wisdom, love of life, opportunities for reaching one's potential, and appreciation of nature's abundant beauty. He decided to defer a decision on romantic love until he understood it better.

He remained at Wivenhoe another six weeks polishing his plays, writing poetry and trying to regain the equanimity he had achieved during his travels.

He rode back to London, where he began to get excited about what was happening in the world of the stage. James Burbage, a former outstanding actor and now the moving spirit of dramas played in tavern-inn courtyards, became upset by the Lord Mayor's proclamation against further performances within London's confines. The Mayor had given in to the pressures of constant Puritan haranguing such as:

Playes are the inventions of the devil, the offrings of idolatrie, the blossomes of vanitie, the roote of apostasy, the foode of iniquitie, ryot, and adulterie. Players are masters of vice, teachers of wantonnesse, spurres to impuritie. Detest them. Loathe them.

Edward was proud of the response by Burbage which was to construct The Theatre in 1576, the first genuine house for plays in England, situated a mile beyond London's walls and thus out of the Mayor's jurisdiction. Soon the ambitious Burbage bought land from the Curtain family and built a second theater nearby, The Curtain. In this invigorating atmosphere Edward created his own company of actors known as Oxford's Players, which he trained and sponsored.

Edward requested an audience with the Queen to discuss his writing. He found her furious, wearing a broad red dress with enormous puffed-up pink sleeves. He wondered why women spent so much time trying to make themselves alluring and ended up as perfumed hippopotami.

"What foul beasts, those Spanish!" she fumed. "How can Philip claim he is a man of God doing God's work?" She took off a shoe and hurled it against the wall.

"Please tell me the cause of your disturbance, Your Majesty," Edward said in a soothing tone.

"'Tis another massacre like St. Bartholomew's Day four years ago. Spanish troops entered Antwerp, plundered and destroyed it, and abused and slaughtered thousands of people all in the name of Christianity!" She bent down her large linen ruff and spat on the floor.

"For what reason?"

"Perhaps to vent frustration over the city's long resistance. God's Passion! I, and England, should do something about it. We are not nearly ready for war but I think now is the time to begin preparing our people's minds for armed conflict."

She paused, and her eyes fixed on his. "Edward, I want you to write a play which will fill our people's minds with the horrors which derive from fanaticism."

He lifted an eyebrow. "Disguise it, yet make sure the audience will equate it with the Spanish fury? That will be new for me."

"Indeed it will," she agreed. "Edward, I find that I am beginning to think of you not only as the Court's main entertainer but also as our chief propagandist. It is time to soar, Edward!"

* * *

Utilizing his intimate knowledge of Ovid, Edward borrowed from *Metamorphoses* the rape and bloody torture of Lavinia. He set his play in Rome and titled it *The historye of Titus Andronicus* . He described the savage mutilation of Lavinia:

'Twill vex thy soul to hear what I shall speak;
For I must talk of murders, rapes, and massacres,
Acts of black night, abominable deeds,
Complots of mischief, treason, villanies . . .
They cut their sister's tongue and ravish'd her,
And cut her hands, and trimm'd her as thou
saw'st.

Speak, gentle niece, what stern ungentle hands
Hath lopped and hewed and made thy body bare
Of her two branches, those sweet ornaments
Whose circling shadows kings have sought to
sleep in .

Titus Andronicus was tried out at The Boar's Head innyard and then staged at Whitehall by Oxford's Players with Edward acting the lead role.

"Marvelous job, Edward," said Elizabeth. "Now you must play it at The Theatre and The Curtain and form road companies to reach cities and towns all over England. If war I must, the people must be eager for it and request it of their Queen."

Both Edward and Elizabeth were exhilarated that audiences all over England were appalled and did identify the horror with Spanish cruelty.

Thus, thought Edward, plays are becoming a political instrument at the monarch's behest. More importantly, drama is being freed from its bondage and low-status vagabondage and elevated by a forward-looking Queen into a respected medium of informational dispersion, intellectual enlightenment and cultural enhancement.

Could this be, he wondered, *the beginning of England's artistic awakening?*

Chapter 26

Conception is a blessing but not
as your daughter may conceive.

— Hamlet

Edward began to feel the curious pangs of loneliness as the Christmas season of 1577 approached.
When, therefore, that staunch old friend of his family, Kate Willoughby, Duchess of Suffolk, invited him
to her house for dinner and a winter's afternoon of
talk, Edward accepted gladly.

Edward thought of Kate as a great and lively lady,
the daughter of Lord Willoughby d'Eresby and a
Spanish lady-in-waiting of Henry VIII's first wife,
Katherine of Aragon. Her second marriage was to
Richard Bertie, learned and charming but not noble.
Their son Peregrine had just become betrothed to
Edward's sister Mary.

Kate sat at one end of the table, her black Spanish eyes flashing, her conversation sparkling.

Peregrine was handsome, mustachioed and brown-haired, reserved in manner but with a merry sense of humor. He responded well to Mary de Vere's lively nature and theirs was a true love-match. Mary was comely, not beautiful, with blue eyes and the same auburn-tinted hair as Edward, and a mind adorned with learning. She was outspoken and quick-tempered but, in her newfound happiness, had become quieter and more deferential.

Kate's Puritan chaplain, Robert Brown, sat on her right in black robes. His face reminded Edward of a sucked-in dried apple as he maintained his effigy of remonstrance. He often injected a firm reminder of God's constant watchful presence and gave frequent advice that hell could only be avoided by subjecting every aspect of life to strict New Testament morality.

He was enough to push a person, thought Edward, straight into the realm of all the jolly friars that ever found joy in the Lord's company.

"And as for this wedding," declared Reverend Brown as wine and sesame cakes were being served at the end of a six-course meal, "I most earnestly entreat you to consider a ceremony stripped to its essentials."

"That will surely be included in the festivities in due course," put in Edward with mock solemnity, as Mary's cheeks reddened.

"Yea forsooth, marriage is a license of the flesh, sanctioned only for the continuation of God's unfortunate creatures. The physical exercises of love must never be indulged in, save for the purposes of perpetuation."

"Totally logical," said Edward. "Once a marriage for one child, thrice for three! An incredible saving of national energy!" Edward and Peregrine both laughed as Mary searched for a lost handkerchief.

"By yea and nay, God save you, it is no matter for jesting," Brown said coldly. "I see that you banter. Is it not unseemly to gather a goodly crowd that all may gape and say: 'Behold, two hours hence these two will lie abed together, flesh overlapping flesh?' Nay! A thousand times, nay! Let them go quietly to a Justice, lay hands on the Holy Book and promise faithfulness unto death."

"And eternal chastity," interrupted Edward, who felt that the chaplain fulfilled all criteria of a motley-minded, prating minimus.

"And come away married," continued Brown, with a level voice but a withering look at Edward. "No foul Popish ring, no bell of Satan, no veil of vanity, no flaunting candles, nothing but pure spirit joining pure spirit."

"Oh, Reverend, that might be well for angels but not for carnate beings," said Kate, darting a look of mingled reproof and amusement at Edward. "Shall we move to the drawing room?"

"Your Grace," said the chaplain, "I have writing to do and, as this is a family gathering, I now thank you and beg to take my leave. But one final word: For your own sake and God's, hold firm against the devil!"

"Yea, yea, forsooth," said Edward to Peregrine and Mary as they walked into the drawing room, "take your leave to the farthest off-shore rock of uninhabited England and live in ecstatic happiness with the bleak blackness of your thoughts and prayers. And may the wet gloom of darkness fall upon ye and a virgin seagull keep thee company!"

All three laughed loudly.

Kate entered the room laughing at the laughter. "Edward the incorrigible, the dagger-thrower, the wit-hurler, how can I take you into my family? I know now why the Queen calls you her allowed fool! Your jocularity is fun and contagious but some of it might best be saved for The Boar's Head!"

"You have an ample sense of humor yourself," answered Edward, "when the chaplain isn't around! Veres and Berties should make a laugh-filled mating, yea forsooth, one hopes more than just a witty mating!" Edward and Peregrine laughed. Edward rarely refrained from laughing at his own jokes—an inborn trait difficult to suppress. Why restrain it, he felt, when one's own laughter brings forth laughter in others?

Mary and Peregrine sat on a cushioned bench near the fire, holding hands. They make a charming enough pair, thought Edward, content as two cooing doves nestled on a perch. A servant passed honeyed pastries and small gold cups containing a sweet Italian almond liqueur.

"This liqueur penetrates to the very center of my aromatic soul," Edward said. "It must have been blended by Titian or Tintoretto."

The room became silent, settling into a new mode after the verbal parry and thrust provided by Puritanical prudery. Kate hesitated, then broke the silence.

"I hope this does not embarrass you, Edward, but you are among close admiring relatives and friends. What is the current status of your publicly unacknowledgable son?"

The question settled him into a reflective mood. "He is two and a half years old." He could scarcely believe that so much time had passed since Henry's birth. "He has green eyes, orange hair and a very appealing personality. He lives in a noble household. I am allowed to visit him whenever I want but no public hints as to his true parentage are allowed."

"Few in higher echelons don't know the truth," said Kate.

Edward nodded solemnly. "In this generation, yes. But by the next, the truth will be forgotten."

"Do you see anything of yourself in him?" asked Mary.

"Just a few minor traits such as keen sense of humor, stunning intellectual precocity and irresistible charm!" Although Edward joined in the laughter, he felt a brief gut-wrench of inner loss.

"Richard and I were going to stage a surprise for you by brightening up our home during these days of Christ-tide with a special guest," Kate said.

"Christ-tide?" asked Edward.

"My dear Edward, you would not say Christ-mass, would you? That would be Popery indeed!"

"Good word-origin! Who was your special guest going to be?"

"Your daughter, Lizbeth. But then we had second thoughts."

Edward's eyes went wide with surprise. "I would have had third and fourth thoughts, as well!" He offered Kate a thin smile. "But open discussion is vastly preferable to behind-the-back taunting with contemptible cuckold signs. Why did you decide against it?"

"Because of what Peregrine learned while carrying out your requested investigation." She turned to Peregrine. "Have you told him yet?"

Peregrine got up and stood before the fire under a large portrait of Henry VIII as a handsome young king with hands on his hips. "I found what I think you suspected, Edward. There is no birth certificate for Lizbeth. Two whole pages of the birth register are missing—one for July and one for September."

"So the only record is in Burghley's personal diary for July with a copy in his own handwriting in his permanent files, which I have seen," said Edward, shaking his head. "Thus history is made and documented."

Kate sipped her liqueur contemplatively. "I am aghast to hear how powerful politicians change history so deftly and so routinely. What can one believe? Did William the Conqueror's victory at Hastings really occur? Caesar's invasion of England? One wonders."

"Did any of you see Anne between March and late September last year, or see her with the baby in July or August?" asked Edward. A phrase formed in his brain: *Maiden virtue rudely strumpeted* .

"I know for a fact," answered Kate, "that she was at Theobalds the entire time. No visitors were allowed nor was anyone invited to the baptism which took place on September twenty-ninth."

"Almost three months after Burghley says Lizbeth was born on July second! Doesn't Burghley feel constrained to follow his own law, backed by the Church of England, requiring baptism in a parish church before a baby is one month old or punishment will ensue?"

"Apparently not," answered Kate. "Although all other Cecil babies followed that law."

Edward frowned. "The circumstantial case is substantial that Lizbeth was born eleven months after I last was with Anne in October."

"But . . . it seems so unlike Anne," Mary said.

"But very much like her father," Edward said. "Burghley must surely have worried that I might die of some strange disease while overseas. Then my estates would have belonged to you, Mary, and not to the Cecils—a thought which our eminent robber-baron couldn't tolerate."

Silence ensued and hung in the air until Peregrine broke it hesitantly. "So . . . you're saying that Burghley . . . *arranged* for Anne to become pregnant?"

Edward's mind had already made the painful journey through Burghley's tangled motives and possible actions. Anne's most favorable quality was the purity of her thoughts, free from malice, which is why Edward could not believe she was primarily responsible for Lizbeth's conception by someone other than her husband.

"God knows who the real father is," he said. "Perhaps Anne herself doesn't know. Unstained thoughts do seldom dream on evil. My suspicion is that Anne, whose trust in her father is complete, simply followed his commands and allowed herself to be inseminated in the anonymous darkness of night by an impregnator of Burghley's choice. But, considering the necessity for familial resemblance, I fear there are other even worse alternatives. . . ."

A stunned stillness penetrated the room as they sipped their liqueur and pondered the possibilities.

Finally Mary cleared her throat and asked, "How will you treat Lizbeth?"

"If Anne and I ever get together again, I will treat Lizbeth like an adopted child, with all the love and affection I can muster. It is not the child who is illegitimate. It is the parents."

Chapter 27

She speaks poniards and every word stabs:
if her breath were as terrible as her terminations,
there were no living near her; she would infect
to the north star.
- Much Ado About Nothing

"I am trying so hard to be a good wife for you," Anne said plaintively. "Please tell me what you want me to do."

She and Edward sat in the formal living room of recently re-opened Oxford Court, with four large gold-framed portraits of Earls of Oxford looking down on them. The oak floor was darkstained. A harpsichord made in Antwerp stood in the corner. The tall windows were hung with deep purple drapes and a fire blazed within the black marble fireplace.

Anne sat with knees tight, hands in her lap, looking at him with red-rimmed eyes as she waited for his answer. Edward was saddened by her helplessness, which he tried to view sympathetically as the result of completely dominating parents.

Finally yielding to Burghley's entreaties, Edward had agreed to live with Anne again on a trial basis. It was December, 1576, almost eight months since his return from his travels. They had been married for five years but had spent little time together.

"Just be yourself, Anne," he said gently. "A person can't daily change his or her character in order to please someone."

"We seemed to be such good childhood friends," she said, as if she had not heard. She shifted position in her chair frequently. Anne's face was sad and glum, her lonely sorrows having taken all the livelihood from her twenty-year-old cheeks, now further attenuated by a Puritan sieve of gloom. Her religious beliefs, obtained from her rigid, dour, unsmiling mother, often conflicted with his spontaneity and zest for life.

He got up from his chair and warmed his hands over the fire. "Our childhood remembrance is different, Anne. The six-year difference in our ages made close friendship almost impossible as children. After I was forced to move to Cecil House at the age of twelve, I merely tried to be kind to you."

"I was forced into our marriage as much as you were, Edward. I thought I was too young and you were too smart, too bookish and of too lofty a background." She shifted her legs restlessly.

"Your father insisted that young people should obey the choice of their all-wise elders and that love inevitably comes drifting down from heaven." He paused, and turned to face her. "But you know very well that your father had other motivations."

Anne's cheeks flushed. "You seem to blame my

father for everything! He works day and night for the Queen and for England."

"And his jobs pay him very handsomely!" he retorted. "He will soon be England's richest man! Look at his mansions. Where do you think the money comes from? He is sucking the lifeblood out of my lands and those of his other wards. He now owns many of my estates under false names."

Putting her hands together as if in prayer, she said, "Oh, Edward, please be good to my father and mother. They both like you. They just don't understand you."

Edward looked directly into her innocent eyes. "Is that why your mother was heard to wish me dead and why your father has set spies on me for many years, including on my travels?"

"Spies?" She looked genuinely astonished. "That can't be true, Edward. Why would he spy on you?"

"Why not ask him? He knows almost everything I say or do. I suspect he uses you as a spy, doesn't he?"

"Of course not! That's a monstrous idea!" She folded her arms across her chest tightly and crossed her legs. He thought how ludicrous she appeared. It was as if she had turned into a sealed box.

Edward walked to the window and looked out at the steady downpour. Although he theoretically agreed with Euripides that among mortals second thoughts are best, he often found it difficult to suppress his first thoughts.

"Let us pursue it further," he said, turning again to face her. "After we are together, doesn't he casually ask you what we talked about, what my beliefs are and with whom I am spending my time?"

"Yes," she admitted with a quick dismissive flick

of her hand. "But that is because he is interested in you as his son-in-law."

"And do you tell him about such private matters?"

"Yes, Edward, of course. He is my father."

Edward walked the room, hands clasped behind him. "Then what's the difference between you and a spy? Did he ever mention to you the mysterious disappearance of my marriage contract with Mary Hastings?"

Anne's pupils dilated. She sat upright in her ornately carved walnut chair and gripped the armrests. "What? What marriage contract?"

"You mean your ennobled father did not share that information with his doting daughter? Since childhood, Mary and I had a completely legal marriage contract. Each of us had to agree to marriage to make it valid."

"You had a choice?" There was bitterness in her tone.

"Yes. Following the contract's requirements, we became secretly engaged in 1568 when I was eighteen. In early 1571, after my repeated requests for military service and travel were turned down by your father and the Queen, we agreed to marry that Christmas."

Anne stared in shocked disbelief. "Before our marriage was arranged?"

"Several months before. Your father found out and soon thereafter I was forced to marry you against the laws of England."

The wrath-kindled thought occurred to him that Burghley was a fox in stealth, a wolf in greed and a lion against his quarry. Edward felt certain that Henry Hastings was appointed President of the North at the instigation of Burghley to keep Henry—and his knowledge of the marriage contract—away from the Queen. And what of the family friend to which his father had entrusted the third copy of the contract? Bought off by Burghley, too, no doubt. The bitterness of personal bile burned like acid inside Edward.

"You were forced to marry me?" Anne asked. "How was that accomplished if it was illegal?"

Edward set his jaw. "By the only way possible. On direct orders from the Queen. She is the law."

Anne turned and stared into the fire. "Is that why you disappeared at the time of our planned September wedding?"

"Of course!" he said impatiently. "Why don't you ask your father about all of this? I have many faults but you know I always tell the truth! *Vero Nihil Verius.*"

On the subject of truth, he nearly broached the question of Lizbeth's paternity. Then he closed his mouth tightly and decided that veracity was an unlikely outcome. Anne had previously answered such questions with red-cheeked silence, severe anxiety, or feigned offended pride.

Over the next few weeks Anne, as instructed by her father, pleaded with Edward to give love a chance. She frequently came to his room at night so they might create a de Vere son.

She did admit that her father had hemmed and hawed awkwardly when asked about spying and the Hastings contract. She told Edward it was the first time in her life that she had any reservations about her father's truthfulness.

Over a period of time, their relationship slowly began to mellow and improve. He began to enjoy her company as she relaxed and allowed her finer qualities to emerge.

But Edward had difficulty coping with the harsh

views of Lady Mildred Cecil who reminded him of Reverend Brown. She saw the world as a perpetual conflict between Biblical moral correctness and wickedness. Inevitable dis-ease and turmoil followed in her wake. When visiting Oxford Court, she saw grievous sin in Giulio Romano's lusciously wanton banquet scene from *The Loves of Psyche,* muraled so impressively in the Palazzo Ducale in Mantua that Edward had it copied and hung as a painting on his study wall.

She was even more horrified by a miniature Roman statue of a rollicking nymph and satyr. "It is bad enough having to put up with such an invasion of intimate privacy in order to create children," she stated during a visit. "But to display it publicly in the sanctity of your home ensures you the everlasting fires of hell."

Edward had no doubt that her facial tartness would sour ripe grapes. He wished that his horse had the speed of her tongue. "I will gladly drape in black all murals and statues, Lady Mildred, even the whole house prior to your visits, if that would please you."

"If that is the entirety of your vaunted sense of humor, you should drape yourself in black!" she shot back instantly. "The unsullied taintlessness of our Puritan beliefs can withstand your Bohemian attack, my very immature Lord Edward!"

Ah, what thorny stings are in your mildest words, thought Edward, *like an overly sharp sauce leaving the biting aftertaste of rue. Yet what rich writing material you do provide!* Although she had several virtues and had treated him with tact, consideration and hospitality as an adolescent, Mildred was now sour and sullen.

"But surely, Lady Mildred, should not a private home rightly reflect the beliefs and personality of the owner and be protected against any form of intrusionary attack?"

"As poor Tom Bricknell well found out!" She stood abruptly. "Let us go, Anne. It is time for you to return home to religious and domestic peace. A sow's ear never made a silk purse, nor a boar's tusk the key of a spinet to make sweet music."

Anne and Lizbeth returned to Cecil House to live.

At Court a few days later, Edward saw Mary Hastings, now a maid of honor and as handsome and dignified in demeanor as in face and form. He mentioned to her his conversations with Anne.

Mary sighed. "It is all behind us now, Edward."

"I've heard that your brother Henry has returned from the North on a visit."

She nodded. "I will see him tomorrow."

Mary was right, Edward told himself. It mattered little now, for the past was pervaded with too much acrid sadness. Yet he could not resist saying, "When you see your brother, ask him about our marriage contract and why he never produced it."

*   *   *

Edward decided to try out *The Historie of Error*—begun at Malcesine, worked upon in Vulcano, and completed at Wivenhoe—in the central courtyard of The Boar's Head tavern. He then presented it before the Queen at Hampton Court on January 1, 1577. In addition to directing it, he played the role of the Duke of Ephesus.

On February 17, 1577, he staged his play about Timon of Athens, *The Historie of the Solitarie Knight,* at Whitehall Palace. A special platform was constructed at one end of the great hall, with members of the court sitting on tiers of seats along the walls. For lighting, a large chandelier was partially lowered over the stage and lowered even further between acts for candle-trimming.

The Queen sat on a tapestried dais in the middle of the hall. Wearing her jasmine-scented Venetian gloves and a necklace of emeralds, she sat enthralled by the lovely wording and simple moral message. The Court enthusiastically congratulated Edward.

Two days later, on Shrove Tuesday, he directed and played the lead in *The historye of Titus Andronicus* at Whitehall.

At Elizabeth's suggestion, James Burbage eagerly agreed to have the three plays featured in repertory at The Theatre and The Curtain.

Edward continued to act in *Titus* and in *Error*, as well as attend to his duties as courtier and as Elizabeth's favorite.

The Queen finally told him, "Edward, you look exhausted. It is past time for you to take a well-deserved vacation. Then you can start writing plays for the next Christmas season, including one new play set in England."

"A vacation? But . . . Your Majesty, I dislike wasting time."

Elizabeth rubbed her hands together and took a deep breath. "I am increasingly excited by your inborn poetic talent and genius for words. You are now combining your gifts in a dramatic form which can and will touch the hearts and minds of all classes of English people."

"You are most kind, my Queen."

Elizabeth walked over to the wall of her privy chamber and looked reflectively at a portrait of herself at the age of thirteen adorned with pearls and

wearing an orange and red dress with intricate designs. She turned around slowly. "Oh, Edward, the
vast potential of your magnificent art form seems
unlimited! Your goals of aesthetic beauty and helping to lead England's artistic rebirth are merging into
my own long-held ambition for an illuminated and
culturally illustrious reign."

Full of thoughts, with hands clasped behind his
back, Edward walked slowly and pridefully to his room
in Whitehall. He felt that he and Elizabeth were both
ahead of their times and were among the very small
percentage of each generation who had a broader
vision, able to view their epoch from above.

Chapter 28

I know a bank where the wild thyme blows,
Where oxlips and the nodding violet grows,
Quite over-canopied with luscious woodbine,
With sweet musk-roses, and with eglantine.
- A Midsummer Night's Dream

Telling no one and following a misleading route to avoid Burghley's spies, Edward rode to his hilltop hideaway at Bilton near Rugby. He asked Wilfred and his wife, long-time family servants and caretakers, to fix all of his noon meals, keep the kitchen stocked with simple foods and bring in a good supply of firewood. Otherwise, he craved delicious aloneness.

Edward did nothing productive for a week. He slept long hours and rambled over the lovely countryside with its irregular hills, oak and elm forests, and rushing muddy Avon. He often postponed his daily walk until a heavy late April rain began, so he could see, hear and smell nature imbibing her abundant refreshment.

He loved the red brick simplicity of Bilton Hall which had come into the de Vere family through the fifteenth Earl's marriage to Elizabeth Trussel. The house had two wings, a steeply gabled shingle roof, tall square chimneys and a large garden extending down toward the river, bordered by brick walls to keep out wandering sheep. Flowers and herbs grew near the house, with orchards below. No fancy hedged-mazes or fountains, just a single birdbath and uncomplicated quiet beauty.

His mind washed clean, he began work on *A Morrall of the Marryage of Mynde and Measure,* which he had started in Malcesine. He enjoyed infiltrating his writing with falconry's special vocabulary, as by Petruccio describing his tactics in taming the resisting shrewish Kate:

> *My falcon now is sharp, and passing empty;*
> *And, till she stoop, she must not be full-gorg'd,*
> *For then she never looks upon her lure.*
> *Another way I have to man my haggard,*
> *To make her come, and know her keeper's call.*

Next he revised *The Historie of the Rape of the Second Helene,* the first draft having been written in Vulcano. He compacted his verses, improved their rhythm, and subtitled it *All's Well That Ends Well.* He included further topical references to current events and people.

He was increasingly convinced that to rise above short-lived Court entertainment, his plays must dramatize the fascinating strengths and weaknesses of human nature and also document the history of the times, both good and bad.

In the serene surround of Bilton, he finished the two plays in five weeks.

*   *   *

After sleeping late one morning, he sat shirtless on the sunny flagstoned verandah. It was now early May of 1578, and the oaks and elms were bursting with new foliage, the hawthorn trees in full blossom white.

"How lovely," said Mary Hastings, who had entered through an iron gate in the brick wall. "No wonder you love it so and find the peace and contentment here to create your poems and plays."

"Mary!" he exclaimed. "What a wonderful surprise!" He stood and feasted his eyes on her lovely 25-year-old dignity. To Edward her beauty was both real and mythological, part gracious human purity and part goddess-Aphrodite. He embraced her warmly and gave her an enthusiastic kiss. Their lips wore the familiar taste of comfortable harmony as she kissed him back and nestled her head against his neck.

"Oh, Edward, how many years I have dreamed of this, just the two of us with arms wrapped around each other, oblivious to all mankind! We should have been married almost six years by now, surrounded by little boy and girl de Veres, dogs and ponies!"

"A wonderful and much-desired fantasy which should have been reality. How did you find me?"

"You forget that I can put myself into that quirky head of yours. I waited a month and a half but the urge to be with you alone overpowered me, especially after I talked with my brother Henry. Ned Somerset,

'R

my sweetest brother-in-law, accompanied me to Rugby and made sure we were not followed, disguises and all!"

"I am eager to hear the details but first let's take your horses to the barn and carry your things into the house."

Back on the verandah a short time later, Mary continued. "I did as you asked, Edward. I cornered Henry one evening and asked him why he had never brought forward our marriage contract, especially when Cecil and the Queen were scheming against our love. He seemed reticent and embarrassed. I filled his wine glass until his tongue finally loosened."

"I think I know what's coming." He kissed her gently on the lips. Even with that brief kiss, he recognized the glimmering of Mary's long-suppressed passion and eager love. *Oh, what might have been!*

"Henry confirmed the contract's complete legality," she went on. "Three copies were made, one given to Judge Elliott Winchester of the Court of Chancery, one kept by your father, and one by Henry. When I told Henry that your copy had disappeared from your doubly-locked chest, he angrily threw his wine glass into the fireplace."

"Indeed! What happened then?"

Mary watched a hummingbird hover over a cuckoo flower. Her hand gently caressed a stray lock of hair that flirted with the temptation of her neck. Her composure regained, she continued. "He left the room for a few minutes, then returned and handed the contract to me. It read precisely as we had been told."

Although this was exactly as Edward had suspected, hearing it spoken aloud made his heart thump in his chest. "What else did he say?"

"The very day that he received word of Burghley's announcement of your betrothal to Anne, he quickly rode to the Court of Chancery. He told Judge Winchester that we were fulfilling the contract at once and asked if he would marry us within the week." She reached for Edward's hand and held it tightly. "Henry was going to seek your approval the next day."

"An excellent and courageous response!"

"The judge reluctantly admitted that Cecil had called upon him four years before, asking to borrow the marriage document for copying, since yours had been lost. Cecil later returned, apologized that his foolish librarian had accidentally destroyed the document, and asked if five hundred pounds would be sufficient to cover the loss. The judge was aware of Cecil's remorseless use of power and felt that he had no choice."

Edward felt the sudden heat of anger surge through him. He was not surprised that even Judge Winchester, one of his father's most trusted friends, had succumbed to Burghley's tactics. "And then?"

"Henry felt morally outraged and immediately rode to Cecil House. He confronted Burghley, who claimed he was completely unaware of any such contract and that you and his sweet Anne were a love-match which only the Queen could countermand."

"Good God! What a repulsive snake!" Edward leaped up and began pacing back and forth, kicking gravel off the path.

"Henry sought an immediate private audience with the Queen. I know you realize, Edward, that Henry's credentials for being monarch are quite possibly better than Elizabeth's. She sent out a message that she was too busy to see him. The very next morning, Henry was appointed President of the North, a prestigious post he still holds."

"By Jesu," exclaimed Edward, reaching his arms toward the sky. "What a vile insect Burghley is! Now it all becomes clear! No wonder that lad Tom Bricknell was scared out of his wits and his speech when I caught him going through my storage chest! He knew that Cecil would kill him if he told the truth and I would kill him if he didn't!"

"The poor lad was totally innocent."

"Burghley must have asked a locksmith to copy the keys to my chest, and later stole the document himself when I was at Gray's Inn studying law."

"I think we should keep this to ourselves, Edward," Mary said. "He has done far worse since. As a favor to me, please don't mention this again during my visit, even though it changed both of our lives so cruelly. My entire soul winces in pain when I think of it."

He lifted her up and embraced her. She put her head on his chest and they clung together in the silence of the room. "How long can you stay, Mary? I want you and need you."

"You know my feelings," she replied softly. "I can stay for several weeks but only if you make two promises to me."

He drew back and gazed into her eyes. "Pray tell, what are those?"

"Firstly, that you spend your usual daily hours writing."

He nodded. "And the other?"

"That we refrain from consummating our togetherness."

He drew her to him again. "I was afraid you'd say that. Not an easy promise to make, since I care for you so much."

"You know I have loved you since childhood, Edward. I have dreamed of being your wife ever since I was told of the contract when I was only eight." She kissed him softly on the lips. "But I want our love to be pure and untainted. If God allows us ever to be married, it will be more beautiful and meaningful this way."

He drew a breath and released it in a long sigh. "I accept your heartfelt wishes, Mary. You are my lady, and I am your chivalric knight. My love and respect for you continue to grow."

After their noon dinner, Edward suggested that she must be tired from her long trip. He guided her to his room and they took off their shoes.

"Now lie down with me and take a nap."

They stretched out together on the bed. Edward kissed her with tenderness, put his arms around her, snuggled into her body and they slept for an hour.

As they awoke, she rolled on top of him and kissed him with warm sleepy gentleness. Edward kissed her more forcefully and both felt his excitement growing. She put her arms around his shoulders and pressed downward into him, returning his kiss with greater ardor. She found her body beginning to move in its own rhythm.

"This is so new and so marvelous, Edward," she whispered. "I don't want to stop."

Edward put his hands on her buttocks and helped her move. She buried her face in his neck and concentrated all of her attention on her thrilling new feelings as the two of them moved in blended harmony.

"Oh, Edward. Oh, yes, yes!" She gripped him with her fingernails as she felt a rapture not experienced before. She held on tightly, lingered, and then reluctantly rolled off, breathing deeply. "Edward, that was thrilling! What glorious sensations, so ecstatic, so powerful."

He smiled. "And so natural, my love!"

"I feel so secure and peaceful with you, Edward, as if we had blended together all our lives." Then her eyes dropped. "But that was my fault for letting it happen. It's not fair to you, darling. You were so manly and strong, I just couldn't control myself. Please forgive me."

"I was thinking of you the entire time, Mary, thrilled to be able to share in this exciting new arena of your life. It was very exhilarating."

"I need distracting!" Her eyes lifted to his again, and now her smile had returned. "Let's do something we used to do as children at Hedingham. I remember so well lying in the soft grass with you on sunny days absorbing the beautiful surround, sometimes holding hands."

Edward returned her smile as a rush of love upwelled within him like a tidal surge. He felt overwhelmed with joy. "Let's play our old game, taking turns describing up to three aspects of nature—sight, sound, feel, taste or smell."

"Agreed!" They walked to the verandah. "You start," said Mary.

"Gentle breeze rippling birdbath and your goddess-like hair."

"Broken rule!" she admonished, laughing. "People are outlawed!" She paused to think. "Tiny yellow-green willow warbler fanning its wings and singing in cherry tree."

"He picked the leaves from two plants. Enticing spicy smell of thyme, strong and repugnant taste of rue."

"Tiny black spider with long legs running across hot tawny flagstone."

And so they went on happily. Edward finally smiled broadly and said, "Time to stop, Mary. We could go on forever in this sensory-filled island of quietude."

"That was fun, Edward." She hugged him. "We were happy carefree children again."

*   *   *

They spent the days roaming the countryside catching up on each other. Each evening, Edward asked Mary to join him in his room where they sat on the green settee in front of the fire and quietly talked, holding hands. He kissed her goodnight at the door between their rooms, each night with greater intensity. After a week, he changed into his velvet night robe and asked her to do the same.

"Why is watching fires never boring?" he wondered aloud.

"Perhaps it's the unpredictability of the flame," Mary said with a gentle breeze of laughter.

Edward turned to her. "I love you so, Mary. Adequate words escape me."

"I know your heart, dear Edward. But more importantly, I understand your inner soul." She kissed him fervently.

Edward added logs to the fire. They gently explored each other's fingers and sipped spicy hippocras.

"I want you closer to me, Mary. Could we sleep together in the same bed tonight?"

For a moment, she did not reply. Then with her eyes still on the dancing flame, she asked, "Can we restrain ourselves? If only you knew how much I want

all of you, Edward! I have had absolutely no experience with any man. I don't even know what men
look like when they make love."

Edward stood, removed his robe and was about
to remove his long white night-shirt when Mary's hand
stopped him.

"Please, Edward." Mary stood and embraced
him with gentle loving intensity. "Take off my robe,
darling, but leave the nightgown alone. Guide me
to your bed but please help us keep our bargain.
The beauty of our spiritual love will illuminate our
togetherness."

And so it did.

*   *   *

Edward and Mary walked barefoot alongside the
clear blue Avon on a warm June morning. He picked
up a small flat rock and skipped it across the water,
then joined Mary's hand in his and said, "It hardly
seems possible that we have been together for a
month."

A solitary kingfisher sitting on a nearby branch,
unaware of the beauty of its salmon-red belly and
greenish-blue wings, flew briskly downstream.

Edward led her to a favorite place of his. The
Avon swirled rapidly over shallow rocks; the bank was
covered with soft grass and brightly colored flowers.
A faint smell of wild thyme tanged the fragrant air. A
natural trellis of yellow and pink honeysuckle
dangled sweetly from overhanging black poplar
branches.

"Oh, Edward, it is so lovely! Why did you wait until
our last day to bring me here? I suddenly feel as if I
am being overwhelmed by nature's beauty and my

love for you." She pulled a honeysuckle to her, inhaling its fragrance and slowly fondling the leaves. She put her arms around him and kissed him fervently. She felt overcome by a force beyond her control and could not pull herself away.

Finally she stepped back, took in all the beauty around her, and gazed longingly at Edward's eyes as she took off all her clothes. She lay down among the flowers.

Edward disrobed, plucked a white musk rose, handed it to her and lay down beside her. They kissed eagerly and touched and explored and shared and loved . . . and forgot their promise. Edward guided Mary slowly and prolongedly along the exciting pathway of love. At the apex of fulfillment, Mary moaned loudly as she spasmed repetitively. She gripped him with trembling exhaustion until they fell asleep in each other's arms.

When they awoke, they made love again. Mary was astonished at the heights of intense excitement which resided within her, dormant for so long. She moved her lips but no sound came forth. In broken breaths she whispered, "I can't speak! My God, Edward, what unutterable glory!"

They lay intertwined for long minutes. Mary kissed him and stroked his hair softly. "Edward, you have brought forth new dimensions in me and have replenished my heart and soul. My dream of being your wife remains a dream but now I understand what beauty that would comprise. It greatly surpasses my reveries."

* * *

Leaving Bilton the next morning, they arrived at London's city wall three days later, exhausted but glowing with their newly magnified love. Edward gazed adoringly into her eyes, enfolded her tenderly and gave her a lingering kiss.

Mary pulled slowly away, then grasped his hands and kissed them. "Edward, our beautiful togetherness and exquisite intimacy must rest. We may enjoy our casual encounters at Court to the fullest degree but we must give up any thought of clandestine meetings. I do not want our love debased in any manner. In the meantime, I will feast upon delicious memories and give thanks to God for giving us these wonderful days and nights together. I shall never marry anyone else."

Chapter 29

There's language in her eye, her cheek, her lip;
Nay, her foot speaks. Her wanton spirits look out
At every joint and motive of her body.
                                  - Troilus and Cressida

One month later as he dined with the Queen in her privy chamber, Edward said, "To broaden and beautify our rather sparse English vocabulary, writers must be encouraged to experiment with language, then publish and disseminate their works." He sipped his beer and wondered whether water did, indeed, hinder digestion as the Court thought.

"I certainly agree. Continue." She picked up two roasted crabapples from a plate and dropped them into her goblet of weak ale.

"I plan to gather together and sponsor, financially and intellectually, a group of writers not only to produce plays but also to publish poetry and books of prose." Edward began to eat his pieces of lamb smothered in a thick spicy gravy.

"I wholeheartedly concur, my Turk," the Queen responded without hesitation. "I will encourage your plans to the best of my ability. As you know, your non-noble writing associates may publish using their own names. In your case, because of your very special proficiency and productivity, I will do everything in my power to find a way for you to publish your works with your name attached despite your noble rank."

"That would be my wish, Your Majesty. The concept of anonymity is odious abomination and totally incomprehensible."

"Also to me, Edward," she said as she ate her toast covered with scrambled egg yolks, finely chopped veal kidney, ginger, cinnamon and sugar.

He stared at her and wondered whether he should pursue it. She seemed in a good mood, an essential prerequisite before posing forthright questions to an absolute monarch who did not fulfill all of Plato's criteria for a Benign King. They had discussed this subject several times. She usually seemed sympathetic but no action had been forthcoming.

"Then why haven't you done something about it?" he asked boldly. He swirled his gooey fingers in rose water and dried them with a towel.

"In your case, I intend to, Edward. I do not want you to be anonymous! I shall not allow it! But Burghley and other nobles have strong feelings. I do not want to alienate them, especially at this critical time with the Spanish threat looming ominous."

"Other nobles? Burghley will always be a commoner to me, Your Majesty! He thinks I squander my time with useless poetry and drama whereas I find them mind-elevating art."

"I know. He is an excellent adviser but regards most art, music and creative writing as 'manual labor' and beneath the dignity of nobility. And most of the untalented upper class agrees, preferring to concentrate their talents on war and jousting. What nonsense! But tell me more about your writing plans, Edward." She suddenly fished a crabapple out of her goblet and popped it in her mouth.

Edward caught a transient glimpse of his own face on that crabapple. He cleared his throat. "Regarding the writing group I plan to assemble, official encouragement by the ruler is the *sine qua non* of artistic rebirth. Patronage is the second key to success, especially since most writers have no means of support. Might they ever count on your financial help?"

Elizabeth wiped her hands on the linen table cloth. "Not yet, Edward. But if your writing friends produce quality products, I will find funding."

Edward thanked her but was not fully reassured. He knew that unfulfilled promises were quite fashionable in Elizabeth's Court and wondered how many time-delaying excuses the Queen would find.

* * *

Since 1573, Edward had rented apartments in the old Savoy Hospital for Thomas Twyne and Thomas Watson, the two writers he was sponsoring. He now rented eight adjacent rooms on a long-term basis and remodeled two of them to serve as a conference room.

The Savoy, a place of shelter for the city's poor, was situated on the Thames in Westminster next to Ned and Elizabeth Somerset's manor house and across the Strand from high-turreted Cecil House.

Knowing Burghley's repeated comments about

his "lewd" friends, Burghley's synonym for "uneducated," Edward now began gathering a group of university graduates. He sought out 24-year-old John Lyly, the Archbishop of Canterbury's best copyist and patcher-and-joiner of old manuscripts. Lyly had two degrees from Oxford and a fledgling interest in writing. He was almost destitute and readily agreed to move into free lodging at the Savoy. Edward asked him to become his literary secretary.

Edward soon added Anthony Munday, also twenty-four, of facile wit and quill, and the flamboyant Robert Greene, red-haired and wild, only nineteen, from Cambridge and all taverns on the way to London.

"Gentlemen," said Edward on a windy September afternoon in 1577, "we are assembled here for the modest purpose of enlarging, complexifying and beautifying the English language. Our native tongue is too simple, arising as it did from our farms and fishermen, our hamlets and handymen, out of the linguistic quagmire of invading Angles, Saxons, Frisians, Jutes, Vikings and finally our charming Normans!"

"I'll drink to that," said Greene, lifting an imaginary glass.

Edward walked over to the small brick fireplace, turned and continued. "This is a noble and ennobling task, but a formidable one. Greek and Latin became enriched over hundreds of years through the eloquence of their poets, dramatists, orators and writers. We will try to accomplish this task by specific intent in a single generation. We have the complete encouragement of our many-languaged Queen. I will provide all necessary funds for lodging, food and drink."

"I'll drink to that!" cried Greene with a broad smile. "And I shall also remind you what Horace said, that no poems can please nor endure with vitality which are written by water-drinkers!" They all laughed.

"We are going to eat, sleep and breathe language," Edward continued. "We all have studied classical rhetoric. Initially I am asking you to dissect each principle from the new perspective of linguistic inventiveness. How can we challenge and change these traditional concepts to enrich our modern tongue? Each of us will lead a separate discussion on antithesis, alliteration, puns and dozens of other topics such as using adjectives as nouns and how to change nouns into verbs."

Outside, a sudden summer storm bounced hail off the windows. Lightning and shattering thunder interrupted the discourse.

"Even Zeus sends his loud heavenly approval!" Edward exclaimed. Everyone laughed as he continued, pacing back and forth in growing enthusiasm. "How are similes and metaphors contrived? Most importantly, how are entirely new words best created? Must they all be derived from Greek and Latin? Is it appropriate to birth them without antecedent?"

"I think I'm beginning to lose my thirst!" said Greene.

"There is no more fascinating task on earth! We will write our new constructions in such an intriguing manner that our readership will begin to use the new vocabulary. It is only through usage that words and new grammar become an enduring part of language."

"It sounds rather difficult," said Lyly. "An example or two might help."

"Indeed," Edward agreed. "Your request is *premeditated*—taken directly from the Latin *praemeditatus,* past participle of *praemeditare*—'to think upon before.' Another word which I recently derived is especially apt for this group: obscene—from *obscenus* meaning 'towards or about filth.' What could be simpler or more fun? English needed the words and now it has them!"

"I think it looks easier than it is," commented Anthony Munday a bit sullenly.

"New words respond to necessity or subtlety of thought. In Ovid's *Metamorphosis,* I introduced many new words, including heedless, hapless and pleasureless .

"I'm already beginning to feel hapless, helpless and hopeless!" added Munday. Greene slapped him on the back and laughed.

"One comment further," continued Edward. "You were chosen not only for your brains but also for your good fellowship and joy of life. As Aristophanes said, 'Birds of a feather, all together.' We will be living and working in a small space and must happily stimulate each other. A sense of humor is essential."

"What will we call ourselves before Burghley tests our linguistic skills on the rack?" asked Greene.

"Right on cue!" said Edward. "We are the Euphuists and our new art-form is Euphuism, from the Greek *euphyes,* meaning 'of good formative parts' or 'formed well.' We will structure our words well, creating elegance and eloquence of linguistic and literary style with sufficient flamboyance to excite people's imagination and get them using new words and word-combinations."

"May I pose just one question, Edward?" asked

Greene. "Are we now supposed to smile, applaud, groan or weep?" They all laughed.

* * *

After a year of diligent effort, they completed their first product, which Edward titled *Euphues: The Anatomy of Wit,* using the word *wit* in its original Danish and Frisian sense of intellectual prowess. Edward wrote and dictated most of the book himself, with significant contributions from Greene and Munday. Edward was unable to get permission to print the book under his own name so it was published as being *compiled* by John Lyly, who was the chief transcriber of the work but the meagerest contributor.

Edward requested permission to read excerpts to the Queen. For the occasion he wore an Italian padded purple doublet, a violet velvet cape and a small green oyster-shell cap set at a rakish angle.

When he arrived in the Queen's private chamber she was seated on a high tapestried chair. Behind her stood the four gentlewomen of the chamber wearing green hooped dresses, with the youngest dark-haired girl being dressed in ruby unhooped silk. Seated on cushions on the floor were her white-clad maids of honor. The scene reminded Edward of a Titian painting and he was briefly saddened by the memory of Titian dying at age 89 of the plague a year after Edward left Venice.

The Queen motioned Edward to a cushioned stool in the center of the semicircle.

"We understand that you wish to change the tongues of ten ladies tonight and then the speech of all women in England! A formidable task for our young Paduan troubadour. Our tongues twitch with anticipation. Please start, Viscount Verbally-Fearless!"

Edward began reading. "There dwelt in Athens a young gallant that deemed himself so apt in all things that he gave himself almost to nothing but practicing sharp wits, fine phrases, smooth quipping, and merry taunting, using jesting without mean and abusing mirth without measure."

As he read, he became aware of someone intensely gazing at him with dark eyes under her sharply arched black eyebrows. The girl in ruby silk smiled subtly, her sensitive lips parting slightly. She was handsome, not beautiful, but her face was keen and compelling. *Like a haggard*, thought Edward. She had high cheekbones, an aquiline nose, a narrow chin and dark hair piled high in a pyramidal coiffure. Edward could feel her pulsing esprit.

He continued. "Here my youth determined to make his abode: whereby it is evidently seen that the fleetest fish swalloweth the delicatest bait and that the highest soaring hawk traineth to the lure."

He read excerpts from *Euphues* for almost twenty minutes.

"That's enough for now, Your Majesty. Just a taste of a new style, a different approach to word usage."

"It's a bit fancy like your attire," said the Queen with a regal smile. "But it does appeal to my love of words and I hope it will begin to elevate the staid simplicity of our tongue. You have well and unusually entertained us." She turned to the girl in ruby silk. "Mistress Anne Vavasour, go fetch your uncle Knyvet and any available courtiers for some cards before retiring."

The girl arose and left the room, her walk supple and full of serpentine ripples.

When Edward bade goodnight and left, the girl, her deep cleavage amply bared, was standing at the outer door, her hand gently caressing the knob. She gave him a tantalizing smile.

· "So, 'tis Anne Vavasour, niece to Thomas Knyvet, cousin of Francis Southwell and to my own cousin, Henry Howard. Greetings, coz!"

Anne let her fingers slide sensuously off the door-knob, curtseyed and raised her head to a proud tilt. "Greetings to you, my Lord of Oxford, famed at Court for wondrous words and sabered satire. Were it better that I flee and perhaps seek safety with the Queen's bodyguard?" She smiled and curtsied again.

"I'll be your bodyguard with pleasure," said Edward, bowing.

"I'll choose my own body's protector," she countered. "*En garde*, sir! None shall keep my inner keep, save solely myself! Drawbridge is up!"

The words were a refreshing echo of Edward's own independence. He laughed heartily as he thought that there never had been an up-drawbridge that didn't eventually come down. "'Tis a gamesome lassie with a flame-quick tongue and spirit!"

"Whose embers are controlled with iron will!"

"May you fire my fancy and enflame my forge! Whence derives such swift and apt responses from one so young? Wide reading or tempered experience in the conflagrations of life?"

Edward saw his answer in her twinkling eyes and alluring head-tilt.

"When shall I see you again, Mistress Anne?"

"At the same moment I see you, my Lord!" With a high laugh and a quick look over her shoulder, she slowly ambled away.

As she reached the door, aware that Edward was

staring intensely at her, Anne chuckled to herself and thought that the highest soaring hawk doth indeed train to the lure!

Chapter 30

And now what rests but that we spend the time
With stately triumphs, mirthful comic shows,
Such as befits the pleasure of the court?
Sound drums and trumpets—farewell, sour annoy!
- Henry VI, Part 3

As the royal barge moved slowly upstream on a sunny morning in May, 1578, Elizabeth and Edward threw pieces of bread into the Thames. Several hundred white swans, forgetting their graceful appearance, fought viciously over the unexpected feast.

"Now, my Italianate Fantastico, I need your conversation, wit, sense of humor and sparkling courtiership on my Progress," the Queen said. "Is it meet that you be absent when I visit your own de Vere territory of Essex and Suffolk?"

Edward admired the richly canopied, silk-cushioned royal compartment and watched the ten black-and-white-clad barge rowers. "But Your Majesty, I believe I can make a greater contribution to England by writing than dancing!"

Elizabeth was singularly unfamiliar with the answer "no" to her requests. "Your Queen would appreciate your presence for the first six weeks. Then you may return to your writing and your University Wits. The Court missed your plays last season in your enthusiasm for Euphuism."

Edward knew he had no choice. His loyalty to the Queen hid any words of displeasure. "Of course, Your Majesty."

"And to show the Queen's gratitude for the success of your diplomatic work in Venice and Istanbul, and for the excellence of your plays, all of which reflect most well upon this Court, I give you this."

Edward opened up the scroll and read that she had granted him the Manor of Rysing and adjacent lands, yielding 250 pounds in annual rents. He suppressed the bitterness that welled up, since the previous owner had been his good friend and cousin, Protestant Tom Howard, Duke of Norfolk, beheaded by the Queen at the personal insistence of Burghley for considering a possible marriage with Catholic Mary, Queen of Scots.

But Edward accepted the award graciously. "That is a large sum of money for a writer of mere frivolity, Your Majesty, but your generosity will disburden a portion of my weighty financial concerns."

"I would only ask, Edward," she added, "that you write another play based upon English history to help infuse our people with increasing patriotic fervor."

* * *

Elizabeth used consummate skill to achieve the main purpose of Royal Progresses, which was to establish a personal relationship with the English people. This was especially important since she spent so much time sequestered in walled-off palaces. Progresses also relieved her treasury by forcing the nobility to host her very expensive Court of several hundred people for two to four months every year or two. She was not unmindful that wealth meant power. Reducing their excess wealth held nobles in check, decreasing chances of threats to royal authority.

In late June the Royal Progress approached the quaint and wealthy wool and weaving town of Lavenham in Suffolk, with its thatched daub and wattle houses, its cobbled streets and its many taverns. Its people and those from the entire area lined the road boisterously for a mile out from town.

In front of Lavenham's entrance gate was a forty foot wooden placard, its borders painted with scenes of sheep at pasture, sheep being clipped, and the several stages of wool being processed into cloth and shipped overseas. In large black letters in the center was inscribed:

THE CAUSES OF THIS COMMON-WEALTH ARE :
>   GOD TRULY PREACHED.
>   JUSTICE DULY EXECUTED.
>   THE PEOPLE OBEDIENT.
>   IDLENESS EXPELLED.
>   LABOUR CHERISHED.
>   UNIVERSAL CONCORDE PRE-SERVED.

The Progress was led into town by trumpeters and drummers, followed by black-robed Lord Treasurer

Burghley riding alone on his old sway-backed horse. He always requested that the Queen place him in the lead so he could protect her from any foul assassin.

Next came thirty mounted yellow-and-red-clad yeomen of the guard, each carrying a pike or musket. Forty gentlemen pensioners followed in long black cloaks and large white ruffs, their right hands holding the distinctive weapon of this honored noble bodyguard: a shining gilt battle-axe. The Queen rode in their midst.

White-dressed maids of honor rode by next, followed by the ladies in waiting, courtiers, nobles, then various royal servants, workers, and pages. Last came two miles of baggage-carts, pulled by horses and oxen, and over 2000 pack horses.

The mayor made a brief welcoming speech in poorly-pronounced Latin. The Queen answered graciously in English, saving her Latin for universities and larger cities. Her friendly tone and cheerful countenance put everyone at ease. She ended with: "I am visiting all of you, every person in this lovely town and all surrounding villages. Feel free to talk to me and tell me your problems and your wishes."

An elderly white-haired man tried to push through the pensioners saying, "Good Queen, I *must* talk with you today!"

The pensioners quickly crossed their battle-axes in front of him but Elizabeth immediately said, "Let him through! What is it, Mister Must, which is so important?"

"My name is Andrew, Your Highness. I am a shepherd. My granddaughter told me that if I didn't kiss your hand today, she would never hug me again!" The crowd laughed. Elizabeth put out her hand.

Andrew bent down on his knees and kissed it as the people cheered.

As the Court passed through the shire of Essex, when anyone shouted "God save the Queen," Elizabeth looked the citizen straight in the eye and answered, "Thank you, my good man" or "You're very kind, my good woman, I love you all." Disregarding her personal security, she often walked smilingly among the crowd, breaching the guards to shake hands and form a truly personal bond with her subjects.

Edward was filled with nostalgia, for this was the land of his illustrious ancestors. He guided the Queen through the elegant Church of St. Peter and St. Paul. The first Aubrey de Vere had initiated construction almost five hundred years before. The great Thirteenth Earl had beautified the clerestory with 108 brightly colored stained-glass shields depicting historical achievements of the de Vere family and allied nobles.

Surrounded by so many reminders of the accomplishful Vere heritage, Edward reviewed his life. A de Vere must first show his mettle with metal, with valor and courageous battle-deeds in defense of monarch and country.

For his non-existent achievements, Edward thought his great-great-grandfather might have given him a clear glass window in the clerestory for parishioners to watch ravens flying by. Or perhaps no glass at all—just the lead-surround, an empty space for an empty life.

*   *   *

A stag hunt the next day diverted his gloomy mood. When Elizabeth's usually trusty aim went awry and her arrow missed the full-antlered red deer, Edward brought it down with his arrow. He offered the Queen his knife for the ceremonial incision across the throat. She angrily grabbed the knife, straddled the animal and not only cut the throat but slashed open the entire abdomen and smiled with grim satisfaction as the bowels billowed out.

Edward was quick to note that the blood of the deer contrasted strikingly with the pale ivory of Elizabeth's skin. It was fascinating to watch as she briskly and without hesitation wiped the blood on her bright yellow dress. It was a reminder of her quick fury and her power of life and death over all of her subjects, both animal and human.

Edward knew that he and Elizabeth shared the traits of moodiness, easy anger and vanity. Their major differences lay in the realms of mendacity, deception, cruelty and power. But they shared many positives, including love of languages and words, quick humor and laughter, insight into human character, and intense pleasure in life. They blended well, each fueling and inspiring the other's best attributes and aspirations.

The last stop on the Progress for Edward was the mansion of Audley End and a visit with Sir Thomas Smith, Edward's first tutor at age three. Gabriel Harvey of the Cambridge faculty gave long welcoming tributary speeches in Latin to the Queen, to Leicester and to Burghley.

But Harvey reserved his most glowing praise for Edward:

"Thy splendid fame, great Earl, demands even more than in the case of others the services of a poet possessing lofty eloquence. Thy merit doth not creep along the ground. It is a wonder which reaches as far as the heavenly orbs.

Let that Courtly Introduction, more polished even than the writings of Castiglione himself, witness how greatly thou dost excel in letters. I have seen many Latin verses of thine, yea, even more English verses are extant. Neither in France, Italy nor Germany are there any such cultivated and polished men.

Thine eyes flash fire, thy will shakes spears. "

Edward looked down at the ground, feeling awkward over such compliments in the Queen's presence but, inwardly, he glowed with the praise. He wondered, *Be it a sin or a noble virtue to covet honor?*

Elizabeth also felt proud over this public affirmation of her most talented courtier.

*   *   *

Edward returned to the Savoy and his Euphuists full of newfound energy and optimism. He completed his unfinished plays and soon started work on a play based on the history of Cunobelinus, or Cymbeline, who reigned as King of Celtic Britain for thirty-five years beginning in 33 BC. Edward included a chastity-oriented plot from a tale by Boccaccio and topical references to contemporaneous historical events.

When writing, Edward emoted with his characters, sometimes crying when he described personal tragedy. He felt this was characteristic of great artists, which he was trying to be. Didn't Raphael weep when he painted his Madonnas? Didn't Michelangelo threaten his statues when they did not breathe?

He staged *An History of the Crueltie of a Stepmother,* the comic-tragic play about Cymbeline, before the

Queen and her Court at Richmond Palace, thirteen miles upriver from Whitehall Palace. Elizabeth appreciated the requested play based on English history, entirely captivated by the imaginative world of stage-drama, far removed from the cares of state.

Four days later, on January 1, Edward directed A *Morrall of the Marryage of Mynde and Measure,* the story of Petruccio's taming of his shrew, performed at Richmond by his acting group, Paul's Boys.

On January 6, he produced before the Court his third original play in ten days, *The Historie of the Rape of the Second Helene* with its sub-title of *All's Well That Ends Well* .

In early March, he staged at Whitehall *A Maske of Amazones and a Maske of Knights,* which he had started in Vulcano as *A Pleasant Conceited Comedie Called Love's Labour's Lost* . Edward had updated the play to include material from the recent Progress. He had rhymed almost half of the lines. He couldn't refrain from characterizing Thomas Knyvet, the haughty knight he had defeated in his first tournament and whom he detested. Knyvet was known for greeting the Queen's palace-guests with pretentious mannerisms and a smile too broad:

> *This fellow picks up wit as pigeons peas,*
> *And utters it again when God doth please . . .*
> *He can carve too, and lisp: why, this is he*
> *That kiss'd away his hand in courtesy;*
> *This is the ape of form, monsieur the nice,*
> *That, when he plays at tables, chides the dice .*

In late March, Edward staged *The History of Murderous Mychaell* at Whitehall, based upon a story in Holinshed's recently printed historical Chronicle describing the cruel murder of Arden of Feversham. Edward and his good friend Tom Radcliffe, Earl of Sussex, acted the leads.

After the performance, the Queen led Edward into the presence chamber. A heavy spring rain was harshly pounding the mullioned windows. Edward noted that the floor-reeds were old and rancid, and that some of the wall-bouquets were wilted.

Notoriously sparse in giving compliments except to Edward, the Queen said, "My Turk, I am rarely at a loss for words but your remarkable literary output and dramatic imagery quite overwhelm me and my Court."

Edward basked in the praise. He never ceased to appreciate the magnificent opportunity afforded him as a writer by having such a special intimate access to monarchy, royal Court and English government. He placed such a thought in the words of Posthumus in the Cymbeline play :

> Many dream not to find, neither deserve,
> and yet are steeped in favours;
> so am I, that have this golden chance
> and know not why.

He was aroused out of his reflections by a sudden brusqueness in the Queen's tone.

"Edward, the time has come to alter certain aspects of our relationship. I need you as Court dramatist and learned courtier, elevating the cultural level of my Court. I have enjoyed our happy intimate times together but they will now cease forever."

"Yes, Your Majesty," Edward said, trying to sound sorrowful. He knew well the Queen's attitude about carnal relationships. She was incapable of sustaining an endless physical relationship with any man, regarding it as feminine weakness.

As the Queen twirled her long double-stranded chains of pearls with fingers beginning to gnarl, Edward breathed a quiet sigh of long-anticipated relief.

Chapter 31

Most dangerous
Is that temptation that doth goad us on
To sin in loving virtue. Never could the strumpet,
With all her double vigour—art and nature—
Once stir my temper; but this virtuous maid
Subdues me quite .
- Measure for Measure

Now that he had been set free from the anchoring constrictions of his physical relationship with the Queen, Edward moved out of the palace and back to Oxford Court. He took John Lyly with him from the Savoy as his secretary and manager of Paul's Boys. This was the acting group chosen from St. Paul's choir for their voices and dramatic ability primarily to play the roles of women, since women still were not allowed to participate in the shameful occupation of acting.

With renewed vitality, Edward increased the

number of University Wits. Anthony Munday and Thomas Kyd joined Lyly and Edward at Oxford Court while Thomas Lodge, George Peele and Thomas Watson joined Robert Greene at the Savoy, making a total of seven. All were educated at Oxford or Cambridge except Thomas Kyd who had attended the Merchant Taylors' trade school. None were of noble blood so all could publish their writings under their own name.

Enthusiastically encouraged by the Queen, Edward now turned his attention to the patriotism-inspiring English history plays he had decided upon, beginning with *Henry VI* . While the Wits worked on the first part of *Henry VI* , Edward worked on part two. He crowded the play with relevant allusions to the times and nationalistic commentary.

After preliminary presentations in the tavern-innyard at The Bull, he staged *The Second Part of Henry the Sixth* as the first play of Whitehall's Christmas entertainments in mid-December.

Two weeks later, after tryouts at The Boar's Head, he presented his romantic comedy entitled *A History of the Duke of Millayn and the Marques of Mantua,* which he now sub-titled *The Two Gentlemen of Verona.* Edward played Valentine, one of the two gentlemen leads, adding amusement to his role by speaking with an Italian accent. The play included several Commedia dell'Arte tricks and plot twists.

＊　＊　＊

A minor incident had recently occurred which annoyed Edward because he felt it was mostly his fault and because it was blown out of proportion.

He was playing a second set of tennis with Ned Somerset at Whitehall when Philip Sidney walked onto the court with Fulke Greville and stood quietly at the side. The rules stated that with players waiting only two sets were allowed. There was no rule defining where waiting players should stand but it was the custom of nobility to remain outside of the court.

Edward's concentration was interrupted, he became disturbed and he hit the tennis ball, made of white leather stuffed with dog hair, into the net three times in a row. He felt that Sidney was impugning his honor by watching closely to prevent a third set. "You are intruding, Philip. Get out of the court and wait in the proper place."

"And are great earls of the realm resistant to all rules, not only of tennis but of politeness?" responded Philip.

"God's blood, Philip! Tennis is for relaxation of the mind and spirit, not for arguments with the likes of you! In the name of Christ, get out and get out now! You will have your court in due course!"

"The likes of me? Am I despoiling your air with my lesser rank? Perhaps a new Euphuistic epithet would frighten me off the court! Whereas a polite request would have initially sufficed, we now find great comfort here. We intend to remain until your second set is finished, which should be quite soon the way you are playing!"

Edward reddened, slammed his short-handled racket on the court and shouted, "God's Wounds, what an insolent puppy you are!"

Visiting French Commissioners, in a conference room above, were now staring down at the court. Edward was not aware of this but Sidney saw the listeners and said, "Sir, I believe you have offended me but to make sure my ears have not deceived me, would you repeat what you just said."

TR

"*Puppy*," Edward shouted, "and a deaf one at that!"

"All the world knows, Edward of Oxenford," Philip said in a loud firm voice, "that puppies are begotten by dogs, by bitches, while children derive from humans. I charge you, Sir, with lying in your throat!"

A sudden silence fell over the court as each reflected on what had transpired and its implications. An innocent tennis diversion had now become a provocation to an unavoidable deadly duel. According to the honored rules of chivalry, giving the lie was an irrevocable challenge which only bloodshed could appease.

Now one must kill the other? They were not good friends but certainly not enemies, frequently interacting on amicable terms. Edward and Philip were struck mute, heads lowered and staring at the court surface. Philip's partner and intimate friend, Fulke Greville, took him by the elbow and led him away. Edward and Ned also left the court in silence.

When the Queen heard, she sent out a regal command forbidding any duel. She then gave them three days to cool off. She first talked with Edward alone in her privy chamber and calmly chastised him for conduct unbecoming the Seventeenth Earl of Oxford.

"You *must* learn to control your temper, Edward, before it wounds or kills you. I have spent years keeping you out of foreign frays, preventing spilling of your blood uselessly in a false drama of heroic splendor. To die foolishly on English soil is hardly of service to Queen and country."

"It was both our faults, mine particularly, but I felt he was mocking our difference in degree. Too quickly, this triggered my ire. I apologize to you for my intemperate behavior. I promise I will apologize to Philip eventually but I cannot do so now."

As he walked out, Edward thought, *By Jesu, why is it that I cannot brook the accent of reproof except my own self-censure? But what right did Philip have to trample on my court and my dignity? God's wounds, the age is grown so picked that the toe of the peasant comes so near the heel of the courtier that he blisters his soul!*

Don't rank and noble status matter any more? What next? Will pseudo-noble Burghley ride his mule onto the tennis court, tether it to the fence and both start hee-hawing at my tennis strokes? Are social order and our knightly society beginning to unravel?

He reached his room, sat his desk for a few moments, took his quill and added new lines to *Troilus and Cressida*:

> *O when degree is shaked,*
> *Which is the ladder to all high designs,*
> *The enterprise is sick. How could communities,*
> *The primogenity and due of birth,*
> *Prerogative of age, crowns, sceptres, laurels,*
> *But by degree stand in authentic place?*
> *Take but degree away, untune that string,*
> *And hark what discord follows.*

The Queen summoned Sidney and reminded him that there was a difference in status between gentlemen and nobles. A society functioned best when each level, top to bottom, recognized the importance of maintaining ordered hierarchy. "Being of lesser degree, Philip, you should have backed away from the argument. Lack of respect for nobility teaches the common people to insult both, which can lead to revolution."

"I would never presume to argue with you but I was faultless!"

Elizabeth beckoned him to rise. "From his perspective, you were disrespectful and intrusive."

"But Edward insulted my honor! Isn't personal pride worth defending, according to the laws of chivalry?"

"Such outmoded rules of so-called satisfaction and honor have caused far more deaths and tragedies than any benefits derived."

"I yield to Your Majesty's wisdom but we are brought up with such concepts. You know I have always been a dutiful courtier. May I respectfully request a leave of absence so that I may visit my sister at Wilton to put together a literary work?"

"Well spoken and granted, Philip. I hold in high regard your forthrightness and courage in expressing your viewpoint."

* * *

After the success of his plays Edward felt ripe for feminine adventure. He decided to seek out Anne Vavasour who had swirled delectably in his mind since their first meeting, enhanced by subsequent interactions in the palace.

He found her in the privy chamber, to which he still had open access. Her bodice was cut low and loosely tied, her full breasts bulging.

"Well," said Anne, subtly swiveling her inviting hips, "are we Zeus or Vulcan today? Do I dodge thunderbolts from hands, or hot breath of volcanic fire attacking timid lips of an innocent Yorkshire shepherd-girl?"

He laughed to himself at his next thought, *I think I'll pursue Anne merely for the material it will provide for my plays!*

To Anne, Edward said, "I was forming the unblemished thought that sweet words are the key to a woman's heart. May I suggest a truce? Perchance we might enjoy each other's company more as friends than as knights at the wit-game barrier."

"A welcomed concept, Edward. Agreed. What is your suggestion?"

"Tonight let's wander through the streets and note the qualities of people. Let us meet at the wardrobe room of the revels, change clothes and do the town as two young lads out for a lark."

This brought a smile to her lips. "I have not often played the role of a boy!"

"Perhaps I can show you a slice of life not yet experienced, at taverns and the Bermoothes. We will savor each diversion until we have had our fill and preserve some excitement for a later occasion."

"I like your wording, Edward," Anne said with a wink.

Edward returned to his room and lay on the bed, eagerly awaiting the evening's adventure. What was it about Anne Vavasour that held such strong attraction, especially at her tender age of seventeen? Her face was striking but not gorgeous. Her slender well-formed body was alluring and exuded animal attraction, yet Edward knew that what most enticed him was her mind. It was quick and darting, full of jest and taunt, leaping to those swift associations which formed the basis both of humor and flirtation. What a combination—alluring mind with a supple sensuous body and the tantalizing mannerisms of a skillful seductress!

Anne was certainly a tempter, sometimes granting him a quick kiss which hinted a fervency of desire. Sometimes while talking, she would move forward into his body and slide a hand gently upward along his thigh and then pull away with a come-hither smile. She was an intellectual prober and enhancer yet full of play and fun, responsive to his own moods and vagaries. And she described to him intimate vignettes of scenes behind the Queen's closed doors witnessed in her role as a gentlewoman of the royal bedchamber, providing potential material for his dramas.

Edward knew that Anne was from Copmanthorpe in Yorkshire and that the Vavasours, whose name meant Chief of Vassals, were an old and distinguished Catholic family, directly descended from Mauger le Vavasour, who came over to England with William the Conqueror and Alberic de Vere. She was intellectually precocious and spoke five languages, including Greek and Latin. She was the Cleopatra-kind of woman who had been irresistible mistresses of kings through all of history.

They were both well aware that physical interaction was a dangerous pastime in palaces, considering the Queen's strong rules against liaisons for anyone other than herself, and with rampant gossip by over a thousand court personnel.

* * *

Anne knew she must act her role well to entice the premier earl of England. It was a golden fish she was luring and the bait must be dangled and withdrawn cleverly. She must keep him unfulfilled but sufficiently fascinated to accomplish her Catholic mission.

Cousin Henry Howard had promised her a necklace of topaz and emeralds if she prevented his return to Anne Cecil, and if she successfully drew Edward closer to the True Church. Henry had given her a complete list of Edward's likes and dislikes, capabilities and weaknesses. He even hinted that she should use all of her feminine wiles to achieve her goal.

Anne laughed. "Anne of the Vavasours needs lessons in enslaving emotions of the species, Man? Go teach the moon to fetch tides from the sea, Cousin Henry! I accept your assignment because I admire you, because Edward intrigues me, and because jewels hold special appeal. I might add that if I exceed your expectations, diamonds go well with my sparkling eyes!"

She was precocious in other arenas of life, as well. At the age of ten, she had witnessed through an open bedroom door conjugal relations between her parents. She was fascinated and couldn't pull herself away, becoming strangely excited as she observed the details. Later that day, she told her mother what she had seen and requested enlightenment.

Her mother explained everything. After answering Anne's many questions, she said, "And my advice to you is to investigate the functions of your own body. Learn to take charge of them and enjoy their pleasures. My mother taught me the opposite and my life is the worse for it."

From that time forward, Anne began to practice by herself. She learned to control the immense potential of her body and drew forth a range of responsiveness which amazed her. At a young age, she sought and obtained practical experience from older men, including a relative.

*   *   *

Edward and Anne met at the appointed time that evening in the wardrobe room for Whitehall theatricals and chose their costumes.

"Since blue has been a color of servitude since Roman times, let's wear blue and pretend our master has given us the night off," said Edward. He put on long simple breeches, a plain doublet with sleeves attached, and a jerkin.

Anne watched him. "No codpiece, Great Lord?"

"Not for servants, Anne!"

"I know. I was just teasing. In my experience, the larger the codpiece the smaller the cod! Would you like to watch me undress?"

"You surprise me!" He laughed and added, "Of course!"

Anne picked up her costume, walked directly to Edward, moved her body into his and began changing. She was so close that he couldn't see anything except her face.

"You're a teaser, Anne," he said, laughing again.

"Perhaps, but with occasional rewards for patience!" She took his hand and put it on her bare breast. He gently caressed it but she chuckled, turned the other direction and finished dressing.

They rode out of Whitehall onto King Street, past the back of Henry Howard's house and onto the Strand. They turned left on Drury Lane and stopped at The Phoenix.

Anne, with her long black hair tucked carefully under her brown cap, absorbed the atmosphere of the noisy tavern full of men from all walks of life.

Shortly, a priest asked to join them. Father Leo

saw through every stitch of Edward's costume. "What have we here, a play, my Lord, a jolly drollery?"

"We are disguised to experience the Play of Life, Father," Edward told him. "It is the toil of writers to capture the smallest details, the hum and murmur, the dialects, the tongue-roll, gestures, even the smells. As Seneca said, a writer must hold a mirror up to nature."

"Be careful! The mirror shows governmental spies everywhere."

"I take note of people to use in dramas for the Queen's pleasure. You, on the other hand, try to influence their souls for the Pope, to the Queen's displeasure."

"Use prudence, Edward," the priest cautioned. "It is said that you walk narrowly between safety and danger and that only the Queen protects your barbed writings. These times are perilous for my teachings of God's word but I have no choice. You do." He turned to look at Anne. "And who is your quiet companion?"

"Just another innocent vassal," said Edward, "a carpenter by trade."

The priest reached across and shook Anne's satin-smooth hand. He lifted it, looked at it closely and laughed. "A fair sweet hand for a carpenter!" He lifted the cap from Anne's head and her raven hair came tumbling down around her shoulders. "Ah, my playful child! Take care, Mistress Anne, take care!"

"I sin not, Father," she said. "We seek life's enchanting varieties. Please give me your blessing."

"I bless you, Anne Vavasour, and also my Lord Edward whenever he may request it." He rose from the table, bowed his head and departed. Anne rearranged her hair and became a lad again.

Edward and Anne soon left, mounted their horses and headed out Drury Lane to the Bermoothes, with its narrow lanes, dark basements full of illegal liquor stills, brothels, dingy taverns, sailors, dock-workers and wandering vagrants. A few were like Edward, just out for adventure in a world quite different from their own.

Anne was amazed at Edward's relaxed, friendly joking manner with these underworld denizens. He told her to remove her hat and introduced her as his cousin Annie. They knew him well under his own name, and the carefree banter continued for two hours.

After initial trepidation, Annie joined in the fun and soon was holding her own in repartee and laughter. *Wouldn't the white-dressed maids of honor be surprised,* she thought as she grabbed Edward's elbow and motioned that it was time to leave. She was invited to return—next time without her prudish elderly cousin.

Riding back to Whitehall, Edward felt strangely content. When he was moody, Anne rose like a bird from the fowler's net of his sadness and sang her lyrical song of happiness above him until the wings of his own spirit rose to frolic with hers. He could see that she understood the devastating impact on his free spirit of endless years of oppressive wardship under Burghley and a compelled unloving marriage. Like himself, she was similarly at ease with queens and paupers, nobility and the downtrodden. Tonight they clearly felt an undeniable pull of attraction for each other.

When they returned to the wardrobe room, Edward waited until Anne had removed her costume, then swept her into his arms and kissed her fully.

She drew him close, returning his ardor. Were her feelings genuine? He aimed to find out.

"I like what I feel, Edward," she said, a little breathlessly. "It does excite me and I had a wonderful time with you tonight."

"Anne, I want to savor more of you, and now! There is a stage-bed in that corner which is meant for us."

She shook her head. "Not now, Edward. Our evening is happily complete as it stands."

"But we have known each other for months!" Edward felt the pull of her heat and craved blending his own fire with hers.

"You will be rewarded soon, Edward. I want you to visit me in Copmanthorpe. My home will be empty for six weeks except for my old and forgetful father."

Edward could not hold back a prolonged sigh as he forced himself to say, "With knightly chivalry, I reluctantly yield to your wishes." He bowed to Anne in the moonlight streaming through three small windows. "I will translate my dampened zeal into a creative surge with quill and parchment. I will happily visit you in the north country, perhaps with a brace of maids of honor in case you're still in a tormenting mood!"

Her smile glistened in the silver moonlight. "Not necessary, my patient courtier. Instead, I would suggest you prepare yourself as if you were about to perform in a strenuous and lengthy tournament."

Edward walked slowly back to his room. She had been such an excellent companion tonight and then the evening ended so abruptly! *Are all women fickle man-ipulators? Is the Yorkshire invitation just a trick to evade my eager clutches? How could she change so quickly from honest ardor to negative rebuff?*

The trickle of a thought rippled through the remote portions of his mind that, in his woman-deprived state, were his eyes somehow beclouded with foggy naiveté? *Is another drama being played here which is murkily unclear to me?*

Chapter 32

Age cannot wither her, nor custom stale
Her infinite variety. Other women cloy
The appetites they feed, but she makes hungry
Where most she satisfies.
     - Antony and Cleopatra

In the crisp coolness of mid-September, Anne Vavasour welcomed Edward with the grace of long-traditioned hospitality to her family's old brick country manor in Yorkshire. She proudly showed him the smoke-darkened oak beams, worn tapestries and soft leather chairs of a home well-used for several hundred years and smelling of age and history.

Anne spoke gently and deferentially to her forgetful father, who kept repeating to Edward that "Yorick was a great city when London was only a swamp."

Edward listened carefully for usable quaint turns of speech but his mind was on Anne. The weather was cloudy and cool for three days. Edward paced through the house and tried to read but could not concentrate.

Their togetherness by the fireside after her father had gone to bed became increasingly passionate but Anne insisted on the proper setting for their first complete sharing.

The fourth morning was clear and windless. Anne prepared a picnic lunch and they rode off. The Yorkshire countryside was rough and hilly, with irregular moors containing clumps of heather, witches' broom, gorse, wild-rose hedgerows and occasional stunted oaks. They rode past small cliffs, shadowy glens and flocks of blackbirds.

"Look, Edward, Jackdaws' Crag!" Anne spurred her horse and disappeared down an almost vertical path.

He followed and found himself in a sunny glen covered with elderberry, laurel, ferns and pink-flowered foxglove. Wilting purple thyme tinged the air with a subtle savory aroma. The glen was boundaried by a semicircle of gray-white perpendicular cliffs mottled with caves. A pebbled stream meandered slowly through the glen, soft grasses growing along its banks. Beyond was a fragrant forest of tall, flat-topped Scots pine which nature had spaced and tended well, allowing giant bellflowers to form a fading blue-violet canopy beneath. The world seemed far away.

Anne settled herself in the grasses, her riding skirt of red and black velvet swirling around her. "It is beautiful and peaceful here, Edward. I used to come here with my brothers and sisters. We swore an oath of secrecy not to tell anyone about it."

He sat down and kissed her neck.

"First you must play the echo-game," she said. "Vere! Vere!" she shouted, and back came the clear, repetitive echoes.

"Anne! Anne!" called Edward, and the cliffs returned her name resonantly. He turned and watched her take off her riding boots and stockings, her dress, then a white bodice so that only a thin lace shirt remained. She walked slowly to her horse and removed the picnic basket and two blankets. She placed the basket underneath a willow, spread the blankets and sat down.

She turned and exclaimed, "Will E. Vere love me ever?"

"E. Vere! Ever!" echoed the rocks. Anne smiled and then laughed that even cold stone responded to her magic.

How strange, almost mystical, is an echo, like a shadow of invisible sound, thought Edward. He reached for a tablet underneath his jerkin. The small diamonds set all around the Queen's medallion sparkled.

Anne's eyes responded with a similar glint. "Oh how beautiful!"

"The Queen's gift. She gave it to me as my prize at the tournament eight years ago. I only use it on special occasions."

"This will be a special occasion for you, Edward. I love diamonds! They are like glistening ice, yet aflame with passion. Very similar to me . . .don't you think?"

"Indeed, yes!" He hesitated, then handed her the tablet. "You may have it, Anne." He felt only a slight pang in memory of the Queen and his great day of triumph.

Without further words Edward, already aroused, removed his clothes. Anne watched him and nodded approvingly. He lay down next to her, kissing her gently at first, then with increasing enthusiasm. He whispered to her, eased off her shirt and began massaging her. When he moved his hands lower, she began to move rhythmically, barely perceptible at first, but gradually increasing in intensity. Her breath came faster and faster. She sighed and repeatedly trembled.

At last she said, "My turn, Edward. Let me show you why making love is an art-form and why I, too, am a dramatic artist."

Her fingers wandered slowly, playing his body like a spinet, delving into new and sensitive areas. With her lips and tongue, she blended a symphony of sensations that Edward was almost unable to withstand. She teased and tantalized and finally captured him and conducted him eagerly and expertly into a world of crescendoing passion. At times she stopped moving her body completely, allowing her continuing excitement to squeeze and ripple vibrantly around him.

She frequently changed position, guiding him with the slightest touch into new and exciting posturings. She was lost in a powerful world of motion and uninhibited wildness interrupted with shudders of increasing force, during which she gripped her fingers into his back or arms and cried out or groaned loudly and uninhibitedly.

Overwhelmed by the unrestrained joy of her expertise, Edward immersed himself in the fiery harmony of intense sensations, simultaneously trying to distract his growing excitement. He counted the branches of pines and elms, watched a hawk circling, then poetized to himself Anne's unbridled exclamations of ecstasy:

And now she beats her heart, whereat it groans,
That all the neighbor caves, as seeming troubled,
Make verbal repetition of her moans,
Passion on passion deeply is redoubled .
"Ay me!" she cries, and twenty times, "Woe, woe!"
And twenty echoes twenty times cry so.

The force began to overpower Edward. All of their lust, all of their longing merged in a crucible of passion. Their final turbulent rapture was explosively incandescent. They clutched each other tightly and collapsed into wondrous exhilaration, clinging together almost desperately as their rapid heavy breathing subsided.

Edward felt overwhelmed by a basic elemental force. Before drifting off to sleep he saw that the sun had moved a considerable distance across the almost cloudless sky.

They slept for an hour. Edward awoke and fetched the picnic basket from beneath the willow. "I propose we have lunch and nourish our depleted bodies," he said with a laugh.

"Our bodies are not yet depleted, my new hero! I have something else in mind."

"But your hero is quite happily spent." *How glutton-like she feeds, yet never filleth,* he thought as she pulled him to her ravenously. The cliffs repetitively echoed their approval of Anne's endless ecstasy until Edward finally groaned loudly several times and crumpled into her arms.

Later, as the shadows migrated across the canyon, they ate their picnic sparingly. Edward shook his head in silent exhausted amazement. Anne chuckled to herself.

* * *

They returned to Jackdaws' Crag each time the weather was clear. They made love frequently wherever they were. Edward tried to cope with her seemingly inextinguishable demands, her remarkable ingenuity, and an almost continual tingling of his body.

On the last evening of the three-week visit, they sat in front of the fireplace after supper and created the poem which they had discussed since their first visit to the echo-glen:

Echo Verses made by the Earl of Oxford
and Anne Vavasour

O heavens, quoth she, who was ye first that bred
    in me this feavere? Vere.
Who was the first that gave ye wound whose
scar I wear for evere? Vere.
What tyrant, Cupid, to my harm usurps thy
golden quivere? Vere.
What wight first caught this heart and can from
    bondage it deliver? Vere.
Yet who doth most adore this wight, oh hollow
    caves tell true? You.
What nymph deserves his liking best, yet doth in
    sorrow rue? You.
May I his favor match with love; if he my love
    will try? Aye.
May I requite his birth with faith? Then faith-
ful will I die? Aye.

After finishing their poem, Edward gently touched her fingers. Anne kissed him tenderly on the lips. She put her head in his lap and for the first time in her life spoke words of heartfelt affection.

As the fire burned down, Edward knew they had created an unexpected bond of endearment. He wondered whither it would lead.

Chapter 33

Invest me in my motley. Give me leave
To speak my mind, and I will through and through
Cleanse the foul body of th' infected world,
If they will patiently receive my medicine.
                                            - As You Like It

Throughout the year, Edward carried on his secret love affair with Anne Vavasour. He found both
the affair and the secrecy arduous but filled with the
overwhelming allure of supreme excitement and
new heights of sexual satisfaction spiced with the thrill
of danger. Anne's inexhaustible talents and insatiable
lust fed his manly hunger and kept him always wanting more.

Edward's greatest concern was queenly wrath
which was hurled like Zeusian thunderbolts upon
any who played amorous games at Court. She was
the Queen bee who demanded constant feeding of
flattery and adoration by her loyal drones. With divine

approval by definition, she held in her hands all the purse-strings, all the keys to success—and also the keys to the Tower. She held the power of life, death and freedom over all citizens, especially members of her Court to whom she provided a glittering lifestyle. In return she expected and demanded obeisance and veneration.

Edward was thoroughly enjoying his enviable status as the admired Court dramatist and favorite courtier when an unforeseen occurrence detoured his steady ascent. The Queen was making notes in a velvet-bound tablet when Eleanor Bridges, a gossipy maid of honor who was attending her, exclaimed, "A lovely tablebook, Your Majesty, but not so pretty as Anne Vavasour's with your portrait on it and emeralds and diamonds all 'round it!"

"My portrait?" the Queen replied, at first merely surprised. Then her demeanor changed as she remembered the gift she'd given to Edward. "Surrounded by emeralds and diamonds? I will have a look at Mistress Vavasour's table-book! Go tell her to fetch it for me *now* !" Her voice had climbed to the high clear octaves of fury when she issued the command.

The order was relayed to Anne. Her heart was thumping when she unlocked the chest in her room and took the table-book from under a heap of silken scarves. She had a strong impulse to destroy the evidence or rip off the diamond portrait cover. She finally tore out, very carefully, the pages of Echo verses and several sonnets written to her by Edward.

With her heart still pounding heavily in her chest, she knelt before the Queen and handed her the tablet.

The Queen's face immediately reddened and she

shook the tablet in front of Anne's face. "You call this yours? Yours?" Her voice was as shrill as the defiant shriek of a falcon stunning its prey.

"It is not mine, Your Majesty. It is but a loan."

"Who loans my gifts loans me! It is yours no longer, nor his to whom I gave it. Go to your chamber!"

In her room, Anne scribbled a note and found a Court page to slip it under the door of Edward's room.

He was far more disturbed than Anne, being all too familiar with the Queen's quick temper and remorseless vindictiveness, especially when jealous. He hurried to the stable and galloped away. His mind was racing faster than his horse as he began to create a sonnet to Elizabeth, explaining that her image was etched forever in his heart and brain and needed no tablet to record it. He asked forgiveness for his mistake.

The next morning, a page delivered the sonnet to the Queen. Edward was summoned to her private presence a few hours later.

"I like not your giving away my imaged tablet," she said. "But 'twas a cunning sonnet. More to the point, why this recipient of the tablet?"

"An innocent child reaching for shiny baubles, sweet liege," he answered. "A mere butterfly of a summer's hour, a . . ."

Elizabeth measured her words carefully. "Be prudent, Lord Edward, lest you become the vassal-slave of a Yorkshire temptress! Her mirror does not image innocence to *my* eye! I have Tudor blood in me, as you well know, and am quite aware of human needs and emotions. But I will *not* have my Court become a love-nest of amours and paramours, mistresses and mattresses, like the French Court and others throughout history."

"I understand, Your Majesty—"

"I want my Court to become the *cultural envy of the world*, and I *am* going to succeed. But I need you, Edward, above all others, to reach that goal."

Edward remained silent, hoping only for a tongue-lashing.

Elizabeth slowly opened and closed her fan. "Don't you yet understand, Edward, that your destiny is to write the beauty which flows so naturally from your mind and heart into your golden pen? You are already changing England's cultural interests and values."

"Your words humble me, Your Majesty."

"And I will guarantee that you will *not* be forced into anonymity or pseudonymity. I will protect you from the detractors and literary nihilists who cannot see beyond their near-sighted spectacles and whose only sense of beauty is stacks of money!"

"My mistake overwhelms me, Your Majesty. You are very patient with my still-untempered faults."

"Have your dalliances, as humans must, but *not* on regal territory. And beware of the Vavasours. They are a close northern clan. You have not well-befriended Anne's uncle, Thomas Knyvet, whom you have bested in a tournament and mocked in writing. He is loyal to his Queen; his over-perfumed mannerisms may be overlooked."

"Yes, Your Majesty."

"Anne appears gifted in arenas which may bode you ill. Listen to me well: tread carefully and in the opposite direction!"

The Queen's sage admonition was not as powerful as Anne's primeval dynamism. The wardrobe room of the revels was irresistibly convenient. Edward again discussed with Anne the necessity of avoiding pregnancy. Anne assured him that she was following a time-honored Yorkshire recipe, drinking at least a pint of apple cider a day and half a cup of vinegar.

*   *   *

Edward returned to Oxford Court, continuing to stimulate and critique his University Wits and sponsor them financially so they could devote full-time to their writings. He had to sell five more of his estates to fulfill his patronage obligations, finance his lifestyle and produce plays. He knew he had little talent with investments or other financial matters and even less regard for wealth for its own sake. He wrote in his tablet for future use:

> *By Jove, I am not covetous for gold,*
> *Nor care I who doth feed upon my wear;*
> *It earns me not if men my garments wear;*
> *Such outward things dwell not in my desires.*

He was also reminded that his all-powerful father-in-law was continuing to siphon his estates and illegally preventing Edward's escape from wardship despite his age of twenty-nine. There was nothing he could do about it.

Edward began a new play based on the theme of usury, with Shylock as the eloquent and forgivable villain and Portia as the romantic heroine. Titling his play *The Jew,* it was given its stage try-outs at The Bull and then performed before the Queen and her Court on February 2, 1580, in the great hall of Whitehall Palace.

This was followed two weeks later by *Ptolome,* his play on Antony and Cleopatra in which, for the first time, he did not caricature or lampoon anyone.

The dramas were staged in repertory at The Theatre and The Curtain, then played all over England by traveling companies. Elizabeth walked with a prideful step when, for the first time, she heard the term "Elizabethan Theater."

Edward searched his mind for new dramatic ideas and techniques. These he discussed with his University Wits once a week at the Savoy and once a week at Oxford Court, often followed by less serious sessions at The Boar's Head or the Stillyard.

Edward's protégés began to publish works and dedicate them to their patron, as Thomas Watson did with his *Book of Passionate Sonnets* and Anthony Munday with his *Zelauto*. Edward was amused by Gabriel Harvey's parody of him in *Speculum Tuscaniami*, the first time he felt the brunt of his own lampooning style.

What excited Edward was the beginning of a burst of literary output never before seen throughout the long history of England. Nothing was happening in painting, sculpture or music.

Edward had an increasing sense that words were truly becoming his facile servants. His vocabularial strength was steadily increasing through the creation of new words and new word-usages. As he continued to observe and encounter life's joys and tribulations, he felt that he was writing with greater feeling and dexterity about the entire spectrum of human experience.

Having passed through the tablet incident being burned but not blistered, Edward again became happy and productive, enjoying the Queen's highest admiration and favor.

He had a dim premonition, however, that life was proceeding too benignly for him.

R

Chapter 34

Then was I as a tree
Whose boughs did bend with fruit : but in one night,
A storm or robbery, call it what you will,
Shook down my mellow hangings, nay, my leaves,
And left me bare to weather.
My fault being nothing, as I have told you oft,
But that two villains'. . false oaths prevailed
Before my perfect honour.

                                        - Cymbeline

Edward had been in awe at the skill with which the Commedia dell'Arte actors played their performances so adroitly. They were constantly being challenged to respond immediately and cleverly to sudden shifts in plot and interaction. Roles were copied mainly from Menander's standard characters in ancient Greece such as the greedy lawyer, the unfaithful husband, the foppish fool, the seductive maid. Wit and comedy were based upon a myriad of possible contorted plot-directions with each actor having the opportunity to extemporize at will.

Serena had repeatedly pointed out to Edward an obvious basic premise of the Commedia, that their humor was aimed in diverse ways at the characteristics of all humanity. Living individuals were not skewered. How long would the Commedia have lasted if it had targeted the narrow-mindedness of a Doge or the scheming greed of particular politicians?

Although Edward had several times reaffirmed his decision to characterize real people, he was still fighting his inner struggle. At times he saw himself being choked and made invisible by Vulcano's overpowering sulfurous fumes. Was he like a swan on the Thames, swimming with fruitless labor against the strong outgoing tides, futilely wasting his strength against over-matching power?

It is easy to forget, thought Edward, *especially being in such a privileged position as the premier earl, that England is not a democracy but an authoritarian dictatorship.*

Was his special relationship to the Queen and his growing word-power engendering an increasing feeling of immunity against reproach? Was he putting his life's work in jeopardy by insisting on documenting the times and its leading characters?

But by God, some people are born to be lampooned and by their actions deserve it! To hell with stock characters! My plays must tell the truth to counteract the scurvied distortions of glory-seekers and unscrupulous self-enhancers. If I don't , who else will?

Historians are often such fools, he thought, *writing "true" histories of the past, totally believing falsified records of those in power, slavishly following the intentions of the deceivers.*

What better choice for a comedy than to satirize

Christopher Hatton, whose dancing agility fancied by the Queen had started his climb to success and whose conversational content of an infinity of nothing had enhanced it?

Hatton's face is not worth sunburning! He is a conniving parasitic flatterer whose pia mater is not worth the ninth part of a sparrow!

Despite his flossy mannerisms and absent sense of humor, Hatton had rapidly advanced in Elizabeth's hierarchy through steadfast loyalty, ardent love-letters, refusal to marry anyone else and endless compliments. He was now Vice-Chamberlain of England.

Such are the ways of this Queenly Court, thought Edward, *with its many admirable qualities but where sugared words and professed adoration are the keys to advancement along the pathways of power and wealth.*

As Edward started his new comedy, a severe earthquake struck London. It set all the tower bells jangling and people tumbled like frightened ants out of their houses. The Puritans wagged their fingers and shook their black hats, declaring that it was God's warning against the moral looseness of plays and playgoers. Since people enjoyed plays, by definition they must be sinful. Edward smiled, shrugged his shoulders in amusement and continued his pen-work.

He so enjoyed writing his buffoonery about Hatton that loud laughter could be heard emanating from his room. His caricature was blatantly obvious, calling Hatton a dev'l puritan, an affectioned ass that cons state, and a rascally sheep-biter.

*   *   *

Shortly after the earthquake, the Jesuit Fathers Edmund Campion and Robert Persons arrived on England's shores from France. Edward was invited to meet them and hear them speak at Henry Howard's house. Both were brilliant, articulate, persuasive preachers, appealing to Edward on a spiritual as well as an intellectual level. He decided to rejoin the group for their secret Catholic services.

One September morning, arriving early at Howard House, Edward overheard low talking in the chapel. He stopped to listen and was astounded to hear Henry Howard advocate rebellion, freeing Mary Queen of Scots, marching on London and seizing Queen Elizabeth. Francis Southwell declared that Elizabeth must be killed quickly. Charles Arundel pointed out the necessity of immediately executing Burghley and the Privy Council.

Edward recognized the voice of the Spanish Ambassador, Guerau de Spes, describing Burghley as false, lying, full of artifice and utterly unscrupulous. Campion and Persons stated that the Spanish navy would blockade all English ports to prevent any escapes.

Stunned, Edward's brain swirled with options. *Should I promptly inform the Queen? I am an artist, not a spy,* he told himself uneasily.

He saw a possible solution in another play on Henry VI, describing the same kind of treasonous plotting. This would be his sword of words. He would write forceful lines to go straight to the Queen's ear and mind which would clearly reveal, through its analogy, that dangerous schemes were brewing.

That evening, Edward asked the Queen's permission for a month's leave to prepare entertainments for the Christmas season.

Sitting on her gilded throne Elizabeth spoke affectionately. "We shall miss your presence, my Turk, but we like what you do for the mind's pleasuring and stimulation."

He rushed to Anne Vavasour and told her that he had some wonderful new ideas and must go off alone to the country to write. Anne begged to know what the ideas might be but an inner voice warned him to keep silent.

"But you must take me with you, Edward!" she cried. "How often have you told me I am your inspiration and muse!"

More my a-muse than muse, he thought but he answered, "I would love your companionship but my creativity demands absolute quietude."

"But you must take us . . . *both of us!*"

"Both of us?" Edward repeated in startled tones. Immediate feelings of trepidation and remorse swept over him as he visibly blanched and waited for the inevitable to erupt from her lips.

"I am carrying your son, Edward. He already kicks like a warrior spurring his horse!"

Edward was rendered utterly speechless. For a long moment, adrift in a sea of conflicting emotions, he could only stare at her. Part of him was pleased. The creation of life was, after all, the greatest miracle.

But what took away his voice were deep concerns about the reaction of a distempered vengeful Queen. He had seen her wrath too many times. Relatives and friends had been beheaded for less.

"God help us," he finally managed. "God help all three of us."

On December 19, he staged his play, *The True Tragedy of Richard, Duke of York and the Death of Good King Henry the Sixth.* In the play he could not refrain from reminding the Queen of the execution of two de Veres and the steadfast loyalty of the Thirteenth

Earl of Oxford to the ruling house of Lancaster. He tried to warn her about treachery against the throne.

But the Queen clearly failed to receive the play's message. Perhaps there were too many implicit warnings about Catholicism, suggesting an ineffectiveness of her broad-minded religious policy. She arose as soon as the play ended, exuding cold severity. She did not applaud and left the hall immediately.

Now Edward was in a quandary. He debated his choices. To inform against friends or relatives was against the code of chivalry, a code within which he was nurtured. Nothing was more important than a man's honor; betrayal was dishonorable. But did not Castiglione himself point out that it was a true courtier's major function to resist tyranny, inform and educate his monarch, and protect him or her from danger? It was plainly his essential duty to notify the Queen.

The next day he talked with the Queen alone. He took off his cap and knelt before her. "Your Majesty, I must confess to you that I have recently found comfort in the Catholic religion of my ancestors. I now realize my error. I beg forgiveness and wish to return fully to the Church of England."

The Queen put her hand on Edward's shoulder. "I knew you were searching, Edward. I have always allowed freedom of worship in private, as long as it did not breed disloyalty."

"That is why I am here, Your Majesty. I have attended private mass at Henry Howard's home on many occasions." He drew a steadying breath and hoped she could not hear the heavy thudding of his heart. "Recently I overheard scheming to eliminate you and the Church of England and re-install Catholicism."

To his surprise the Queen laughed. "Come now, Edward! At cousin Henry's house? And who might be the plotters?"

"Henry himself, Charles Arundel and Francis Southwell, along with Ambassador de Spes and Fathers Campion and Persons. The plans are well advanced and your own personal safety is in danger!"

"God's blood but you are a dreamer and imaginer! I'd sooner believe my own hand would take me by the throat than cousin Henry. He has always been loyal and most attentive to me, as has Charles Arundel."

"I would also like to disbelieve it but I know what my ears heard!"

She shook her head. "Sheer delusion! Impossible! Watch your words, Edward, lest you reach heaven aforetime!"

"Your Majesty, why do you find it so difficult to believe that a Howard can plot?"

The Queen frowned, taken aback. Quickly she recalled three consecutive generations of executed Howards, the most recent being Henry Howard's brother Tom, Duke of Norfolk.

"Show me your proof, Edward!" she demanded at last. "Queens do not react rashly to flimsy rumors or conjectured distortions of the truth!" She spat on the floor. Edward watched as her royal saliva congealed. He slowly took a clove from his kirtle pocket and put it in his mouth, carefully plotting his verbal strategy as he straightened his light brown breeches and pulled up his long green stockings.

"This courtier does not lie, Your Majesty. How does one prove a conversation overheard? I tried my best to warn you with my play. My duty is now done."

As he bowed and left the room, he remembered

the words of Tertullian, *"Cum odio sui coepit veritas. Simul atque apparuit, inimica est."* The first reaction to truth is hatred. The moment it appears, it becomes an enemy.

* * *

Despite her ire that anyone should imply treason against her by those held in high esteem, the Queen notified Principal Secretary Walsingham of Edward's accusations. Based on evidence from informers, Walsingham requested the temporary house-detention of the three chief suspects.

Henry Howard and Charles Arundel, unable truthfully to deny Edward's accusations, fabricated a long list of discrediting allegations against Edward to divert attention from themselves. These included that he was very seldom sober; that he boasted so greatly of his accomplishments in Flanders and Genoa that his listeners rose from the table laughing; that he had accused the Queen of having the worst singing voice of any woman; and that he had denied the divinity of Christ.

Without explanation, in a show of power Elizabeth had Edward thrown in the Tower for one day and night. Astounded, Edward belched the bitterness from his heart by bold words which poured forth into his tablet:

> *My life thou shalt command, but not my shame.*
> *The one my duty owes, but my fair name,*
> *Despite of death that lives upon my grave,*
> *To dark dishonour's use thou shalt not have.*
> *I am disgraced, impeached, and baffled here,*
> *Pierced to the soul with slander's venomed spear.*

Edward learned a few days later, in a private talk with the Queen, that Henry Howard had done such an eloquent job of self-exculpation and character-blackening of Edward that all three plotters were released from detention. Elizabeth chose to be loyal to the accused three who seemed so faithful. Once again, Edward had become a fable of the world, this time by adherence to his basic honor and principles.

So much for Cicero's dictum, thought Edward, *that fame comes from being a loyal citizen and serving the republic devotedly, thus earning praise, respect and love.*

After release from the Tower he suffered that most bitter of experiences: exile from the good will of his fellows. The Court had to follow the Queen's lead and shun him. He had lost honor, so especially esteemed by de Veres.

When Edward walked down palace corridors or entered any room, even the maids of honor averted their glances or turned their backs. He tried to assuage his ire by writing in his tablet :

When in disgrace with fortune and men's eyes, I all alone beweep my outcast state, and trouble deaf heaven with my bootless cries , and look upon myself and curse my fate.

The scowling scheming face of Henry Howard appeared in his imagination, and Edward thought, *O treason of the blood! O villainous cousin, thou art a dissentious rogue! May your tongue rot that speaks against truth and me!*

* * *

On the twelfth night of the Christmas season, Edward staged his play parodying Hatton, *Call It What You Will* . The Court felt it was a justified and witty lampooning of Hatton but all were afraid to laugh because of the Queen's displeased countenance.

Edward knew the play was a failure despite its clever humor.

Edward walked the streets of London, oblivious to the din, filth and penetrating smells. He was assailed by cries of "What d'ye lack?" sounded forth by street vendors and craft apprentices. He walked slowly, arms behind him, a heavy weight on his chest, oppressed and disparaged by forces beyond his control.

"I feel like a tiny island of defeated truth," he muttered to himself, "surrounded by an ocean of inundating mendacity." From the highest level of esteem and popularity with Queen and Court, he was now shunned like a leper, all for being honest.

He felt a tugging on his breeches and looked down into the grimy but smiling face of a street urchin.

"Y'look sad, Sir," said the boy. "What d'ye lack?"

Edward bent forward, patted the boy on the head, handed him a shilling and said, "What do I lack? The esteem of my fellow man, complete freedom in creative writing, the right to sign my own name to my artistic productions, and a sense of purpose in life!"

The urchin was puzzled. He looked at the shilling, looked at Edward and looked at the shilling again. Then he ran up the cobbled street, dodged a horse-drawn cart, turned and waved, and disappeared around the corner.

Chapter 35

Yet again, methinks
Some unborn sorrow, ripe in fortune's womb,
Is coming towards me.
                              - Richard II

Although Edward had spent only one day and night in the Tower, its dark locked rooms led to bleak and cynical thoughts which long overlasted the time of Edward's arbitrary authoritarian incarceration.

He thought bitterly, *How quickly eyes of approval can change to disapproval, the paean of praise to the deriding glance of scorn! Without truth and honor, life is meaningless. How could the Queen believe the false syrupy words of Henry Howard and Charles Arundel and not feel the venom in their hearts?*

Edward sat at his desk in Oxford Court and pondered the immense importance of personal esteem. After a few minutes' reflection, he removed from his drawer the third feather of a goose's wing.

He sharpened the edges of the tip with his dagger, softened it with spit and wiped the edges smooth with a cloth. He dipped his new pen in his inkwell and wrote:

> *Good name in man and woman, dear my lord,*
> *Is the immediate jewel of their souls.*
> *Who steals my purse steals trash; 'tis something,*
> *nothing;*
> *'Twas mine, 'tis his, and has been slave to*
> *thousands.*
> *But he that filches from me my good name*
> *Robs me of that which not enriches him*
> *And makes me poor indeed.*

*   *   *

One early dawn in January, 1581, Ned Somerset brought Edward the news that the combined spy networks of Walsingham and Burghley had uncovered abundant evidence that Edward's accusations had been wholly justified. All trails led to the black-clad, unsmiling, ascetic King Philip of Spain.

Charles Arundel had successfully escaped to Paris, where the traitor now lived a life of luxury on a pension from Philip. Henry Howard's eloquent self-exculpation, saturated with falsehood, convinced the Queen of his innocence.

So broad-minded had been Elizabeth's religious policies that she was profoundly shocked by the new revelations. Edward's warnings had triggered the investigation which finally awakened her from long years of dangerous, slumbered disregard of repeated advice from Burghley.

The Queen issued a sweeping anti-Catholic

proclamation warning that Jesuits who henceforth ventured into England would be hunted down and executed. Catholics could still worship freely in private but fines were to be imposed for non-attendance at Protestant services.

That evening Edward was invited to sit at the Queen's right at a banquet at Whitehall. Despite one of her severe headaches which had put her to bed for the previous twenty-four hours, she seemed in good spirits.

"Queens who rule by Divine Guidance need not apologize, Edward," she told him, "but we are not immune from error. You have served us well."

Elizabeth then rose in front of the two hundred and gave a toast "to those excellent citizens whose loyalty to Queen and country rise above personal constraints in order to stave off grave threats and serious peril to the realm."

Edward was quick to note that she did not mention his name.

Despite his restoration to favor, he viewed his treatment at her hands a vivid example of unrestrained abuse of power. He was disillusioned about the behavior of so mercurial a monarch. He wrote in his tablet:

With every minute you do change a mind,
And call him noble that was now your hate,
Him vile that was your garland.

Her rapid vacillations reminded him of a cobra swaying gently to enchanting music with full power to strike in an eye-blink.

* * *

Philip Howard, son of the executed Tom and cousin of Edward, now issued a friendly general invitation to a tournament in honor of his newly inherited earldom. The challenge was designed to show his own knightly honor and loyalty to the Queen at a time when the behavior of Howards was once again being severely tested.

"I must accept that chivalric jousting challenge, Ned," said Edward at Ned Somerset's elegant three-story manor house.

"Be careful, Edward," Ned warned. "It is true that eyes are once more sliding toward you in friendship. But there is justifiably a deep resentment against you in the Howard clan, you being the chief thwarter of their long-laid plans. You won your only tournament but that was ten years ago."

"Mind and strategy are as important as strength," Edward replied. "But the real key to winning tournaments is being totally as one with your horse."

"Caution yourself, Euphues!" said Ned, putting his hand on Edward's shoulder. "Grapes and amorous grapplings do not graft well with tilting lances and swords!"

Edward officially accepted the tournament invitation and asked Philip Sidney to joust on his side as the White Knight. Edward had previously apologized to Sidney for the tennis court incident; it was accepted and never mentioned again.

New bleachers had been built at the north end of the Whitehall tiltyard. Edward had hidden himself before the ceremonies in a stately tent of orange taffeta embroidered with silver. Elaborate pennants flew from the pinnacle, proudly displaying his symbols of the five-pointed mullet star of Aubrey de Vere at Antioch; the fierce Bolebec lion sejant brandishing the broken spear of his vanquished enemy; and the de Vere heraldic crest with his motto: *Vero Nihil Verius* .

After the other contestants had made their entrances and their pages had made speeches to the Queen, the spectators cheered as Edward exited from the tent in gilded armor and stood next to a large bay-tree planted adjacent to the tent. The tree trunk and all of its branches and leaves were also gilded, brilliantly shining in the sun of a crisp winter day. Alongside the tree stood twelve golden spears.

After the playing of stirring marching music which he had recently composed, Edward mounted his courser, Bucy II, richly draped in gold and decorated with boars and silver stars. He rode to the base of a new staircase built up to the second story of the palace and bowed to the Queen.

He then declared that his Tree of the Sun bore only one fruit, Virtue, and that he would rather die upon the points of a thousand lances than yield one jot in constant loyalty.

The crowd cheered. Edward was very popular with the commoners, being the only nobleman they knew, as tavern-frequenter, story-teller, prankster and actor. He was often secretly pleased when he walked or rode through the streets of London with other nobles or with the Queen on state occasions, because a ripple of laughter accompanied him in happy remembrance of his many roles.

Sidney performed well and tilted to a draw with Philip Howard and Sir William Drury. Edward was clearly the favorite and a major reason for the unexpectedly large gathering.

With the sun glinting off his golden armor, spear and horse, and with his own honor and the honor of the Knight of the Tree of the Sun at stake, Edward's skill and special unity with his horse led him to a resounding triumph, defeating both Howard and Drury by a significant margin, unhorsing both.

The crowd jumped up and down on the scaffolding and cheered. Edward's heart once more beat with the joy of triumph. Once again his victory was unexpected by the majority at Court because of their continuing premise that intellectual introspective poets who spend their time finding rhymed meaning in the universe, tides, flowers and flights of birds are not supposed to be athletic courageous tournament champions in a dangerous sport.

He mounted the stairs to receive the Queenly prize: a golden inkwell studded with small rubies and diamonds. Trumpets signaled the end of the tournament. The crowd began to rush out of the stands since by tradition anything left on the field of battle was theirs for the taking—this time the lure of the tent's fine taffeta and the glittering gilded tree.

Suddenly the air was rent with shattering sounds of splitting wood and shrieks of pain and terror as the new north bleachers crumbled under the large crowd's sudden surge. Bones shattered, some protruding through the skin. Head injuries killed four and a sharp piece of wood transfixed one woman. Twenty spectators were crushed to death by the piles of struggling groaning bodies.

TR

* * *

Sitting in front of his fire at Oxford Court that night reviewing the day's events, Edward felt a sense of gloom as he thought about the bereavement in so many homes of the onlookers.

He also felt a sense of personal foreboding as he contemplated Anne Vavasour's pregnancy. He had tried his best during the last six months to convince Anne to have her baby in Yorkshire.

"For God's sake, Anne, feign illness! Make up any story, but leave Court and have your baby at home!"

"For God's sake or for yours?" she retorted. "*My* baby or *our* baby?" She spat the words with contempt, using the same passion she'd once applied in setting the original trap.

"So much for cider and vinegar! Did you ever vacation in the Tower?"

Anne would not budge. On Edward's accusation, she admitted her complicity with Henry Howard but swore to Edward that she had come to love him. She then lured him to the wardrobe room, entwined herself around him coil-of-Circe tight and exhausted his manly energies with new prolonged techniques of fiery ardor. She did not tell Edward that she had followed Henry Howard's suggestion to discontinue the cider and vinegar.

It was now clear to Edward that Anne was determined to have the baby publicly recognized as his. If she had her baby in Yorkshire, he could claim that the father was a shepherd or stable-boy. She knew that she had to stay at Court to the end and immediately name her son after him. Her reasoning had merit, he mused. Although he had no intention of denying paternity, in similar circumstance others would.

She appeared to have no comprehension that she was endangering all three of them. Having not seen Elizabeth disembowel a stag or send an innocent like Tom Howard to the chopping block, Anne did not understand the brutality of omnipotent rage.

He finally offered her a thousand pounds to disappear. Anne vented a mocking laugh, patted her abdomen, and walked away with a slow confident gait which infuriated him, as did all inescapable encirclements. He wrote part of a sonnet:

> *For I have sworn thee fair and thought thee bright*
> *Who art as black as hell, as dark as night.*

Edward retreated angrily to Oxford Court and wondered how long Anne could effectively conceal her pregnancy. Wide farthingaled dresses were an immense advantage, as proved by the Queen. But as a gentlewoman of the bedchamber, she must interact with so many, including prattle-mouths like Eleanor Bridges, that Edward had strong doubts about effective concealment. Even the Queen had become so worried about the discovery of her own pregnancy, he recalled vividly, that she had fled the Court to Havering-Atte-Bower for the last two months before delivery.

Anne abandoned her clinging muslins and silks and wore full hooped skirts. She continued to do all of her usual duties for the whole pregnancy, interacting on a normal daily basis with maids of honor and even the Queen without the slightest suspicion being aroused.

It was a remarkable performance acted with

panache, thought Edward, but he feared the final scene.

When she went into labor on March 21, she tried her best to keep it noiseless, but couldn't. The secret spread rapidly among the ladies in Elizabeth's retinue. Dr. Julio was summoned from within the palace and soon Anne's baby was delivered.

"A boy!" said Dr. Julio. "A fine healthy boy!"

"Praise be, I knew it!" Anne whispered wearily.

Dr. Julio immediately reported the birth to the Queen.

"God's Wounds and God's Death!" screamed Elizabeth in her shrill metallic voice. "A baby born behind the Queen's private doors! What next?" She took a long stride and kicked the wall. She massaged her left temple, trying to attenuate an impending headache.

"What is your wish, Your Majesty?" asked Eleanor Bridges.

"Get Walsingham now, and I do mean *now* !" She slapped her hands forcefully against her thighs, rocking her farthingaled dress briskly from side to side. Elizabeth's headache threatened to devour her as she paced back and forth like a lioness.

Francis Walsingham soon appeared, his austere unsmiling face and pointed beard blending well with his black clothes of a devout Calvinist. "At your service, Your Majesty. What has happened that I may alleviate?"

"Alleviate? You're nine months too late for that! Anne Vavasour has just given birth to a son not a hundred feet from here! I know who the father is but I want it spoken from her own lips. Use any means necessary to find out! Holy Jesu! Babies dropping all over the floor in my own chambers! Get them out of here *tonight* and commit them to the Tower!"

Walsingham bowed and left the privy chamber.

Elizabeth clenched her fists and shouted at the ceiling, "God's Blood! That scheming Yorkshire vamp successfully kept it a secret from me and from all of us, right here in my own apartments, with her clever farthingales!" Despite her anger, her mouth expressed a subtle smile, recalling her own regal trickery.

Anne had fallen asleep with her chubby son, swaddled in a linen petticoat, lying beside her. She was vigorously roused by the rough hands of Walsingham who glared down at her with pitiless piercing eyes.

"I come at the Queen's command. Who is the father of this child?"

Anne held her baby tightly and answered, "Honored Mr. Secretary, is this an appropriate time to conduct an inquisition, at the panged bed of birth? Let me rest awhile."

"Merely utter the name of the father, then you may sleep. I ask by the Queen's order and it must be obeyed!"

"Why not put the baby on the rack and ask him?"

"How dare you, impudent girl!" Walsingham snarled. "Nineteen years old in the Queen's intimate service and you would challenge her authority? Give me the name of the father immediately or you may never lay eyes on your baby again! The Thames runs dark and cold tonight." He reached for the baby with his bony hands.

"No! No!" Anne clutched her son more tightly to her. "I will tell you! I am truly overwhelmed by your saintly Calvinist feelings of kindness and love!"

Walsingham scowled and grabbed for the baby. Anne swung her body over it in protection.

"Don't you dare contaminate the noble virtue of my baby, you foul spymaster and torturer! The father is Edward de Vere and the baby's name is Edward Vere. Now leave our sanctuary and continue your loathsome work elsewhere!"

Walsingham appeared stunned and hesitated for a moment. He turned and left the room.

Anne penned a brief message and asked Martha Howard to get it to Edward. Martha hurried to the Greenwich stables and paid a groomsman to ride to Oxford Court and deliver it to Edward.

Although Edward had been expecting such news at any day, it was still a jolt. He could find no pleasure in being a father again—to a son whom he would barely know. *Affliction clings to me like an inevitable inamorata,* he thought. *I seem wedded to calamity.*

Walsingham reported to the Queen.

"As always, faithful Francis, you have performed speedily and well in my service," she praised. "Have your men complete the mission with Anne and the baby *now*! Tomorrow, fetch the errant fornicator and escort him to his new lodgings in the Tower."

Within an hour, Anne and her baby were strapped to a litter and carried through the cold rain to the stone water-stairs. As they were taken by boat upstream to the Tower of London, Anne thought of all those who had spent their final days there, having offended an all-powerful sovereign whose whim was mightier than any law of man or God.

Edward had no intention of trying to flee. *Escape what? The chance-begetting of a child out of wedlock, such a common event and so familiar to sovereigns of either sex, especially Tudors?*

He had done his best to prevent its public knowledge but Anne's agenda had prevailed. *So be it! Admit responsibility, exclude oneself from Court for a short time and then make something good come from it. For over two thousand years, had not philosophers pointed out repeatedly that every affliction of life fosters new opportunities for the well-disposed mind?*

Three days later, Edward heard horses' hooves in his courtyard. From his window, he was surprised to see, in addition to Sir Francis Walsingham, a contingent of armed soldiers as well as William Brooks, the Seventh Lord Cobham. Assuming that Edward would attempt escape, they had spent two days blocking roads and searching ports, not thinking to look for him at home.

He changed into purple and yellow clown-clothes as his visitors waited impatiently. He greeted them boldly: "Welcome, agents of benevolent sovereign authority! Your cheerful countenances bode well for a happy citizenry!"

Lord Cobham, a staunch Puritan and great grandson of Sir John Oldcastle, whose name appealed to Edward for use in his plays, was taken aback. "Come to your senses, my Lord of Oxford! Are you out of your reason quite? Our business with you is no laughing matter. I am told that severed heads rarely laugh!"

"When or where did a Puritan *ever* laugh, Sir Stodgy Cobcastle?" said Edward. He looked at the puffed red cheeks and trembling lips of Cobham and thought that he would someday immortalize that sputtering facial expression.

Walsingham thrust forth a paper stamped with the Queen's seal. Edward read the parchment commanding his conveyance to the Tower. The Queen's predictable over-reaction left him undismayed and he responded, "I will find you twenty lascivious turtles ere one chaste man!"

"Surely you can't jest at a time like this," said Walsingham, unsmiling.

I dare not laugh, thought Edward, for fear of opening my lips too wide and inhaling the infected air. "Ah, what a witty, outwitting devil the Devil is! Just when my mind was beginning to bulge with new writing ideas, he provides me England's ultimate peaceful surroundings: good old Willy the Conqueror's thick-walled, moated Chapel of Silence, perfect for an errant playwright!" Edward bowed low to Walsingham and Cobham.

His audience looked at each other in bafflement. Then Cobham said, "Methinks Bedlam might be more appropriate, Sir Francis. But let us carry out our task quickly, before he quips himself to death and deprives us of the pleasure of locking him up!"

Edward recalled the words of Quintus Ennius that freedom is having a pure and dauntless heart. He exhorted himself to unmuzzle his innate reflective wisdom. He must make himself believe that he was going to the liberty of aloneness and not to the confinement of prison.

Edward smiled, shook the hand of each, and said, "Gentlemen, I forgive you for participating in this grievous and unreasoned command from our Queen, who has so many graver problems with which to deal. Although you tread upon my patience, I yield myself into your hands."

When they arrived at the Tower, Walsingham led him toward the usual entrance of Traitors' Gate. Edward suddenly leapt to the side, pulled out his rapier, stood with feet apart against the stone wall and calmly but forcefully said, "Neither you, nor your contingent of soldiers, nor an entire army will convey Edward de Vere, Seventeenth Earl of Oxford, through Traitors' Gate alive! I am *not* a traitor, nor have I been charged with such! Is decapitation the new penalty for being half-responsible for the creation of a child? If so, the Royal Court will abruptly shrink in size! Continue in this direction and prepare to die!"

Walsingham, Cobham and the soldiers all stepped backwards from the fiercely menacing tournament champion, shocked into silence.

Walsingham spoke at last: "As England's Principal Secretary, I like not being threatened with rapier when carrying out the Queen's orders. But your point is well made. Sheathe your weapon, Lord Edward, and we will enter through another gate."

Chapter 36

Sweet are the uses of adversity,
Which, like the toad, ugly and venomous,
Wears yet a precious jewel in his head.
                                        - As You Like It

When the heavy wooden door slammed shut and the iron latch was bolted gratingly into place, Edward walked slowly through his new accommodations. Since he had not been charged with a specific crime, he was assigned a two-room apartment in guarded lodgings.

He had a view of the inner courtyard but not the broad moat. He could see the executioner's block but also trees, grass and the ever-present ravens which landed on his windowsill. They had the audacity to peck at his window, begging for food. He knew that those facing death feel a greater kinship with any form of life. Previous prisoners had clearly fed the ravens' ravenous appetites.

A simple chair was in each room. The windows

were covered with iron grills. His bed was too hard but the fireplace was ample. He asked his servant to bring the large Turkish carpet he had bought at dockside from the first English ship returning from Istanbul. He had learned in Turkey that the proper place for carpets was on the floor, not draped over furniture as in England. He installed his writing desk and two bookcases filled with his favorite velvet-covered books.

Edward contemplated the dramatic difference between the ocean's predictable tides and the totally capricious currents of human life. He recalled the words of Aemilius Paulus, third century BC Roman, that courage and resolution are not merely to resist weaponry in battle but to cushion the many shocks of ill fortune in life.

The Tower pulsed with the vibrant history of heroes and villains and so many executions of guilty and innocent, including de Veres. Even Queen Elizabeth had spent ten weeks in the Tower, fearing that at any moment her life would be snuffed out by her half-sister, bloody Queen Mary.

It was March 24, 1581, and in this splendid silent solitude, Edward decided that he must make his creative quill shine! Only his freedom was imprisoned and the interrupting world was also solidly walled out. In time, he knew the Queen would relent and he wrote in his tablet:

In time the savage bull sustains the yoke,
In time all haggard hawks will stoop to lure,
In time small wedges cleave the hardest oak,
In time the flint is pierc'd with softest shower,
And she in time will fall from her disdain,
And rue the suffrance of my friendly pain.

Anne Vavasour and her baby were not so fortunate, having been thrown into a dank, fungus-smelling, stone-walled basement room with meager fireplace, furniture and food. She was allowed no visitors.

Edward bribed the guard to take extra blankets to Anne and the baby but his requests to the Queen for better accommodations for them fell on jealousy-thickened royal eardrums.

He found himself wrestling with his feelings toward Anne. She had deliberately tried to ensnare him and lure him into the treacherous embrace of scheming Catholicism. It was hard to believe she had confederated with a disreputable pack of England's traitors just to acquire jewels but that was undeniably the case.

Edward was unable to dismiss her quickly. Reasoned analysis of her negatives were quickly vaporized by thoughts of the steaming cauldron of her allure. She held him by deep attraction powered by the blistering fuel of passion and the mystique of verbal interplay.

But he damned her for publicly staining his character and he wrote in his tablet:

> *Reputation, reputation, reputation!*
> *O! I have lost my reputation .*
> *I have lost the immortal part of myself.*

*   *   *

Edward spent three days reading his velvet-covered Geneva Bible, making more notes in the margins and marking further passages he could use in his plays. After another two days of reflection on the vagaries of human emotions, Edward sat down at his desk. Although it entailed certain risks, what better time to write about authority and its abuses and perversions?

He began a play on morality and corruption of virtue in high places. He pushed up his sleeves and wrote strong words to call attention to the misuse of power by politicians like Burghley:

> *This outward-sainted deputy would appear a pond as deep as hell.*

Edward soon finished *Measure for Measure*. He well knew, as all writers did, that revisions were an integral part of good writing and would tone down certain over-emotional lines. But where such lines were so richly deserved, as in Burghley's case, he would let them stand.

He took two days off to read ancient texts and converse with the ravens to see which species could learn the other's language first.

* * *

One evening while reading Plutarch he decided to write a play about Coriolanus and Rome in the fifth century BC. It would involve banishment, integrity and heroism, all relevant to his own situation.

He filled the play with political critique and commentary on human emotions such as arrogance, courage, tenderness and veracity. He felt confident that time would unfold what plighted cunning hides.

Edward's writing and thinking made time pass quickly and he was given back his freedom after two and a half months. But for reasons quite unclear to

Edward, the Queen forbade his access to the Court indefinitely.

Anne Vavasour and her baby were not released until Christmas and she was banned from Court forever.

Edward ascertained that it was largely due to Burghley's efforts that he had been released from the Tower earlier than anticipated. He wrote to his father-in-law and thanked him. Edward was continually perplexed by Burghley's admixture of patriotism and self-centeredness, good and evil, wisdom and narrow-mindedness, and hard grinding work for England combined with endless acquisitive greed.

Despite his tormenting inner conflicts about his wife, Edward began to admit to himself that much of his antagonism should have been directed toward her father. He and Anne Cecil were both innocent victims of the misuse of power. Divorce was an unattainable option in a Burghley-and-Queen-enforced marriage. If Edward wanted heirs to the ancient and honored de Vere heritage, he must re-unite with Anne, who certainly had major and justified grievances against him.

He began writing to her and soon Anne and her daughter Lizbeth joined him at Oxford Court.

Now married for ten years with a six-year-old daughter, 25-year-old Anne had lived with her husband for only a few months. She had not requested the marriage, had only followed parental orders and had tried to love her husband according to current custom and her Puritan religion. But how does one love an absent husband who, for most of those years, has led a life entirely apart? Her once-cheerful face of childhood had metamorphosed into stiffened lips and shadowed eyes. Time, heredity, and Puritanism had imprinted a solemn doleful cast on her features.

Edward was determined to make amends for his severe faults as Anne's husband. Why could he impale his own character-flaws so readily in his plays and yet so unchangingly maintain them in real life? Except for the source of Lizbeth's paternity, which Edward strongly believed had been forced upon Anne against her will, what had she done wrong except to be herself and be true to her Puritan beliefs? *What a miserable decade I have inflicted upon her,* he concluded.

His two months of exile had changed his perception toward life. He knew that happiness and true affection were entities that one must earn. He realized that he had been selfish, caring little for the needs of others and mainly for his own. With this awareness came a new maturity.

He must treat Anne with the affection and respect which was her due as his wife and mother-to-be of his children, including sons. When she came to him at night, wasn't she affectionate and tender? During the day, wasn't she often kind and forgiving of his labile moods and harshness?

Edward knew it was essential to their co-existence that he avoid the word-battles she could not win. He must never again openly question Lizbeth's spurious paternity although he might allude to his grim concerns in his plays. He should accept Anne's Puritan piety without negative comment, laud her guilelessness, and even give love a chance to develop—although he considered that as hopeless as a year without rain in England.

*   *   *

Edward sent his Oxford Players around the country and allowed his old plays to be staged at The Theatre and The Curtain. But since he was exiled from Court by the Queen, he decided that no new play of his would be staged anywhere.

He used his abundant free time to continue writing plays. He knew he was in an unparalleled position to see the avarice, sycophancy, perpetual lying and constant scheming of politicians and courtiers from the inside. He knew that few, if any, writers in history had found themselves in similar situations, being brought up in the household of the country's leading politician, married to his daughter, and being in an intimate relationship with the ruler on many levels.

Edward once again found reasons for not listening to the subconscious voice which warned him against over-forthrightness and the easily recognizable personal characterizations he included in his plays. Mary Hastings had several times lovingly cautioned him about the potential hazards of such portrayals. Serena had repeatedly urged him to reconsider that dangerous tactic, as had the Queen.

In his more introspective moments and sometimes in dreams, Edward visualized himself being engulfed by overwhelming blackness, with no illuminating light of escape by which he could shine forth.

He was aware that he was overlooking one of history's lessons, that often it is best that truth hath a quiet breast. He wondered whether he truly understood that fires should not be built so dangerously that one can burn oneself.

At times Edward felt almost intoxicated with the power of his quill. Only in fleeting moments did he wonder whether his intellectual and creative exhilaration were making him disregard the abundant weaponry of amoral politicians who could smother and obliterate those who chose to be defamatory. In one such moment he wrote:

> *The eagle suffers little birds to sing,*
> *And is not careful what they mean thereby,*
> *Knowing that with the shadow of his wings*
> *He can at pleasure stint their melody.*

Chapter 37

O God, that men should put an enemy in
their mouths to steal away their brains!
                                    - Othello

"Please don't go back to London now, Edward," said Anne de Vere on a frosty March day in 1582 as they strolled the long gallery of Castle Hedingham's manor house. "I have bad feelings about it."

Anne had successfully urged Edward to move to Castle Hedingham when the plague struck London in January. She hoped that living in such meaningful surroundings, away from her parents, might enhance their marriage. They must ignore the predations of some of the castle's valuables by Robert Dudley, who had bought the right to plunder it from Burghley, who was Edward's guardian of record, albeit illegally for many years.

Edward glanced at a faded tapestry showing the signing of the Magna Carta in which Robert, Third

Earl of Oxford, had played a prominent part. "Is this the Ides of March? Am I to be surrounded and stabbed to bloody death at the age of thirty-two?"

"You know I can't debate with you," said Anne. She was dressed in dark blue and black of Puritan piety. She reached for his hand. "Oh, Edward, I do care for you and honor you as my husband. Don't you think our love for each other is growing now that we are both trying to give it a chance? Won't you wait until the plague in London is surely over?"

Edward felt the pious coolness of her hand and something inside him turned obstinate. "My intentions are to travel where and when I like!" he heard himself exclaim. But as he glanced down and saw the hurt reflected in her still-innocent face, the pillar of his own stubbornness weakened. "But if it would please you, I will postpone my leaving."

He heard her breath exhale a sigh of relief as he paid rare homage to her feelings.

* * *

It was difficult for Edward to accept his irrational banishment from Court after all of his loyal service as a devoted courtier. He tried but failed to be as consistently philosophical during his exile as Dante, who had found the security of his spiritual home wherever the sun shined.

Edward realized that his writing was becoming richer and more concerned with significances, with the impact of character upon fate, rather than the Greek emphasis on fate impacting character.

Creation of new words now came very easily. He felt that his writings were beginning to breathe softly with the mellow aroma of classical antiquity blending smoothly with new forms of English grammatical usage.

As spring began to break early over Essex County, Edward became restless once again for company other than Anne and the charming but time-demanding Lizbeth. In early March, he invited young Horatio Vere for a visit. He was now a robust lad with calm self-control and a quick hand with his rapier, and he was leaning toward a military career. He and his older brother Francis, Edward's first cousins, were still his favorite relatives.

During the happy visit, a letter arrived from Ned Somerset stating that the Queen had ordered Edmund Tilney, Master of the Revels, to form a Queen's Company of actors and pluck away several of Edward's best performers.

Edward gritted his teeth at the unwelcome news but knew there was nothing he could do. Being at odds with Elizabeth was as futile as a scrawny monkey challenging a lioness!

Edward invited Horatio to journey with him to London to look for replacement actors. They attended a play at The Theatre and talked with two of the best actors. Edward then suggested a bit of camaraderie at The Bull. They immediately spotted Tom Sackville and Ned. At another table sat Ferdinando Stanley, the 23-year-old son of the Earl of Derby, and his younger brother William. Both brothers had enthusiastic interests in literature and theater. Edward suggested that they all join together in The Jester, a private room upstairs.

As they were convivially talking and drinking beer, the wine master, Charles Grenville, entered with two carafes of Spanish sherry. "These are gifts from a gentleman downstairs who wishes to remain anonymous. Take care, for the sweet aroma belies a hidden strength."

Edward poured every goblet full of the golden-brown wine. "Smell that fascinating fragrance! It is perhaps Spain's only cultural contribution to the world under King Philip. A toast to the Queen: May she forgive her errant knight and his wandering weaponry!"

"This is potent brew," said Ferdinando. "Sip with prudence."

"May not an exile, like Ovid banished by Tiberius, mollify his sorrows with fine wine?" Edward downed his glass and refilled it.

Time passed rapidly as anecdotes and earthy humor prevailed. Another anonymous pair of carafes were brought by Grenville, who asked, "Said I well? Is this not a fine wine?"

"Who is our generous benefactor?" slurred Edward as he relinquished his soul to the wine.

"Or malefactor," suggested Tom Sackville. "Beware of strangers bearing grapes!"

"There is too much Spain in these goblets," said Ned. "Let's quit this place and head for my home. You must see Elizabeth and our five children!"

Edward felt a brief pang as he thought of still-unmarried Mary Hastings. *What a glorious life we would have had together . . .*

At that moment, Thomas Knyvet minced into the room, disregarding the time-honored custom of English taverns that when guests took over an entire room, it was considered their temporary personal property.

He bowed low. "*Avec* my compliments, *messieurs. Bon après midi!* I hope you enjoyed my mild aperitif, especially our unrepentant writer without a palace he can call home."

"Courtesy requires our thanks of you, Thomas Knyvet," said Edward. "The sherry was of fine quality, particularly appreciated by me."

"Then I chose wrongly. *Pardonnez-mois* to you other noble four."

"A jester," said Edward, "must be clever and witty, not a fool! Now take your bastard French and our thanks and leave."

"So, you call me a fool, insolent Lord! How dare you insult a gentleman of the Queen's own chamber!" His chin quivered, his nostrils flared.

Edward stood up. "God's blood! How long must I endure these coxcombs, these curtseying roosters, these pseudo-Gauls that gall?"

"And you, you over-proud debaucher, how dare you use the word 'bastard' in front of me after savagely deflowering my innocent eighteen-year-old niece and having her forbidden for life from Court."

"Innocent, you say? You mock those words in reference to Anne!" Edward shouted.

Both Stanleys rose, grabbed Thomas by the arms, and lifted him toward the door, Ferdinando saying, "Leave now, Knyvet. Your clever scheme is quite obvious and unbecoming a gentleman."

Knyvet replied by shouting, "And must I let our noble Lord Edward fornicate our gentle ladies of the Court until he impregnates seventeen? Did the Thirteenth Earl inseminate thirteen and the Fifteenth, fifteen?"

Edward whipped out his rapier. "Insult both me and my honorable ancestors? Wine or not, that cannot stand! And leave Anne Vavasour out of this!" His tongue was somewhat thick and his balance imperfect but that did not hinder him. "She was a puppet of the treacherous Howards and knew exactly what she was doing. You should have protected her from such traitors!"

"Edward!" exclaimed Tom Sackville. "Take heed! Remember how often you have warned about the dangerous combination of anger and alcohol! You are falling into his nets. Re-scabbard your rapier. He isn't worth it!"

"I will enjoy carving this conniving cowardly ca-pon!" roared Edward. "The Noble Boar against the slimy fecal fowl! Who will prepare the excremental stuffing when he breathes his last?"

"To the yard, vile slanderer and violator of young girls," answered Knyvet with a smug smile. Edward was unaware that for months Knyvet had been tak-ing lessons with London's fencing-master, Rocco Bonetti.

"Edward, reconsider!" pleaded Ned. "You are not fit to fight."

"Uncle Edward, let me take him on for the honor of the Veres!" cried Horatio, his rapier already out.

"Oh, no!" said Knyvet loudly. "This is *our* fight. Let our venomous poet-scorpion show his sting in the time-honored manner!"

The tavern drinkers spilled out onto the over-hanging balconies and into the courtyard. Charles Grenville, who knew that Knyvet had stopped drink-ing when Edward had entered, stepped between them.

"Gentlemen! We don't allow affrays at The Bull! Please settle your quarrel elsewhere!"

"Step aside, Charles. This will be brief," said Knyvet, thrusting his point at Edward without the

.TR

courtesy of a warning *en garde.* Charles left the building immediately to search for the sheriff.

"Too rash," said Ferdinando to his brother. "Edward would never be defeated by him without the intrusion of wine. If he dies, England loses a man with a rare touch of greatness who has much more to write."

"Be ready to intervene," answered William Stanley. "I shall not idly watch a dastardly butchery by such an ignoble wretch!"

The fencing began. Neither pulled his dagger. Edward began to retreat, inviting thrusts and then parrying. He saw a cocky grin on Knyvet's face and immediately realized that his opponent's skills had improved. Edward's own reactions were slowed just enough to mean the difference between life and death.

What an idiot I am, he thought belatedly, *a bird already limed, a plastered patrician steeped in sherry. Is this my end, at the hands of a scheming sycophant?*

Edward continued to retreat, trying to keep his balance. He then attacked, feinting to the leg and attempting a *fleche.* Knyvet skillfully parried. Back and forth they went, circling in the center of the yard, feinting, dodging, leaping forward, locking rapiers, pushing away, thrusting. Edward was clearly clumsy and slow.

Edward feinted left and tried a *mandritto* but missed. The crowd began to murmur and curse as the word spread of Knyvet's sherry strategy. Edward felt lightheaded and his balance worsened. Knyvet quickly aimed a *stoccata* at his abdomen. Edward turned too sluggishly and had to block the rapier with his left arm. His shirt began to redden. He launched a *stramazzone,* but it was too apparent.

Knyvet side-stepped and aimed for the heart, but Edward's overshoot caused the rapier point to bounce off his ribs.

"This is going to be a slaughter," muttered Ferdinando. Edward pretended to lean backwards off-balance. Knyvet took the bait and lunged awkwardly. The opening was perfect but Edward missed Knyvet's liver and thrust his point into Knyvet's upper thigh. The pain and surprise left Knyvet open. Edward struck quickly but missed the chest, slicing into Knyvet's left forearm.

Vertigo began to overwhelm Edward and he broke into a cold sweat. As more sherry was absorbed he felt increasingly nauseated. He put his left hand to his forehead and waved it in front of him, trying to clear his blurred vision. He staggered backwards.

"Enough, Thomas! Wine and I can stand and fight no more. You have won. I concede."

Ferdinando rushed out between them, grabbed Edward with both arms, and turned to lead him inside.

"I have not won until you are dead!" shouted Knyvet. "You cannot run from a fair fight!" With Edward's back to him, Knyvet lunged forward and thrust his rapier into Edward's left flank, quickly withdrew it and thrust again, the point catching Edward behind the left knee. Edward winced when it hit the bone.

"Oh, Ferdinando, why hold me thus defenseless?" said Edward as he twisted away. "Sniveling hyena! Putrid coward, to blade a man with his back turned! Take that, and that!"

Knyvet was off balance and caught two *stoccatas* into his right upper arm and shoulder as his rapier fell to the ground. Edward pitched forward and landed next to it.

"Stop, I say, in the Queen's name, stop!" said the sheriff in a booming voice as the crowd parted to let him through. "All men assembled here in arms this day against the Queen's peace, we command you to cease at once. Continue under grave penalty. Repair to your dwelling places!"

Knyvet picked up his rapier with his left hand and swirled it, with head held high. "So much for poet-weaklings!" He walked out of the courtyard as several in the crowd sent muttered oaths after him:

"Loathsome, unmanly son-of-a-bitch!"

"Whoreson dogfish!"

"Villainous bastard!"

Copious blood was flowing out of Edward's left leg wound. He tried to get up but fell again.

Ned removed his belt and bound Edward's upper leg tightly. "Keep his blood-flow staunched while I ride and get Dr. Julio."

As they carried him upstairs, Edward said, "Thank you, friends. How stupid! A fool bereft of sense!"

Charles Grenville led them to a third-floor room.

"Let me at least walk to my bed of sherry and shame," said Edward. They put him into the standing position. He took two steps and fell forward to the floor. "What in hell is happening? I am full of wine but not *that* drunk!" He tried again with the help of Tom Sackville and Horatio. He then looked down and said, "My God, my left foot isn't moving!"

Tom and Horatio removed Edward's bloody shirt, pulled down his long stockings and applied pressure to the bleeding wounds.

When Dr. Julio arrived, he checked Edward over and said, "Nothing looks serious above the knee.

A couple of inches here or there and you could have been in big trouble, Edward. But I don't like what I see in the left leg. He obviously sliced a nerve. I don't see any movement in your foot at all. We'll take you home in the morning. In the meantime, I'm binding your wounds with herbs. If we are fortunate, infection won't set in."

A pensive Edward remained silent for a few moments before shouting, "O thou invisible spirit of wine, if thou hast no name to be known by, let us call thee Devil!"

Chapter 38

The only soil of his fair virtue's gloss . . .
Is a sharp wit matched with too blunt a will,
Whose edge hath power to cut, whose will still wills
It should none spare that come within his power.
                                    - Love's Labours Lost

It was now the second anniversary of Edward's release from the Tower. His wounds had fully healed but his left foot-drop paralysis was permanent. There were also emotional scars that lingered. His knowledge of life's imperfections and demands haunted him and at times he had an overwhelming sense of futility and dishonor.

He lingered in the richly tapestried presence chamber of Greenwich Palace for a private Sunday dinner with the Queen, by her invitation. He looked out of the windows at the sky-blued Thames directly below and admired the myriad colored sails of pleasure craft and merchant ships of all sizes moving in both directions.

As organ music wafted into the room from the Queen's chapel service, Edward wondered what Elizabeth's true religious beliefs were. She had told him more than once that she regarded theological conjectures as ropes of sea-slime leading to the moon. However, he thought she was devout in private.

While waiting, he watched the daily ritual of the formal dinner ceremony, an elaborate sequence with servants clad in blue and white bringing in turn the tablecloth, silver saltcellar and stacks of plates, kneeling three times between each trip. A maid of honor and lady in waiting then rubbed each plate with bread. Scarlet-clad yeomen of the guard brought in heaping platters of food. Each was tasted with a knife given them by the women as twelve trumpeters and two kettle-drums announced the food's arrival. Edward appreciated the formality and charm of this royal custom.

"Good day, Lord Edward," said the fifty-year-old Queen. "Please be seated. Are you well-recovered from your wounds?"

"Physical wounds heal well in a few months, Your Majesty. Other wounds require longer. But my limp, I fear, will be with me to my grave." He admired her tall rippled orange wig laced with jewels and wondered whether the rumors were true that she was almost bald. Her still-handsome face showed more wrinkles. He noted the yellowing of her teeth, worse on the right, despite her attempts to keep them white by washing them twice a day with a mixture of white wine and vinegar boiled in honey.

"I am sorry that my fine tournament champion

and sprightly dancing-partner is marred. Has the lesson been well-learned?"

Edward cut a piece of mutton and began eating it with his fingers. He briefly thought about the 20,000 sheep consumed by the royal Court each year, along with four million eggs, 600,000 gallons of beer and not a single drop of water.

"Every day is a veritable encyclopedia of learning," he replied. "Wine, scheming reptiles and swords mix not well. A coward is worse than a cup of sack with lime in it."

"I like not any continuation of your street-battles with Knyvet and his men. I trust that my royal edict shall be obeyed."

"I shall comply, Your Majesty, although I would rather carbonado his shanks! I shall always regard him as a greasy white-livered scoundrel . . . but I shall reserve future comments for my pen."

"Oh, Edward, you and your golden pen have been sorely missed by me and my Court," she said. "But some of your acidities and acerbicies have not. Have your various tribulations affected your writing?" She sipped her favorite red alicant wine from Spain although she always tried to drink wine sparingly so that her faculties would not be clouded.

"I believe my style is becoming more effective as it incorporates the broad spectrum and impact of life, including the serious and tragic."

Elizabeth admired her new ribbed plaster ceiling with designs of royal crowns intermixed with lions and falcons. "My Turk, I realize I have been hard on you, banishing you for two years. We now invite you back. What writings do you have in mind?"

He had been hoping for the invitation to return to Court and hearing it from her lips was a great relief. Trying not to be too obvious about it, he answered, "Many plays, Your Majesty, both light and dark. I feel our English language bursting its bonds of restrictive simplicity, don't you?"

"Indeed I do! And how are your University Wits?"

"My writing group is producing quite good work. Greene, Lodge, Watson, Munday, and Peele write very well and are quite inventive. Thomas Kyd is bright but needs nurturing, as does Lyly."

The Queen finished her fowl pie dyed bright yellow with saffron and containing capon, mallard, woodcock and teal. She dipped her fingers in a silver basin of water and dried her hands. "My dream of a cultured and literary Court has suffered a relapse because of your temporary absence. May I now officially request a great outpouring of new plays and other writings by you and your group?"

"My quill vibrates with anticipation," he said truthfully.

"But must you insist on portraying real people? Future generations may have difficulty recognizing whom you are describing, but not ours!"

Edward put a clove in his mouth. "I believe a false history is being created of your era for the untrue glorification of others. My own eyes have seen it. If I disguise my characters completely, my plays will not be true chronicles of the times. The most eminent writers throughout history have richly documented their eras, to the benefit of posterity."

"Doing so is not always without danger," she pointed out.

"Aristophanes named his characters directly. If he were living now, Burghley would have him earning his living hopping headless in one of West Smithfield's side-shows!"

Elizabeth fidgeted with her spoon. "Your wounded leg has not modulated your frontal assaults! Be prudent and flexible, not intractable, Edward. Impaling strong individuals is risky and I may not always be able to protect you."

"Even Socrates used living examples to portray human nature." He sighed. "But I do often fail to realize how much an ill word may empoison liking."

She began eating a sugary pudding. "Most people do not want their flaws described for all time. Venomed spears are revenge-triggering. Be wary of hemlock in the hands of the mighty!"

"I shall be wary, Your Majesty. But as I wrote in *As You Like It*:

> *I must have liberty*
> *Withal, as large a charter as the wind,*
> *To blow on whom I please, for so fools have;*
> *And they that are most gallèd with my folly,*
> *They most must laugh.*"

"It is time to change the subject, Edward. I have decided we should spread more of your plays throughout England, staging them in cities, towns, even villages and hamlets. We must kindle the flames of patriotism to help repel the rapacious Spanish invaders."

Edward, always eager to follow the de Vere tradition of service to country and loyalty to the monarch, pushed up his sleeves and began rubbing the boar ring on his left thumb. "How may I best serve you, Your Majesty?"

"Write more dramas of English history, stirring sagas which foster ideas of courage, fidelity to the crown and inspired allegiance to our country."

"An exhilarating challenge! I will revise my drafts of *King John* and *Richard III* , then pen more King Henry plays." He paused, then added, "But *never* Henry VII because he so maliciously crippled my family financially, leading to encumbered estates which are still in lien today."

She nodded. "Godspeed, Edward. Use your sword of words to fight our Spanish enemy and glorify our England." With a flourish she exited into her private chambers.

* * *

Edward immediately discussed the new royal charge with his University Wits. All were fired with enthusiasm. They eagerly agreed to remain together to continue the invigorating cross-fertilization of ideas in the academic atmosphere they had created.

Edward, therefore, disregarding the cost, bought Fisher's Folly, located just beyond London's wall on the road to The Theatre and The Curtain. The large extravagant house included ten acres of ornate pleasure gardens, a bowling alley and a tennis court. Edward felt that living well in an intellectually stimulating environment would best enhance creativity.

John Lyly, Thomas Watson, Robert Greene, Anthony Munday, Thomas Churchyard, Thomas Kyd and Thomas Lodge all moved into Fisher's Folly. Edward worked there five days a week but returned to Oxford Court to be with his wife and daughter on weekends.

To remind himself always to strive for enduring excellence, he purchased for his desk an oval piece of amber encasing a perfectly preserved bee. He placed it beside the golden inkwell studded with small rubies and diamonds which he had won in 1581 in his second tournament. He was proud that he had been victorious in all three of his tournaments and had been the reigning champion of England for more than a decade.

John Lyly, still Edward's secretary, managed Edward's two acting groups, Oxford's Players and Children of St. Paul. He leased space for rehearsals and performances at The Blackfriars, a former monastery on the Thames near Westminster which also contained the Revels Office.

Edward now completed *The Most Excellent and Lamentable Tragedy of Romeo and Juliet* . The story had intrigued him since the age of ten when his mother had given him Luigi Da Porto's *Historia Novellamente Ritrovata di Due Nobili Amanti* about the beautiful but fatal youthful romance in Verona in the early 1300's. He followed the general pattern of *Tragicall Historye of Romeus and Juliet* , his first published work at age twelve.

He decided to revise *Hamlet* , begun three years previously, his autobiographical play set at Castle Kronberg in Denmark. He poured himself, his own life history, his own being, his own thoughts and ideas into the lead character. He portrayed Burghley as a bumbling councilor to the King, naming him Corambis, double-hearted, in reference to Burghley's coat of arms motto, *Cor Unum Via Una*, One Heart One Way. He could not restrain himself from depicting Corambis as a stuttering repeater of inanities:

> Hamlet: *Do you see yonder cloud that's almost in shape of a camel?*
> Corambis: *By th' mass, and 'tis like a camel, indeed.*

Hamlet: *Methinks it is like a weasel.*
Corambis: *It is backed like a weasel.*
Hamlet: *Or like a whale.*
Corambis: *Very like a whale.*

Edward decided to make a hardly-disguised reference to Burghley's favorite techniques for stealing land, in the words of Hamlet, when the gravedigger unearths a skull:

> *This fellow might be in 's time a great buyer of land, with his statutes, his recognizances, his fines, his double-vouchers, his recoveries. Is this the fine of his fines and the recovery of his recoveries, to have his fine pate full of fine dirt? The very conveyances of his lands will hardly lie in this box.*

Edward could not refrain from having Hamlet slay Corambis when he catches him spying behind a tapestry, thrusting his sword through the tapestry in the same manner in which Edward had killed Burghley's apprentice cook and coerced thief, Tom Bricknell.

Edward fully realized he was throwing down the gauntlet. But what difference could it make? Burghley had already mal-influenced his entire life.

Edward started to revise *The Troublesome Reign of John, King of England* , who ruled from 1199 to 1216. Fulfilling Elizabeth's request, he included new lines on nationalism and anti-Catholic commentary: *Tell him this tale and from the mouth of England add thus much more, that no Italian priest shall tithe or toll in our dominions.*

He ended his play with a flourishing call to patriotism:

> *This England never did, nor never shall,*
> *Lie at the proud foot of a conqueror.*
> *And we shall shock them. Naught shall make*
> *us rue*
> *If England to itself do rest but true.*

As Edward wrote, he became increasingly enthusiastic about Elizabeth's now-sweeping assignment to stimulate and enhance the whole country's pride and loyalty in a perilous time of threatened invasion. What an opportunity to influence the minds and hearts of an entire nation!

Books and plays were pouring forth from the University Wits and from other English writers. Edward believed that his goal of a true literary eruption, akin to the great Italian artistic rebirth, was now actually in process in England.

Chapter 39

O, it is excellent
To have a giant's strength, but it is tyrannous
To use it like a giant .
                    - Measure for Measure

As Edward stood at the edge of the Thames in front of Whitehall and looked down into the crystal clear blue waters on a sunny day in June, 1586, a feeling of pride permeated him. Hadn't he and his University Wits amply met the Queen's stimulating challenge and already produced a large number of loyalty plays and books?

He raised his eyes, gazed at the church-steepled skyline of the London he had grown to love, and wondered why the Queen had suddenly requested his presence for a royal interview.

*   *   *

The day previous, paunchy white-bearded Baron Burghley, the Queen's trusted chief councilor for twenty-eight years, had limped into the presence chamber and asked to speak to her alone. He prided himself on tempered emotions but he was red-cheeked and spoke loudly, with unaccustomed firmness.

"My Gracious, Gracious Sovereign, I beg you to stop your playwrighting favorite, yes, your noble allowed fool, from slandering me!"

The imperious Queen quickly dismissed her attendants. "Leviathan, you must stop defaming the finest poet and playwright England, and perhaps the World, has ever produced. He does great honor to our country."

Despite his inflamed feet, Burghley remained standing as his face reddened further. "Honor by writing plays and poems? Surely a work for Court dunces!"

"God preserve you, my gouty Spirit! Your pain seems to have frothed your usual controlled restraint." She fingered the scented pomander hanging from her waist by a silver chain.

"Begging pardon, majestic Majesty, but de Vere's childish verses are vilely repugnant when they make repeated mock of me."

"Childish verses? The endless panorama of human drama so beautifully scripted by unmatchable talent at the Queen's own urging?" She began pacing back and forth.

"Such writings must be *totally destroyed* when they attack those in authority." His face became deep red.

How intriguing, thought Elizabeth, that as a

stutterer loses his stutter when talking with his dog, Burghley loses his slow, repetitive, ponderous speech on those rare occasions when he is angry. "Take care, councilor. I like not your demeaning commentary. Those whom sovereigns elevate out of the dirt of commonality can easily be cast back into the muck of poverty."

Burghley's eyes opened widely and he took a deep breath. He nervously tapped his white staff on the floor as he fought to control his emotions. "A thousand pardons, most benevolent Queen! An unbearable mental pain was inflicted upon me yesterday by watching our Seventeenth Earl of Oxford's play, *Hamlet* , at The Theatre, hearing the raucous deriding laughter elicited by Corambis. Everyone knows that the shallow-headed, imbecilic Corambis represents me, your esteemed Lord Treasurer."

Elizabeth chuckled to herself, remembering some of Corambis' foolish lines. "But Leviathan, laughter keeps our blood flowing and prolongs our lives! Edward makes fun of my frailties and those of other sovereigns in a manner which highly amuses me! We are getting old, Spirit! Relax and bring laughter into your life!"

"His barbed attacks on me are merciless," Burghley blurted, his face now purple. "Please allow me to obliterate all of his plays! Yes, demolish them for all time!"

"Never! Not as long as I am Queen!" She set her lips firmly.

"But his plays discredit England! After I die, if he tries to publish his plays, then I beg you to stop him, or force him to publish anonymously or with a false name attached. Yes, such a misleading name that no one in times ahead, not ever, will guess the true author. Then they will not know whom he mocks and history will accord me my due." He stomped his foot forcefully on the floor and groaned in pain.

"History will not forget you, Spirit. You have served England more than well. Together we have steadied an able course for England during troubled times."

The Queen walked thoughtfully to the window, looked down upon the fountain jetting in her courtyard, and silently mulled her options.

After several moments she said, "Spirit, I must tell you that when the time is right, I will do all in my power to help him publish his works which I deem a national treasure. They are a beautiful triumphant tribute, perhaps the most permanent and inspiring, to my reign."

"But what about the authorship, my gracious Queen?"

With eyes downcast and in somber voice, Elizabeth continued. "Out of fairness to you and those whom Edward has rather parboiled in his plays, I will now promise you this: By royal command, I will forbid him from attaching his own name to any of his literary works. I have formidable doubts about the wisdom of this decision and in the past, I have led him to believe quite otherwise. But for greater harmony of the court and for necessary smoothness of our country's governing, especially in the face of an imminent threat of Spanish invasion, I give you my word."

"Thank you, Your Majesty."

*   *   *

A fight between two male swans brought Edward back to the moment. It was time for his appointment with the Queen.

Edward entered the presence chamber and gazed admiringly at Elizabeth, magnificently attired in a broadly-hooped, bejeweled green skirt, a broad white linen ruff and her many-tiered orange wig intertwined with pearls glistening in the blazing firelight.

Edward felt the power which emanated from the strong face and regal bearing of Elizabeth, now fifty-three and Queen since the age of twenty-five. He studied her high forehead, thin eyelashes, narrow mouth and somewhat prominent Tudor nose just beginning to hook. She sat in her richly ornamented chair of state, rapidly opening and closing her ivory-handled fan. She was talking in Latin with the German ambassador.

Edward recalled the Queen telling him once, "I am more afraid of making a fault in my Latin than of the Kings of Spain, France, Scotland and all of their confederates." As the last foreign emissary arose and backed away, Edward's name was called.

The Queen waved everyone out of the room. Edward kneeled at her feet and tried to disregard the odors of rotting food and animal excretions emerging from the reed-covered floor, not overcome by numerous bouquets of herbs and flowers.

She looked down at Edward and fondly recalled her first glimpse of him in his early childhood when his father was a courtier and his mother a lady in waiting. Elizabeth bade him rise as she looked at his handsome face, auburn hair, mustache and short brown beard tinged with gray. She smiled at his un-orthodox attire, this time bright yellow with black hose.

"I have a reward for you, my talented Lord, well earned and richly deserved. Your writing abilities are exceeding even my own high expectations. Your plays and poetry are a shining ornament to my reign and now your words are helping defend our kingdom against the Spanish."

"Thank you . . . Your Majesty." Edward breathed deeply and smiled, basking in her praise.

Elizabeth presented him with a Privy Seal Warrant which paid tribute to his unspecified continuing service to crown and country and granted him one thousand pounds annually and indefinitely from special secret funds unknown even to Burghley.

Edward was stunned. The sum was far larger than that paid to most high-ranking public officials and ambassadors. Over the years, he had sold off many estates to finance his writing group, produce plays and live as a ranking nobleman and courtier. The Queen had pledged funding many times to allay his expenses, as she did for so many of her courtiers, but had come through only once. Discouraged, he had recently written in *Hamlet* :

> *I eat the air, promise-crammed.*
> *You cannot feed capons so.*

"Your largesse overwhelms me, Your Majesty," he said at last.

The Queen tapped her fan nervously and Edward felt a sudden chilly certainty that she was about to say something he would not like.

"There is only one condition." She paused, her

jaw tightening. "You may only publish your works with a pseudonym. That must be a solemn and covert agreement with your Queen."

Edward stood up with eyes wide and brow furrowed. "But Your Majesty, would history have benefited from Aristotle, Plato and Socrates being known to the world as Lusty, Lout and Longbottom? Did Michelangelo and Leonardo da Vinci sign their works with an 'X' ?"

"Edward, this decision is irrevocable." She looked away, for once too steeped in shame and chagrin to meet his eyes.

His mind was racing, his breathing rapid and his heart pounding. They both had agreed so many times that anonymity was nonsense! She was his primary motivator, pledging repeatedly that his authorship would be publicly acknowledged in print as a reward for his artistic enrichment of her Court.

He could not give up with silent acquiescence. "Your Majesty, is it not a normal human attribute to desire credit for one's own artistry at any level of sophistication? Surely this is not yourself talking, considering our many discussions in the past!"

Elizabeth turned her eyes downward. "Queens make hard lonely decisions every day and need not explain themselves. I am accountable to God alone."

"But Your Majesty . . ."

"My decision in this matter was exceedingly difficult, Edward. I will tell you that the Lord Treasurer was red-cheeked and fuming when he talked with me yesterday after seeing *Hamlet* at The Theatre. He described the jeering laughter elicited by the shallow-headed Corambis and said that everyone in the audience knew that Corambis represented him."

"He was correct!" Edward confessed readily. "Our

English play audiences are becoming more sophisticated all the time, even the penny-paying groundlings!"

"Don't you see the lack of wisdom in such characterizations, Edward? He called you malicious and slanderous. I had to remind him that you are the finest poet and dramatist in England."

"You humble me, Your Majesty." Having been tempered in the crucible of royal deceit, Edward visualized himself as the Queen's playwrighting steer, fattened with compliments before being led to beefy slaughter.

Elizabeth rose from her chair and walked briskly back and forth, hands tightly clenched around her fan. "Burghley pleaded with me to have the plays destroyed or published anonymously. His unusual anger finally upset me and I reminded him that his titled nobility could be revoked at any time."

"Did that make his gizzard quiver?" asked Edward. The thought of Burghley losing both his status and his ill-gotten wealth was enough to bring a thin smile to Edward's lips.

"He calmed down immediately but reminded me that he had given his entire life to his country."

"He has paid himself amply!" Edward said firmly. "He is now the richest man in England!" Edward recalled with disgust Elizabeth's statement to Burghley on making him her Principal Secretary in 1558 when she became Queen, *This judgment I have of you, that you will not be corrupted by any manner of gift* .

Elizabeth drew in a breath and released it in a sigh. "I grow weary, Edward, and I feel a headache coming on. Burghley has been my strong right arm for my entire reign. I understand how you feel but from his perspective, his points are well taken. You have repeatedly impaled the powerful with your skillful rapier-wit."

Edward knew that debating the Queen was futile. He could see that she was feeling guilty, a rare sight, but her mind was clearly made up.

He decided to make one final sortie. With head bowed, he said in a low voice, "Is my literary anonymity what you truly wish, Your Majesty, as a shining memorial to your monarchy, while Burghley marches gloriously unscathed and triumphantly into history?"

Elizabeth reddened and gritted her teeth. "My decision is *final*, courtier! Your pseudonymity will be coerced, even though I have assured you otherwise in the past. It is essential for the tranquillity of my Court and for our country's smooth governing in this time of imminent Spanish invasion. Your authorship may be known by any other name but your own."

Edward felt completely crushed. He kept his head low and did not speak for a few moments. Finally he said, "Your majesty, a rose may smell as sweet by any other name but *not* my plays. They are full of allusions, characterizations and references to our times that future readers will not understand without knowing the true identity of the author."

Elizabeth walked to the window and looked down upon the Lancaster red, Yorkist white, and blended pink roses in Whitehall's inner courtyard.

After several minutes of silence, she said quietly, "Why was I born a Queen rather than a merry carefree country milkmaid? To wear a crown is more glorious to those who see it, than it is a pleasure to them that bear it."

She turned and walked slowly back to Edward and put her hand on his shoulder. "Edward, you are already the most eminent creative artist in your generation, or in any generation in England's history. You are known by everyone in Court and many throughout England and the continent. Your reputation and fame *can not and will not die* !"

"You are kind to say so, Your Majesty," he said, his eyes lifting at last to hers. "But anonymous obscurity appears more likely to me."

The Queen did not reply. She swung her pomander and let it wrap and unwrap around her index finger.

Edward finally knelt and kissed Elizabeth's hand. "De Veres have been totally loyal to their monarchs for five hundred years, as you well know, Your Majesty. Though I disagree one thousand per cent with your verdict, I accept it and will continue my best efforts to beautify and adorn your Court and deserve your trust."

*   *   *

Edward walked slowly to his palace room, several times stopping to gaze at portraits of England's monarchs. *How could Elizabeth so shamelessly and disloyally rescind her repeated promises to me over so many years?*

With a tight grip on his pen, he sat quietly at his desk and then wrote:

> *Time is the author both of truth and right,*
> *And time will bring this treachery to light .*

He paused to think over events that had brought him to this point. He had struggled for years with the dilemma of whether or not to portray real people in his plays and had always decided that he must do so. Could a writer of significant literature be considered worthwhile if he did not enrich future generations by including the thoughts, deeds and singularities of his own times?

Was it, however, a fatal flaw to disregard discretion and insist on depicting the frailties and faults of the mighty?

He picked up his pen and began to write new lines for Hamlet to soliloquize, for Hamlet was himself:

> *So, oft it chances in particular men*
> *That, for some vicious mole of nature in them,*
> *By the o'ergrowth of some complexion,*
> *Oft breaking down the pales and forts of reason,*
> *Or by some habit that too much o'erleavens*
> *The form of plausive manners, that these men*
> *Carrying, I say, the stamp of one defect,*
> *Shall in the general censure take corruption*
> *From that particular fault .*

He gazed at his stained glass windows for long minutes and reaffirmed that throughout his life he had repeatedly decided that he must be true to himself: *Vero Nihil Verius*. He could *not* refrain from characterizing the times and the people in power, especially amoral politicians such as Burghley.

Are greed, deceit, corruption and hypocrisy immune from dramatization? With paid historians writing from selected and falsified documents, will anyone else depict my era accurately if I do not? The great sweep of history deserves the truth.

He had been warned against negative portrayal by the two great loves of his life and by a literature-loving monarch but he had chosen to ignore their caring advice. As one who had several times himself felt the pain of life's often undeserved misfortunes, lines formed in his mind which he thought he could use in a new tragedy he was beginning to plan, *Macbeth*: :

> *I am one, my liege,*
> *Whom the vile blows and buffets of the world*
> *Have so incensed that I am reckless what*
> *I do to spite the world.*

Edward pondered whether his coerced pseudonymity was the result of fate, being born into the only culture in the world which forbade authorship-identity, or the result of his own basic character defect, his own mole of nature.

Both, he decided.

Was he now, therefore, powerless to prevent his lifetime of literary creativity from being blown by the dark treacherous winds of fortune, scattered forever in the cold silent universe of anonymity?

Chapter 40

'Tis very true, my grief lies all within
And these external manners of laments
Are merely shadows to the unseen grief
That swells with silence in the tortur'd soul.
— Richard II

The Thames was unusually high, lapping half-way up the algaed bricks. White-crested waves crashed forcefully into the river wall sending sheets of spray flying into the wind.

It had been two weeks since the Queen commanded his pseudonymity and Edward, depressed and unable to sleep, had spent most of every night pacing the floor and staring into the fireplace.

It was difficult for him to believe that, as in his compelled marriage, Burghley was again holding sway over the Queen of England, influencing her to make decisions contrary to her own true self.

Edward was sure that Elizabeth had *never* wanted

him to remain anonymous! Selfish and egotistical she may be, but the Queen had always said that she wanted them both to share in any credit or glory deriving from a brilliant literary flowering in England.

How incredible that in so many areas, the son of Henry VIII's wardrobe keeper and grandson of a tavern-owner is more powerful and influential than a divinely-inspired Tudor monarch!

Staring at the dark turbulent water, Edward briefly thought about leaping into the Thames but it was against his nature to run from life's adversities.

With another appointment requested by the Queen and scheduled for tomorrow at Greenwich, he knew he needed something dramatic to distract his mind and get it back into harmony with the three ancient virtues: *Aequinimitas, Sobrietas, Temperitas.*

So, Edward decided to *shoot the bridge* . Ned Somerset reluctantly agreed to accompany him on this cold morning.

"Would you mind telling me what I am doing here at dawn on this miserable day when I could be back in my warm canopied feather bed creating my tenth child?" Ned groused. "I must be crazy to continue to pretend you are my friend!"

Ned and Edward were both dressed like fishermen in dark green jackets, overpants and oiled leather boots. They were standing on slippery cement stairs as Andy the waterman rowed his fourteen-foot boat into their waiting hands.

"All right you crazy earls, hop in and let's get this adventure going!" Andy called to them. "It's a high tide for sure and excellent weather for a drowning or two!"

Edward laughed. Andy was an old friend from river ferrying and The Boar's Head. Edward held the prow while Ned jumped in and sat in the middle. Edward followed and kneeled in the bow.

"Let's go, Andy!" he shouted. "The tide is moving out splendidly. Our timing couldn't be better. Ned is a timorous trembling landlubber! It has taken me years and uncounted barrels of beer to bolster up his courage."

They were two hundred yards above London bridge and picking up speed as Andy rowed to the center of the roiling river and turned downstream. The bridge, topped by five-story dwellings and shops, was supported by eighteen stone arches. Underneath were long oval-shaped wooden starlings which narrowed each opening to a few feet. More than half of the Thames' width was effectively blocked. On an outgoing tide, water backed up above the starlings and drained out rapidly below them, creating a thunderous waterfall four to seven feet high. The rushing water operated force pumps supplying water to London's inhabitants.

Edward knew that shooting the bridge was considered dangerous and unwise, suitable only for daring adventurers and fools. The crashing roar of the waterfall grew louder as they were swept toward the bridge. Edward enthusiastically raised his clenched right hand while Ned crouched low with a tight grip on the sides of the boat.

Andy steered carefully into the center of an opening with only eighteen inches on each side, shouting, "Steady, steady . . . hold on lads, here we go!"

The boat leaped out over the edge of the waterfall, hesitated in the air, then pointed almost straight down and fell six feet into the swirling water. The front half of the boat disappeared under the water as Andy tried desperately to steady it. The boat shot upwards, tilted to the left and turned over, hurling its occupants into the cold briny river.

Edward bobbed up first, then Ned and finally Andy. All were good swimmers and swam quickly to the left bank before their heavy clothes could drag them down.

"Fantastic!" shouted Edward as they were helped out by two of Andy's watermen-friends. "Let's do it again!"

Three others in their boats, arranged in advance by Andy, an experienced bridge-shooter, waited downstream to retrieve the oars and overturned boat.

Edward wiped the water out of his eyes and started laughing at Ned's appearance. "You look like a baptized basset hound, Ned—only with sadder eyes! For sheer excitement, where can you equal that? If Andy hadn't belched as we were going over the falls, we would have made it!"

*   *   *

Elizabeth had summoned Edward to meet her in the apple orchard of Greenwich Palace. She stood near the central fountain wearing a pink and white summer dress.

"I know how sad you are over the pseudonym decision, Edward," she said. "My informants tell me you are morose and gloomy which is not like you."

Edward nodded assent but did not respond. He thought how incredible it was that seeking honor for the Queen's Court, for England and for himself was so disgracing that a cloak of suffocating anonymity was royally mandated.

Elizabeth sat down on a white marble bench and gestured for him to sit next to her. She had brought a book with her and now opened it and said, "Far be it for your Queen to embarrass such a sensitive soul, but you may not have seen William Webbe's new work, *A Discourse of English Poetry* . He states:

> *I may not omit the deserved commendation of many honourable and noble Lords and Gentlemen in Her Majesty's Court, which, in the rare devices of poetry have been, and yet are, most skillful; among whom the Right Honourable Earl of Oxford may challenge to himself the title of most excellent among the rest.*"

"How did that survive Burghley's raptor-grip on censorship?" Edward asked bitterly.

"Queens still have *some* power, Edward!" she said sharply, laying aside the book. "To swell your head even further, the French ambassador told me that scores of Frenchmen have seen you act and regard you as the finest *acteur comique* not only in England but in all of Europe."

Edward forced a smile. "That is exhilarating, Your Majesty, but less so when garmented with oblivion."

Undeterred by his tone, she looked directly into his eyes and said fervently, "Bring your own spirits up to their usual high level, Edward, and keep the vitality of my people burning with patriotic fire! Let all Englishmen feel the radiant energy of your literary creativity! Continue to write of the great kings and soldiers of England. Regard yourself as a warrior and the golden pen I gave you as your golden sword in our time of impending crisis."

Edward offered no response.

With a sigh, Elizabeth stood and walked slowly around the many-tiered fountain several times. Twice she started to speak. Finally she gently waved her bejeweled arm at Edward and walked away. The interview was over.

* * *

In early October the Progress was cut short when a new Catholic plot was discovered. The Court moved to the Queen's favorite Richmond Palace with its many blue-cupolaed towers and peaceful view of the Thames. Elizabeth invited Burghley for conference.

"With Babington and his six traitorous co-plotters executed less than a week ago, is it necessary to bring Mary Stuart to trial?" she asked. "Threatening a twice-monarched queen with execution is not to my liking, especially one who has been an accepted exile in England for sixteen years. Why not continue permanent house-arrest?"

"As long as she lives there will be plots against Your Majesty's person and your realm," Burghley said firmly. "Her complicity is proven beyond doubt!"

"By the usual document-altering? I can hear my mother's beheaded voice telling me that the treachery of falsified testimony pervades a realm and mars a ruler."

"She is guilty of treason by all reasonable standards, Your Majesty," Burghley insisted. "It is time to cut off the serpent's head to save your own." He stroked his white beard and his eyes flitted about.

"Save *my* head or *yours* ? My informants tell me you are first on the list of those to be killed if the Catholics succeed."

"The thought had occurred to me, Your Majesty," he admitted with a thin smile.

The Queen laughed in her high shrill tone. "Your annual smile! Hooray, by St. George! I thought we might miss it this year! Your loud guffaws once more resonate our chambers and rattle our mullioned panes!"

The thin smile disappeared. "Your Majesty, the time has come to eliminate the indigenous Catholic threat once and for all. Mary *must* be exterminated since she is the focus of all Catholic plots."

"All right, I will sign the document for a trial of Mary but do *not* proceed with it until I give my final word. I need more time to think it over."

"One thing more, just one, for your magisterial consideration, your Majesty. As we all sadly know, Philip Sidney now lies mortally wounded at Zutphen and is not likely to survive."

"Yes, a foolish heroism on the bloody fields of war, more akin to stupidity when one removes one's armor and rides into battle to show zeal and courage. I believe he was seeking death, construing it as a noble and glorious hero's end when he found his pen inadequate."

The seated Burghley pulled a hand from his staff and began stroking his silver beard, his eyes shifting with every stroke. "Cleaving Mary's Stuart's head could cause Catholic unrest. May I make a suggestion?"

"Proceed, my Lord. I smell foxiness."

"When Sidney dies, we should embalm and cold-storage him. If Mary is executed, I suggest we distract our populace by staging a magnificent hero's funeral for Sidney immediately afterwards, with eulogies far surpassing his life's accomplishments. Then command a period of national mourning."

"Your plan is well thought out and quite Machiavellianly masterful. It certainly would please Sidney, who is clearly dying to be a hero!"

*   *   *

Edward did not relish any role in the trial of Mary, Queen of Scots, but all the leading earls were required to participate and vote "guilty" or their own fortunes would be at stake. All were reluctant to try a former Queen of France and Scotland, someone who was given a safe haven as a guest of England. All were affected by her tragic life, with her own intrinsic weaknesses bringing misfortune. In an authoritarian state dominated by Burghley, the doctored evidence was always overwhelming in a treason trial and the verdict predetermined.

Mary, deprived of any warning, legal counsel or her own papers, made a dignified, eloquent, moving speech in her defense. Edward's eyes made direct contact with Mary's several times and there passed between them an invisible wave of sympathetic understanding, respectful admiration, compassion and futility. The verdict was unanimous. Death by axe. The whole scenario was orchestrated by Burghley without seeking the Queen's final verbal approval.

Edward was appalled at the flimsy altered evidence used to murder a former Queen of both France and Scotland. He immediately wrote a testimonial verse, aimed at Burghley, to include in *The Winter's Tale* :

> *It is an heretic that makes the fire,*
> *Not she which burns in't. I'll not call you tyrant;*
> *But this most cruel usage of your Queen—*
> *Not able to produce more accusation*
> *Than your own weak-hinged fancy—something*
> *savours*

Of tyranny, and will ignoble make you,
Yea, scandalous to the world.

As Edward listened to the resounding organ at St. Paul's during Philip Sidney's funeral, he sat in wonderment at the political process of hero-making. He recalled the mediocre quality of Sidney's writing, his frequent plagiarism of French writers such as Ronsard and Desportes, and the high likelihood that the best of his writing was actually done by his more gifted sister, the red-haired Mary Herbert, Countess of Pembroke.

Sidney's national funeral took place on February 16, 1587, eight days after Mary Queen of Scots' execution and four months after his death.

* * *

Edward's family had grown considerably. Lizbeth was now twelve years old, Bridget three, and Frances two when, during an unusually rainy day in late May, Susan was born. Anne remained unwell after the birth.

Only a few months later, while a fierce wind rattled the shutters, Frances died of pneumonia. Edward had watched over her for three sleepless nights as she struggled to breathe. She finally lay cold and unmoving. Edward was grimly reminded of their only son, stillborn several years before.

Anne was devastated by the loss. Edward tried his best to comfort her. He spent more time at Oxford Court and added extra servants but Anne was almost constantly tearful.

"It's all my fault, Edward. Two of our children have died, and I have not been able to give you an heir. Why is God punishing me?"

Edward had long ago concluded that self-professed archangels like Puritan Bible-quoters fared no better in life than anyone else. "It's not your fault, Anne."

A severe pang of deep internal pain went through Edward as he thought of Mary Hastings who had recently died from sweating sickness, still unwed, still waiting for him. Through all this death and pain, he used creative writing to distract himself from the cruel realities of life.

Edward turned to Anne. "These are perilous times for adults as well as children. Think how many will die if Spain invades."

Anne threw herself on his bed and buried her face in a pillow. Edward patted her shoulder and stroked her back. Her frail spine relaxed beneath his touch. With sorrow he realized how rarely he had given her such affectionate tenderness during their marriage.

* * *

The next day he walked to Fisher's Folly and started to plan further writings. His mind flashed back to Serena. He arose from his desk, walked to his walnut chest with inlaid designs of tusked boars, and pulled out the promised drama he had written in her honor, *The Tempest*.

He began the play with a vivid description of the shipwreck scene which he and Serena had watched in the wind-whipped strait between Vulcano and Lipari. He depicted the flaming lava streaming into the ocean which they had witnessed while visiting the constantly active volcano on Stromboli. He described the stark lava bleakness of the island of Vulcano, with its scattered vineyards and fruit trees midst strangely intoxicating sulfurous vapors.

He sent a copy to Serena, along with a sonnet which included the thought that love is an ever fixèd mark that looks upon tempests and yet is never shaken.

.Edward decided there was sufficient material to transform *The Famous Victories of Henry V* into three new plays. He promptly began work on *The History of Henry IV-Part 1*, including the Gads Hill episode. He particularly liked writing the comedy parts, featuring Sir John Oldcastle and Mistress Quickly, hostess of The Boar's Head. To hold the attention of the nut-crunching, apple-munching groundlings standing noisily in the oiled sawdust pit in front of the stage, Edward used quaint language which he knew would appeal to them:

Prince Harry: *Why, thou clay-brained guts, thou knotty-pated fool, thou whoreson obscene greasy tallow-catch.*

Sir John: *'Sblood, you starveling, you elf-skin, you dried neat's tongue, you bull's pizzle, you stock-fish—O, for breath to utter what is like thee!*

He made final revisions to *Henry V*, which he planned to keep off the drama circuit until the Spanish invasion was truly menacing. He identified closely with Henry V's esprit and charisma. Even his own limp could not dissuade him from playing the lead in the rehearsal at Blackfriars. He decided this would be his last acting role and he wanted it to be triumphant.

Free admission to dress rehearsals guaranteed a full house so the actors could fully absorb the reaction of the mainly working-class audience, who enjoyed plays almost as much as bull and bear baiting.

This time all of the Wits, including the recently joined Thomas Nashe, Christopher Marlowe, John Marston, Thomas Dekker and George Chapman were in attendance.

Vastly outnumbered by the French and wearied by weeks of battles, Henry V refused to surrender and chose to fight a final battle at Agincourt. With chin held high and in a voice trembling with fervor, Edward gave Henry's pre-battle speech to his weary troops:

> *This day is called the Feast of Crispian.*
> *He that outlives this day and comes safe home*
> *Will stand a-tiptoe when this day is named*
> *And rouse him at the name of Crispian.*
> *He that shall see this day and live t'old age*
> *Will yearly on the vigil feast his neighbors*
> *And say, 'Tomorrow is Saint Crispian.'*
> *Then will he strip his sleeve and show his scars*
> *And say, 'These wounds I had on Crispin's day.'*
> *Old men forget; yet all shall be forgot,*
> *But he'll remember, with advantages,*
> *What feats he did that day. Then shall our names,*
> *Familiar in his mouth as household words . . ..*
> *Be in their flowing cups freshly rememberèd.*
> *This shall the good man teach his son,*
> *And Crispin Crispian shall ne'er go by*
> *From this day to the ending of the world*
> *But we in it shall be rememberèd,*
> *We few, we happy few, we band of brothers.*
> *For he today that sheds his blood with me*
> *Shall be my brother; be he ne'er so vile,*
> *This day shall gentle his condition.*
> *And gentlemen in England now abed*

*Shall think themselves accursed they were not
here,*

*And hold their manhoods cheap whiles any
speaks*

That fought with us upon Saint Crispin's day.

With the thundering applause of the standing ovation ringing in his ears at play's end, Edward stood on the platform gazing at the wildly enthusiastic audience, reflecting deeply on the familiar ebbs of life's ups and downs, both for Henry V and himself.

He wondered why the term "common stage" was still prevalent. *Is the human drama common—its lords and simple folk, its traitors and heroes, its failures and triumphs, its tears and laughter, its follies and boundless grandeur?*

Chapter 41

Were't aught to me I bore the canopy,
With my extern the outward honouring.
                                    - Sonnet 125

When *Henry V* played before the royal Court at Whitehall over the Christmas holidays of 1587, no prior play had ever captured the tenor of the times so well nor received such a pervadingly ardent reception.

After the performance, Elizabeth walked to the stage with tears in her eyes and on her cheeks and embraced Edward. She immediately ordered all available acting companies to spread out over the entire country and present *Henry V.*

All English people were apprehensive over the impending Spanish invasion by the world's strongest navy and army. England's patriotic fervor was rising with perfect timing towards the expected arrival of the Armada in the coming summer.

* * *

Edward continued to be pleased with the literary productions of his writing group. The first part of Christopher Marlowe's *Tamburlaine* had been published and Edward thought it excellent. Lyly was still not able to script a play by himself nor was 29 year-old Thomas Kyd, but both were gaining in confidence. All of the Wits were non-nobles, so all could publish their works under their own names.

Thomas Nashe, only twenty, a graduate of Cambridge, had a facile pen. He blasted the Puritans for trying to block the loyalty plays of Edward and the Wits, and extolled the virtues of plays, especially in a time of national crisis:

> *In Playes, all strategems of warre, all the canker-wormes that breede on the rust of peace, are most lively anatomiz'd: they shew the ill successe of treason, the fall of hasty climbers, the wretched end of usurpers, the miserie of civil dissention.*

Edward gathered his eleven University Wits at Fisher's Folly in early January, 1588 and urged them to finish their writing projects and then volunteer for war duty.

"As for myself, *Henry V* will be my last patriotic play. This time, I shall enter the fray and not be blocked by Burghley or the Queen! My ship and I are going to war!"

With a skeleton crew, he sailed the *Edward Bonaventure* down the Thames into the North Sea, then around the lower end of England past Portsmouth, Southampton and the Isle of Wight to the harbor of

Plymouth. Here, he oversaw the modernizing of the ship he had owned since 1581 to battle the Spanish.

Before the work was completed, Edward was forced to return to London because of his wife's poor health. He left Ronald Hargraves, the ship's First Officer, to complete the job of bringing the ship up to battle-readiness.

Dr. Julio had recommended against any more children for Anne, confirming her worst fears, and her father's, that she could not provide a de Vere son to inherit his noble name and title. She had been morose for months, had trouble sleeping and became susceptible to minor infections.

Edward wished there were more he could do. He asked her lady friends to visit. All felt that she had lost the will to live.

In late May, London experienced another epidemic of sweating sickness. To escape it, Edward immediately took Anne and the children by boat to Greenwich but Anne became ill with high fever and coughing.

Edward stayed by her bedside, reflecting upon their unhappy marriage, derived solely from scheming connivance by the two most powerful persons in England.

There were moments when he bargained with God and times when he pleaded with a near-comatose Anne, begging her to continue her tenuous hold on life. He wept real tears for the prolonged sadness of her destiny and his own unsought role in it. More than once he cradled her in his arms and apologized for his misdeeds and shortcomings.

After three short days, on June 5, 1588, she died holding his hand. She was thirty-one.

Burghley insisted upon Anne's burial in

Westminster Abbey. With the entire royal Court in attendance, Edward listened to the religious readings and tributary sermon. There was little to say about her almost invisible life, without focus of remembrance.

He sat somberly between Lizbeth and Bridget. He accepted condolences from the Queen and left the abbey quietly with his tearful daughters.

* * *

The tide was at the height of flood. Bosun's pipes squealed as the crew raced to their stations, as eager as their captain to wipe out the Spanish Pestilence once and for all! The Armada was approaching England and the Queen had given her permission for the *Edward Bonaventure* to join the fleet.

"Up anchor!" barked the bosun.

The messenger rope tightened as weathered hands heaved on the bars driving the giant double capstan, bringing the ship around slowly.

"Short stay," shouted the second mate from the forecastle. "Heave and paw," he yelled to the men at the capstan bars.

First Officer Ronald Hargraves gave orders from the quarterdeck rail. "Away aloft."

Edward's heart soared as he watched the men scramble up the rigging and fling out the sails. The main and fore topsails began to fill and then the jib, as the mud-covered anchor rose dripping to the cathead.

Bonaventure began making headway, heeling over in the light southwesterly breeze and gliding gracefully out of Plymouth, keeping the headland well to starboard. Edward stood on the prow, inhaled the tangy salt air, and planned the command he would assume on days of battle. *By God, at last I'm going to fulfill my military destiny and become a true de Vere! Bring on those murderous Spanish invaders!*

Edward had received instruction on new naval tactics from Francis Drake, sub-commander and chief tactician, and John Hawkins, commander. Their sleeker, faster, more mobile ships were built to out-maneuver the top-heavy galleons of the Spanish, who were still imbued with the ancient concept of grappling and boarding the troops carried on each Spanish ship.

The huge Armada was first sighted off the tip of Cornwall on July 29, behind schedule because of unusually stormy weather. By a stroke of good fortune, the English fleet had favorable winds from the northwest, allowing them to remain windward of the Spanish.

Edward's ship was ordered to the left rear flank of Drake's attacking line. Edward felt very frustrated, especially after the first day's action which saw Drake attack and sink two Spanish galleons. The Spanish were confused by the speed and quick tacking ability of the English ships.

The next day, the galleons sailed into their consolidated crescent formation and proceeded up the channel. By swift pinnace, Edward requested permission to join the attack but was denied. He stood at his bow and watched Admiral Howard form a single line of ships along the north flank of the crescent, with Drake attacking from the rear. They darted around out of range of the Spanish guns, firing longer-range culverins at the clustered Spanish ships. Most cannonballs missed by a wide mark. To save money, Burghley had forbidden practice shooting.

On the evening of the third day, a pent-up Edward walked alone to the prow and stood under the swelling foretopmast sails. The wind seemed to fill each sail with bulging opportunities for action and distinction. Clouds were piling up for a storm but a rift streaked a fanned ray of sunlight onto the rear ships of the crescent, the Biscayan and Andalusian squadrons.

Edward watched the brightly painted ships with their yellow banners and red crosses of St. Andrew as they became their own sunset against the silver-gray of water and sky. *War from a distance can be so dramatic and colorful! But I want personal involvement!*

The next morning, Edward climbed to the crow's nest and watched the third encounter, this time off the Isle of Wight. The English ships sped past the crescent inflicting little damage.

Edward and all English captains knew that the Spanish invasion plan was to land Parma's army of 20,000 battle-hardened troops on the beaches of Kent and advance toward London. The Armada would enter the Thames and destroy everything in its path. The Spanish were aware that Leicester had many troops, but only 5,000 rifles. Most English soldiers were armed only with small bows and arrows, pikes and sickles.

Edward let the wind fill his chest and felt all-powerful, imagining himself and his ship taking on the entire Spanish fleet and sinking every one of them, thus saving England from sure slaughter.

First Officer Hargraves snapped Edward out of his reverie, pointing to port and shouting, "Milord, a royal dispatch boat appears to be heading in our direction."

Edward analyzed the boat by telescope and had a quick premonition of deprivation of glory.

"We must lose her!" he yelled.

"But Sire, she is flying the commander's flag!"

Edward glowered and gritted his teeth. "Mr. Hargraves," he bellowed, "you have your orders. Head for that squall line! Look to it!"

Hargraves could not disobey his captain nor could he ignore a message from the commander. He headed the *Bonaventure* at an angle to allow the dispatch boat to catch them just before hitting the squall. Edward realized it too late. Before he could clamber down and lash out at Hargraves, the dispatch boat pulled alongside as the rain struck.

Admiral Howard ordered Edward to return to port and load his ship with ammunition to supply other ships. In the first three days, the English had consistently over-fired and had little ammunition left. The two-mile wide Spanish crescent was continuing up-channel, virtually undamaged, to their rendezvous at Calais with General Parma and his large army.

Edward reluctantly followed orders and sailed his ship toward Portsmouth. He became surer and surer that the Queen had ordered Howard to keep Edward's ship in the back lines, out of range of any action.

It took two days to load the ship and two days to reach the English fleet. The night before, Drake had sent eight fire-ships loaded with explosives under full sail into the midst of the Spanish ships which were anchored side by side in the harbor of Calais. In terrified panic, most Spanish ship captains disobeyed orders, cut loose their anchors and fled northwards.

After hearing the news, Edward retired to his cabin with mixed emotions. How proud to be an Englishman in one of England's glowing moments!

But how sad and gut-wrenching that his last chance for military distinction was lost forever.

*   *   *

When Edward returned to Fisher's Folly, he was met with depressing news.

John Lyly had been the first University Wit and Edward's trusted Secretary and manager of his acting groups. For years, Edward had shared his innermost thoughts with him.

He now learned that Lyly had been in Burghley's pay as a spy from the very beginning. Once lured by money into the entrapping nets and sinister threats of England's most powerful man, few could escape. Edward and the other Wits were stunned. Lyly silently packed and left.

Edward lived alone at Oxford Court, spending his time reading and reflecting. His inkwell remained dry.

He was summoned out of his seclusion to take part in the royal procession and celebration of National Thanksgiving decreed by the Queen. Evidence had accumulated to declare a magnificent victory over the Armada. Two-thirds of the fleeing Spanish ships sank or went aground trying to escape around the Shetland Islands and down the Irish coast through the battering seas of frightful storms.

Some Irish beaches were littered with hundreds of bodies, and most of the pathetic survivors were slaughtered by the English and Irish under orders from Burghley's Privy Council.

On Sunday, November 24, Edward rode in black and gold cape and golden hat to join the triumphal gathering. Leading the procession rode trumpeters, aldermen and judges, Bishops and Barons, and Sir William Segar, Lord Mayor of London.

Side by side rode the two Senior Earls of the Realm, George Talbot, Earl of Shrewsbury, and Edward de Vere, Earl of Oxford, Lord Great Chamberlain of England. The major duties of the Lord Great Chamberlain were to assist the monarch at the time of coronation and, on major ceremonial occasions, to hold the magnificent canopy over the Queen's head or walk ahead carrying the Great Sword of State.

The earls were followed by the Queen's company of fifty gentlemen pensioners carrying battle-axes. Elizabeth rode in her gilded coach, followed by her handsome new favorite, thirty-three years younger than herself, Robert Devereux, Earl of Essex. Her white-clad maids of honor rode side-saddle alongside the coach.

Edward had never seen such a spectacle of joy. It was a momentous occasion and the multitudes lining the Strand cheered lustily. The gloomy threat of invasion by Spain, which had oppressed the spirit of the English people for twenty years, had ended. Whether it was Elizabeth, or the Navy, or the storms of Divine Providence, or all three, mattered little to the jubilant crowds. England was triumphant!

The bells rang from every church. Bands added their discordant music. For the whole length of the freshly sanded streets, from Whitehall Palace to St. Paul's Cathedral, painted cloths, bright tapestries, flags, banners and emblems hung from windows and rippled along walls.

The people shouted themselves hoarse: "God save our Queen!" and "God save Your Majesty!" Many had known no other monarch. The people cast flowers at the royal coach, threw their caps high in the air, capered and danced. Edward waved his hat at the crowd, and once, with the Queen out of view, he leaped off his horse and danced with them despite the paralysis of his left foot.

At the west door of St. Paul's, the company dismounted and the Queen was officially welcomed by the Dean of the Cathedral. Shrewsbury and Edward awaited the Queen just inside the portal.

As Edward walked slowly alongside the Queen holding the tasseled canopy as she made her majestic walk down the aisle to the royal box, he thought that Elizabeth deserved the triumph of a victory well-achieved. It should have been a high moment for Edward, also, occupying one of England's three most important posts in this great pageant. All of those in the church might well envy the holder of the Queen's golden canopy. But, he thought, what was it to him that he bore the canopy? His external ritual behaviors were being honored but none of his own life's accomplishments.

In his mind, on deeper levels, he wondered what honors he had truly achieved to add to the luster of his family name. What was the real value of his few dramas of comedy, patriotism, and tragedy? Were they not mere trifling revelries for the frivolous Court's fleeting pleasure?

He stood beside the Queen's open cabinet along the north wall of the cathedral listening to the Bishop of Salisbury preach from the appropriate Biblical text: "Thou didst blow with Thy winds and they were scattered."

The inspiring words of the ceremony began to stir Edward's thoughts. *Soon, in the emancipated solitude of my study, I must begin again to write plays and poetry to capture the broad sweep of human emotions and experience. I must continue to spin threads of beauty despite the dark cocoon of enforced anonymity.*

Chapter 42

I may not evermore acknowledge thee
Lest my bewailèd guilt should do thee shame.

- Sonnet 36

Every wall of Whitehall's Great Hall was decorated with captured Spanish banners. A large replica of St. Paul's Cathedral, made entirely of sugar, was placed next to the royal chair in honor of God's role in destroying the invaders. In tune with the happy glow of rejoicing over the Armada's destruction, the Queen decided that only light entertainment would be arranged for Christmas.

Edward revised and staged three comedies: *As You Like It; Much Ado About Nothing*, which he had originally named *A Historie of Ariodante and Genevora*, and *Merry Wives of Windsor*, which was first staged before Elizabeth in the Somersets' house in 1584 as *An Antick Play and Comodye* . Edward had originally written the latter play in two weeks at the special request of the Queen because she so enjoyed the character of Falstaff that she asked for a comedy showing Falstaff in love.

After his last play, Edward sought an audience with Elizabeth to discuss an important matter with her. He had spent several days pondering the best way to broach the subject. After much debate with himself, he had decided on the direct approach.

"Your Majesty, I beg your gracious leave to leave the Court."

"To leave?" she repeated, her voice shrill with surprise. Then her brow lowered and she fidgeted with her fingers.

"I am now thirty-eight years old and have been a courtier for twenty-two years. I have decided that I should enter a new phase of my life. I would like to move to the country. Lizbeth, Bridget and Susan will stay at Cecil House with Burghley. He is quite willing to do this and has arranged a fine group of tutors for his granddaughters."

Elizabeth took a moment to absorb this. As Queen, she could deny his request but Edward had been a courtier far longer than most. "You speak from conviction, my Turk," she said at last. "What are your plans?"

"To revise my plays, many of which are young immature efforts. I will try to elevate and beautify them into literary works for reading and study, not just for stage-presentation. They also need to be kept current with recent events to chronicle our times."

After another long pause, she nodded affirmation. "My Court will never be the same, Edward, but permission is granted." Queen Elizabeth reached for Edward's hand and held it warmly.

"Your long years of service have been unique, exemplary and irreplaceable."

* * *

Edward gathered his eleven University Wits for one final session at The Boar's Head: Thomas Lodge, Thomas Nashe, Thomas Kyd, Thomas Watson, Anthony Munday, Kit Marlowe, Robert Greene, George Peele, Thomas Dekker, John Marston and George Chapman.

When all tankards were filled with beer, Edward stood at the end of the long table and said, "I urge you to concentrate your attention on new word usages and particularly new words, a true enrichment of our English vocabulary. I am asking each of you to try to create at least one new word every week. As for myself, I plan to create one new word each day."

"What are your latest?" asked Greene. "Any new drinking words?" They all laughed. Greene was now a popular figure around London with flaming red hair and pointed beard, fancy-colored coats, silk stockings and irrepressible laughter. He also wrote well and prolifically.

"How about an *auspicious, disgraceful, gloomy, gnarled, lackluster, laughable bump* !" Edward replied. "And verbs so easily turned into nouns: *bite, blink, stink, walk,* and *talk* !"

"More, Gentle Master Will! More!" shouted Greene, using Edward's nickname among the Wits. "I'm toasting every one!"

"It is not difficult at all! Transform nouns into verbs, a mere flick of the quill: *gossip, shovel, worship,* and *lust* ."

"Entirely new words must be more difficult," said Kyd.

"Nimbly and quickly accomplished, with merely a thimble of thought!" Edward said with a smile. "How about *assassin* from the Arabic word hashshashin, a secret sect of Mohammedans who carried out murders of crusaders while under the influence of hashish? Now let's *assassinate* this beer!"

At evening's end, Edward made a final tributary statement.

"Your magnificent writing production has played a vital role in preserving England against Spanish aggression. The Queen and I are immensely proud of your creative abilities. Never stop writing! Now I am leaving the city's hectic pace and seeking rural peace. I will visit with you when I come to London."

* * *

Edward decided to spend the spring, summer and early fall at Castle Hedingham to achieve aloneness and pay a final tribute to his ancestry. The great two-story banquet hall on the second floor of the unlooted castle tower became both his study and his bedroom. Its magnificent many-ribbed stone supporting arch curved over the room.

He set his writing desk under the arch facing the huge chevron-molded fireplace. On his desk he put his gold and ruby pen, ambered bee, and golden inkwell studded with rubies and diamonds. He placed his usual two stained glass panes in the windows next to the fireplace: the ox fording the brook, and the de Vere heraldic crest with its silver star and *Vero Nihil Verius* .

He placed his old four-posted bed on the dais at the opposite end of the hall where plays used to be staged by the de Vere family troupe of players, often including himself when he was a child. He reveled in the memories of his happy youth, so brief and so long ago. He hung tapestries showing the Norman invasion of England copied from portions of the eleventh century Bayeux tapestry. To the wall above the fireplace, he attached a recently commissioned three-foot-high wooden carving of the Bolebec crest showing the courageous lion sejant shaking the broken spear of his subjugated enemy.

The 480 year-old room was graciously old, permeated with a smell of ancientness and a feeling of history exuding from the oak floors and stone walls.

He wandered his childhood haunts but few familiar faces remained. An endless passage of rapidly moving clouds brought new rainstorms just as the previous downpour ended. It was good writing weather but he was somber and insomniac, worrying about his uncertain anonymous future.

Between revisions of his plays—including *Othello,* first written in 1583—Edward often spent an entire day thinking, lying on his bed staring at the timbered ceiling. He felt quite out of kilter with his society, unable to synchronize his talents with the mores of his times.

He knew that his culture's values would change but probably not in his lifetime. It occurred to him that innovators are rarely successful the first time; perhaps a whole generation must die off before a new idea can take hold.

* * *

Mildred Cecil died on April 4, 1589 and was buried alongside Anne in the Chapel of St. Nicholas in Westminster Abbey. Edward attended the services.

The outward relationship between Burghley and his wife had always been cordial but formal and distant. Burghley spent most of his time alone at his Canon Row townhouse, close to Whitehall, working on state matters and creating his wealth. Though Edward had never seen a sign or touch of affection pass between them, neither had he heard or witnessed anything of unkindness or criticism.

When Edward visited the chapel six months later, the tomb completely designed by Burghley had been finished, including side-by-side effigies of Mildred and Anne, so similar in appearance. Small kneeling statues of Edward's three living daughters were in front of the tomb. In gold characters on bronze tablets, Edward read the Latin inscriptions composed by Burghley for each. For Elizabeth:

> *Lady Elizabeth, daughter of the most noble Edward Earl of Oxford and Anne his wife, daughter of Lord Burghley, born 2nd July 1575.*

Edward blinked his eyes in wonderment. Burghley had now made permanent Lizbeth's fictitious date of birth, so historians could never disagree!

The inscription for Susan:

> *It is only now that she is beginning to recognize her most loving grandfather, who has the care of all these children, so that they may not be deprived of a pious education or a suitable upbringing.*

In large gold letters in Westminster Abbey? Edward sighed and shook his head.

*   *   *

Edward often visited his daughters at Cecil House. Lizbeth was nearing marriageable age and Edward felt strongly that she should choose her own husband. Burghley disagreed, believing that arranged marriages would more likely reflect family values and foresightful prudence, not impeded by unnecessary emotions such as love or affection.

Edward also visited with his son by the Queen, fifteen-year-old Henry Wriothesley, Third Earl of Southampton. The young earl had lived as Burghley's ward since the age of eight, acquired free of charge through the generosity of the Court of Wards of which Burghley was still Master.

Henry had the green eyes and orange hair of his mother and Edward's prominently arched eyebrows and thin sensitive lips. He was outgoing and smiling with engaging charm and was about to graduate from Cambridge. Edward had spent considerable time with him on his visits to Cecil House during the past seven years, introducing him at an early age to the theatrical stage. Watching plays was now his major hobby. Henry rarely saw his mother.

"Let's attend a play today!" said Henry enthusiastically during one of Edward's visits.

"Grand idea! Do they stage such idolatrous frivolities in England?"

Henry laughed, radiating his infectious smile. "I like all plays but especially yours. The complex plots, allusions and word manipulations are great fun and a real challenge."

"What shall we see?" Edward asked, basking in his son's words of praise.

"*As You Like It* at The Curtain. I have seen it once

but I enjoy understanding something new every time I see one of your plays." Henry paused, and his face took on a thoughtful expression. "May I ask you a question?"

"Of course!"

"Why are you allowed to visit with me but never acknowledge me as your son? Other sons born out of wedlock, even to royalty like Henry VIII, have usually been recognized and brought up without secrecy."

The question did not surprise Edward. Henry had learned about his parentage some years back but this was the first time he had asked a direct question about it. Edward liked the boy's candor and the fact that Henry felt comfortable enough with him to broach the subject in an open way.

"Your mother made a sad decision long ago," he replied. "She felt that the English people needed to respect and venerate their Queen, especially in the light of Henry VIII's dishonorable beheading years. She thought it would be disruptive to her reign and do harm to national unity to mar the illusion of The Virgin Queen."

"I hardly ever see her!" Henry protested. "I don't agree with that."

"Nor do I," said Edward, rubbing his boar ring. "But she did what she thought best for England. What are your plans now?"

"Attend Gray's Inn to learn to drink and perhaps acquire a bit of law!" They both laughed.

* * *

Edward visited Ned Somerset and family for two days. Ned still gleamed with the happiness of a loving marriage. He was without mustache, beard or pretense. He had tried being a courtier, hadn't liked the contrived atmosphere, and retired in his early twenties to live the life of a gentleman as Earl of Worcester. He remained a quiet Catholic, never letting religion interfere with his loyalty to the Queen.

His wife Elizabeth was still sprightly and elegantly handsome, with dark hair and eyes and an enthusiastic zest for life. Edward had never seen a couple so warmly affectionate. They now had eleven children.

Edward loved visiting the Somerset family even though Elizabeth was a painful reminder of her sister Mary and of a loss from which Edward knew he would never fully recover. For Edward, the love and marital happiness that Ned and Elizabeth shared was a reflection of that loss.

The gardens of their stately brick home on the Strand extended down to the Thames. On a sunny afternoon, Elizabeth Somerset and Edward sat on a stone bench in the garden on the riverbank. Sailboats and rowboats were taking passengers to the other side. Boats of all sizes were waiting for the incoming tide to head upstream.

"Oh, Edward, how I wish Mary had lived longer and that you both hadn't fallen victim to Burghley's self-serving malignant use of power. She never looked at another man, refusing a number of marriage offers."

"We would have been immensely happy," Edward said, staring out at the Thames. "And what joy and spontaneity we would have had with you and Ned and all of your children."

"For years, Mary held the rights to buy the Savoy Hospital. She had the Queen's permission to tear it down and build a manor house. We would have been next door neighbors!"

"She never told me that!" Edward took a moment to reflect, then turned to face Elizabeth. "What was she like after our weeks together at Bilton in 1577?"

Elizabeth smiled. "She was absolutely glowing. She shared with me the beauty of her visit. She seemed spiritually complete and a peace settled over her. She was so regal in grace and charm!" Elizabeth shook her head sadly. "Fate was indeed cruel to remove her from the human scene at so young an age. Just before she died . . ." Elizabeth's voice caught and she turned away to look out at the boats crossing the river. "Just before she died, she whispered to me to tell you how sorry she was, not to be able to wait for you any longer."

Edward lowered his head as he felt the sudden sting of tears in his eyes. For a long time he sat quietly, lost in thoughts about a spirit passing great and of what could have been.

*   *   *

In early 1589, Edward spent two weeks at Bilton with Anne Vavasour and their son. At Edward's insistence, they had met briefly once a year for the past seven years so that he could know the acknowledged son he was fully supporting. Edward Vere had Anne's eyes but the rest of his pleasingly handsome face was de Verean. His animated personality was an intriguing mixture of serious and humorous. He had intellectual curiosity, loved books and had a bent for languages, especially Greek. Edward discussed with Anne the possibility of sending him to the continent for his university education.

Anne had bounced from man to man and was now living with elderly Sir Henry Lee, for many years the Queen's tournament champion. Edward discovered that her unrestrained vitality, sensuality and endless amorous appetite had not changed. Edward wrote in his tablet:

She paragons description and wild fame,
one that excels the quirks of blazoning
pens, and in th'essential vesture of
creation does tire the engineer.

In the cold gray light of wintry days and his own life-hardened maturity, Edward was able to appraise Anne's self-centered hedonism more realistically. Although he had encountered many liars at Court, Anne Vavasour was second only to Burghley as the champion liar of his life. She was also calculating, wanton and promiscuous. He had written dozens of sonnets to her during the past ten years in an effort to cleanse his feelings of impurity and negativity.

Now he decided it was time to free himself from her passionate grip on his body, soul and pen. This, he told her firmly, would be their final interaction. He agreed to continue his generous support for their son and she agreed to let father and son meet whenever desired.

* * *

Edward returned to Castle Hedingham feeling relieved and relaxed. As he gazed around the keep's banquet hall he could visualize its vivid history, including the entertainment of royalty for hundreds of years.

If he couldn't write creatively and dramatically in this atmosphere, he should retire his pen and frame it on the wall.

He never wrote sonnets to or about Edward Vere,

despite their warm relationship. But now he began a sonnet to his son Henry Wriothesley:

> *Shall I compare thee to a summer's day?*
> *Thou art more lovely and more temperate.*

He ended with a thought on the immortality of written words:

> *So long as men can breathe or eyes can see,*
> *So long lives this, and this gives life to thee.*

He still considered it remarkable that printed words could outlast buildings constructed so solidly by man, and he thought: *Not marble nor the gilded monuments of Princes shall outlive this powerful rhyme.*

*   *   *

With the fire blazing in the old Norman fireplace in his banquet hall hideaway one cold afternoon, Edward thought about his future. He wanted a year or two of an artist's best friend, solitude—alone in the world of creative imagination, the corona around the head of fact.

He still wrestled with the Queen's decree of anonymity. The thought of having his works published under a pseudonym repulsed him. But he felt a sickening certainty that any attempt to publish under his own name would be blocked by Burghley or destroyed. Anonymous publications stood a good chance of being scattered and lost, crushing any hope that his writings would live on and speak to future generations.

Perhaps it would be best to follow the Queen's command and use a pseudonym. At least all of his plays would be attributed to one person. Having reached that reluctant conclusion, he now had to choose a suitable pen-name.

He sat motionless in the silent banquet hall and allowed his mind to wander freely through possibilities. He wanted to feel a connection with whatever name he chose and yet he knew it could not be too obvious.

His eyes moved around the room, touching shadowed corners and ancient walls. He found himself contemplating the origin of drama, both comedies and tragedies, in glorious ancient Athens. Pallas Athena, the Greek goddess of the theater and fine arts, had sprung forth from the brow of Zeus fully armed, shaking her spear. It was an image he had always found compelling.

Something else came to mind: the tribute Gabriel Harvey had paid him in front of the Queen's entire entourage on Royal Progress in 1578:

"Thine eyes flash fire, thy will shakes spears."

He looked up at the strong determined lion of his wooden Bolebec crest hanging between two torches above the chevroned stone fireplace. He visualized himself as that lion, shaking his spear courageously and defiantly at the narrow, self-seeking and self-protecting minds of those who would distort truth and tongue-tie art.

He contemplated the name "Willy" which was often applied to poets, and his own nickname of Gentle Master William or Will, used for years by the University Wits when referring to him.

He gazed at the Oxford and de Vere stained glass panes, then once again studied the bold spear-shaking lion which had been his favorite family symbol since earliest childhood.

He pounded his fist on the desk. The decision was made. His writing name would be *William Shakespeare* !

Chapter 43

Through tattered clothes great vices do appear;
Robes and furred gowns hide all.
Get thee glass eyes, and, like a scurvy
politician, seem to see the things thou
dost not . . . Plate sin with gold and the
strong lance of justice hurtless breaks.
- The Tragedy of King Lear

While sun-bathing next to the largest of Castle Hedingham's fish ponds, Edward wondered whether he had the capacity to outstrip his own defects. He continued to worry about his inability to avoid rapiering people with written words. *But,* he thought, *how difficult not to skewer those who are so juicily skewerable and so richly deserving of my basting and barbecuing.*

As a haggard is given an extra piece of mallard breast for a superior stoop, should not a writer be rewarded with that special quilled joy of a pointed characterization captured in print forever?

He knew this was his basic character flaw, but concluded that he was just as powerless to suppress it as he was incapable of lying. *Vero Nihil Verius!* Nothing Truer Than Truth—Nothing Truer Than Vere.

Edward decided that he would endure no new entangling personal alliances. Why distract his independent mind from savoring the delights and harmony of living alone? If any woman tried to lure him into her hazardous web, he would use cold brusqueness as a form of pest-control.

He was aroused from his musings by a courier riding up the driveway and handing him a letter from the Queen.

My Dear Edward:

Civil strife between Catholics and Protestants is heating up again in France with the murder of the Guises. I have a diplomatic mission for you to Paris. The enclosed may elevate your spirits!

-Elizabeth, Regina

Enclosed was a quotation from *The Arte of English Poesie,* just published by Lord John Lumley, which Edward had not seen:

> *In these days Poets and Poesie are despised, subject to scorn and derision. In Her Majesty's time are sprung up a crew of Courtly makers, Noblemen and Gentlemen of Her Majesty's own servants, who have written excellently well if their doings could be found out and made public, of which number is first that noble gentleman Edward, Earl of Oxford.*

Edward shook his head in amazement that the book had escaped Burghley's vicious talons. Clearly, Elizabeth was exerting her queenly powers to protect Edward and announce to the world the literary glories of her reign. Then why was she so adamant about his pseudonymity?

During the past few months of solitary contentment at Hedingham, he had relived his happy childhood, steeped his soul in the ancient flavor of de Vere history and tradition, and created poetry and literature in his familial castle-surround. The time was now ripe to see his children and interact again with his protégés, after which he would retreat to Bilton and continue revising his plays.

As he rode out of the arched brick entrance gate of Castle Hedingham, Edward looked back at the stately manor house and castle-keep indenting the clouded sky. Its formerly barren hillsides, kept treeless for centuries so besiegers could not hide, were now dotted with young elms and oaks, a tribute to Elizabeth's basically peaceful reign. Leaves were beginning to turn yellow and orange as the weather cooled.

He had a powerful feeling that he would not see Castle Hedingham again. He turned away slowly to confront what lay ahead but before he did, he saluted a heart-felt farewell to the majestic castle of his forebears and himself.

* * *

After a year and a half writing in the quiet beauty and invigorating solitude of his Bilton home above the Avon, Edward returned to London despite a plague epidemic. The Court and most nobles had fled the city, allowing the poor to battle the plague alone.

This time he decided to see the horrors of the plague firsthand. Shouldn't a writer view all aspects of life, including its calamities?

Edward knew that from the first red spots on the skin through the rapidly progressive pneumonia with its fever, marked prostration, and unstoppable bloody coughing, to death could take only two or three days. What initiated an epidemic, no one knew.

What had been obvious for centuries was the marked contagiousness of the pneumonic form, with entire families dying together. Black-gowned and masked physicians did little more than organize the disposal of bodies and dispense the bitterest of concoctions which only sickened the weak and weakened the sick. Constant church bells rang out for the newly dead.

Edward watched with a forced grim detachment as distorted bodies were hurled into the filthy streets from as high as the third story, to be picked up by masked cartmen with long metal tongs and thrown quickly onto ox-drawn death-carts. Bodies sprawled like piles of giant dolls until they were unceremoniously dumped into large pits, covered with lime and quickly shoveled over with dirt.

The permeating stench of death and putrefaction overwhelmed even London's usual loathsome smells. None of London's characteristic street cries could be heard: "Hot fine oatcake," "I have fresh cheese and cream," "Radishes or lettis, two bunches a penny." Not even "What do ye lack?" the most appropriate answer to which was "Life."

Edward returned to his sparsely furnished apartment near St. Paul's and lit the fire. Juniper smoke began to fragrance the air as he lay down on his Turkish carpet. Overwhelmed by the plague's horrors and by the narrow line separating life from death, he grabbed his tablet and wrote lines for *Macbeth*:

> *Tomorrow, and tomorrow, and tomorrow*
> *Creeps in this petty pace from day to day*
> *To the last syllable of recorded time,*
> *And all our yesterdays have lighted fools*
> *The way to dusty death. Out, out, brief candle.*
> *Life's but a walking shadow, a poor player*
> *That struts and frets his hour upon the stage,*
> *And then is heard no more.*

* * *

Edward was now confronted by Burghley with his final bill of wardship. The total was a staggering 21,000 pounds, enough to build a number of palatial manor houses. Included under "other obligations" was 3,000 pounds owed to Burghley by Edward for marrying Anne, rather than the promised dowry to Edward of 10,000 pounds. The size of the bill represented authoritarian finality and was not arguable.

Out of the total, Edward figured Burghley would keep at least 12,000 pounds for himself, with the Queen lucky to get 3,500 even though the whole purpose of wardship was to enrich the regal treasury. Over the past twenty-nine years, he knew that Burghley had appropriated tens of thousands of pounds of income from Edward's properties and had secretly transferred many of Edward's lands to his own hidden assets. Edward took out some of his frustrations by writing:

Whilst you have fed upon my signories,
Disparked my parks and felled my forest woods,
From my own windows torn my household coat,
Razed out my imprese, leaving me no sign,
Save men's opinions and my living blood,
To show the world I am a gentleman.

Burghley had started his life in politics owning one piece of property. Utilizing a skillful combination of power, unmatched greed and multiple illegal strategies, he now owned over 300 estates, most under disguised ownership, making him the wealthiest man in England.

Edward derived some of his calculations from a piece of paper with one burned edge which he had spotted in the library fireplace one day while browsing books at Cecil House. The paper was a summary of six months' transactions of the Court of Wards in Burghley's handwriting, showing that he had taken 25,000 pounds for himself, 60% of the total. He had given 20% to other committee members for their help and their silence, 11% to the Queen, and spent 9% for expenses. At the bottom of the paper was a memo to himself: N.B.: BURN THIS.

Edward had considered taking the evidence to the Queen. But he had bitter memories of the time he had tried to warn her about the plot hatched by Henry Howard and others to bring Mary Queen of Scots to the throne. So he dropped the idea.

Burghley was certainly not a person to trifle with. He was the most powerful man in England and anyone who crossed him was likely to endure dire consequences. Besides, the Queen already knew of Burghley's greed and acquisitive habits—just not their extent. Her toleration showed that she valued

Burghley's counsel more than the loss to the Royal Treasury.

Edward craved being free of Burghley once and for all. In order to raise the money to pay the exorbitant sum, Edward sold family jewels and more properties, including his beloved Wivenhoe. He also disbanded his two acting companies.

He finally achieved his freedom from Burghley and the Court of Wards in early 1591 at the age of forty-one, twenty years beyond the legal age-limit for wardship. He was free at last! Edward felt that a great criminal yoke had been removed from his shoulders and shackles from his shins.

If the Queen only knew how much more I could include in my plays about her esteemed chief councilor, Edward thought. But out of reverence for her, he would give a sparing limit to his pen, suppress the smoldering embers of his anger and try to rise above the on-going outrages to himself and his countrymen.

At this time Edward's friend, poet Edmund Spenser, published his long narrative poem *Fairie Queen*. His repeated attempts to get financial sponsorship by the Queen were persistently blocked by Burghley. An exasperated Spenser then published an open attack on Burghley in Mother *Hubberds Tale*.

> *The cloak was care of thrift and husbandry,*
> *For to increase the common treasure's store;*
> *But his own treasure he increasèd more*
> *And lifted up his lofty towers thereby,*
> *That they began to threat the neighbor sky . . .*
> *For men of learning little he esteemed;*
> *His wisdom he above their learning deemed.*

This resulted in confiscation and destruction of all of Spenser's literary works which Burghley and his agents could lay their hands on, including several popular plays. Edward was aghast at the power of authoritarian censorship in England and at what could happen to his own writings.

Lord Chancellor Christopher Hatton, whom Edward still felt had more ear-wax than brains, took great pleasure in declaring Edward bankrupt. However, he was shocked into a fatal decline of his diabetes when the Queen, greatly disturbed at what was maliciously happening to her leader of England's great literary surge, demanded back from Hatton all of her Queenly gifts to him, amounting to many thousands of pounds. This left him disillusioned, destitute and terminal.

*   *   *

When Edward learned that some of his University Wits were in dire financial circumstances, he rented furnished rooms for them on St. Peter's Hill and provided a food allowance.

Whenever Edward was in London, he gathered with the Wits at the Stillyard for unrestrained storytelling and drinking. One evening Thomas Nashe arose and gave a toast: "Friends, all of us have received the longtime benefits and generosities from our noble patron despite his falling upon hard times imposed by greedy power-mongers. All rise and join me in a toast to our Gentle Master William: To the most generous benefactor of writers and most skillful poet-dramatist of our time. May the foul perpetrators of his enforced anonymity soon realize ruination and an early greeting from the blazing fires of Hades!"

Edward remained thoughtful for a few moments while absorbing the rich atmosphere of the Stillyard and the captivating smell of roasting beef. He then passed the carafes and stood up next to a stack of German wine-barrels. "Gentlemen, the toast honors not me alone but all of us who have joined together to dedicate our lives to writing. Your literary development and remarkable facility with creative pen are more than commendable. Few, if any, more talented groups of writers have ever simultaneously graced any society in history."

Robert Greene, who could induce laughter at will because of his own contagious laughter, once again said: "I'll drink to that!" Then he added, "Seriously, Lord Edward, your flock of quilled protégés renders you much-deserved gratitude. To use Spenser's words about you, may your 'gentle spirit, from whose pen large streams of honey and sweet nectar flow,' never be quelled by the forces of ignorance and darkness."

"Thank you, Thomas," said Edward, deeply moved. "We shall persevere. Like Plautus, we must infuse our works with our utmost genius and make them breathe with innovative alliances of words, clever and resourceful imagery, and skillful invention of new words to bejewel our native tongue. We must fulfill our own literary destinies and also give help to unripened writers. England's artistic surge is just beginning!"

* * *

Edward spent several days visiting Henry Wriothesley and Lizbeth, Bridget, and Susan at Cecil House. Henry detested Burghley not only personally but for his greedy dishonesty, having discovered that Burghley was rapidly siphoning the wealth from his inheritance as Third Earl of Southampton.

Edward tried hard to be cordial to his father-in-law, but the wide gulf between their ethics and lifestyle made the relationship tenuous, at best.

Burghley suddenly announced, without consulting the involved individuals, that Henry and sixteen-year-old Lizbeth, now a maid of honor, were engaged. An angry Henry immediately declined the impossible arrangement between presumed half-siblings and was fined 5,000 pounds by Burghley's Court of Wards. Burghley nodded his head happily and took the money for himself which he had already put aside from Henry's dwindling holdings. One of Burghley's heirs could build a nice manor house with that sum.

During this visit, Edward spent considerable time in the extensive Cecil House library which contained Burghley's carefully biased records of the reign of Queen Elizabeth since her coronation in 1558. Edward confirmed his gravest suspicions about document selection and altering by Burghley and the private librarian who had worked for him anonymously for thirty-three years.

While borrowing a book from Burghley's study-library one day, Edward noted with interest that a single tapestry had been added to the room, directly over Burghley's antique desk. It showed a muscled Hercules wearing his lion skin, large club in hand, achieving the third of his twelve labors: overcoming the fierce boar of Erymanthus by tiring it in a field of snow and then throwing a noose around its neck.

* * *

After Edward's departure, Burghley summoned his bright serious son, Robert Cecil, for a conference.

Twenty-nine year-old Robert appeared in black, walking with a white staff. He had a lean, serious, good-looking face with high forehead and pointed chin, black beard and narrow mustache without any of his father's disquieting features. He was of short stature and leaned to the left because of his curved spine and hunched back.

"Good morning, Father," said Robert.

"A good morning it is for short-and-long-range planning. I now want you to apprentice full-time with me and gradually take over all of my official work. Attend all meetings of the Privy Council and Court of Wards, learn the financial intricacies of petitions, wardships and all Queenly dealings. When it comes time for Elizabeth to choose my successor, there will be no one to compete with you."

"Isn't this premature, Father?" Robert spoke loudly because of his father's deafness.

"Not at all! I am old and tiring of my duties. And we must nip any competition in the bud! For anyone who appears promising, like Robert Devereux or Walter Raleigh, we will lay traps or arrange foreign assignments. By the time I die, you will be indispensable to the Queen."

Robert knew that Theobalds and half of his father's estate would be his if he followed his father's advice, even though he was the second son. "And what if she dies first?"

"She won't," answered Burghley. "She is almost indestructible. But you must play the key role in choosing the next monarch. Select King James of Scotland before anyone else does. He will be a weak ruler and therefore easy to persuade and manipulate. Correspond with him secretly so you will appear to be solely responsible for his coronation. To reach the pinnacle of power and wealth, you must attain my two jobs."

Robert got up from his chair and walked around the room. "Although I already appreciate the wisdom of Machiavelli, you will have to train me."

Burghley stroked his white beard slowly and rhythmically, seeming to pump his eyes from side to side. "To reach the family goals I set, it was essential to use every strategy, however harsh, no matter who got crushed. You must do the same."

Robert nodded, watching his father. "Something else seems to be on your mind, Father."

"You must develop the ability to pry open men's brains and out-fox them. Edward has been reading our bound historical volumes and his look suggests he has discovered some discrepancies, some modifying, which is our privilege. Those who make history have the right to edit it!"

"Are you sure about Edward, Father? He has always hated the concept of snooping and spying."

"Quite. Yes, quite sure. Now I want you to scour all governmental offices, all places where Edward may have left any trail, and bring all relevant papers to me. Then you and I will burn all that are adverse to us or in praise of him."

Robert hesitated, his eyes dropping to the floor. "Is that really necessary, Father? Despite our thirteen-year difference in age, he was very kind and respectful to me as a child when others were mocking my deformities. He interested me in poetry and took me to plays when Mother thought that would lead me to depravity."

"It is absolutely essential, Robert," Burghley shot back. "To be more specific, I want you to borrow, in my name, all records of Privy Council meetings between June, 1582 and February, 1586. We spent considerable time discussing Edward's historical propaganda plays, created at the Queen's urging, which did have an impressive nationalistic and anti-Spanish effect. They all require obliteration. Get into the Office of the Revels and bring back their records of play productions for the past fifteen years. They need burning, also."

"But he is a great dramatist and a credit to the Queen's reign!" Robert protested.

Burghley whacked his long staff on the floor. "He is our sworn enemy, Robert! Not only did he wreck the life of our sweet Anne but he has also depicted me in his plays as a scheming, bumbling, inane fool. He has maliciously described the methods I have used to achieve greatness and wealth. With his cleverly worded lies, he plans to discredit my proper role in history."

Robert frowned doubtfully. "Are you sure you are interpreting him correctly?"

"Absolutely! How naive and vulnerable you are! I will change you! Anyone who stands in our way must be eliminated!"

"Is there no alternative?"

Burghley stared at his son for a long moment. When he spoke again, his voice was low and intense. "Robert, listen carefully. I have no intention—yes *no* intention—after a lifetime of dedicated work for England and my family, to allow the noble Cecils to be slandered back into the vacuum of faceless anonymity. That is where our Seventeenth Earl belongs, and that is where he will end! Yes! Not with God's help but with yours and mine!"

Chapter 44

For what is wedlock forced, but a hell,
An age of discord and continual strife?
Whereas the contrary bringeth bliss,
And is a pattern of celestial peace.
                                        - Henry VI, Part 1

Edward was busy writing in his London apartment a month later when he heard a knock on his door. A courier handed him a letter from the Queen :

My Dearest Turk,

My Court and I are enjoying relaxed summer pleasures at Hampton Court. My spies from Istanbul tell me that you are leading the life of a solitary monastic poet rarely graced with spicier fare.

I and a few of my retinue will be spending five days at Windsor beginning on Friday of this week. Please cross the Bosporous and join us. Bring wit and poetry of life; leave quill and harem behind.

                                        -Elizabeth, Sultana

Edward had visited the Court only twice since returning from Bilton. Such personal invitations from the Queen were infrequent. Although her tone was light, he dared not refuse.

Edward felt at home in Windsor Castle, originally constructed by William the Conqueror and rebuilt in the 1100's in gray stone. He was shown to his elegant chambers in Elizabeth's newly added royal apartments. He changed clothes and presented himself to the Queen.

"It is good to see you, Edward. The first time I entertained you here, you could hardly grow facial hair. Now your slightly silvered beard and mustache are most distinguished! The next five days are for relaxation." She noted that his serious but handsome face still had a merry twinkle in the eyes. She wondered why his Roman nose had remained straight while hers was beginning to bend like an eagle's beak.

"No play-assignments, Your Majesty?" he inquired with mock surprise. "I am shocked silent!"

"I don't want your silence! That's when you are most dangerous, honing your sword of words!"

"Just relax and be myself? Who are your guests?"

"Ned and Elizabeth Somerset and a few others, including a maid of honor or two." Edward knew the Queen selected her maids of honor from noble families for attractiveness, education, languages and social graces.

He spent the rest of the afternoon wandering the palace grounds, gazing over expansive views of an England largely at peace. He bowled with the Somersets, his closest friends. Wistful memories and fantasies of life with Mary Hastings were inevitable companions. She had been a fine-faceted jewel held only for an instant in the hand of time.

Life is indeed fleeting, Edward thought, *and one must grasp quickly at any leaves of happiness which flutter by on the gusty and unpredictable winds of fortune. But all of my plays need revision: more eloquence, more insight, more philosophy, more linguistic novelty! Why am I wasting five days?*

*   *   *

The Queen was in a strangely exuberant mood. She had arranged supper for her nine guests in her privy chamber. Edward was seated on her right, next to Elizabeth Somerset. Beth Trentham was seated across the table next to Ned. She was the senior maid of honor, having been with the Queen for ten years since the age of seventeen. Edward recognized her by sight but knew little else about her.

"Beth, how good to see you and how lovely you look tonight," Edward said, surprised at his rare compliment. She had dark brown hair rolling softly down to her shoulders, curled outward at the ends. Her face was refined and beautiful with iridescent blue eyes, a smoothly contoured nose and full lips. She radiated serenity, warmth and dignity.

"Edward, I do believe you're staring!" said the Queen laughing, placing her left hand underneath her chin to hide the wrinkles in her neck. "You've known Beth for ten years!"

"You do me great honor to seat me here, Your Majesty," said Beth. "I am pleased to have the opportunity to talk with you, Lord Edward. I don't believe a hundred words have ever passed between us. In the halls, you were usually deep in thought, your eyes on the floor."

"How boring I must have been!" Edward said with a laugh.

She smiled gently. "You were preoccupied, my Lord."

"Tell me something of yourself," Edward said as he settled comfortably into his chair.

"My father was Sir Thomas Trentham of Stafford-shire, not far north of your writing hideaway at Bilton."

Edward was charmed by her sincere listening face. Their eyes met and lingered. "Do you know the innermost secrets of all courtiers?" he asked.

"Maids of honor are distinguished by their white clothing, their knowledge of most secrets of the Court, and their discretionary silence."

After supper they listened to music and danced in the Queen's ballroom, tapestried from wall to window into a smaller more intimate area. When the Queen was not dancing vigorously herself, she sat on damask cushions and beat time to the music.

Edward spent the entire evening with Beth, impressed with her combination of stately elegance and natural unaffected charm. By the end of the evening, he was overwhelmed by unaccustomed emotions. Beth was exciting and fascinating, bright and quick, intriguingly gentle and appealing.

"What is happening to me?" he asked the Somersets. "I am besieged with strange feelings which poets write about but seldom experience. Have I been alone too long and thus need rescuing?"

"You don't need rescuing, Edward," said Elizabeth Somerset with a smile. "We have been watching you two all evening and the glow is evident."

"But this does not happen at my age, especially to a hardened cynic!"

"It happens at any age, Edward," said Ned. "But the opportunities are rare since most marriages are arranged so early in life. Elizabeth and I were fortunate. Allow it in! Beth is a charming, gracious woman with a very compatible personality and background."

The next morning, Edward sought audience with the Queen. "I need to talk with you, Your Majesty."

She nodded, amused by his seriousness. "I know. Queens have eyes, and even their steely hearts can feel."

"I earnestly request your permission to pay court to Beth. Aphrodite seems to have smitten me! I went back to my room last night and wrote:

> *Her sight did ravish but her grace in speech,*
> *Her words yclad with wisdom's majesty,*
> *Makes me from wond'ring fall to weeping joys,*
> *Such is the fullness of my heart's content."*

"The luminescence around you two reminded me of my loud and elated utterance taken from the 118th Psalm when I was notified that I was Queen: '*A Domino factum est istud, et est mirabile oculis nostris.* 'This is the Lord's doing and it is marvelous in our eyes'. But last night was not only the Lord's doing!"

Edward lifted an inquisitive eyebrow. "Your meaning, Your Majesty?"

"Oh, Edward, are all poets, with their minds in the clouds, so naive in earthly matters? Is the boar's snout so clogged with Euphuistic linguistic conspiracies against the English tongue that he can't sniff out a collaboration between the Queen and Venus?"

Edward knelt and kissed Elizabeth's hand. "I am verily overwhelmed! Your Olympian scheming quite surprises me! Was Beth aware of it?"

"Not at all, nor anyone else here. Now I want to say something private, Edward, for your ears alone.

I made a mistake with you, through my own vanity and selfishness, and it has rankled within me. I let Burghley convince me that you should marry his Anne after he denied the existence of any Hastings marriage contract. I now know that to be untrue. Elizabeth Somerset showed me the Hastings' copy of the contract."

Edward drew a breath to calm his suddenly conflicting feelings. The Queen had just given him the closest to an apology that she was ever likely to offer to anyone. Edward felt a brief surge of wrath but was able to control it. "I am glad you verified the marriage contract and my family motto of truthfulness," Your Majesty.

"Edward, at that time I was quite taken with you as a courtier, a writer with powerful potential, and as a man," the Queen continued, sensing the depth of his feelings. "With Anne as your wife, I knew I could easily detain you at Court. You and Anne were completely mismatched. Cecil achieved his eagerly sought noble status but, as a result, you two have a deep enmity which, I fear, will never be assuaged."

Edward, suddenly overwhelmed with anger, nodded agreement, tried hard not to show his ire, and deemed it best not to speak.

"Mary Hastings would have been perfect for you. She was the epitome of loveliness. She worked loyally and graciously for me for fifteen years, never showing any resentment. But that era is over. Beth Trentham is from a similar mold and the two of them were good friends. I think you need and deserve a harmonious mate."

"The word 'harmony' does have a nice ring to it, my Queen, deriving from the Greek, *harmonia,* meaning concord, as in the lovely fitting together of two parts of a bony joint."

"Yes, Beth will be a concordant partner for you. She is beautiful, honest, spiritually pure, totally loyal and from a noble and wealthy family. She has refused several excellent offers of marriage, wanting a love-match or none at all. I recently asked her brother's permission for my little plan, and he wholeheartedly agreed. He warned, however, that success in such aphrodisian strategy is uncommon."

"It would make a wonderful play but I'm afraid the Greeks are two thousand years ahead of us. I will proceed with caution and keep you informed of the major plot-line." He smiled as he added, "But not the finer scenarios!"

The Queen laughed.

Edward continued. "My appreciation is un-bounded. Our long association since my childhood is replete with the whole spectrum of life's pageantry. I must confess that you have done to me everything a woman can do to a man except bore me!"

Edward and Beth took long walks along the Thames and through meadows blossoming with dai-sies, goldenrod and wild basil. They talked of their childhoods, life at Court, his writings and their in-terests. She held his hand or put her arm through his in private and in public. Their affection blossomed like the summer flowers. When they parted at the end of five days, they kissed and held each other tightly.

As Edward rode back to London, he knew he was about to enter a new and probably final phase of his life which would determine not only his personal happiness but also his literary destiny. He was con-sumed by a joyful thought, *I wonder if the lame old boar*

*can indeed capture the young beauteous maiden in white
who has intersected my life so unexpectedly.*

* * *

After a lively interchange of letters with Beth,
Edward joined the Royal Progress two months later.
The warmth of summer had dissipated but not the
warmth of happiness and love between Edward and
Beth. Many members of the Court retinue quietly
came to each and voiced their enthusiastic approval,
including sixteen-year-old Lizbeth de Vere, whom
Beth had befriended as a new maid of honor.

One week later, with the Queen and her retinue being entertained at the inherited home of the
Third Earl of Southampton in Titchfield, Edward and
Beth became engaged. They received the enthusiastic approval of Henry as well as the Queen, and
were given leave to break off from the Progress and
proceed to Beth's home in Staffordshire. Permission
was promptly given by Beth's older brother Thomas,
a poet and country squire. Their father had recently
died.

In October, 1591, after three months of court-
ship, Edward married Beth in a small church in the
town of Rocester. Ned Somerset was best man, Elizabeth Somerset stood with the bride, and Thomas
Trentham escorted his sister down the aisle.

As dowry, Thomas paid off all of Edward's remaining mortgages, which amounted to 10,000
pounds. For the first time in his life, Edward's properties, albeit significantly diminished in number,
were completely his own. With a generous inheritance from her late father, Beth was now wealthy in
her own right.

The new couple bought a modest temporary house in Stoke Newington on the outskirts of London, just beyond The Theatre and The Curtain. It was daub and wattle, with two acres of land including a garden and apple orchard. Beth now supplied the atmosphere of harmonious love in which Edward could polish and refine his writings with an unfettered mind and a happily overflowing heart.

They often saw plays, as did an average of 15,000 persons per week in the London area. With an admission price of only a penny to the central theater-pit, plays had become very popular with English people and visitors from every walk of life including merchants, travelers and sailors. All of Edward's expectations were being realized in this explosion of interest in drama despite continuing negative efforts by Burghley and the Puritans.

The more popular the plays, the more vociferous the Puritans. As one London preacher said: "The cause of plagues is sin, if you look to it well; and the cause of sin are plays; therefore, the cause of plagues are plays."

One day in their garden, Edward said to Beth, "Isn't it strange that the Puritans feel so constrained to force their views on others? What they need is their own island. Maybe that's what I need also, since so much of my life has been in ideational conflict. But you have provided me with our own isolated island of peace right here, where I am now free to concentrate my total energies on writing and on you!"

"I certainly have no complaints about your energies with me!" she replied with a smile. "You have contented and fulfilled me most admirably."

Edward walked over to a cluster of roses, picked a red one, and handed it to Beth. "Even though my creative life is through words, when I'm with you I don't seem able to express adequately my love. I would call it Anglo-Saxon reticence except that I am a Norman Viking!"

"Edward, I can tell your feelings by the unsaid words of your touches and your expressive eyes. I know what is in your heart."

"It is strange how locked up my verbal romantic words often are, yet when I write, complete stanzas and whole pages may appear in their entirety. At times, when the setting and mood are in special unity, I can visualize whole poems or acts of plays all at once in a strange and wondrous simultaneity. Today these lines came to me suddenly as part of a sonnet to Henry, my unacknowledgeable son, encouraging him to marry:

> *Look in thy glass, and tell the face thou viewest*
> *Now is the time that face should form another.*
> *For where is she so fair whose uneared womb*
> *Disdains the tillage of thy husbandry?*
> *Thou art thy mother's glass, and she in thee*
> *Calls back the lovely April of her prime.* "

Beth kissed him with gentle ardor. "Speaking of forming another," she said, patting her abdomen, "our rural aloneness may be happily interrupted one of these days by your own husbandried tillage of *my* womb!"

"How marvelous!" he shouted. He held her tightly and kissed her enthusiastically. "Your life-drama is so much more joyful and creative than my dramas! And certainly less controversial!"

Edward smiled and added, "I wonder whether we will be coerced into giving our child a pseudonym!"

Chapter 45

The time is out of joint. O cursèd spite
That ever I was born to set it right!
                                    - Hamlet

Having heard of Edward's choice of William Shakespeare as his pen name, Burghley talked to the Queen about making Edward even more anonymous.

By sleuthing with his spy network, Burghley learned that there lived in London a 28-year-old grain merchant named William Shaksper, a former butcher's apprentice from Stratford. Burghley asked the Queen to consider requesting Edward to pay Shaksper an annual sum to serve as the pretended author of the plays so there would be a real person attached to the name.

"The camouflage will be more authentic than a mere pseudonym," said Burghley, leaning on his cane and stroking his beard. "There will be less chance of someone uncovering our little plan, Your Majesty."

"Do you really deem it necessary, Leviathan? Isn't anonymity enough?"

"After thirty-four years of dutiful and devout service to you and to England, my most Gracious Queen, it seems precious little to ask."

The next day, Elizabeth called Edward to Whitehall and proposed it to him as a harmless personal Queenly request. He dutifully acquiesced, suppressing his temper, and arranged a meeting with Shaksper.

Edward was unimpressed with Shaksper's simple appearance and crude speech but admired his pluck in coming to London to compete as a merchandiser. Edward offered him a hundred pounds a year, a large sum for someone in the lower class, to feign authorship. Shaksper eagerly accepted. The matter was settled.

Edward regarded the agreement as a traitorous coerced perversion of truth and art, and was certain the idea had originated with Burghley. He returned to his room, lay on his bed and stared at the ceiling. Finally he shouted, "O curséd spite, that truth-threatened men, with cunning vengeful power in their hands, can so easily obliterate my name!"

He started his fire, sat on the bare oak floor, leaned his elbows on his knees and his face on his clenched fists, and ruminated. By the time the fire had dwindled to a mere glow, he had decided it was definitely time to include authorship identity clues in his plays. When possible, he would use the word "ever," really meaning "E. Vere." He went to his desk and composed two tentative new lines for *The Winter's Tale,* writing in his tablet:

Autolycus: *O, that E. Vere I was born!*
Clown: *I' th' name of me!*

He wrote part of a new sonnet:

Why write I still all one, E. Vere the same
And keep invention in a noted weed,
That E. Very word doth almost tell my name.

He added new lines to *Hamlet*:

The time is out of joint. O cursèd spite
That E. Vere I was born to set it right!

And:

Hamlet: *I am glad to see you well, Horatio, or I*
do forget myself.
Horatio: *The same, my lord, and your poor ser-*
vant E. Vere.
Hamlet: *Sir, my good friend; I'll change that*
name with you.

After further revision, Edward submitted to the censors his narrative poem of 1,200 lines, *Venus and Adonis* . He had worked on the poem intermittently for many years, describing in lusty detail Elizabeth's conquest of him as a bashful youth. Because he used his invented name of William Shakespeare for the first time and provided no indication to the reader that the heroine was the Queen, it passed the censors and was published in 1593.

By placing no author's name on the title page and only using it under the dedication, he hoped his readers would deduce it as a pen-name. Edward had made friends over the years with several print-ers who agreed with him that anonymity was a per-verse literary farce and that authorship clues in print-ing the cover and preliminary pages were as justifi-able as in the text.

The English readership, not used to such printed eroticism, eagerly bought *Venus and Adonis,* which promptly required five printings. Edward dedicated this first published use of the name William Shakespeare to his son, the Third Earl of Southampton, referring to his pseudonym as "the first heir of my invention":

> *Right Honourable, I know not how I shall offend in*
> *dedicating my unpolished lines to your lordship,*
> *nor how the world will censure me for choosing so*
> *strong a prop to support so weak a burden. But if*
> *the first heir of my invention prove deformed, I*
> *shall be sorry it had so noble a godfather.*

*   *   *

"A legal heir, at last," Edward shouted as he kissed Beth. "I do love you so!" With the help of a midwife, Beth delivered their son at home.

"I am so happy for you and for us, Edward," she said wearily. "I will leave the naming to you while I get some rest."

He almost chose Aubrey, after several famous de Veres, but decided that this son should have a stir-ring name that walked proudly through English his-tory. Henry Wriothesley had been named by the Queen, and Edward liked the name. He decided to name this son Henry also, after Henry V with whom he closely identified.

Edward enjoyed playing with Henry, watching him grow and attain new skills, having missed so much of his daughters' development. He and Beth attended Court only for special occasions, such as the knighting of Ned Somerset in April, 1593.

Edward was informed that Elizabeth had wanted to knight him at the same time but Burghley had pleaded with her not to render an official stamp of approval to his poison pen.

Edward, Thomas Nashe and Robert Greene were drinking Rhenish wine and eating cheese and pickled herring at the Stillyard one night when the gifted Greene, only thirty-four but already author of eight published novels, had a heart attack. He died four weeks later. Thomas Watson had died in 1592. In May 1593, the talented 29-year-old Christopher Marlowe was killed in a fight.

Edward decided to gather his University Wits at The Boar's Head.

"My good friends, remember what Seneca said: 'Vita brevis est, ars longa.'. Only too poignantly, how well we all know that life is brief, as fleeting as a shadow, but that our art is long and will endure. This is now an excellent time to publish despite being tongue-tied by censorship."

"Hamstrung by insecure authoritarians and hammered by narrow-minded fanatics who are disgraces to English culture and English artistic aspirations," added Thomas Nashe.

"Many wearing fiercely menacing rapiers are afraid of our diminutive goose-quills," continued Edward. "But the English people have become excited readers and playgoers. We have created the greatest literary torrent in English history. But we must urge ourselves onward, since attitudes change so swiftly with change of monarchs."

"And politicians," added Thomas Lodge.

"I know all of you are concerned about my enforced pseudonymity. It is extremely displeasing to me but it is *my* battle. We must delight in our good fortune to live in an era in which literature is appreciated and encouraged by royalty. As long as the Queen lives, she has promised to guarantee publication of our writings and to fill the post of Master of Revels with an ally to enhance the printing of our work."

"What about the literary executioner Burghley?" asked Thomas Kyd.

"I believe Elizabeth will try to control his censorship prudently. And you, Tom, of course, can publish any work of yours using your own name."

"It seems so unfair and absurd to discriminate against noble authors," added Kyd. "The logic mystifies me."

Edward pushed up his sleeves. "With the beauty of our words, we are reaching the soaring heights of the great Italian painters. Our language is enlarging and beautifying much more rapidly than I dreamed! Continue to reach for the sun, fly higher than the peregrine and be true to yourselves but with a wary pen. Use my example as a lesson."

"Writing or drinking example?" asked Nashe, and they laughed.

"I can not, to be true to my honor and my motto, refrain from writing about real people and their fascinating foibles, both good and bad. As I wrote recently in *The Rape of Lucrece* :

Time's glory is to calm contending kings, to
unmask falsehood and bring truth to light. "

"Hear, hear!" exclaimed Nashe.

"The result, however," continued Edward, "is suffocating pseudonymity. But rest assured that our powerful words will long outlast the unenlightened restraints of frightened, empty-headed, double-hearted politicians."

*   *   *

In January 1594, Edward sent a copy of his long poem, *The Rape of Lucrece,* to Burghley to read, and called on him a few days later.

Now seventy-three, he sat at his desk with his usual plate of cheese between two high stacks of papers.

"Your Lordship, I thank you for reading my latest work," said Edward. "I know you are not overly fond of poetry, but my poem is true to the real events that occurred in 509 BC, and I seek your permission to publish it with my own name attached."

Burghley stroked the brown rabbit fur on the collar of his lugubrious black robe. "Edward, you know that is impossible. Rules are rules. Laws are laws. Successful societies are those which follow their own rules, else anarchy follows."

"Surely it is no ill-reflection on England to have my name attached to an accurate historical poem about events in ancient Rome!"

"If you were skilled in governmental matters, Edward, a world more realistic than yours, you would understand the need for order," he said, fondling his snow-white beard. "Why would a great earl risk a loss of respect merely to have his printed name attached to ideas contained in a foolish 2000-year-old poem?" He smiled ingratiatingly.

Edward thought, *There are daggers in men's smiles. A false face must hide what the false heart doth know.*

His stomach tightened and he tasted acid. He watched Burghley's roving eyes and the image formed in his mind of an innocent flower with a serpent under it. "Poems add elegance, linguistic invention and often lofty thoughts to a culture."

"Only to poets," answered Burghley. "Others think differently."

Edward briefly thought that Burghley's mouth would make a good mousetrap, so much did it smell of cheese. He hesitated and then decided to take the risk so often accompanying truth. "If it is sinful to have one's name attached to pieces of paper, why have you hired a full-time librarian for the past thirty-six years to file and bind documents most of which have *your* name on them? And I understand that you have just hired a second historian, William Camden, to write a biography of you at a high fee, with sources limited to those which you provide."

Burghley sat up straighter in his chair. "That is something quite different, Edward, quite different. History is history, poetry is poetry, and plays are plays."

Edward studied the falsity in Burghley's expression and thought, *It is easy to find the mind's construction in the face* . "Poetry and plays are just as much a product of the times as your carefully edited documents!"

"Carefully edited, my insulting Lord? There is no sorting or editing!"

How easily liars lie, Edward thought. "Meaning no offense, but I tried to retrieve my letters to Anne recently and was told they had all been destroyed."

"Imagined happenings can be dangerous, Edward. Anne did not share with me such private matters. She probably destroyed them herself because you were so cruel." Burghley began to shift his legs restlessly.

Too much conversation with this embossed carbuncle might infect my brain, thought Edward. "Hundreds of letters and not one remains? She told me she always gave them to you for your perusal."

"She was mistaken, Edward. Yes, she was mistaken. Her unhappy marriage confused her, yes, confused her and made her mis-speak."

Listening to this deceptive drivel bitters my mouth, thought Edward, as if I had just licked the inside of an old green copper bell.

Realizing that Burghley would never give his approval to *Lucrece,* Edward decided to challenge him. "I found in your library fireplace not long ago a half-burned note written by Sir George Buc of the Revels Office describing me as 'a magnificent and very learned and religious man.' Does that opinion threaten you in some manner, so that it must be destroyed? Are you obliterating me from history?" Edward stroked his boar ring.

Burghley took his long white staff which was leaning against his desk, squeezed both hands around it and began rocking back and forth. "You are mistaken! Have you lost all sense of reality?"

Edward leaned against the bookcase and persisted. "I note that none of my letters to you were kept except for an occasional excerpt in your handwriting, complimentary to you. A rather selective history, one might say! I also encountered a letter in your handwriting, supposedly from Anne to me which I never received, proclaiming for the historical record her utter innocence of any misdeed, deception, or extra-marital conception during my travels. How say you, your Lordship?"

His face as red as a ripe radish, Burghley bellowed, "That is libel!"

Edward contemplated that this egotistical man with endless cold avarice had kept him in degrading wardship until the age of forty-one, stolen a major part of his inheritance, forced him into an empty unfulfilling marriage, and was suppressing and trying to annihilate his artistry. It was clearly time to take a firm and moral stand no matter what the consequences.

"Did you not, sir, steal my totally legal marriage contract, lie to the Queen and force me to marry your daughter, guaranteeing our mutual unhappiness?"

Burghley's cheeks bulged and turned purple and his jaw tightened. He slammed his hand on his desk as he blubbered, "I say you are very mistaken! Yes, delirious! Were you at The Boar's Head all night? My God, this is more than libelous! It is slanderous!"

"Am I troubling you, sir? Do go on." Edward put his hand in his pocket and rubbed a clove softly, trying to keep from smiling at the theatrical drama unfolding before him.

"You are crazy! Crazy!" Burghley shouted. He struggled up out of his chair and limped to the door, stomping his staff loudly.

"You mean crazed by the insanity of truth, Your Lordship?"

Burghley turned rapidly, stumbling against the door. "Think you, demented poet, I have not work of greater import than childish rhymes and false hallucinations? Unprovable accusations can be hazardous! Yes, most hazardous! Beware of those more mighty than you. I have a few years left and am capable of Herculean weaponry." He left the room and slammed the door.

As Edward left Cecil House and walked out into a cold rain, he thought of his lines in *Julius Caesar*:

> *There is no terror, Cassius, in your threats,*
> *for I am armed so strong in honesty that they*
> *pass by me as the idle wind.*

Chapter 46

These our actors,
As I foretold you, were all spirits, and
Are melted into air, into thin air;
And like the baseless fabric of this vision,
The cloud-capped towers, the gorgeous palaces,
Yea, all which it inherit, shall dissolve,
And, like this insubstantial pageant faded,
Leave not a rack behind. We are such stuff
As dreams are made on, and our little life
Is rounded with a sleep.
                              - The Tempest

In the flickering light of tapers, with the back-drop of a magical flowering forest, the circling dance concluded the play. As the fairies converged upon the Queen and white-gowned Lizbeth sitting to-gether, Edward's heart, for a charmed moment, glowed like the setting sun. He had grown close to Lizbeth despite her never-identified paternity.

She was marrying William Stanley, Sixth Earl of Derby, learned, distinguished and traveled, a talented friend of Edward and of Royal Tudor blood. Lizbeth had chosen the man she loved. He was also the second richest man in England.

The nuptials were celebrated with great splendor at Greenwich Palace on January 26, 1595, the wedding banquet followed by Edward's fanciful forest fantasy, *A Midsummer Night's Dream,* first acted before the Queen ten years before under the title *A Pastorall of Phillyda & Choryn.* Edward had revised it into a light frolicsome play suitable for a wedding, involving fairy kings and queens, country bumpkins and starcrossed lovers happily rejoined.

* * *

In the previous year, the long narrative poem *Lucrece* had been published. As with *Venus and Adonis,* the name William Shakespeare was printed only under the dedication, not on the title page.

Edward's son, Henry Wriothesley, Third Earl of Southampton, was now a dashing red-haired courtier very popular with the maids of honor. Edward also dedicated *Lucrece* to him :

> *The love I dedicate to your lordship is without end, whereof this pamphlet without beginning is but a superfluous moiety. The warrant I have of your honourable disposition, not the worth of my untutored lines, makes it assured of acceptance. What I have done is yours; what I have to do is yours, being part in all I have, devoted yours.*

No matter how many times he went over it in his mind, Edward was still mystified by the concept of artistic anonymity, a brief inexplicable moment in English history. Why had such an un-human and in-human doctrine coincided with his life?

Shaking his head, he recalled what John Lumley recently stated in his Introduction to the *The Arte of English Poesie* :

> *I know very many notable gentlemen in the Court that have written commendably, and suppressed it again, or else suffered it to be published without their own names to it, as if it were a discredit for a gentleman to seem learnèd.*

* * *

On Edward's birthday, a sunny and flower-per-fumed April day, Beth asked him to join her for a coach-ride to the adjacent town of Hackney in the Stratford-at-Bow region of London's suburbs.

"What a magnificent manor-house and what a surprise!" he exclaimed.

Beth had been waiting for the right opportu-nity to use some of her inherited wealth to pro-vide suitable lodging for Edward's monumental task of revising more than thirty-seven plays. He needed seclusion but also nearness to his writing associates and the stimulating atmosphere of London's theater district.

"Our new home is called 'King's Place' because of its association with Henry VIII," Beth told him. "He liked its location only two miles from London, so he confiscated it from a wealthy cleric and remod-eled it extensively."

Beth showed him the two inner courtyards, the elegant wide balustraded staircases curving grandly upward, its twenty rooms and the long gallery with its ceiling of lovely molded swans, stags, horses and bulls. Edward's study overlooked its 270 acres of orchards, pastures and large formal gardens laid out by the previous owner, Lord Hunsdon, cousin of the Queen.

"Here is where you will walk with me in winter on Trentham Days," she said, taking his hand.

"And what, pray tell, is a Trentham Day?"

"If you could have your childhood Bolebec Days, then surely I may suggest that each Thursday be Trentham Day, totally devoted to your wife and son. We will refresh and re-create your gifted but weary brain!"

He laughed delightedly. "You are a wonder, Beth. I don't say nearly often enough how much I love you. I should keep my golden pen in my mouth to remind me to verbalize my feelings! These lines from *Romeo and Juliet* certainly apply to you:

> *Her eyes in heaven would through the airy*
> *region stream so bright that birds would*
> *sing and think it were not night."*

When Edward first sat at his study desk in King's Place, surrounded by his familiar books, he was a happy man. He had a mutually enhancing, loving marriage, a healthy three-year-old son, and freedom from financial problems. He also had uninterrupted tranquillity away from the turmoil and backstabbings of Court.

Edward continued to sonnetize the Third Earl of Southampton, the son he could never acknowledge as his own:

Your name from hence immortal life shall have,
Though I, once gone, to all the world must die .
The earth can yield me but a common grave
When you entombèd in men's eyes shall lie .
Your monument shall be my gentle verse,
Which eyes not yet created shall o'er-read .

On their first Trentham Day, Edward, Beth and Henry wandered through the village, introducing themselves to the merchants, bakers and butchers as Edward's father used to do.

At the end of the day, Edward said to Beth, "After a rather tumultuous and jagged life, you are turning me into a truly contented husband, something I hardly thought possible!"

That evening, after putting Henry to bed, Beth and Edward sat sipping hippocras on a soft leather sofa in front of their bedroom fire. Edward was pensive and sat in silence with his eyes on the fire. Beth tried to cheer him up.

"Speaking of authorship clues, my dearest Edward, let me read you an excerpt from Richard Barnefield in a book I bought for you today, *A Remembrance of Some English Poets* :

And Shakespeare thou, whose honey-flowing vein
Pleasing the world, thy praises doth obtain .
Whose Venus and whose Lucrece (sweet and chaste)
Thy name in fame's immortall booke have plac't .
Live ever you, at least in fame live ever :
Well may the body die, but fame dies never ."

"Quite amazing, Beth. I am truly surprised that Barnefield escaped Burghley's ever-watchful censors.

Our magnificent literary and linguistic rebirth is being sieved, sanitized and Cecilized."

She nodded agreement. "I'm afraid you have trod too often on the gouty toes of the mighty!"

Edward sipped wine faster when he was keyed up. "I would wish it otherwise but the pious arrogance and unrestrained dishonesty of dim-sighted Burghley galls my gallbladder!"

He remained silent for a few moments. "I see serious trouble looming for England. Burghley has been a fine governmental partner for the Queen in difficult times but England is sinking farther into debt."

"Isn't that King Philip's fault?"

"Only partially. The endless greed of politicians and sycophants with their huge mansions is playing a key role. Taxes, poverty and vagrancy are increasing, as is corruption. Parliament is being asked for more money without a voice in governing. I sense conflict ahead, perhaps revolution."

"Revolution? After decades of relative peace under Elizabeth?"

"History's lessons are obvious. The mighty know they can postpone the societal results of their greed to a later generation. They care little for their country or countrymen and use them merely as stepping stones to personal wealth, high social position and distorted historical greatness."

After putting Henry to bed, they bathed together in a tub built by Henry VIII, followed by a fervent and prolonged expression of their love.

* * *

During the next five years, from 1596 to 1601, Edward tried to achieve a balance, giving ample time to his happy home life and working hard to polish and publish his plays as literature. He continually updated his dramas to include new topical references and real people, often targeting himself.

Using as his preceptors the scrupulous revisers Virgil, Horace and Ovid, whose lives overlapped in the great era of Caesar Augustus, Edward used meticulous care and creativity in his revisions. He discovered that it often took longer to elevate the quality of his plays to a new level than did the original writing.

Following the example of Plautus, the third century BC genius of comedy and language, he continued to experiment with word combinations and new grammar, adding a cascade of hundreds of new words to English, exceeding his goal of one new word a day. He attached new meanings and subtleties to old words, making them transcend their simplicities and achieve new elegance and flexibility.

Edward's goal was to infuse his native language with the dignified refinement and sophistication of classical Greek and Latin while retaining the charm of indigenous multi-origined English.

The Curtain still existed but Burbage tore down The Theatre and used its timbers to build The Globe adjacent to the Thames across London Bridge. The tall circular playhouse open to the sky now joined The Rose, The Swan, The Fortune and The Red Bull. This excited Edward, all new theaters being built within five years to accommodate the explosive surge of interest in drama.

Edward's versions of *Henry VI Part Three, Richard II, Richard III, and Romeo and Juliet* were published anonymously at the insistence of the new Principal

Secretary, Robert Cecil. *Love's Labour's Lost* was published in 1598 with his full pseudonym.

In Edward's officially published plays thereafter, some were printed anonymously at the whim of censors and some were blocked indefinitely without explanation, for instance *As You Like It* . Several plays were printed without his permission by play-pirates, usually under Shake-speare, the hyphen indicating a pen name.

Edward found out that his once-friendly brother-in-law, Robert Cecil, was silently wiping out most records of his playwriting and of his very existence as far back as he could find material to destroy. He also learned that Cecil had burned all available publications of Gabriel Harvey and Thomas Nashe, annihilating their scurrilous descriptions of the truth.

Edward was amazed that Cecil had allowed Francis Meres to publish his *Palladis Tamia* in which he analyzed the eruption of English literature:

> As the Greek tongue is made famous and eloquent by Homer, Hesiod, Euripides, Aeschylus, Sophocles, Pindarus, and Aristophanes, and the Latin tongue by Virgil, Ovid, Horace, and others, so the English tongue has been mightily enriched and gorgeouslie invested in rare ornaments. The best for Comedy among us be Edward, Earl of Oxford.

He was proud that Meres also commended several of the University Wits including Greene, Nashe, Lodge, Munday and Chapman.

* * *

Baron Burghley died in 1598 at the age of seventy-eight. A fastidious planner in death as in life, many years previously he had arranged the fine details of his own funeral in Westminster Abbey. His magnificent closed purple-palled casket rested in the Abbey choir for six days while the multitudes paid their final respects, followed by funereal eulogies in front of Elizabeth and her Court.

Unknown to any, even the Queen, the casket was empty. Burghley had already been buried in St. Martin's Church in Stamford, far away from his Puritan wife and daughter. He was laid to rest in a new crypt built to hold future noble Cecils.

In the nave, Burghley had created a huge ornamental tomb, his sculpted likeness resting majestically in marbled grandeur, without competition from Kings and Queens.

Chapter 47

Fear no more the heat o'th'sun
Nor the furious winter's rages .
Thou thy worldly task hast done,
Home art gone and tak'n thy wages .
Golden lads and girls all must,
As chimney-sweepers, come to dust .
— Cymbeline

Elizabeth was dressed in black with a flaming red wig. She was in a bitter mood, her green eyes glaring as she shrilled, "God's Death, Edward! Southampton has fine attributes and great charisma. He could have reached any pinnacle he set his mind to, but now his brazen behavior in Ireland and London makes that impossible."

Edward spoke with Elizabeth alone in Whitehall's privy chamber. It was February, 1601, and Edward noted how inadequately the flickering wall torches lighted the room or illuminated the darkness of his mind.

"Your Majesty, must I sit as jurist in yet another pre-decided trial, this time with agonizing personal poignancy both for you and me? All Southampton and Essex desired was to express their viewpoint and serve their Queen more meaningfully."

Edward wondered whether the close relationship between Essex and the Queen, despite their thirty-three year age-gap, was a physical union or merely based upon platonic courtley love. He had heard the Court gossip that Essex often came not to his own lodging till the birds sang in the morning.

Essex and Southampton had been outraged when, despite falling for the romantic flattery of the dashing Essex, the Queen made Robert Cecil Master of the Court of Wards in addition to being Principal Secretary. They soon learned that Cecil was secretly pilfering at a rate of 70,000 pounds a year, an incredible sum, even greater than the annual rate of misappropriation by his father. *Simil pater, simil filius,* concluded Edward. Like father, like son.

Essex and Southampton had angrily left their unfinished war in Ireland, to which Cecil had sent them while Elizabeth was making up her mind on new appointments, and stormed home. When blocked by Cecil from even talking with the Queen, they tried to force their way into the palace to express their grievances about Cecil to her. They were captured and now, to Edward's shock and dismay, both were about to stand trial for treason at Cecil's insistence.

The Queen exclaimed loudly, "They were carrying weapons and meant to breach my personal guards!" She stomped her foot hard on the floor.

"Their brashness was a fit of temper against

Robert, not you. Southampton would never . . ." He left the words *harm his own mother* unsaid.

As she strode briskly back and forth she said defiantly, "No monarch can allow that to stand! God's Wounds!!" She ripped off one of her high corked chopines and threw it against the wall.

"So you will instruct them by decapitation? Good preparation for humility in the next life, perhaps, but hardly a heady learning experience for this one!"

Elizabeth paused and looked at her throne. "Do you forget the ancient codes of honor that the crown, the state, must endure no stain, no spot of infection, else the disease may spread through the whole body politic? No monarchy can hold its majestic pattern without obedience."

Edward knew he must appeal to her on another level. "But what about your private feelings for the two attractive talented courtiers, including your own flesh and blood? They have ably enhanced your Court and have risked their lives repeatedly in defense of England."

For a long moment, she said nothing. When she turned to him, some of the fury in her eyes had been replaced by pain. "You are quite aware, Edward, that I am not made totally of iron. This is *extremely* distressing to me. You well know how fond I am of both, and why. But this is a regal drama and each of us must play our role—you as judge and I as Queen, in saddened dissonance."

"I beseech you, Your Majesty, listen compassionately to these words on mercy from *The Jew*, which I now call *The Merchant of Venice* :

> *The quality of mercy is not strained,*
> *It droppeth as the gentle rain from heaven*

Upon the place beneath. It is twice blest .
It blesseth him that gives, and him that takes.
It is enthroned in the hearts of kings;
It is an attribute to God himself."

Elizabeth felt cold sweat on her forehead and her heart began to race. She had trouble getting her breath. Without replying to Edward she swirled and strode rapidly from the room.

* * *

The two conflicting streams of orderly justice and human forgiveness flowed through Edward's mind and heart during the one-day trial. The judges were pre-rehearsed, much of the evidence concocted or altered. Edward wondered how future generations would view this form of authoritarian justice, with mandatory guilty verdicts required from the noble jurors on threat of loss of wealth and status.

Essex was a threat to the power of Robert Cecil, and Cecil leaped out from his hiding-place behind a wall-tapestry and demanded death for traitors to the Queen.

When the winter night's shadows had fallen behind the high windows of Westminster Hall, darkening the twenty-four carved angels leaning from the rafters, it was time for the Commission of Noble Judges to make their decision. The presiding Lord High Steward was Edward's friend, Thomas Sackville, now a dignified, even more portly Lord Buckhurst.

Edward tightened his jaw as Sackville stood and requested a roll-call. As each judge pronounced the word "Guilty" in subdued tones, Southampton was completely composed and gave Edward a reassuring smile. In that smile, Edward could see the boy he'd visited so often over the years, the son he loved in sonnets and in life.

Edward suddenly felt dizzy and noted prickly sensations in his right arm. He briefly wondered whether his time had come. His right arm kept tingling but the dizzyness cleared.

The Seventeenth Earl of Oxford was the last to be polled. If this were a play, the timing would have been perfect for an epic ennobling speech on the concepts of unencumbered justice, truth, honor and mercy.

Edward had prepared such a speech but it now seemed scrambled. All eyes were upon him in the strained silence as he pushed himself upright with hesitance, his right arm feeling strangely clumsy and not his own. His words seemed sparse and far away.

"Guilty," he said softly, looking directly at Robert Cecil, and sat down.

The final judgment was formally rendered by Lord Buckhurst who, since Essex and Southampton had been found guilty of high treason by their peers, sentenced them to be laid upon a hurdle and drawn through the midst of the city to the gallows, there to be hanged. When half-dead, they were to be taken down, disemboweled and, after their heads were cut off, quartered, with the heads to be dealt with according to the Queen's pleasure.

Glinting silver flashed in the torchlight as the officer of the axe turned the sharp edge toward the two guilty men who were no longer earls, only honor-and-wealth-stripped traitors to England.

Each was given an opportunity for final words and each spoke calmly and eloquently. Essex declared that he never had any treacherous or disloyal intentions toward her Majesty. He primarily entreated with his jury to intercede with the Queen and ensure that his best friend was granted a pardon.

The Earl of Southampton stood, the torches gleaming on his golden hair. He glanced at Edward, nodded and looked forgivingly at the entire jury. In a quiet voice he explained that loyalty to his friend had made him choose the wrong pathway and he expressed penitence.

He closed by saying, "Since I am found guilty by the law, I do submit myself to death, yet not despairing of her Majesty's mercy; for I know she is merciful, and if she please to extend mercy to me, I shall with all humility receive it."

As the bells of St. Margaret's began to toll in melancholy tones, announcing to the hostile crowd the verdicts against the popular nobles, Edward leaned on the arm of his son-in-law, who asked him to spend the night with Lizbeth and him on Cannon Row. Edward declined, so William rode with him back to Hackney.

Beth immediately noted his slightly thick speech and, with a stunned look upon her face, said, "Oh, Edward, you're too young to have a stroke! You're only fifty-one!"

"Don't worry, Beth," he reassured her. "It is minor and I will recover in a few days."

His speech normalized completely over the next month, but his right hand remained slightly clumsy, an annoying inconvenience which slowed his writing.

He learned that the Queen spared Southampton's life but committed him to the Tower indefinitely. The rash Essex was executed, a harsh penalty for youthful imprudence but not in a continuing *Regnum Cecilianum*. And at Whitehall, lonely forlorn sighs were heard emanating from the Queen's private chambers.

In his study at King's Place, Edward thought about the death of Essex. He pondered the miracle of life and its split-second transience in the never-ending universe. He thought of a phrase he had used in *Troilus and Cressida : One touch of nature makes the whole world kin* .

Edward looked out of the window, appreciating the many shades of green which made a garden pleasing in winter. He watched a robin hop, stand still with head cocked, then quickly dart his bill unerringly to beak a worm.

How intriguing, he thought, *that man, the highest form of animal, should be so out-eared by common robins, so out-nosed by mongrel dogs, and so out-eyed by high-flying peregrines.*

He recalled his father's words forty years before as they admired the lovely Essex countryside, that de Veres tended to die within four years of their first chest pain or paralysis. It certainly had been true of his father, who died at the age of forty-five, one year after his first symptom.

Edward thanked God that his mind was completely unaffected. In whatever time he had remaining, he felt he had further important creative work to do before his silent exit from the stage.

Chapter 48

My name be buried where my body is,
And live no more to shame nor me nor you;
For I am shamed by that which I bring forth.
                                    - Sonnet 72

Edward sat at his desk and looked down at the statue commissioned by Beth for their garden's center, featuring a white marble de Vere boar, front hoofs elevated, head reaching upward toward a fluttering black marble Trentham raven kissing the boar's lips.

Edward stared at his wooden plaque of the Bolebec lion shaking the broken spear. He liked the lion's expression of proud defiance. Although Henry de Vere had been Viscount Bolebec for ten years, Edward had held the title for forty-three years. He still felt that the Bolebec hereditary crest best symbolized his own spirit struggling honorably against governmental subterfuge, cruel use of power, mendacity, boundless greed, suppression of literary artistry, and coerced pseudonymity.

In the past two years, Edward had not experienced a single medical symptom. At times he became glum when reflecting on his career, its barriers, turmoils and absence of traditional de Verean achievements. He summarized some of his life's negatives in partial sonnet form :

> *And gilded honour shamefully misplaced,*
> *And maiden virtue rudely strumpeted,*
> *And right perfection wrongfully disgraced,*
> *And strength by limping sway disabled,*
> *Tired with all these, from these would I be gone,*
> *Save that to die I leave my love alone.*

Robert Cecil informed him that the name Corambis for the spying inept politician in the first edition of *Hamlet* had to be changed. Edward authorized a name-change to Polonius, derived from ponderous, ending his letter to Robert, "I hope truth is subject to no prescription, for truth is truth though never so old, and time cannot make that false which was once true."

He liked these words, so he added two new lines to *Troilus:*

> *Nay, it is ten times true,*
> *For truth is truth to th' end of reck'ning.*

The next day was Trentham Day. He told Beth he needed a morning walk alone with their son. As they climbed up a low, gently curving hill, Edward explained the state of family finances. He also described the de Vere family health history with its four-year guideline for death after the first chest pain or episode of weakness. He mentioned his own minor occurrence two years before.

Henry's facial features were more Beth's than Edward's, although he had Edward's wavy brown hair with an auburn tint, and his brown eyes. "When you die, Father, what kind of death would you prefer?"

Edward thought for a moment. "I think, as Julius Caesar once answered, a sudden unexpected kind."

"Have you any further thoughts for me?"

"The world is changing fast, Henry. The days of castles, knights in armor and tournament jousting will disappear in your generation. Ours was a marvelous era in some ways and dreadful in others, like most epochs."

As they looked out over Hackney and Stoke Newington towards nearby London, Henry asked, "What career would you recommend for me, Father?"

"I was taught that military heroism was a nobleman's duty and the true path to glory. That futile pursuit dominated much of my life. The most important goal is to maintain truth and honor and remain steadfastly faithful to your monarch. I hope you will choose a career more harmonious with the times than mine. To be out of kilter with one's peers leads to many painful thorns and festering wounds."

That afternoon, Edward told Beth for the first time the four-year death guideline for de Veres.

"Oh, Edward, I wish you had shared that with me sooner!"

"Why, my love? I didn't want to disturb the even flow of our congenial times together. I have overcome adversity so often in my life, why shouldn't I be able to break that precedent? The great Thirteenth

Earl, despite a lifetime of tumult, lived to seventy-one!"

The next morning, Edward began final revisions of *Hamlet*. His intuition told him that this might be his final opportunity for meaningful reflections and forthright allusions to his times. Since the play was autobiographical, he included his feelings toward his father who died so prematurely, toward his mother who re-married less than two months later, toward Burghley the evil cancer of his life. He also included dialog with his two favorite cousins, Francis and Horatio, cast in the play as the soldiers Francisco and Horatio.

*   *   *

Late one afternoon, Ned Somerset arrived at King's Place and told him that the Queen was dying. Edward invited him to spend the night. As Edward went to bed, resting his head against Beth's shoulder, he knew that an era was ending, not only Elizabeth's but his own.

For several months, Elizabeth's spirits had been on the wane. She would sometimes sigh, stand up, grab a sword hanging on the wall and jab it into a tapestry. The court-sustaining dynamic force of the Queen's personality was disappearing. In late January, she became more brooding and moved the Court upriver to Richmond Palace.

Edward and Ned rode in the sun through a foot of snow and wind-whipped snowflakes along the frozen Thames, past sparkling forests glistening with ice-covered branches. It was as if Time itself were freezing to prevent the inevitability of royal demise.

Edward requested a private talk with the Queen. She was slumped in a low chair in her privy chamber, the floor covered with a large red and gold Turkish carpet.

She smiled and pointed to the carpet. "Your handiwork, my Turk! Our trade with Istanbul is going well, thanks to you!"

He was saddened by her appearance: scalloped cheeks, right side of mouth flattened, deep-set gloomy eyes, teeth missing or blackened. "How are you feeling, Your Majesty?"

"My brain seems strangely turned upside down. I think something is growing inside my head, making my right side weak and depriving me of myself. Would you bring me that mirror?"

Edward hesitated. "I have been told you have not looked in a mirror for twenty years."

"My maids of honor find excuses not to bring it to me. They must think I am bereft of all senses. Think they I cannot feel the sagging skin on my face and neck, nor see the disfigured joints of once-dainty fingers?"

Edward briefly considered dropping the mirror but how frustrating it must be at the end of one's life to be debased with dissembling. He handed the mirror to her.

"My God, it is worse than I thought!" she said hoarsely, peering at her reflection. "I always liked my face in portraits. Now I am already an Egyptian mummy!"

Edward knelt. "I have come to pay my final respects, Your Majesty. I have always been honest with you. Our earthly work is almost finished."

She nodded slowly, and her mouth twisted into a wry smile. "Yes, my most noble courtier, I feel creeping time at my gate. Life's great play is coming to a close."

"Yes, my Queen, the pageant is nearly over."

"What thinkest thou, my Golden Pen? Was it a comedy or a tragedy?" She clumsily opened and closed her fan.

"A mixture of both, as is all life. What a sponsorship and partnership you have provided for me, Your Majesty! What an opportunity! What a time to live! And what stimulating leadership you gave, with all of England the recipient!"

"Perhaps true, but my own sea-girded audience is small and temporary; yours is the world and timeless! Someday you will shine forth, my dear Edward, as the singular greatest tribute to my reign."

"I deem it likely that my true name will sink quietly into the sea like the setting sun, and my writings will remain anonymous forever. Your name and regime, however, will gleam in glorious radiance. And well they should, as England continues to explode in national splendor!" He looked at the boar ring on his left thumb and caressed it slowly and thoughtfully.

Elizabeth slipped down in her chair. "Now listen to *my* words as I have so long been inspired by yours. My Lord of Oxford, you are the most supremely gifted and accomplished of all of your distinguished lineage. Your writings will soon override their transient pseudonymity by their own nobility, magisterial power and inspired beauty." She futilely tried to raise herself with her right hand. "I am beginning to tire."

"My deepest gratitude, Your Majesty, for tolerating my uneven intemperate nature and for encouraging me to poetize our age, its fascinating players and the endless variety of the human spirit."

Elizabeth's countenance became briefly regal as she raised her head. "And may you be praised for not frivolizing your last words to me! Thank you, Lord

Edward de Vere, for illustering my reign, illuminating our England and well-contenting your three hardest taskmasters: your God, your Queen and yourself. Let us both be at peace."

Edward stood, bowed, and kissed her hand. She climbed down from her chair and crawled over to three satin pillows on the carpet, one red, one white and one pink. He walked towards the door, turned and saw her sitting on the center pink pillow with arms crossed and jaw clenched, as if challenging Death to battle.

He could feel her still-emanating power as he visualized the entire panoramic script of her 45-year reign. *What a drama! What a stage! And what a role for thee and me!*

As he took one final look at Elizabeth, he said in a soft voice, cracking with emotion, *"Atque in perpetuum, Regina, ave atque vale."* And forever, My Queen, hail and farewell.

Three days after, still seated on her cushion with arms folded, she became completely speechless. The next day, on March 24, 1603, Queen Elizabeth died, the last of the Tudors.

* * *

Fifteen months later, on a sunny June 26, Edward and Beth were sitting on a stone bench near the marble boar-and-raven statue enjoying the brightly colored flowers.

Forgetting his usual reticence, Edward said, "You look especially lovely today, Beth, with the sunlight glinting off your hair and the joyous expression on your face. But I feel a bit chilly and a sonnet is forming. I think I will write it in my study."

"What is the subject of your verse?" she asked.

He smiled. "The usual philosophic thoughts. Poets tend to be rather repetitive."

Beth sat in the garden a while longer. Then, humming to herself, she picked a bouquet of flowers, took it inside and placed it on the dining table. She went upstairs and walked quietly down the hall. As she passed Edward's study, she saw him writing intensely, shirt sleeves pushed up, frequently dipping his golden pen into his golden inkwell. She never tired of these silent glimpses of his creativity.

A few minutes later, Beth walked by his study again, glanced through the door and gasped. Edward was slumped over his desk, not moving, not breathing. A shaft of afternoon sunlight shining through the five-pointed silver star of Aubrey the Second beamed upon his right hand, glimmering his pen.

She walked slowly across the room, put her hand on his shoulder and lifted a parchment from the desk. In a soft, choking whisper she read his final sonnet which addressed the brevity of time and life, ending with: *This I do vow, and this shall ever be, I will be true despite thy scythe and thee* .

She stroked his back with her tender love and recalled Edward's words in *Henry V*:

> *Small time, but in that small most greatly lived*
> *This star of England. Fortune made his sword,*
> *By which the world's best garden he achieved.*

Beth leaned over Edward, kissed his cheek and noticed a piece of tablet-paper in his left hand, his left arm draped over his beloved *Hamlet* manuscript. She pulled the paper from his hand and realized he must have had a warning after completing the sonnet.

This provided just enough time to scribble a final addition to his favorite play :

Horatio, I am dead, thou liv'st .
Report me and my cause aright to the unsatisfied.
O God, Horatio, what a wounded name,
Things standing thus unknown, shall live be-
hind me!
If thou didst ever hold me in thy heart,
Absent thee from felicity a while,
And in this harsh world draw thy breath in pain
To tell my story .

* * *

On a blustery afternoon in July, 1604, with only his family and the Somersets in attendance, Edward de Vere, Seventeenth Earl of Oxford and Lord Great Chamberlain of England, was buried in St. Augustine Church, Hackney. By command of Principal Secretary Robert Cecil, the coffin was placed in a grave unmarked.

VERO · NIHIL · VERIUS